MERCY

MERCY

ANDREA DWORKIN

FOUR WALLS EIGHT WINDOWS
NEW YORK

A FOUR WALLS EIGHT WINDOWS FIRST EDITION.

First Printing August, 1991.

Excerpts from this novel have appeared in *The Michigan Quarterly
Review,* Vol. XXIX, No. 4, Fall 1990 and *The American Voice,*
No. 21, Winter 1990.

Mercy was first published
in Great Britain by Secker & Warburg in 1990.

The author and publisher are grateful to the following for
permission to quote from copyright material: Olwyn Hughes for
"Daddy," in *Collected Poems* by Sylvia Plath, published by Harper
& Row, Publishers, © 1965, 1981; Pantheon for Anna Cancogni's
translation of *Sartre: A Life* by Annie Cohen-Solal, © 1987
Random House, Inc.

Library of Congress Cataloging-in-Publication Data
Dworkin, Andrea.
    Mercy : a novel / Andrea Dworkin.
        p.   cm.
    ISBN 0-941423-69-7 : $22.00
    I. Title.
PS3554.W85M4   1991
813'.54—dc20   91-18157
                                                          CIP

Four Walls Eight Windows
P.O. Box 548, Village Station
New York, N.Y. 10014

Printed in the U.S.A.

For Judith Malina
For Michael Moorcock
In Memory of Ellen Frankfort

Daddy, daddy, you bastard, I'm through.
"Daddy," Sylvia Plath

For a small moment have I forsaken
thee; but with great mercies will I gather
thee.

In a little wrath I hid my face from
thee for a moment; but with everlasting
kindness will I have mercy on thee, saith
the Lord thy Redeemer.

Isaiah 54:7–8

Contents

Not Andrea: Prologue

Now I've come into my own as a woman of letters. I am a
committed feminist, of course. I admit to a cool, elegant
intellect with a clear superiority over the ape-like men who
write. I don't wear silk, of course. I am icy and formal even
alone by myself, a discipline of identity and identification. I do
not wear myself out with mistaken resistance, denunciation,
foolhardy anguish. I feel, of course. I feel the pain, the sorrow,
the lack of freedom. I feel with a certain hard elegance. I am
admired for it—the control, the reserve, the ability to make
the fine point, the subtle point. I avoid the obvious. I have a
certain intellectual elegance, a certain refinement of the mind.
There is nothing wrong with civilized thought. It is necessary.
I believe in it and I do have the courage of my convictions. One
need not raise one's voice. I am formal and careful, yes, but
with a real power in my style if I do say so myself. I am not, as
a writer or a human being, insipid or bland, and I have not sold
out, even though I have manners and limits, and I am not
poor, of course, why should I be? I don't have the stink on me
that some of the others have, I am able to say it, I am not effete.
I am their sister and their friend. I do not disavow them. I am
committed. I write checks and sign petitions. I lend my name.
I write books with a strong narrative line in clear, detailed,
descriptive prose, in the nineteenth-century tradition of
storytelling, intellectually coherent, nearly realistic, not
sentimental but yes with sex and romance and women who do

something, achieve something, strong women. I am committed, I do care, and I am the one to contend with, if the truth be told, because my mind is clear and cool and my prose is exceedingly skillful if sometimes a trifle too baroque. Every style has its dangers. I am not reckless or accusatory. I consider freedom. I look at it from many angles. I value it. I think about it. I've found this absolutely stunning passage from Sartre that I want to use and I copy it out slowly to savor it, because it is cogent and meaningful, with an intellectual richness, a moral subtlety. You don't have to shout to tell the truth. You can think. You have a responsibility to think. My wild sisters revel in being wretched and they do not think. Sartre is writing about the French under the German Occupation, well, French intellectuals really, and he says—"We were never as free as under the German Occupation. We had lost all our rights, and, first of all, the right to speak; we were insulted every day, and had to keep silent. . . . and everywhere, on the walls, the papers, the movie screen, we were made to confront the ugly mug that our oppressor presented to us as our own: but this is precisely why we were free. As the German poison seeped into our minds, every just thought we had was a real conquest; as an omnipotent police kept forcing silence upon us, every word we uttered had the value of a declaration of rights; as we were constantly watched, every gesture we made was a commitment." This is moral eloquence, in the mouth of a man. This applies to the situation of women. This is a beautiful truth, beautifully expressed. Every just thought is a real conquest, for women under the rule of men. They don't know how hard it is to be kind. Our oppressor puts his version of us everywhere, on walls, in the papers, on the movie screens. Like a poison gas, it seeps in. Every word we utter is a declaration of our rights. Every gesture is a commitment. I make gestures. I experience this subtle freedom, this freedom based on nuance, a freedom grotesquely negated by a vulgar, reckless shout, however sincere. He didn't know that the Jews were being exterminated, perhaps, not then. Of course, yes, he did know that they had been deported from France. Yes. And when he published these words much later, in 1949, he did know, but one must be true to one's original insights, one's true experiences, the glimpses one has of freedom. There is a certain pride one takes in seeing something so fine, so subtle, and saying it so well—and, of course, one cannot endlessly revise backwards. His point about freedom is elegant. He too suffered during the war. It is not a cheap point. And it is true that for us too every word is a declaration of rights, every gesture a commitment. This is beautifully put, strongly put. As a woman of letters, I fight for my kind, for women, for freedom. The brazen scream distracts. The wild harridans are not persuasive. I write out Sartre's passage with appreciation and excitement. The analogy to the condition of women is dramatic and at the same time nuanced. I will not shout. This is *not* the ovens. We are *not* the Jews, or, to be precise, the Jews in certain parts of Europe at a certain time. We are not being pushed into the ovens, dragged in, cajoled in, seduced in, threatened in. It is *not* us in the ovens. Such hyperbole helps no one. I like the way Sartre puts it, though the irony seems unintended: "We were never as free as under the German Occupation." Actually, I do know that his meaning is straightforward and completely sincere—there is no irony. This embarrasses me, perhaps because I am a captive of my time. We are cursed with hindsight. We need irony because we are in fact incapable of simple sincerity. "We were never as free as under the German Occupation." It gives the right significance to the gesture, something Brecht never managed incidentally. I like the sophistication, the unexpected meaning. This is what a writer must do: use words in subtle, unexpected ways to create intellectual surprise, real delight. I love the pedagogy of the analogy. There is a mutability of

3

meaning, an intellectual elasticity that avoids the rigidity of ideology and still instructs in the meaning of freedom. It warns us not to be simple-minded. We were never as free as under the German Occupation. Glorious. Really superb. Restrained. Elegant. True in the highest sense. De Beauvoir was my feminist ideal. An era died with her, an era of civilized coupling. She was a civilized woman with a civilized militance that recognized the rightful constraints of loyalty and, of course, love. I am tired of the bellicose fools.

ONE

In August 1956
(Age 9)

My name is Andrea. It means manhood or courage. In Europe only boys are named it but I live in America. Everyone says I seem sad but I am not sad. I was born down the street from Walt Whitman's house, on Mickle Street, in Camden, in 1946, broken brick houses, cardboard porches, garbage spread over cement like fertilizer on stone fields, dark, a dark so thick you could run your fingers through it like icing and lick it off your fingers. I wasn't raped until I was almost ten which is pretty good it seems when I ask around because many have been touched but are afraid to say. I wasn't really raped, I guess, just touched a lot by a strange, dark-haired man who I thought was a space alien because I couldn't tell how many hands he had and people from earth only have two, and I didn't know the word rape, which is just some awful word, so it didn't hurt me because nothing happened. You get asked if anything happened and you say well yes he put his hand here and he rubbed me and he put his arm around my shoulder and he scared me and he followed me and he whispered something to me and then someone says but did anything happen. And you say, well, yes, he sat down next to me, it was in this movie theater and I didn't mean to do anything wrong and there wasn't anyone else around and it was dark and he put his arm around me and he started talking to me and saying weird things in a weird voice and then he put his hand in my legs and he started rubbing and he kept saying just let me . . . . and someone says did anything happen and you say well yes he scared me and he followed me and he put his hand or hands there and you don't know how many hands he had, not really, and you don't want to tell them you don't know because then they will think you are crazy or stupid but maybe there are creatures from Mars and they have more than two hands but you know this is stupid to say and so you don't know how to say what happened and if you don't know how many hands he had you don't know anything and no one needs to believe you about anything because you are stupid or crazy and so you don't know how to say what happened and you say he kept saying just let me . . . . and I tried to get away and he followed me and he . . . . followed me and he . . . . and then they say, thank God nothing happened. So you try to make them understand that yes something did happen honest you aren't lying and you say it again, strained, thicklipped from biting your lips, your chest swollen from heartbreak, your eyes swollen from tears all salt and bitter, holding your legs funny but you don't want them to see and you keep pretending to be normal and you want to act adult and you can barely breathe from crying and you say yes something did happen and you try to say things right because adults are so strange and so stupid and you don't know the right words but you try so hard and you say exactly how the man sat down and put his arm around you and started talking to you and you told him to go away but he kept holding you and kissing you and talking to you in a funny whisper and he put his hands in your legs and he kept rubbing you and he had a really deep voice and he whispered in your ear in this funny, deep voice and he kept saying just to let him . . . . but you couldn't understand what he said because maybe he was mumbling or maybe he couldn't talk English so you can't tell them what he said and you say maybe he was a foreigner because you don't know what he said and he talked funny and you tried to get away but he

followed you and then you ran and you didn't scream or cry
until you found your momma because he might hear you and
find you so you were quiet even though you were shaking and
you ran and then they say thank God nothing happened and
you don't know why they think you are lying because you are
trying to tell them everything that happened just the right way
and if you are a stubborn child, a strong-willed child, you say
the almost-ten-year-old version of fuck you something happened all right the fuck put his hands in my legs and rubbed me
all over; my legs; *my legs*; me; my; my legs; my; my; my legs;
and he rubbed me; his arm was around my shoulder, rubbing,
and his mouth was on my neck, rubbing, and his hand was
under my shirt, rubbing, and his hand was in my pants,
rubbing, and he kept saying just let me . . . . and it was a
creepy whisper in some funny language and he was saying
sounds I didn't understand and then they say the child is
hysterical, something must have happened, the child is
hysterical; and they want to know if anything came inside or
was outside and you don't want to tell them that he took your
hand and put it somewhere wet on him in his lap in the dark
and your hand touched something all funny and your hand got
all cold and slimy and they say thank God nothing happened;
and they ask if something went inside but when you ask inside
where they look away and you are nearly ten but you are a
fully desperate human being because you want to know inside
where so you will know what happened because you don't
know what he did or what it was or how many hands he had
but they don't ask you that. And your mother says show me and
you don't know if you should put your arm around her
shoulder, rubbing, or rub your head into her neck, and she says
show me and you try to whisper the way he whispered in a deep
voice but you are too far away from her for it to be like him and
you don't know what he said so you are crying and a little sick
and you point to your legs and say here and she says show me
where he touched you and you say here and you point to your

7

legs and she says did he put anything in and you say his hands and she says anything else did he put anything else in and you don't know how many hands he had or if he put them in or in where and you are wearing bermuda shorts because it is hot, hot summer, August, black ones, too grown up for a girl your age she told you but you are always fighting to wear black because you want to be grown up and you are always fighting with her anyway and this time she let you because she didn't want to fight anymore, and she wants to know if he touched your knee and she points to your bare knee and you say yes and she wants to know if he touched higher and you don't know how high because you were sitting down and you say my legs and she asks you if he touched your bermuda shorts and you say yes and she asks you if he took them off and you think she is trying to trick you because you were at the movies and how could someone take your bermuda shorts off at the movies and she asks you if he touched under the bermuda shorts and she wants to know what he touched you with and it was dark and you couldn't see and you don't know what he touched you with or how many hands he had but she doesn't ask you that and afterwards sometimes you think he was from outer space because people from earth have two hands and when you make a drawing of him with crayons or pastels you draw a stick man with a big face and big hands, lots of hands, and sometimes you make another hand in the sky coming down and you never tell that you are drawing him and you say that he rubbed you with something inside your legs, no, not there, higher up, and she cries, your beautiful mother cries, with her long hair, with her black hair down to her shoulders, and her cotton summer dress with flowers on it from when she was young, she cries and she sits across from you and she holds your hands in hers and you feel so sorry because you always do something wrong and make her angry or sad and this was a special day when she let you go to the movies by yourself for the first time because you said you were mature enough and she let you wear black and you made her cry so you say momma I'm sorry momma nothing happened momma nothing happened he didn't hurt me momma I'm fine momma honest momma nothing happened it didn't momma honest nothing; and she says "pregnant" something; and I am punished, in my room, put alone in my room and not allowed to come out and she doesn't like me anymore, and I cry, I am going to cry until I get old, I am crying for God to see, I am afraid the man will come again because he came from nowhere the first time and he disappeared into thin air and if he is from outer space he can go anywhere or maybe he followed me like they do on television and I couldn't see him because he hid behind trees and cars and God would know if he had followed me and maybe God could stop him from finding my room or it could be like when someone is killed on television and you think he is dead and then it gets all quiet and he isn't dead and he attacks again with a knife or a gun or he is real strong and it is real quiet but suddenly he appears from nowhere so I cry but I keep my eye on the door so I will be alert in case he is just pretending to be gone but really he sneaked inside the house and he is just waiting or he could come in the window; and something hurts me like when you fall down and scrape your knees and the skin is all scraped off and it is all bloody and has cuts in it and dirt in it and your mother cleans it off and puts iodine on it and says it won't hurt but it burns and she puts a bandage on it; something hurts somewhere where he rubbed but I don't look because I'm afraid and I keep my hands away because I don't want my hands to touch me and I don't want to touch anywhere in my legs because I'm afraid; and I couldn't say something was hurting because I didn't know if something was hurting or not or where it was because maybe I was making it up because it hurt like a scraped knee but it hurt somewhere that didn't exist. I wanted God to see me crying so

9

He would know and it would count. I asked God if there were men from outer space on earth because He knew if there was life on other planets but He didn't answer me; and I knew there weren't but I knew He could have made them if He wanted to and I knew people only had two hands and I didn't know how many hands this man had and I couldn't figure it out no matter how much I tried because if he was rubbing in some places how could he be rubbing in so many places and I couldn't count how many places and if he was from outer space he could come into my room now through the air or anytime from nowhere. I wanted God to tell me the truth because I was afraid. I was trying to tell God I was hurt because I thought God should know and let me stay in my room and keep the man away and I wanted to stay in my room a long time, until I got old, and I wanted God to keep my mother away because she didn't like me anymore and I didn't want to take off my bermuda shorts or show her any more and I didn't want her to look at me anymore, and I thought God should know I needed Him and where was He? I thought maybe the man wasn't a bad man because they said nothing happened after all and I looked grown up so how could he know I was just a child and I wasn't sure if he thought I was a child or not because I did look very grown up and act very grown up but I told him I was a child and he should go away but I said it in a very grown-up way. I cried because they said nothing happened and because I didn't know if the man knew I was a child and I cried because I wanted God to know something had happened and I was a child and I wanted God to say why it was less bad if I wasn't a child because I was still the same me if I was or if I wasn't. And for the first time I didn't want to be grown up because all the adults said it was less bad. I cried because I didn't see how it could be less bad; and if I grew up were men going to be putting themselves on me in movies only it wouldn't be bad because I wouldn't be a child anymore. I cried because God was busy somewhere else and didn't come and if I cried He would know I was hurting so much somewhere that didn't exist and He could find it because He lived somewhere that didn't exist and He would know what I meant even if I couldn't say it and I wouldn't have to point here and here and here and so I kept crying in case He didn't know yet that He should be coming to me now even though people were sick and hungry all over and He had to see them too. I used to talk to God, especially when my mother was sick and in the hospital and my daddy had to be working so hard all day and all night and God would be pretty near me, in the same room, near me, and I wanted to know things like why anyone had to die or be poor or starve in China, and if China was real or just a story adults made up, and why colored people were treated so bad, and why so many Jews were dead; and I can't remember what He said but I always thought someday I would understand if I kept trying to pin Him down and maybe I could convince Him not to have things be so bad; and I had complicated discussions with Him about why He made things the way He did, because I didn't think He did it right, and I wanted to be a scholar when I grew up and write things about what God meant and intended and He would listen to my questions and arguments but the adults wouldn't; and I heard Him inside my head, and it was like He was in the room, but it was never scary and it always made me peaceful even though I thought He hadn't done things completely right and I would get calmed down and quiet even when I had been begging Him to let my mother get better or at least not die. I talked to Him a lot when my mother was in the hospital for an operation that might kill her and they told me she might die right then and I had a high fever and appendicitis and a rash and the adults told me I had to tell her over the phone that I was all right because she must not worry and die and I knew it was wrong to lie, especially because she might die right then or that night or the next day, and my last words to her would be lies, and I wanted to cry to her, but the adults said I wasn't allowed, and it didn't matter if God said it was wrong to lie if adults said you had to lie because you had to do what adults said not what God said. You had to be careful not to tell anyone you talked with God because they might think you were crazy and you had to make sure nobody heard you talking to Him and you had to remember not to tell the doctor. They told you to believe in Him and you were supposed to pray and they sent you to Hebrew School and you had to go to the children's services where girls weren't allowed to do anything anyway but He wasn't supposed to talk to you. He talked to Moses and Abraham but you were just Andrea from Camden even though Abraham had just been a boy herding sheep when he figured out there was one God. He had been staring up in the sky trying to think about God and he thought God was the moon but the moon disappeared when night was over and then he thought God was the sun but the sun disappeared when the day was over and then he figured out God had to be there all the time so He couldn't be the sun or the moon or any king because they died or any idol because you could break it and you weren't so different from Abraham before he grew up. Except that you didn't understand how he knew God couldn't be air because air is everywhere all the time and the teacher didn't know but they never say they don't know, they just make you feel stupid for asking something. You were supposed to pray but you couldn't lead the prayers because you were a girl and you couldn't read from the Torah so a whole bunch of boys who were a lot stupider than you got to do all the important things and you weren't supposed to argue with God although the rabbis did it all the time but you were a girl and you weren't allowed to be a rabbi anyway and all the rabbis who argued with Him were dead anyway and none of the rabbis you ever saw or heard who were alive ever argued with God at all. You thought they just didn't care enough but they kept telling you rules and what you had to do and what you couldn't do and how to grow up and what to think but you knew that the dead rabbis couldn't have been like them and hadn't just learned rules and so sometimes you would write arguments in the margins of books just like the great rabbis because you wanted to make commentaries like they did but you weren't supposed to write in any holy book even if it was for children so you would have to hide your writings and you would have to try to argue with God out loud in person but hiding it but mostly you would talk with God when you were crying for your mother or had had a big fight with her or if you were very scared. I had a big fight with God when I learned in Hebrew School that women couldn't go into the Temple when they had their periods because I got mine when I was nine, I was an adult when I went to the movies alone in the Bible, and it had hurt so terrible, so bad, and still did every month, and I couldn't think when anyone would need God more, and how could He keep me away and say awful things like that I was unclean when He gave you the thing. We were studying Leviticus and I was in class and I was angry with the teacher who sat slumped over the book and told me what God had said which I could see for myself. No one else was upset but maybe they hadn't gotten their periods yet and the teacher never would and he could go into the Temple all the time, the whole month, all slumped over and stupid. When I had it out with God I tried to explain over and over that I really was sincere and why would He want to keep someone sincere like me out of the Temple and there wasn't any good answer that I could figure out except that it wasn't sincerity God was looking for; He wanted people who didn't bleed so why had He made you bleed; and you thought that having a baby would be even worse and hurt even more and He said you were even more unclean and had to stay out even longer but you could solve that by not having a baby. And if you had a baby you would have nine months when you could go into the Temple and make God happy but when it got real bad and you needed Him you couldn't go because once it got really bad and blood came you were unclean. I thought women should have their babies in the Temple where God was because it might hurt less. The teacher said you had to accept things you didn't understand and God didn't have to be fair but if God wasn't who would be and how would they know how? The teacher said that when he went to dinner in people's houses he would take a book out of the people's bookcases and blow dust off it to show the wife the books weren't clean and how lazy and dirty she was. He said the books were always dusty because women were lazy and didn't take care of their husbands' books. I didn't understand why it wasn't rude to blow dust off someone's books and make them feel bad and I couldn't understand how she could stand it after she had made him dinner and been real nice. But he just laughed and said women were unclean and he had just proved it. I asked him if his books were dusty and he said his wife cleaned them and he blew on them. I didn't go to God with the problem of the books and the dust but I didn't think it was fair either. I asked my mother and she said he was my teacher and I should listen to him but I decided not to anymore. Now I had another problem on my mind. Why was what the man did less bad if I wasn't a child? If I was a grown-up and went to the movies and wanted to see the movie, why would it be less bad if the man stopped me and if he scared me and if I had to run away and if he hurt me and if he made me cry and if I didn't want him sitting next to me and whispering or anything. I wanted to know if God thought it was less bad; and I hated the adults for saying it was less bad. I wanted to know where God was when the man was there and why God didn't make the man go away. I wanted to know if God was there too. The Hebrew School teachers said God knows everything and can do anything and He's always there, everywhere. I believed He could do anything and knew everything but I didn't think He was always there because too many bad things happened and if He was there they couldn't just happen; how could they? If I see someone do something bad I'm not supposed to just watch. Momma says call the police or an adult. How could He be in the movies with me when the man came? He wouldn't even come to my room after because He knew all about it and felt ashamed for making such a horrible man. I knew He could do anything and made us all so why did He make that man? Was God there like the teachers kept saying and the rabbis kept saying and did He look or was He looking somewhere else because He could have turned to look somewhere else because it didn't take so long and time for God must be different and it must have been just a small minute for Him to turn away. Or if He had to go to India or somewhere maybe He wasn't there. I sort of thought He was there but I couldn't believe that He'd just sit and watch because that wouldn't be right and God has to do things that are right. Maybe He turned away but maybe He was there. Maybe He looked. I thought He was there, I didn't feel alone, but I couldn't stand to think He had just looked so I stopped thinking it but the only way I could stop thinking it was to think that probably God didn't exist anyway and was only a superstition and there was no God the same way there were no space creatures. I lectured myself that I was a child and I was going to grow up even though I didn't want to anymore and someday I would understand why it was less bad if I wasn't a child unless the adults were just lying, because adults lie a lot to children I had found out. Maybe they were lying about God too and maybe there wasn't one. I sort of thought God had been there though. The theater was empty but it didn't feel empty and there's a special kind of dark that feels like God's in it, it's got dots of light in it all dancing and sparkling or it's almost thick so it's just all surrounding you like a nest or something, it's something alive and you're something alive and it's all around you, real friendly, real close and kind as if it will take care of you. I was so excited to be at the movies by myself. I thought it was a very great day in my life because usually I would be fighting with my mother and she wouldn't let me do anything I wanted to do. I had to play with children and she didn't like for them to be older than me but all my real friends were older than me but I kept them secret. I had to go shopping with her and try on clothes and go with her to see the women's things and the girls' things and there were millions of them, and they were all the same, all matching sets with the dressy ones all messed up with plastic flowers, all fussy and stupid, and they were so boring, all skirts and dresses and stupid things, little hats and little white gloves, and I could only try on things that she liked and I wanted to read anyway. I liked to walk around all over and go places I had never seen before and I would always try to find a way to wander around and not have to shop with her, except I loved being near her but not shopping. Now she was going on a big trip to Lits, the biggest department store in Camden and almost near Philadelphia, right near the bridge, and I loved to be near the bridge, and I used to love to have lunch with my mother at the lunch counter in the giant store because that wasn't like being a child anymore and we would talk like girlfriends, even holding hands. So this time I asked if I could go to the movie across the street while she shopped and come back to Lits all by myself and meet her when the movie was over and instead of fighting with me to make me do what she wanted she said yes and I couldn't believe it because it made me so happy because she didn't fight with me and she had faith in me and I knew I could do it and not get lost and handle the money right and get back to the store on time and be in the right place because I was mature. I had to act like a child but I wasn't one really. She wanted to have a child but I had been on

16

my own a long time so I had to keep acting like a child but I hated it. When she was sick I was on my own and when I was with relatives I was alone because they didn't know anything and when she was in the hospital or home from the hospital I did the ironing and I peeled the potatoes and once when she couldn't breathe and fell on the kitchen floor and it was late at night and my daddy was working I called the doctor and he told me to get her whiskey right away but I didn't know what whiskey was or how to find some so he told me to go to the neighbors and I did and I got her whiskey and I ran like he told me to in the dark at night and I took care of her and made her drink it even though she was on the floor dead and the doctor said if not for how calm I was she would have died but I wasn't calm and I wanted to cry but I didn't. I thought she was dead and I stopped breathing. I had already lived in lots of different houses and you can't act like some normal child even though everyone wants you to be just normal and they don't want you to feel bad but you have to be grown up and not give them trouble and they never know what is in your heart or what you really think about because their children are normal to them and you aren't their children and their children don't know about dying or being alone so you have to pretend. So I was grown up inside and acted grown up all the time except when my mother was around because she wanted to have a child, a real child, and got angry if I didn't act like a child because it upset her to think I had got grown up without her when she wasn't there because she wanted to be the mother of a real child. When I forgot to be a child or didn't want to be I made her very mad at me and very unhappy and she thought I was trying to hurt her on purpose but I wasn't because I loved just being near her, sitting near to her when she drank her coffee, and I was so proud once when I had helped my daddy shovel snow and she let me drink some coffee just like her. I loved her hair. I loved when she talked to me about things, not telling me what to do but just said things to me about things not treating me like a baby. I loved when she let me go somewhere with her and her girlfriends. I loved even when she was sick but not real sick and was in bed for many days or sometimes many weeks and I was allowed to go in and visit her a little and sit on the bed and watch television with her and we would watch "The $64,000 Question," and we were both crazy for Charles Van Doren because he was so cute and so intellectual and we rooted for him and bit our lips waiting for him to answer and held hands and held our breath. Then I had to leave her alone because I had tired her out but I felt wonderful for hours after, so warm and happy, because my mother loved me. We held hands and we sat. But I couldn't stand the stuff she made me do. She made me sew and knit and do stupid things. I was supposed to count the stitches and sit still and be quiet and keep my legs closed when I sat down and wear white gloves and a hat when I went out in a dress. She made me close my legs all the time and I kept trying to get her to tell me why I couldn't sit how I wanted but she said girls must not ever sit so sloppy and bad and she got mad because I said I liked to have my legs open when I sat down and I always did what I wanted even if I got punished. She said I was a relentless child. But if I had to think about closing my legs all the time I couldn't just sit and talk and I thought it was silly and stupid and I wasn't going to do it and she slapped me and told me how I was just trying to hurt her. Sometimes she screamed and made me sit with my legs closed counting stitches knitting and I wanted her to die. I wanted to go everywhere and I would lie and say I was somewhere I was allowed to be and I would go somewhere I had never been just to see it or just to be alone or just to see what it was like or if anything would happen. Once I got caught because two boys who were bigger and older threw a Christmas tree at me and it hit the top of my head and blood started running down all over me. I was walking on a trashy dirt road but it had trees and bushes on it and even some poison sumac on the trees which was bright red and I thought it was beautiful and I used to pretend it was Nature and I was walking in Nature but children weren't supposed to go there alone because it was out of the way. The two boys came running out of the bushes and trees and threw a whole Christmas tree at my head and my head got cut open and blood started running down and I got home walking with the blood coming down and I got put in bed and the doctor came and it wasn't anything, only a little cut with a lot of blood he said. He said the head could bleed a lot without really being hurt bad. But I had been some place I wasn't supposed to go so it was my fault anyway even if I had been hurt very bad. I was supposed to learn that you weren't supposed to go strange places but instead I learned that my head didn't get smashed or cracked open and I wasn't going to die and I could do what I wanted if I wasn't afraid of dying; and I wasn't. I had another life all apart from what my momma said and wanted and thought and did and I did what I wanted and she couldn't stop me and I liked going places she wasn't and I liked not having to listen to her or stay with her or be like some prisoner where she could see me and I liked doing what I wanted even if it was nothing really. I hated her telling me everything not to do and I stopped listening to her and no one knows all the things I did or all the places I went. I liked it when she was away. I knew it was bad of me to like it because she was sick but I liked being alone. I got sick of being her child. I'd get angry with her and yell at her for trying to make me do things. But I was always nice to the other adults because you wanted them to like you because then they left you alone more and sometimes they would talk to you about things if you asked them lots of intelligent questions and made them talk to you. And you have to be nice to adults to show you have manners and so they won't watch you all the time and because you get punished if you aren't nice to them because adults get to punish you if they want and you can't stop them. I knew I had to be nice to the man in the movies because he was an adult and I had to talk to adults in a certain way because I was a child and I got punished if I didn't but I also wanted to act like an adult so they would leave me alone so I had to talk to·him like an adult and not cry or be stupid or act silly or act like a baby or be rude or raise my voice or run away or be scared like a baby. You had to say mister or sir and you had to be polite and if you wanted to be grown up you had to talk quiet and be reasonable and say quiet, intelligent things in a certain quiet, reasonable way. Children cried. You didn't cry. Little babies screamed like ninnies. You didn't scream. Adults didn't scream when someone talked to them quietly. The man talked very quiet. The man was very polite. I was too grown up to scream and cry and then I would have had to leave the movie if I made noise because you weren't even allowed to make any noise in a movie. You weren't allowed to whisper. I couldn't understand how come the man kept talking once the movie started because I knew you weren't allowed to talk during it. My daddy hated for me to cry. He walked away in disgust. My momma yelled at me but my daddy went away. Adults said I was a good child or I was very mature for my age or I had poise. Sometimes they said I was a nice girl or a sweet child or a smart, sweet child with such nice manners. It was a big act on my part. I waited for them to go away so I could go somewhere and do what I wanted but I wanted them to like me. My momma made me talk with respect to all adults no matter what they did. Sometimes a teacher was so stupid but my momma said I had to talk with respect or be quiet and I wasn't allowed to contradict them or even argue with them at all. One teacher in regular school made her pets stand behind her when she was sitting at her desk in the front of the room and you had to brush off her collar, just stand there behind her for fifteen minutes or a half hour or longer and keep brushing her collar on her shoulders with your open hands, palms down, stroking all the whole way from her neck to her arms. She sat at her desk and we would be taking a test or writing something or answering her questions and she would say someone had to come up and stand behind her and she wore one of those fuzzy collars you put on top of sweaters and someone had to stand behind her chair facing the class and with their hands keep brushing the fuzzy collar down, smoothing it down, with one stroke from her neck to her shoulder, the left hand had to stroke the left side of her collar and the right hand had to stroke the right side of her collar, and it had to be smooth and in rhythm and feel good to her or she would get mean and say sarcastic things about you to the class. You just had to stand there and keep touching her and they'd stare at you. You were supposed to like it because she only picked you if she liked you or if you were done your test early or if you were very good and everyone else stared at you and you were the teacher's pet. But my arms got tired and I hated standing there and I felt funny and I thought it was boring and I didn't see why I couldn't do something else like read while I was waiting for the test to be over and I tried to prolong it but I couldn't too much and I thought she was mean but the meaner she was the more you wanted her to like you and be nice to you because otherwise she would hurt you so much by saying awful things about you to the class. And my mother said she was the teacher and an adult and I had to be respectful and do what she said. I had to be nice to adults and do what they said because they were adults and I wanted to grow up so I wouldn't have to listen to them anymore and obey them but the only way to get them to think you were grown up was to obey them because then they would say you were mature and acting like an adult. You had to brush the teacher's collar and no one ever had to say why to you even if you kept asking and they just told you to keep quiet and stop asking. She could make you stand in the corner or sit alone or keep you after school or give you a bad mark even if you knew everything. I wanted to be an adult like my daddy. He was always very polite and intelligent and he listened to people and treated them fair and he didn't yell and he explained things if you asked why except sometimes when he got tired or fed up. But he was nicer than anyone. He didn't treat people bad, even children. He always wanted to know what you were thinking. He listened to what everybody said even if they were children or even if they were stupid adults and he said you could always listen even if you didn't agree and even if someone was dumb or rude or filled with prejudice or mean and then you could disagree in the right way and not be low like them. He said you should be polite to everyone no matter who they were or where they came from or if they were colored or if they were smart or stupid it didn't make any difference. My relatives and teachers were pretty stupid a lot and they weren't nice to Negroes but I was supposed to be quiet even then because they were adults. I was supposed to know they were wrong without saying anything because that would be rude. I got confused because he said you needed to be polite to Negroes because white people weren't and white people were wrong and Jews like us knew more about it than anyone and it was meaner for us to do it than anyone but I also had to be polite to the white people who did the bad things and used the bad words and said the ugly things that were poisonous and made the six million die. My daddy said I had to be quiet because I was a child. My daddy said I had to be polite to my uncle who called colored people niggers and he said I had to stay quiet and when I was grown up I could say something. I watched my daddy and he was quiet and polite and he would wait and listen and then he would tell my uncle he was wrong and Negroes were just like us, especially like us, and they weren't being treated fair at all but I didn't think it helped or was really good enough because my uncle never stopped it and I wanted to explode all the time. My daddy always said something but it was just at the end because my uncle would go away and not listen to him and no one listened to him, except me, I'm pretty sure of that. And once when my mother was sick and going into the hospital and I had to go stay in my uncle's house I cried so hard because I was afraid she would die but also I knew he would be calling colored people bad names and I would have to be quiet and I had to live there and couldn't go away and my daddy told me specially as an order that I had to be quiet and respectful even though my uncle was doing something awful. I didn't understand why adults were allowed to do so many things wrong and why children had to keep quiet all the time during them. I stayed away out of the house as long as I could every day, I hung out with teenagers or I'd just hang out alone, and I prayed to God that my uncle wouldn't talk but nothing stopped him and I would try not to move and not to breathe so I wouldn't run away or call him bad names or scream because it caused me such outrage in my heart, I hated him so much for being so stupid and so cruel. I sometimes had cuts on the inside of my mouth because I would bite down to stop from talking back and I would press my fingernails into my palms so bad they would bleed and I had sores all over my hands so I bit my nails to keep the sores from coming. You had to do what adults said no matter what even if you didn't know them or they were creeps or very bad people. The man was an adult. He wasn't so mean as my uncle in how he talked, he talked nicer and quieter. I was sitting there, acting grown up, wearing my black bermuda shorts. Outside it was hot and inside it was cold from air-conditioning. I liked the cold inside. Our house was hot and the city was hot but the movie was nice and cold and the sweat dried on you and I liked how amazing it felt. The man sat down next to me. There were a million empty seats and the theater was like a huge, dark castle, but he sat down right next to me, on my left. The whole big theater was empty. The usher was a teenager but I didn't think he was cute. He had a light blue uniform and a flashlight. He showed me to my seat. He wanted it in the middle but I kept wanting to go closer to the screen. I sat down in front where I'm not allowed with my parents because they think it's too close but I like it because then the movie is big and it seems like the people are giants and you forget everything looking at them. The theater was so big and the ceiling was so high and you could get lost in it except that the seats were all in rows. The theater was dark but not completely dark. There was dim light but not enough light really to see in or to read my book in. I had a book stuffed in my pocket. I always carried a book. I liked to read whenever I could. You could read almost anywhere but there wasn't enough light even for me so I had to sit and wait for the lights to go down all the way and the movie to start. I crossed my legs because I thought it was sophisticated. I crossed them one way, then the other way. I opened the top buttons on my blouse because I was alone now and I could do what I wanted. The man sat down and the usher wasn't there because I tried to look but I didn't want to insult the man by acting like anything was wrong. I didn't understand why he had to sit there and I wished he wouldn't but you had to be nice to people who sat next to you in a bus or in a synagogue or anywhere and I wanted to move but he hadn't done anything bad and I knew it would be an insult to him and I didn't think I was better than other people. He said some things to me and I tried to look straight ahead and I tried to be polite and not talk to him at the same time and I tried to ask him to leave me alone but not to be rude because he was an adult and it wasn't right to be mean anyway. I didn't understand what was wrong because people sit next to people all the time but I thought he could move over one seat and not be right next to me but I

24

didn't know how to say he should move over without it seeming like I was mean or thought he was dirty or poor or something bad. He said things and I said yes or no or I don't know or I don't think so and kept looking ahead to show I wasn't interested in talking and had other things on my mind and he told me I was pretty and grown up and I said I was just a child really and I had never been to the movies before myself and my mother was waiting for me and I wanted to watch the movie but when someone says you're pretty you have to say thank you. Then the lights went off and it was really dark and the room was dark and big, an enormous cave of darkness, and I felt buried alive in it as if it wasn't good and then the light started flickering across things from the screen and the man put his arm around my shoulder and I asked him not to touch me but I was very polite because I thought he was just being a friendly person because people only touched you if they were your friends or your relatives and liked you and I wanted to scream for the usher to come but I was afraid of making noise because it wasn't right to make noise and I didn't want to do something wrong and insult the man and he did all those things, many things but as if it was one thing with no breaks or stops in it because he just curled and curved and slid all over with his arms everywhere and his mouth all over and his hands everywhere and keeping me in the seat without stopping, and he kept whispering and he hurt me and I didn't know what to do except that grown-ups don't cry or make noise and he pushed his hands in me and I didn't know what to do, except he was hurting me, and he slumped more over me and in my chest and kept pressing me and then he slumped again and shaked and stopped pressing so hard and I pulled myself away from him grabbing on me and I ran and I ran all the way up the aisle in the dark and I found the usher who was all the way in the back and I said the man was bothering me but I was afraid to say what he did and the usher didn't say anything or do anything so I asked if I could sit somewhere else please and could he keep the man from bothering me please because I knew you weren't supposed to talk in the movies and the usher could make you stop and he just stared at me and he took me somewhere else with his flashlight and I sat there making my shirt right and my pants right but I couldn't make them right and wiping my hand dry and I sat there looking all around in the dark and there wasn't enough light from the movie for me to see where the man was and I couldn't look at the movie because I kept looking for the man but I was afraid that if he saw me looking for him he would think I was wanting him to come and I kept trying to see where he was in the dark and if he was going to try to talk to me more and the movie kept going on but I was afraid to watch it because maybe the man would come and I knew I couldn't find my mother because it wasn't time to meet her yet and I had to stay in the movies or I didn't have anywhere to go and then the man came and I was going to scream or hit him or shout but I was afraid to because I was never allowed to hit adults, no such thing could ever happen, and he looked at me and he stared and he walked by and down the aisle and I was afraid he would come back and I got up and I ran, I ran out, I ran into the street, into the cars, into the hot air, into the light, it was like running into a wall of heat and I couldn't breathe, and I ran to the department store and once when I was a little child I had gotten lost in a department store and I was lost from my mother a long time and someone took me to the manager because I was crying and lost and scared and they announced over the loudspeaker for my mother to come find me and she came and this was the first time I was ever so scared since then but I wouldn't cry or make noise because I didn't want the man to find me so I kept running and saying I needed the manager and I needed my mother and it was an emergency but I kept as quiet as I could and I couldn't breathe so they called her on the loudspeaker and then when she came I shook and cried and I tried to tell her and she said, did anything happen, and I kept saying yes and I kept trying to say each thing that happened and then we were on the bus and I kept crying but I wasn't supposed to talk because people could hear and it was something bad, and then we got home and I said how I didn't want the man to sit next to me and I didn't know how to tell him to go away because he was an adult and I didn't mean to do something wrong but I didn't know how to tell the man not to rub because I didn't even know what it was or if it was a mistake because maybe he was making a mistake because it was dark and maybe he thought I was someone else that he knew or it was some other mistake and when I told him he didn't listen to me and he rubbed me and I didn't want him to, I wanted him to go away, and I tried to be polite and act like an adult and not make noise in public and I didn't cry like a child and he had a dark jacket on and they asked me if it was leather but I didn't know what leather was and they asked me what it felt like but I didn't know how to say and he had on a striped shirt and he had on dark pants and he had dark hair and he didn't sit straight even when he first sat down and he had bad posture because he couldn't sit straight and he smoked and he asked me if I wanted to smoke, and I did but I didn't say that to my mother because I just looked ahead of me and said no even though I wanted to and so I was good and I didn't have to say I wanted to, and then he slumped all over me and held me still with his arm around my shoulder and his head pinned under my head so I couldn't move away and I couldn't describe him enough for them but I could still see him; and my mother cried; and now I can see him, almost, I can't remember yesterday as well, even now he's right next to me, almost, on me, almost, the pressure of his body covering my heart, almost, I can touch him, nearly, I could search the earth for him and find him, I think, or if he sat down next to me I would die, except I can't quite see his face, nearly but not enough, not quite, and I can feel his fingers going in, almost, if I touch my face his fingers are more real, and it hurts, the bruised, scraped labial skin, the pushed, twisted skin; and my daddy came into my room after I couldn't cry anymore and said nothing happened and not to cry anymore and we wouldn't talk about it anymore; and I waited to be pregnant and tried to think if I would die. I could have the baby standing up and I wouldn't make any noise. My room is small but I can hide behind the door.

TWO

In 1961 and 1962
(Age 14, 15, 16)

My name is Andrea. It means manhood or courage. In Europe only boys are named it. I live in the U.S.A. I was born down the street from Walt Whitman's house, on Mickle Street in Camden in 1946, after the war, after the bomb. I was the first generation after the bomb. I've always known I would die. Other generations didn't think so. Everyone says I'm sad but I'm not sad. It doesn't make me sad. The houses were brick, the brick was made of blood and straw, there was dust and dirt on the sidewalks, the sidewalks were gray, the cement was cracked, it was dark, always dark, thick dark you could reach out and touch and it came down all around you and you could feel it weighing on you and bumping up against you and ramming you from behind. You moved against the dark or under it or it pushed you from behind. The dark was everything. You had to learn to read it with your fingers or you would be lost; might die. The cement was next, a great gray desert. You were on it, stuck and abandoned, a great gray plain going on forever. They made you fall on your knees on the cement and stay there so the dark could come and get you. The dark pushed you, the cement was the bed, you fell on your knees, the dark took you, the cement cradled you, a harsh, angry embrace tearing the skin off your knees and hands. Some places there is a great, unbearable wind, and the fragile human breaks in it, bends in it, falls. Here there was this dark; like the great, unbearable wind but perfectly still, quiet, thick; it pushed without moving. Them in the dark, the cement was the bed, a cold slat of death, a grave with no rest, the best bed you could get, the best bed you would ever have, you fell forward on your knees pushed by the dark from behind and the dark banged into you or sometimes there were boys in cars flying by in the dark and then coming around from behind, later, the same ones; or sometimes different ones. The dark was some army of them, some mass, a creature from the deep, the blob, a giant parasite, some spreading monster, pods, wolfmen. They called you names and they hissed, hot steam off their tongues. They followed you in beat-up cars or they just stood around and they whistled and made noises, and the dark pushed you down and banged into you and you were on your hands and knees, the skin torn off, not praying, waiting, wanting all right, wanting for the dark to move off you, pick itself up and run. The dark was hissing and hot and hard with a jagged bone, a cold, brutal bone, and hips packed tight. The dark wasn't just at night. The dark was any time, any place; you open your eyes and the dark is there, right up against you, pressing. You can't see anything and you don't know any names, not who they are or the names for what they do; the dark is all you know, familiar, old, from long ago, is it Nino or Joe or Ken or Curt, curly hair or straight, hard hips, tight, driven, familiar with strange words whispered in your ear, like wind lashing it. Do they see you, do they know your name? I'm Andrea you whisper in the dark and the dark whispers back, okay babe; shut up babe; that's cool babe; that's a pretty name babe; and pulls out all the way and drives back in, harder, more. Nino is rough and bad, him and his friend, and he says what's wrong with making love here, right now, on this lunch counter. We are in Lits. I'm alone, a grown-up teenage girl; at the lunch counter, myself. They come up to me. I don't know the name of the other one. I have never heard anyone say "making love" before. Nino takes the salt shaker and the pepper shaker from the counter and he rubs them against each other, slow, and he talks staring at me so I can't move my head away from his eyes and he says what's wrong with it, here, now, in the daytime, on this lunch counter, you and me, now, and I don't know what's wrong with it; is Nino one of them, in the dark? Stuart is my age from school before he stopped coming and went bad and started running with gangs and he warned me to stay away from him and Nino who is older and bad and where they go. Nino has a knife. I write my first poem for Nino; I want it to be Nino; I'd touch him back. I ran away lots of times. I was on the bus to New York lots of times. I necked with old men I found on the bus lots of times. I necked with Vincent and Charles different times, adults, Vincent had gray hair and a thick foreign accent, Italian, and Charles had a hard, bronze face and an accent you could barely hear from someplace far, far away, and they liked fifteen-year-old girls; and they whispered deep, horsey, choked words and had wet mouths; and you crunched down in the seats and they kissed you all over, then with their hands they took your head and forced it into their laps. One became a famous movie star and I went to watch him in cowboy films. He was the baddie but he was real nice to me. I said I wanted to be a writer, a real writer, a great writer like Rimbaud or Dostoevsky. He didn't laugh. He said we were both artists and it was hard. He said, Andrea, that's a pretty name. He said follow your dream, never give up, it takes a long time, years even, and we slouched down in the seats. I knew the highway to New York and the streets when I got there. I knew the back alleys in Philadelphia too but I didn't like Philadelphia. It was fake, pretend folksingers and pretend guitar players and pretend drug dealers, all attitude, some pot, nothing hard, pretend poets, a different attitude, no poems. You couldn't get lost in the dark, it wasn't dense enough, it wasn't desolate enough, it was safe really, a playpen, the fake girls went there to not get hurt, to have regular boyfriends, to pretend they were different or bad; but I was really lost so I had to be lost, not pretend, in a dark as hard and unyielding as the cement under it. In New York I got off the bus dank from old Charles, old Vincent, he walked away, wet, rumpled, not looking back, and I had some dollars in my hand, and I took the A train to Greenwich Village, and I went to the Eighth Street Bookstore, the center of the universe, the place where real poets went, the most incredible place on earth, they made beauty from the dark, the gray, the cement, your head down in someone's lap, the torn skin on your bruised knees, your bloody hands; it wasn't the raspy, choked, rough whisper, it was real beautiful words with the perfect shape and sound and filled with pain and rage and pure, perfect; and I looked everywhere, at every book, at every poem, at every play, and I touched every book of poems, I just touched them, just passed my hand over them, and I bought any poems I had money for, sometimes it was just a few pages stapled together with print on it, and I kept them with me and I could barely breathe, and I knew names no one else knew, Charles Olsen, Robert Duncan, Gregory Corso, Anselm Hollo, Leroi Jones, Lawrence Ferlinghetti, Kenneth Patchen, Robert Creeley, Kenneth Rexroth; and when Allen Ginsberg had new poems I almost died, Allen Ginsberg who was the most perfect and the bravest and the best and the words were perfect beauty and perfect power and perfect pain and I carried them with me and read them, stunned and truly trembling inside because they went past all lies to something hidden inside; and I got back on the bus and I got back to Camden and I had the poems and someday it would be me. I wrote words out on paper and hid them because my mother would say they were dirty words; all the true words were dirty words. I wrote private, secret words in funny-shaped lines. You could take the dark—the thick, mean, hard, sad dark—the gray cement, lonely as death, cold as death, stone cold, the torn skin, you on your knees your hands bleeding on the cold cement, and you could use words to say *I am*—I am, I want, I know, I feel, I see. Nino's knife, cold, on the edge of my skin down my back, the cement underneath: I want, I know, I feel; then he tears you apart from behind, inside. You could use words to say what it was and how it felt, the dark banging into you, pressing up against you, pinning you down, a suffocating mask over your face or a granite mountain pressing you under it, you're a fossil, delicate, ancient, buried alive and perfectly preserved, some bones between the mountain and the level ground, pressed flat on the cement under the dark, the great, still, thick, heavy dark. You could sing pain soft or you could holler; you could use the voices of the dead if you had to, the other skeletons pressed in the cement. You could write the words on the cement blind in the dark, pushed on your knees, a finger dipped in blood; or pushed flat, the dark on you, the cement under you, Nino's knife touching the edge of your skin. The poems said: Andrea, me too, I'm on my knees, afraid and alone, and I *sing*; I'm pushed flat, rammed, torn up, and I *sing*; I weep, I rage, I *sing*; I hurt, I'm sad, I *sing*; I want, I'm lost, I *sing*. You learned the names of things, the true names, short, abrupt, unkind, and you learned to *sing* them, your heart soared from them, the song of them, the great, simple music of them. The dark stayed dark and hard but now it had a sound in it, a bittersweet lyric, music carried on the edge of a broken line. Then my momma found the words I wrote and called me awful names, foul names, in a screaming voice, in filthy hate, she screamed I was dirty, she screamed she wanted me off the face of the earth, she screamed she'd lock me up. I left on the bus to New York. No one's locking me up. When the men said the names they whispered and touched you; and flat on the cement, still there were no locks, no walls. When the men said the names they were all tangled in you and their skin was melting into you the way night covers everything, they curved and curled. There was the edge of Nino's knife on your skin, down your back, with him in you and the cement under you, your skin scraped away, burned off almost, the sweat on you turning as cold as the edge of his knife; try to breathe. She screamed foul hate and spit obscene words and tore up all your things, all your poems you had bought and the words you had written; and she said she'd lock you up; no one locks me up. Men whispered the same names she said and touched you all over, they were on you, they covered you, they hid you, they were the weight of midnight on you, a hundred years of midnight, they held you down and kept you still and it was the only stillness you had and you could hear a heartbeat; men whispered names and touched you all over. Men wanted you all the time and never had enough of you and the cement was a great, gray plain stretching out forever and you could wander on it forever, free, with signs that they had been there and promises they would come back, abrasions, burns, thin, exquisite cuts; not locked up. Under them, covered, buried, pinned still—the dark ramming into you—you could hear a heartbeat. And somewhere there were ones who could *sing*. Whisper; touch everywhere; *sing*.

THREE

In January 1965
(Age 18)

My name is Andrea. It means manhood or courage, from the ancient Greek. I found this in Paul Tillich, although I like Martin Buber better because I believe in pure love, I-Thou, love without boundaries or categories or conditions or making someone less than you are; not treating people like they are foreign or lower or things, I-It. Prejudice is I-It and hate is I-It and treating people like dirt is I-It. In Europe only boys are named Andrea, André, Andreus, but my mother didn't know that and so I got named Andrea because she thought it was pretty. Philosophy comes from Europe but poetry comes from America too. I was born down the street from Walt Whitman's house, on Mickle Street in Camden, New Jersey, in 1946, after the bomb. I'm not sad but I wish everyone didn't have to die. Everyone will burn in a split second, even less, they won't even know it but I bet it will hurt forever; and then there will be nothing, forever. I can't stand it because it could be any second at all, just even this second now or the next one, but I try not to think about it. I fought it for a while, when I had hope and when I loved everyone, I-Thou, not I-It, and I suffered to think they would die. When I was fourteen I refused to face the wall during a bomb drill. They would ring a bell and we all had to file out of class, in a line, and stand four or five deep against a wall in the hall and you had to put your hands behind your head and your elbows over your ears and it hurt to keep your arms like that until they decided the bomb wasn't coming this time. I thought it was stupid so I wouldn't do it. I said I wanted to see it coming if it was going to kill me. I really did want to see it. Of course no one would see it coming, it was too fast, but I wanted to see something, I wanted to know something, I wanted to know that this was it and I was dying. It would just be a tiny flash of a second, so small you couldn't even imagine it, but I wanted it whatever it was like. I wanted my whole life to go through my brain or to feel myself dying or whatever it was. I didn't want to be facing a wall pretending tomorrow was coming. I said it outraged my human dignity to have my elbows over my ears and be facing a wall and just waiting like an asshole when I was going to die; but they didn't think fourteen-year-olds had any human dignity and you weren't allowed to say asshole even the minute before the bomb came. They punished me or disciplined me or whatever it is they think they're doing when they threaten you all the time. The bomb was coming but I had to stay after school. I was supposed to be frightened of staying after school instead of the bomb or more than the bomb. Adults are so awful. Their faces get all pulled and tight and mean and they want to hit you but the law says they can't so they make you miserable for as long as they can and they call your parents to say you are bad and they try to get your parents to hit you because it's legal and to punish you some more. You ask them why you have to cover your ears with your elbows and they tell you it is so your ear drums won't get hurt from the noise. They *consult* each other in whispers and this is the answer they come up with. I said I thought my ear drums would probably burn with the rest of me so I got punished more. I kept waiting to see them wink or smile or laugh or something even just among themselves even though it wouldn't be nice to show they knew it was crap but they acted serious like they meant it. They kept telling you that you were supposed to respect them but you would have had to take stupid pills. I kept thinking about what it meant that this was my life and I was going to die and I thought I could say asshole if I wanted and face whatever way I wanted and I didn't understand why I couldn't take a walk in the fucking spring air if I wanted but I knew if I tried they would hurt me by making me into a juvenile delinquent which was a trick they had if you did things they didn't like. I kept reading Buber and tried to say I-Thou but they were I-It material no matter how hard I tried. I thought maybe he had never encountered anything like them where he lived. I kept writing papers for English on Buber's philosophy so I could keep in touch with I-Thou even though I was surrounded by I-It. I tried to reason it out but I couldn't. I mean, they were going to die too and all they could think of was keeping you in line and stopping you from whispering and making you stare at a wall. I kept thinking they were ghosts already, just dead already. Sometimes I thought that was the answer—adults were dead people in bodies giving stupid orders. They thought I was fresh but it was nothing like what I felt inside. Outside I was calm. Inside I kept screaming in my brain: are you alive, are you zombies, the bomb is coming, assholes. Why do we have to stand in line? Why aren't we allowed to talk? Can I kiss Paul S. now? Before I die; fast; one time? In your last fucking minute on earth can't you do one fucking human thing like do something or say something or believe something or show something or cry or laugh or teach us how to fight the Goddamn Russians or anything, *anything*, and not just make us stand here and be quiet like assholes? I wanted to scream and in my brain I screamed, it was a real voice screaming like something so loud it could make your head explode but I was too smart to scream in real life so I asked quietly and intelligently why we couldn't talk and they said we might miss important instructions. I mean: *important instructions*; do you grasp it? I didn't scream because I knew there might be a tomorrow but one day there wouldn't and I would be as big an asshole as the teachers not to have screamed, a shithead hypocrite because I didn't believe tomorrow was coming, one day it wouldn't come, but I would die pretending like them, acting nice, not screaming. I wanted to scream at them and make them tell me the truth— would there be a tomorrow or not? When I was a child they made us hide under our desks, crawl under them on our knees and keep our heads down and cover our ears with our elbows and keep our hands clasped behind our heads. I use to pray to God not to have it hurt when the bomb came. They said it was practice for when the Russians bombed us so we would live after it and I was as scared as anyone else and I did what they said, although I wondered why the Russians hated us so much and I was thinking there must be a Russian child like me, scared to die. You can't help being scared when you are so little and all the adults say the same thing. You have to believe them. You had to stay there for a long time and be quiet and your shoulders would hurt because you had to stay under your desk which was tiny even compared to how little you were and you didn't know what the bomb was yet so you thought they were telling the truth and the Russians wanted to hurt you but if you stayed absolutely still and quiet on your knees and covered your ears underneath your desk the Russians couldn't. I wondered if your skin just burned off but you stayed on your knees, dead. Everyone had nightmares but the adults didn't care because it kept you obedient and that was what they wanted; they liked keeping you scared and making you hide all the time from the bomb under your desk. Adults told terrible lies, not regular lies; ridiculous, stupid lies that made you have to hate them. They would say anything to make you do what they wanted and they would make you afraid of anything. No one ever told so many lies before, probably. When the Bay of Pigs came, all the girls at school talked together in the halls and in the lunchrooms and said the same thing: we didn't want to die virgins. No one said anyone else was lying because we thought we were all probably going to die that day and there wasn't any point in saying someone wasn't a virgin and you couldn't know, really, because boys talked dirty, and no one said they weren't because then you would be low-life, a dirty girl, and no one would talk to you again and you would have to die alone and if the bomb didn't come you might as well be dead. Girls were on the verge of saying it but no one dared. Of course now the adults were saying everything was fine and no bomb was coming and there was no danger; we didn't have to stand in the halls, not that day, the one day it was clear atomic death was right there, in New Jersey. But we knew and everyone thought the same thing and said the same thing and it was the only thought we had to say how sad we were to die and everyone giggled and was almost afraid to say it but everyone had been thinking the same thing all night and wanted to say it in the morning before we died. It was like a record we were making for ourselves, a history of us, how we had lived and been cheated because we had to die virgins. We said to each other that it's not fair we have to die now, today; we didn't get to do anything. We said it to each other and everyone knew it was true and then when we lived and the bomb didn't come we never said anything about it again but everyone hurried. We hurried like no one had ever hurried in the history of the world. Our mothers lived in dream time; no bomb; old age; do it the first time after marriage, one man or you'll be cheap; time for them droned on. Bay of Pigs meant no more time. They don't care about why girls do things but we know things and we do things; we're not just animals who don't mind dying. The houses where I lived were brick; the streets were cement, gray; and I used to think about the three pigs and the bad wolf blowing down their houses but not the brick one, how the brick one was strong and didn't fall down; and I would try to think if the brick ones would fall down when the bomb came. They looked like blood already; blood-stained walls; blood against the gray cement; and they were already broken; the bricks were torn and crumbling as if they were soft clay and the cement was broken and cracked; and I would watch the houses and think maybe it was like with the three pigs and the big bad wolf couldn't blow them down, the big bad bomb. I thought maybe we had a chance but if we lived in some other kind of house we wouldn't have a chance. I tried to think of the bomb hitting and the brick turned into blood and dust, red dust covering the cement, wet with real blood, but the cement would be dust too, gray dust, red dust on gray dust, just dust and sky, everything gone, the ground just level everywhere there was. I could see it in my mind, with me sitting in the dust, playing with it, but I wouldn't be there, it would be red dust on gray dust and nothing else and I wouldn't even be a speck. I thought it would be beautiful, real pure, not ugly and poor like it was now, but so sad, a million years of nothing, and tidal waves of wind would come and kill the quiet of the dust, kill it. I went away to New York City for freedom and it meant I went away from the red dust, a picture bigger than the edges of my mind, it was a red landscape of nothing that was in me and that I put on everything I saw like it was burned on my eyes, and I always saw Camden that way; in my inner-mind it was the landscape of where I lived. It didn't matter that I went to Point Zero. It would just be faster and I hadn't been hiding there under the desk afraid. I hate being afraid. I hadn't grown up there waiting for it to happen and making pictures of it in my mind seeing the terrible dust, the awful nothing, and I hadn't died there during the Bay of Pigs. The red dust was Camden. You can't forgive them when you're a child and they make you afraid. So you go away from where you were afraid. Some stay; some go; it's a big difference, leaving the humiliations of childhood, the morbid fear. We didn't have much to say to each other, the ones that left and the ones that stayed. Children get shamed by fear but you can't tell the adults that; they don't care. They make children into dead things like they are. If there's something left alive in you, you run. You run from the poor little child on her knees; fear burned the skin off all right; she's still on her knees, dead and raw and tender. New York's nothing, a piece of cake; you never get afraid like that again; not ever. I live where I can find a bed. Men roll on top, fuck, roll off, shoot up, sleep, roll on top again. In between you sleep. It's how it is and it's fine. I never did feel more at home. It's as if I was always there. It's familiar. The streets are the same gray, home. Fucking is nothing really. Hiding from the law and dumb adults is ordinary life; you're always hiding from them anyway unless you're one of their robots. I hate authority and it's no joke and it's no game; I want them dead all right, all the order givers. New York's home because there's other people the same; we know each other as much as you have to, not much. The only other way is the slow time of mothers; facing a wall, staring at a blank wall, for life, one man, forever, marriage, the living dead. I don't want to be like them. I never will be. I'm not afraid of dying and I'm not standing quiet at some wall; the bomb comes at me, I'm going to hurl myself into it; flashfly into its fucking face. I'm fine on the streets. I'm not afraid; of fucking or anyone; and there's nothing I'm afraid of. I have ideals about peace and freedom and it doesn't matter what the adults think, because they lie and they're stupid. I'm sincere and smarter than them. I believe in universal love. I want to love everybody even if I don't know them and not to have small minds like the adults. I don't mind if people are strangers or how they look and no matter how raw somebody is they're human; it's the plastic ones that aren't human. I don't need a lot, a place to sleep, some money, almost none, cigarettes. Everyone in this place knows something, jazz or poems or anarchism or dope or books I never heard of before, and they don't like the bomb. They've lived and they don't hide from knowing things and sex is the main way you live—adults say it isn't but they never told the truth yet. New York's the whole world, it's like living inside a heartbeat, you know, like a puppy you can put your head up against the ticking when you're lonely and when you want to move the beat's behind you. I don't need things. I'm not an American consumer. I'm on the peace side and I have ideals about freedom and I don't want anyone telling me what to do, I've had enough of it, I'm against war, I go to demonstrations, I'm a pacifist, I have been since I can remember. I read books and I go to places in New York, churches and bare rooms even, and I hear people read poems and in my mind I am with Sartre or Camus or Rimbaud and I want to show love to everyone and not be confined and sex is honest, it's not a lie, and I like to feel things, strong things. In New York there's people like me everywhere, hiding where regular people don't look, in every shadow there's the secret people. There are pockets of dark in the dark and the people like me are in them, poor, with nothing, not afraid, I'm never afraid. It's as if every crack in the sidewalk is an open door to somewhere; you can go between the cracks to the hidden world but regular people never even see the cracks. People the same as you go through the cracks because they're not afraid and you meet them there, in the magic places, real old from other generations even, hidden, some great underground city, dirty, hard, dark, free. There's always sex and dope and you can get pretty hungry but you can get things if you have to; there's always someone. I never doubted it was home from the start; where I was meant to come. I'm known and invisible at the same time; fitting in but always going my own way, a shy girl alone in a dark corner of the dark, the dark's familiar to me and so are the men in it, no rules can ever stop night from putting its arms around a lonely girl. I like doing what I want no matter what it is and I like drifting and I run if I have to; someone's always there, kind or otherwise, you decide quick. I love the dark, it's got no rough edges for me. I hear every sound without trying. I feel as if I was born knowing every signal. I'm an animal on instinct lucky to be in the right jungle, a magic animal charged with everything intense and sacred, and I hate cages. I'm the night, the same. You have to hurt it to hurt me. I am one half of everything lawless the night brings, every lawless embrace. I can smell where to turn in the dark, it's not something you can know in your head. It's a whisper so quiet not even the dead could hear it. It's touching fire so fast you don't burn your hand but the fire's real. I don't know much, not what things are called or how to do them right or how people act all the regular times. Everything is just what it is to me with nothing to measure it against and no way to check and I don't have any tomorrow and I don't have a yesterday that I can remember because the days and nights just go on and on and never stop and never slow down and never turn regular; nothing makes time normal. I have nineteen cents, I buy a big purple thing, it's with the vegetables, a sign says eggplant, it's the cheapest thing there is, I never saw one before, I try to cook it in my one pan in a little water, I eat it, you bet I do, it's an awful thing, I see why momma always used vegetables in cans but they cost more. I buy rice in big unmarked bags, I think it's good for you because Asian people eat it and they have lived for centuries no matter how poor they are and they have an old civilization so it must be good but then someone says it has starch and starch is bad so I stop buying it because the man's very disapproving as if I should know better because it makes you fat he says. I just boil what there is. I buy whatever costs what I have in my pocket. I don't know what people are talking about sometimes but I stay quiet because I don't want to appear so ignorant to them, for instance, there are funny words that I can't even try to say because I think they will laugh at me but I heard them once like zucchini, and if someone makes something and hands it to me I eat it. Sometimes someone asks me if I like this or that but I don't know what they mean and I stare blankly but I smile and I don't know what they think but I try to be polite. I worked at the Student Peace Union and the War Resisters League to stop the bomb and I was a receptionist at a place that taught reading and I was a waitress at a coffee shop that poured coffee-to-go and I typed and carried packages and I went with men and they had smoke or food or music or a place to sleep. I didn't get much money and I didn't keep any jobs because mostly I lived in pretty bad places or on the streets or in different places night to night and I guess the regular people didn't like it or wanted to stay away but I didn't care or think about it and I never thought about being regular or looking regular or acting regular; I did what I wanted from what there was and I liked working for peace and the rest was for cigarettes. I slept in living rooms, on cots, on floors, on soiled mattresses, in beds with other people I didn't know who fucked while I slept, in Brooklyn, in Spanish Harlem, near Tompkins Square Park, in abandoned buildings, in parks, in hallways, curled up in corners. You can build your own walls. Even the peace people had apartments and pretty things and warm food, it seemed regular and abundant but I don't know, I never asked them for anything but sometimes someone took me home and I could see. I didn't know where it came from; it was just like some play with scenery. They had plants or pretty rugs or wool things or pots; posters; furniture; heat; food; things around. I tried to live in a collective on Avenue B and I was supposed to have a bed and we were going to cook and all but that was where the junkies kept rolling on top of me because the collective would never tell anyone they couldn't sleep there and I never was there early enough so there wasn't someone asleep where I thought was mine. I never did really

44

sleep very well, it's sort of a lie to say I could sleep with junkies rolling over on top of me, a little bravado on my part, except I fell off to sleep, or some state of less awake, and then it'd happen. You are always awake a little. I lived in a living room of a woman for peace who lived with her brother. He slept in the living room, she slept in the bedroom, but she put me in the living room with him. He breathed heavy and stayed up watching me and I had to move out because she said he couldn't sleep. I stayed anywhere I could for as long as I could but it wasn't too long usually. I slept on benches and in doorways. Doorways can be like palaces in the cold, in the dark, when it's wet; doorways are strong; you feel sheltered, like in the arms of God, unless the wind changes and comes right at you and drives through you; then you wake up already shivering, sleep pulling you down because you want to believe you are only dreaming the wind is driving through you, but you started to shake unconscious and the cold permeates your body before you can bring your mind to facing it. You can't find any place in New York that doesn't have me in it. I'm stuck in the dark, my remembrance, a shadow, a shade, an old, dark scar that keeps tearing, dark edges ripping, dark blood spilling out, there's a piece left of me, faded, pasted onto every night, the girl who wanted peace. Later I found out it was Needle Park or Bed-Stuy or there were whores there or it was some kind of sociological phenomenon and someone had made a documentary showing the real shit, some intrepid filmmaker, some hero. It never happened. No one ever showed the real shit because it isn't photogenic, it doesn't stand still, people just live it, they don't know it or conceptualize it or pose for it or pretend it and you don't get to do it over if you make a mistake. You just get nailed. Fucked or hit or hurt or ripped off or poisoned with bad shit or you're just dead; there's no art to it. There's more of me stuck in that old night than anywhere. You don't just remember it; it remembers you; Andrea, it says, I know you. You do enough in it and it takes you with it and I'm there in it, every night on every street. When the dark comes, I come, every night, on every street, until New York is gone; I'm alive there in the dark rubbing up against anything flesh-and-blood, not a poor, homeless girl but a brazen girl-for-peace, hungry, tired, waiting for you, to rub up against you, take what you have, get what you got; peace, freedom, love, a fuck, a shy smile, some quarters or dimes or dollars. The dark's got a little anger in it moving right up against you. You can feel it pushing right up against you now and then, a burning flash across your thing; that's me, I'm there, Andrea, a charred hallucination, you know the way the dark melts in front of you, I'm the charred thing in the melting dark, the dark fire, dark ash burned black; and you walk on, agitated, to find a living one, not a shade stuck in midnight but some poor, trembling, real girl, hungry enough even to smile at you. That's my home you're misbehaving in with your mischievous little indulgences, your secret little purchases of girls and acts, because I was on every street, in every alley, fucked there, slept there, got drugs there, found a bed for my weary head; oh, it got weary; curled up under something, a little awake. Can't be. No one can live that way. Can't be. Isn't true. Can't be. Was. Was. I wasn't raped really until I was eighteen, pretty old. Well, I wasn't really raped. Rape is just some awful word. It's a way to say it was real bad; worse than anything. I was a pacifist and I didn't believe in hurting anyone and I wouldn't hurt anyone. I had been eighteen for a couple of months; of legal age. It was winter. Cold. You don't forget winter. I was working for peace groups and for nonviolence. It wouldn't be fair to call it rape; to him; it wouldn't be fair to him. I wasn't a virgin or anything; he forced me but it was my own fault. I was working at the Student Peace Union then and at the War Resisters League. I typed and I answered phones and I tried to be in the meetings but they didn't really ever let me talk and I helped to organize demonstrations by calling people on the phones and I helped to write leaflets. They didn't really believe in rape, I think. I couldn't ask anyone or tell anyone because they would just say how I was bourgeois, which was this word they used all the time. Women were it more than anybody. They were hip or cool or hipsters or bohemians or all those words you could see in newspapers on the Lower East Side but anytime a woman said something she was bourgeois. I knew what it meant but I didn't know how to say it wasn't right. They believed in nonviolence and so did I, one hundred percent. I wouldn't hurt anybody even if he did rape me but he probably didn't. Men were supposed to go crazy and kill someone if he was a rapist but they wouldn't hurt him for raping me because they didn't believe in hurting anyone and because I was bourgeois and anything that brought me down lower to the people was okay and if it hurt me I deserved it because if you were bourgeois female you were spoiled and had everything and needed to be fucked more or to begin with. At the Student Peace Union there were boys my age but they were treated like grown men by everyone around there and they bossed me around and didn't listen to anything I said except to make fun of it and no one treated me as if I knew anything, which maybe I didn't, but the boys were pretty ignorant pieces of shit, I can tell you that. I was confused by it but I kept working for peace. These boys all called momma at home; I heard them. I didn't. There were adults, some really old, at the War Resisters League but to me they weren't anything like the adults from school. They were heroes to me. They had gone to jail for things they believed in. They weren't afraid and they didn't follow laws and they didn't act dead and they had sex and they didn't lie about it and they didn't act like there was all the time in the world because they knew there wasn't. They stood up to the government. They weren't afraid. One had been a freedom rider in the South and he got

47

beaten up so many times he was like a punched-out prizefighter. He could barely talk he had been beaten up so much. I didn't try to talk to him or around him because I held him in awe. I thought I would be awfully proud if I was him but he wasn't proud at all, just quiet and shy. Sometimes I wondered if he could remember anything; but maybe he knew everything and was just humble and brave. I have chosen to think so. He did things like I did, typed and put out mailings and put postage on envelopes and ran errands and got coffee; he didn't order anyone around. They were all brave and smart. One wrote poems and lots of them wrote articles and edited newsletters and magazines. One wrote a book I had read in high school, not in class of course, about freedom and utopia, but when I asked him to read a poem I wrote—I asked a secretary who knew him to ask him because I was too shy—he wouldn't and the secretary said he hated women. He had a wife and there was a birthday party for him one day and his wife brought a birthday cake and he wouldn't speak to her. Everyone said he had boys. His wife was embarrassed and just kept talking, just on and on, and everyone was embarrassed but no one made him talk to her or thank her and I stayed on the outside of the circle that was around him to think if it was possible that he hated women, even his wife, and why he would be mean to her as if she didn't exist. You'd thank anyone for a birthday cake. From his book I thought he was wise. I thought he loved everyone. And if he hated women and everyone knew it how come they were so nice to him because hate wasn't nonviolence. When he died a few years later I felt relieved. I wondered if his wife was sad or if she felt relieved. I suppose she was sad but why? I thought he was this one hateful man but the others were the great I-Thous, the real I-Thous; fighting militarism; wanting peace; writing; I wanted to be the same. The I-Its were the regular people on the streets dressed in suits all the same like robots busy going to business and women with lacquered hair in outfits. But when the boys who wanted to be conscientious objectors came in for help there were always a lot of jokes about rape. I didn't see how you could make jokes about rape if you were against violence; maybe rape barely existed at all but it was pretty awful. The pacifists and war resisters would counsel the conscientious objectors about what to say to the draft boards. Vietnam was pulling all these boys to be killers. The draft board always asked what the c.o.'s would do if their mother was raped or their girlfriend or their sister and it was a big joke. The pacifists and the c.o.'s would say things like they would let her have a good time. I don't remember all the things they said but they would laugh and joke about it; it always made me sort of sick but if I tried to say something they wouldn't listen and I didn't know what to say anyway. Eventually the pacifists would tell the c.o.'s the right way to answer the question. It was a lofty answer about never using violence under any circumstance however tragic or painful but it was a lie because none of them ever thought it was anything to have their girlfriend raped or their mother. They always thought it was funny and they always laughed; so it wasn't violence because they never laughed at violence. So I'm not sure if rape even really existed because these pacifists really cared about violence and they never would turn their backs on violence. They cared about social justice. They cared about peace. They cared about racism. They cared about poverty. They cared about everything bad that happened to people. It was confusing that they didn't care about rape, or thought it was a joke, but then I wasn't so sure what rape was exactly. I knew it was horrible. I always had a picture in my mind of a woman with her clothes torn, near dead, on the floor, unable to move because she was beaten up so bad and hurt so much, especially between her legs. I always thought the Nazis had done it. The draft board always asked about the Nazis: would you have fought against the Nazis, suppose the Nazis tried to rape your sister. They would rehearse how to answer the draft board and then, when it came to the rape part, they always laughed and made jokes. I would be typing because I never got to talk or they would act irritated if I did or they would just keep talking to each other anyway over me and I felt upset and I would interrupt and say, well, I mean, rape is . . . . but I could never finish the sentence, and if I'd managed to get their attention, sometimes by nearly crying, they'd all just stare and I'd go blank. It was a terrifying thing and you would be so hurt; how could they laugh? And you wouldn't want a Nazi to come anywhere near you, it would just be foul. *The Nazis*, I would say, trying to find a way to say—*bad, very bad*. Rape is very bad, I wanted to say, but I could only say *Nazis are very bad*. What's bad about fucking my sister, someone would say; always; every time. Then they'd all laugh. So I wasn't even sure if there was rape. So I don't think I could have been raped even though I think I was raped but I know I wasn't because it barely existed or it didn't exist at all and if it did it was only with Nazis; it had to be as bad as Nazis. I didn't want the man to be fucking me but, I mean, that doesn't really matter; it's just that I really tried to stop him, I really tried not to have him near me, I really didn't want him to and he really hurt me so much so I thought maybe it was rape because he hurt me so bad and I didn't want to so much but I guess it wasn't or it doesn't matter. I had this boyfriend named Arthur, a sweet man. He was older; he had dignity. He wasn't soft, he knew the streets; but he didn't need to show anything or prove anything. He just lived as far as I could see. He was a waiter in a bar deep in the Lower East Side, so deep down under a dark sky, wretched to get there but okay inside. I was sleeping on a floor near there, in the collective. Someone told me you could get real cheap chicken at the bar. I would go there every night for my one meal, fried chicken in a basket with hot thick french fried potatoes and ketchup for ninety-nine cents and it was real good, real chicken, not rat meat, cooked good. He

brought me a beer but I had to tell him to take it back because I
didn't have the money for it but he was buying it for me. Then
I went with him one night. The bar was filled and noisy and
had sawdust on the floors and barrels of peanuts so you could
eat them without money and there were lowlife and artists
there. He smiled and seemed happy and also had a sadness, in
his eyes, on the edges of his mouth. He lived in a small
apartment with two other men, one a painter, Eldridge, the
other I never met. It was tiny, up five flights on Avenue D,
with a couple of rooms I never saw. You walked in through a
tiny kitchen, all cracked wood with holes in the floor, an
ancient stove and an old refrigerator that looked like a bank
vault, round and heavy and metal, with almost no room
inside. His bed was a single bed in a kind of living room but
not quite. There were paintings by the artist in the room. The
artist was sinewy and had a limp and was bitter, not sad, with a
mean edge to anything he said. He had to leave the room so we
could be alone. I could hear him there, listening. I stayed the
night there and I remember how it was to watch the light come
up and have someone running his finger under my chin and
touching my hands with his lips. I was afraid to go back to the
bar after that because I didn't know if he'd want me to but it
was the only place I knew to get a meal for small change.
Every time he was glad to see me and he would ask me what I
wanted and he would bring me dinner and some beer and
another one later and he even gave me a dark beer to try
because I didn't know about it and I liked it; and I would stay;
and I would go with him. I didn't talk much because you don't
talk to men even if they seem nice; you can never know if they
will mind or not but usually they will mind. But he asked me
things. He told me some things, hard things, about his life,
and time in jail, and troubles; and he asked me some things,
easy things, about what I did that day, or what I thought, or if I
liked something, or how I felt, or if something felt good, or if I

51

was happy, or if I liked him. He was my lover I guess, not really my boyfriend, because I never knew if I should go to the bar or not but I would and then we'd make love and when we made love he was a sweet man with kisses and soft talk into sunrise and he'd hold me after and he'd touch me. Sometimes he took me to visit people, his friends, and I was too shy to say anything but I thought it might mean he liked me or trusted me or had some pride in me or felt right about me and they asked me things too and tried to talk with me. Eldridge would come into the bar and get drinks and say something but always something cutting or mean so I didn't-know what to say or do because I didn't know if I was supposed to be his friend or not; only that Arthur said he loved him. I would ask him about his paintings but he would look away. I went to the bar for a long time, maybe three months, and I went with Arthur to where he slept in the bed in the living room; and we'd kiss, face to face, and the light would come up. I learned to love dawn and the long, slow coming of the light. One night I went to the bar and Arthur wasn't nice anymore. He brought dinner to me and he brought beer but he wouldn't look at me or talk to me and his face was different, with deep anger or pain or I didn't know what because I don't know how to know what people feel or think. A lot of time went by and then I thought I should go away and not come back but he sat down, it was a Saturday night, early in the night because he usually worked Saturdays until four a.m. but now it was only ten at night and it was busy, very busy, so it wasn't easy for him to sit down; and he said his sister, an older sister, Caroline, was in the hospital, and she had brought him up, and she had cancer, and she had had cancer for a long time but now it seemed she was dying, now, tonight, and he was hurting so bad, he was in bad grief, sad and angry and fucked up, and he had to go to the hospital right now and it was far away up town and it would take most of the night and probably she would die tonight; and would I go to his place, he would take me there to make sure I got there safe, and would I wait for him there—he knew I might not want to and it was a lot to ask, but would I? And I said I was sorry about his sister and I would go there and I would wait for him. He took me there and he kissed me and he showed me with courtesy to the little bed where we slept that was all made up like a sofa in what was sort of a living room, with the paintings all around, and he showed me where some books were, and he thanked me, and I said I would wait, and I was so sorry. I waited many hours. Sometimes I walked around. Sometimes I sat. There wasn't enough light to read really. I looked at the paintings. Then Eldridge came in and he touched me on my face and I pulled away and said no and said I was waiting for Arthur and his sister was dying of cancer and he was at the hospital and she was dying now, dying now, and he said yes but I'm his friend what's wrong with me I'm as good as he is I'm as good; and he limped but he was tall and strong and angry and he forced me down on the bed and he hit me flat out with his fist in my face and I fought him and he raped me and pushed me and he hit me and he was in me, sitting on top of me, upright, my skirt was up over my face and he was punching me; and after I was bleeding on my lips and down my legs and I couldn't move and I could hear Arthur coming and Eldridge said, I'm his best friend and I'll tell him you wanted it, and he said, I'm his best friend and you'll kill him if you tell him, and he said, he'll kill you if you tell him because he can't stand any more. I straightened up the bed fast because I could have been sleeping on it so it didn't have to be perfect and I straightened up my clothes and I tried to get the blood off my face by rubbing it on my sleeve and I sat on the edge of the bed with my hands folded, waiting, and the lights were out, and I didn't know if Arthur would see anything on my face, pain or bruises or cuts, and I didn't know what Arthur would believe; and he said his sister had died; and he sat down next to

53

me and he cried; and I held him; and he asked me if everything was all right; and I said yes; and he asked me if anything was wrong and I said no; and he asked me if Eldridge had bothered me and I said no; and he wanted to make love so we made love in the dark and the pain of him in me was like some hot, pointed branding iron in me, an agony of pain on pain, and I asked God to stop the pain, I had forgotten God but I remembered Him now and I supplicated Him with Arthur in me asking Him to stop the pain; and the light started coming up, so slow, and it fell, so slow, on Arthur's grief-stricken, tear-stained black face, a face of aging grace and relentless dignity, a handsome face with remorse and sorrow in it for what he had seen and known and done, the remorse and sorrow that is part of any decent life, more sorrow, more trouble than white men had, trouble because of color and then the burden of regular human pain—an older sister, Caroline, dies; and I turned my face away because I was afraid he would see bruises or cuts where I was hit or I was afraid he could see I was raped and I didn't know how to explain because I had already lied so it couldn't be true now later and tears were coming down my face and he touched the tears and he asked if I was crying because I loved him and was sad for his sister and I said yes. He slept then and I went away. I didn't come back. There's this girl I loved but she disappeared a long time ago. When we were children we played in the rubble in the street, in the broken cement, on broken glass and with sticks and bricks and garbage, city garbage, we made up mysteries for ourselves and enacted stories, we made great adventures in condemned houses, deserted garages, empty, scary warehouses, we broke into cars and churches, we trembled and held hands, we'd wrestle and we'd fight, we were tender and we were fierce; and then in alleys we would kiss each other a hundred million times. Arthur was my lover in my heart, a city lover, near to her. It made me lonely, what wasn't rape; I disappeared from him and grief washed over me pulling me near to her. She'd died when someone did something, no one would say what; but she was wild and strong, a man did something and she took pills, a beautiful girl all the adults said; it makes you lonely, what isn't rape. He slept, and I left; lonely twice; for both. You can love somebody once and somebody, a little, once. Then it ends and you're a sad, lonely girl, though you don't think about it much. After, the light would come, slow; he'd be kissing my hands.

FOUR

In February 1965
(Age 18)

I live in a funny kind of silence, I have all my life, a kind of
invisible bubble. On the streets I am quiet and there is quiet all
around and no one gets through, nothing, except for the wind
sometimes bellowing in my head an awful noise of cold
weeping. I don't look quiet but I am quiet. People don't see
much so they don't see how still I am. I see the people talking,
all the people of every kind, throwing words at everything,
throwing words at each other, throwing words at time, sitting
over coffee throwing words, peaceful or shouting, smiling or
in pain, throwing words at anything they see, anything that
walks up to them or anything that gets in their way or trying
to be friendly throwing words at someone who doesn't know
them. I don't have words to throw back. When I feel
something no right words come or no one would know what
they mean. It would be like throwing a ball that could never be
caught. They act like words are cheap and easy as if they can
just be replaced after they are used up and as if they make
things all right. If I am caught in a situation so I have to, I say
something, I say I am shy and I smile, but it's not true, I am not
shy, I just don't have these great numbers of dozens of words,
it's so blank inside, so empty, no words, no sound at all, a
terrible nothing. I don't know things. I don't know where the
people come from when the light starts coming through the
sky. I don't know where the cars come from, always starting
about an hour after the first trash can is pushed over by boys

running or cats looking for food. There's no one to ask if I knew how but I can't think how. The people come out first; in drips; then great cascades of them. I don't know how they got there, inside, and how they get to stay there. I don't know where the cars come from or where the people get all their coats or where the bus drivers come from in the empty buses that cruise the streets before the people come out. If it's raining suddenly people have different clothes to stay dry in but I don't know where they got them or where you could go to get them or how you would get the money or how they knew it was going to rain if you couldn't see it in the sky or smell it in the air. I don't know how anything works or how everyone knows the things they know or why they all agree, for instance, on when to all come out of the buildings at once in a swarm, or how they all know what to say and when. They act like it's clear and simple and they're sure. I don't have words except for my name, Andrea, which is the only word I have all the time, which my momma gave me, which I remember even if I can't remember anything else because sometimes I forget everything that happened until now. Andrea is the name I had since being a child. In school we had to write our names on our papers so maybe I remember it from that, doing it over and over day in, day out. And also my mother whispered it to me in my ear when she was loving me when I was little. I remember it because it was so beautiful when she said it. I don't exactly remember it in my mind, more in my heart. It means manhood or courage and it is from Europe and she said she was damned for naming me it because you become what you are named for and I wasn't the right kind of girl at all but I think I could never be named anything else because the sounds of the word are exactly like me in my heart, a music in a sense with my mother's voice singing it right to my heart, it's her voice that breaks the silence inside me with a sound, a word; my name. It doesn't matter who says it or in what way, I am comforted, as if it is the whisper of my mother when I was a baby and safe up against her in her arms. I was only safe then in all my life, for a while but everything ends soon. I was born into her arms with her loving me in Camden, down the street from where Walt Whitman lived. I liked having him there because it meant that once it was somewhere; it meant you could be great; it meant Camden was something; it meant there was something past the rubble, this great gray man who wasn't afraid of America and so I wasn't afraid to go anywhere and I could love anyone, like he said. Camden was broken streets, broken cement, crushed gray dust, jagged, broken cement. The houses were broken bricks, red bricks, red, blood red, I love brick row houses, I love blood red, wine red, crumbled into sawdust; we're dust too, blood red dust. It was a cement place with broken streets and broken bricks and I loved the cement and I loved the broken streets and I loved the broken bricks and I never felt afraid, just alone, not sad, not afraid. I had to go away from home early to seek freedom which is a good thing because you don't want to be a child for too long. You get strong if you go away from where you are a child; home; people say it's home; you get strong but you don't have a lot of words because people use words to talk about things and if you don't have things there's few words you need. It's funny how silence goes with having nothing and how you have nothing to say if you don't have things and words don't mean much anyway because you can't really use them for anything if you have nothing. If you go away from home you live without things. Things never mattered to me and I never wanted them but sometimes I wanted words. I read a lot to find words that were the right ones and I loved the words I read but they weren't exactly the ones. They were like them but not them. I just moved along the streets and I took what was coming and often I didn't know what to call it. We were going to die soon, that was for sure, with the bomb coming, and there weren't words for that either, even though people threw words at it. You could say you didn't want to die and you didn't want them to wipe out the earth but who could you say it to so it would matter? I didn't like people throwing words at it when words couldn't touch it, when you couldn't even wrap your mind around it at all. When I thought about being safe I could hear the word Andrea coming from my mother's lips when I was a baby, her mouth on me because she loved me and I was in her arms but it ended soon. I played in the bricks and on the cement; in rubble; in garbage; in alleys; and I went from Camden to New York and the quiet was all around me even more as if I was sinking under it sometimes; and I thought, if your momma isn't here to say your name there is nothing to listen to. If you try to say some words it is likely people don't understand them anyway. I don't think people in houses understand anything about the word cold. I don't think they understand the word wet. I don't think you could explain cold to them but if you did other words would push it out of their minds in a minute. That's what they use words for, to bury things. People learn long words to show off but if you can't say what cold is so people understand what use is more syllables? I could never explain anything and I was empty inside where the words go but it was an emptiness that caused vertigo, I fought against it and tried to keep standing upright. I never knew what to call most things but things I knew, cold or wet, didn't mean much. You could say you were cold and people nodded or smiled. *Cold*. I tremble with fear when I hear it. They know what it means on the surface and how to use it in a sentence but they don't know what it is, don't care, couldn't remember if you told them. They'd forget it in a minute. Cold. Or rape. You could never find out what it was from one of them or say it to mean anything or to be anything. You could never say it so it was true. You could never say it to someone so they would help you or make anything better or even help you a little or try to help you. You could never say it, not so it was anything. People laughed or said something dirty. Or if you said someone did it you were just a liar straight out; or it was you, dirty animal, who pulled them on you to hurt you. Or if you said you were it, raped, were it, which you never could say, but if you said it, then they put shame on you and never looked at you again. I think so. And it was just an awful word anyway, some awful word. I didn't know what it meant either or what it was, not really, not like cold; but it was worse than cold, I knew that. It was being trapped in night, frozen stuck in it, not the nights people who live in houses sleep through but the nights people who live on the streets stay awake through, those nights, the long nights with every second ticking like a time bomb and your heart hears it. It was night, the long night, and despair and being abandoned by all humankind, alone on an empty planet, colder than cold, alive and frozen in despair, alone on earth with no one, no words and no one and nothing; cold to frozen but cursed by being alive and nowhere near dead; stuck frozen in nowhere; no one with no words; alone in the vagabond's night, not the burgher's; in night, trapped alive in it, in despair, abandoned, colder than cold, frozen alive, right there, freeze flash, forever and never let loose; the sun had died so the night and the cold would never end. God won't let you loose from it though. You don't get to die. Instead you have to stay alive and raped but it doesn't exist even though God made it to begin with or it couldn't happen and He saw it too but He is gone now that it's over and you're left there no matter where you go or how much time passes even if you get old or how much you forget even if you burn holes in your brain. You stay smashed right there like a fly splattered over a screen, swatted; but it doesn't exist so you can't think about it because it isn't there and didn't happen and couldn't happen and is only an awful word and isn't even a word that anyone can say and it isn't ever true; so you are splattered up against a night that will go on forever except nothing happened, it will go on forever and it isn't anything in any way at all. It don't matter anyway and I can't remember things anyway, all sorts of things get lost, I can't remember most of what happened to me from day to day and I don't know names for it anyway to say or who to say it to and I live in a silence I carry that's bigger than my shadow or any dark falling over me, it's a heavy thing on my back and over my head and it pours out over me down to the ground. Words aren't so easy anymore or they never were and it was a lie that they seemed so. Some time ago they seemed easier and there were more of them. I'm Andrea but no one says my name so that I can hear it anymore. I go to jail against the Vietnam War; it's night there too, the long night, the sun is dead, the time bomb is ticking, your heart hears it; the vagabond's night, not the burgher's. I'm arrested in February. It is cold. There is a driving wind. It slices you in pieces. It goes right through you and comes out the other side. It freezes your bones and your skin is a paper-thin ice, translucent. I am against the War. I am against war. I find it easier to do things than to say things. I am losing the words I had about peace. The peace boys have all the words. The peace boys take all the words and use them; they say them. I can't think of ones for myself. They don't mean what they say; words are trash to them; it's hollow, what they say; but the words belong to them. In January I sat in court and saw Jay sent away for five years to a federal prison. He wouldn't go to Vietnam. I sat there and I watched and there was nothing to say. The peace boys talked words but the words were trash. When the time came Jay stood there, a hulking six-foot black man and I know he wanted to cry, and the Feds took him out and he was gone for five years. The peace boys were white. He was afraid and the peace boys were exuberant. He didn't have words; he could barely say anything when the judge gave him his few

61

seconds to speak after being sentenced or before, I don't know, it was all predecided anyway; I think the judge said five years then invited Jay to speak and I swear he almost fell down from the shock and the reality of it and he mumbled a couple of words but there wasn't anything to say and federal marshals took him off and his mother and sisters were there and they had tears, not words, and the peace boys had no tears, only words about the struggle of the black man against the racist war in Vietnam, I couldn't stop crying through the thing which is why I'm not sure just when the judge said five years and just when Jay seemed like he was going to double over and just when he was told he could say something and he tried but couldn't really. I've been organizing with the peace boys since the beginning of January, working to organize a demonstra- tion at the United States Mission to the United Nations. We are going to sit in and protest Adlai Stevenson fronting for the War. The peace boys wanted Jay to give a speech that they helped write and it covered all the bases, imperialism, racism, stinking U.S. government, but it was too awful and too tragic, and the peace boys went out disappointed that the speech hadn't been declaimed but regarding the trial as a triumph; one more black man in jail for peace. I thought they should honor him for being brave but I didn't think they should be jumping for joy; it was too sad. They weren't sad. You just push people around when you organize, get them to do what's best for you; and if it hits you what it's costing them you will probably die on the spot from it. We have meetings to work out every detail of the demonstration. It is a way of thinking, precise, demanding, you work out every possible scenario, anticipate every possible problem, you have the right people at the right place at the right time, you have everything happen that you want to have happen and nothing that you don't; and if something bad happens, you use it. I try to say things but they just talk over it. If I try to say words to them about what we are doing they don't hear the words. I think I am saying words but I must be mute, my mouth makes shapes but it must be that nothing comes out. So I stop saying things. I listen and put stamps on envelopes. I listen and run off addresses for envelopes on the mimeograph machine. I listen and make phone calls to people to get them to come to the demonstrations. I have long lists and I make the calls for hours at a time but if I talk too long or say too much someone makes a sarcastic remark or if I talk too much about the War as if I am talking about politics someone tells me I am not working hard enough. I listen and type letters. The peace boys scribble out letters and I type them. I listen and learn how to make the plans, how to organize; I take it in in a serious way, for later perhaps; I like strategy. I learn how to get people to come and exactly what to do when and what is important and how to take care of people and keep them safe—or expose them to danger if that is our plan, which they never know. I learn how to make plans for every contingency—if the police do this or that, if people going by get violent, if the folks demonstrating get hurt, if the demonstrators decide to get arrested, what to do when the police arrest you, the laws the police have to follow, how to make your body go limp in resisting arrest, how to get lawyers to be ready, how to get the press there, how to rouse people and how to quiet them down. I listen so that I learn how to think a certain way and answer certain hard questions, very specific questions, about what will happen in scenario after scenario; but I am not allowed to say anything about what to do or how to do it or ask questions or the words I do say just disappear in the air or in my throat. The old men really are the ones. They say how to do it. They do all the thinking. They make all the plans. They think everything through. I listen to them and I remember everything. I am learning how to listen too, concentrate, think it hard as if writing it down in your mind. It is not easy to listen. The peace

63

boys talk and never listen. The old men do it all for them, then they swagger and take all the credit while the old men are happy to fade to the background so the movement looks virile and young. The peace boys talk, smoke, rant, make their jokes, strum guitars, run their silky white hands through their stringy long hair. They spread their legs when they talk, they spread out, their legs open up and they spread them wide and their sentences spread all over and their words come and come and their gestures get bigger and they got half erect cocks all the time when they talk, the denim of their dirty jeans is pulled tight across their cocks because of how they spread their legs and they always finger themselves just lightly when they talk so they are always excited by what they have to say. Somehow they are always half reclining, on chairs, on desks, on tables, against walls or stacks of boxes, legs spread out so they can talk, touching themselves with the tips of their fingers or the palms of their spread hands, giggling, smoking, they think they are Ché. I live in half a dozen different places: in the collective on Avenue B on the floor, I don't fight for the bed anymore; in a living room in Brooklyn with a brother and a sister, the brother sleeps in the same room and stares and breathes heavy and I barely dare to breathe, they are pacifists and leave the door to their ground floor apartment open all the time out of love for their fellow man but a mongrel bulldog-terrier will kill anyone who comes through, this is the Brooklyn of elevated subways where you walk down dark, steep flights of stairs to streets of knives and broken bottles, an open door is a merciless act of love; in an apartment in Spanish Harlem, big, old, a beautiful labyrinth, with three men but I only sleep with two, one's a sailor and he likes anal intercourse and when he isn't there I get the single bed in his room to myself, some nights I am in one bed half the night, then in the other bed; some nights between places I stay with different men I don't know, or sometimes a woman, not a peace woman but someone from the streets who has a hole in the wall to disappear into, someone hard and tough and she seen it all and she's got a mattress covered with old garbage, paper garbage, nothing filthy, and old newspapers, and I lay under her, a pretty girl up against her dry skin and bones that feel like they're broke, her callouses, her scars, bad teeth but her eyes are brilliant, savage and brilliant, and her sex is ferocious and rough, a little mean, I find such a woman, older than me and I'm the ingenue and I'm the tough girl with the future; some nights between places I stay in a hallway in a building with an open door; some nights between places I am up all night in bars with nowhere to sleep and no one I am ready to go with, something warns me off or I just don't want to, and at two or four when the bars close I find a doorway and wait or walk and wait, it's cold, a lethal cold, so usually I walk, a slow, purposeful walk with my shoulders hunched over so no one will see I'm young and have nowhere to go. The jail was dirty, dark, foul. I wasn't allowed to make the plans or write the leaflets or draft the letters or decide anything but they let me picket because they needed numbers and it was just being a foot soldier and they let me sit in because it was bodies and they let me get arrested because it was numbers for the press; but once we were arrested the women disappeared inside the prison, we were swallowed up in it, it wasn't as if anyone was missing to them. They were all over the men, to get them out, to keep track of them, to make sure they were okay, the heroes of the revolution incarnate had to be taken care of. The real men were going to real jail in a real historical struggle; it was real revolution. The nothing ones walked off a cliff and melted into thin air. I didn't mind being used but I didn't expect to disappear into a darkness resembling hell by any measure; left there to rot by my brothers; the heroes of the revolution. They got the men out; they left us in. Rape, they said. We had to get them out as a priority; rape, they said. In jail men get raped, they said. No jokes, no laughs, no Nazis; rape; we can't have the heroes of the revolution raped. And them that's raped ain't heroes of the revolution; but there were no words for that. The women had honor. We stood up to the police. We didn't post bail. We went on a hunger strike. We didn't cooperate on any level, at any time. The pacifists just cut us loose so we could go under, no air from the surface, no lawyers, no word, no solace, no counsel, no help; but we didn't give in. We didn't shake and we didn't scream and we didn't try to die, banging our heads against concrete walls until they were smashed. We were locked in a special hell for girls; girls you could do anything to; girls who were exiled into a night so long and lonely it might last forever, a hell they made for those who don't exist. "Ladies," they kept calling us; "ladies." "Ladies," do this; "ladies," do that; "ladies," come here; "ladies," go there. We had been in the cold all day. We picketed from real early, maybe eight in the morning, all through the afternoon, and it was almost five in the evening before Adlai Stevenson came. About three or four we blocked the doors by sitting down so then we couldn't even keep warm by walking around. We sat there waiting for the police to arrest us but they wouldn't; they knew the cold was bad. Finally they said they'd arrest us if we blocked a side door, the one final door that provided access to the building. Then we saw Adlai Stevenson go in and we got mad because he didn't give a fuck about us and then we blocked the final door and then the police arrested us; some people went limp and their bodies were dragged over cement to the police vans and some people got up and walked and you could hear the bones of the people who were dragged cracking on the cement and you wondered if their bones had split down the middle. Then we went to the precinct and the police made out reports. Then the men were taken to the city jail for men, the Tombs, a place of brutality, pestilence, and rape they said; rape; and we went to the women's jail; no one said rape. It was way late after midnight when we got there. We got out of the van in a closed courtyard and it was cold and dark and we walked through a door into hell, some nightmare some monster dreamed up. Hell was a building with a door and you walked through the door. But the men got out the next day on their own recognizance because the pacifists hurried to get them lawyers and hearings, spent the whole day working on it, a Friday, dawn to dusk, and the women didn't get out because the pacifists didn't have time; they had to get the heroes of the revolution out before someone started sticking things up them. They just left us. Then it was a weekend and a national holiday and the jail wasn't doing any nasty business like letting people who don't exist and don't matter loose; we were nothing to them and they left us to rot or be hurt, because it was a torture place and they knew it but they didn't tell us; and they left us; the women who didn't exist got to stay solidly in hell; and no one said rape; in jail they kept sticking things up us all the time but no one said rape, there is no such word with any meaning that I have ever heard applied when someone spreads a girl's legs and sticks something in anywhere up her; no one minds including pacifists. One woman had been a call girl, though we didn't know it then, and she was dressed real fine so the women in the jail spit on her. One woman was a student and some inmates held her down and some climbed on top of her and some put their hands up her and later the newspapers said it was rape because lesbians did it so it was rape if lesbians piled on top of you and lesbians was the bad word, not rape, it was bad because lesbians did it, like Nazis, and it wasn't anything like I knew, being around girls and how we were. Later the newspapers said this women's jail was known as a hellhole torture place and there's a long history of women beat up and burned and assaulted for decades but the pacifists let us stay there; didn't bother them. There was a woman killed there by torture.

There were women hurt each and every day and the news-papers couldn't think of enough bad names to say how evil the place was and how full of cruelty and it was known; but the pacifists let us stay there; didn't bother them; because if you get tortured they don't hear the screams any more than if you talk in a meeting; you could be pulled into pieces in front of them and they'd go on as if you wasn't there; and you weren't there, not for them, truly you were nothing so they weren't worrying about you when you were well-hidden somewhere designed to hide you; and they weren't all overwrought just because someone might stick something up you or bring you pain; and if you got a hole to stick it up then there's no problem for them if someone's sticking something up it, or how many times, or if it's very bad. I don't know what to call what they did to me but I never said it was rape, I never did, and no one did; ever. Two doctors, these men, gave me an internal examination as they called it which I had never heard of before or seen and they used a steel speculum which I had never seen before and I didn't know what it was or why they were putting it up me and they tore me apart inside so I couldn't stop bleeding; but it wasn't rape because it wasn't a penis and it was doctors and there is no rape and they weren't Nazis, or lesbians even, and maybe it was a lie because it's always a lie or if it did happen was I a virgin because if I wasn't a virgin it didn't matter what they did to me because if something's been stuck up you once it makes you dirty and it doesn't matter if you tear someone apart inside. I didn't think it was rape, I never did, I didn't know what they did or why they did it except I knew how much it hurt and how afraid I was when I didn't stop bleeding and I wouldn't have ever said rape, not ever; and I didn't, not ever. The peace boys told me I was bourgeois; like I was too spoiled to take it. The pacifists thought if it was bad for the prison in the newspapers it was good. But even after the pacifists didn't say, see, these girls hate the War. Even these silly girls hate the War. Even the girl who's stupid enough to type our letters and bring us coffee hates the War. Even these dumb girls who walked through a door into hell hate the War. Even these silly cunts we left in a torture pit knowing full well they'd be hurt but so what hate the War. They are too stupid to hate us but they hate the War. So stop the War because these dregs, these nothings, these no ones, these pieces we sent in to be felt up and torn up and have things stuck in them hate the War. The peace boys laughed at me when they found out I was hurt. It was funny, how some bourgeois cunt couldn't take it. They laughed and they spread their legs and they fingered themselves. I wasn't the one who told them. I never told them. I couldn't speak anymore at all; I was dumb or mute or however you say it, I didn't have words and I wouldn't say anything for any reason to anyone because I was too hurt and too alone. I got out of jail after four days and I walked on the streets for some days and I said nothing to no one until this nonviolence woman found me and made me say what happened. She was a tough cookie in her own way which was only half a pose. She cornered me and she wouldn't let me go until I said what happened. Some words came out and then all the ones I had but I didn't know how to say things, like speculum which I had never seen, so I tried to say what happened thing by thing, describing because I didn't know what to call things, sometimes even with my hands showing her what I meant, and when it was over she seemed to understand. The call girl got a jail sentence because the judge said she had a history of prostitution. The pacifists didn't say how she was noble to stand up against the War; or how she was reformed or any other bullshit; they just all shivered and shook when they found out she had been a call girl; and they just let her go, quiet, back into hell; thirty days in hell for trying to stop a nasty war; and the pacifists didn't want to claim her after that; and they didn't help her after that; and they didn't want her in demonstrations after that. They let me drift, a mute, in the streets, just a bourgeois piece of shit who couldn't take it; except for the peace woman. She seemed to understand everything and she seemed to believe me even though I had never heard of any such thing happening before and it didn't seem possible to me that it had happened at all. She said it was very terrible to have such a thing happen. I had to try to say each thing or show it with my hands because I couldn't sum up anything or say anything in general or refer to any common knowledge and I didn't know what things were or if they were important and I didn't know if it was all right that they did it to me or not because they did it to everyone there, who were mostly whores except for one woman who murdered her husband, and they were police and doctors and so I thought maybe they were allowed to even though I couldn't stop bleeding but I was afraid to tell anyone, even myself, and to myself I kept saying I had my period, even after fifteen days. She called a newspaper reporter who said so what? The newspaper reporter said it happens all the time there that women are hurt just so bad or worse and remember the woman who was tortured to death and so what was so special about this? But the woman said the reporter was wrong and it mattered so at first I started to suffocate because the reporter said it didn't matter but then I could breathe again because the woman said it mattered and it couldn't be erased and you couldn't say it was nothing. So I went from this woman after this because I couldn't just stay there with her and she assumed everyone had some place to go because that's how life is it seems in the main and I went to the peace office and instead of typing letters for the peace boys I wrote to newspapers saying I had been hurt and it was bad and not all right and because I didn't know sophisticated words I used the words I knew and they were very shocked to death; and the peace boys were in the office and I refused to type a letter for

70

one of them because I was doing this and he read my letter out loud to everyone in the room over my shoulder and they all laughed at me, and I had spelled America with a "k" because I knew I was in Kafka's world, not Jefferson's, and I knew Amerika was the real country I lived in, and they laughed that I couldn't spell it right. The peace woman fed me sometimes and let me sleep there sometimes and she talked to me so I learned some words I could use with her but I didn't tell her most things because I didn't know how and she had an apartment and wasn't conversant with how things were for me and I didn't want to say but also I couldn't and also there was no reason to try, because it is as it is. I'm me, not her in her apartment. You always have your regular life. She'd say she could see I was tired and did I want to sleep and I'd say no and she'd insist and I never understood how she could tell but I was so tired. I had a room I always stayed in. It was small but it was warm and there were blankets and there was a door that closed and she'd be there and she didn't let anyone come in after me. Maybe she would have let me stay there more if I had known how to say some true things about day to day but I didn't ask anything from anyone and I never would because I couldn't even be sure they would understand, even her. And what I told her when she made me talk to her was how once you went to jail they started sticking things up you. They kept putting their fingers and big parts of their whole hand up you, up your vagina and up your rectum; they searched you inside and stayed inside you and kept touching you inside and they searched inside your mouth with their fingers and inside your ears and nose and they made you squat in front of the guards to see if anything fell out of you and stand under a cold shower and make different poses and stances to see if anything fell out of you and then they had someone who they said was a nurse put her hands up you again and search your vagina again and search your rectum again and I asked her why do you do this,

71

why, you don't have to do this, and she said she was looking
for heroin, and then the next day they took me to the doctors
and there were two of them and one kept pressing me all over
down on my stomach and under where my stomach is and all
down near between my legs and he kept hurting me and
asking me if I hurt and I said yes and every time I said yes he did
it harder and I thought he was trying to find out if I was sick
because he was a doctor and I was in so much pain I must be
very sick like having an appendicitis all over down there but
then I stopped saying anything because I saw he liked pressing
harder and making it hurt more and so I didn't answer him but
I had some tears in my eyes because he kept pressing anyway
but I wouldn't let him see them as best as it was possible to turn
my head from where he could see and they made jokes, the
doctors, about having sex and having girls and then the big
one who had been watching and laughing took the speculum
which I didn't know what it was because I had never seen one
or had anyone do these awful things to me and it was a big,
cold, metal thing and he put it in me and he kept twisting it and
turning it and he kept tearing me to pieces which is literal
because I was ripped up inside and the inside of me was bruised
like fists had beaten me all over but from within me or
someone had taken my uterus and turned it inside out and hit it
and cut it and then I was taken back to my cell and I got on my
knees and I tried to cry and I tried to pray and I couldn't cry and
I couldn't pray. I was in God's world, His world that He made
Himself on purpose, on my knees, blood coming down my
legs; and I hated Him; and there were no tears in me to come as
if I was one of God's children all filled with sorrow and
mourning in a world with His mercy. My father came to get
me weeks later when the bleeding wouldn't stop. I had called
and begged and he came at night though I had shamed them
and he wouldn't look at me or speak to me. I was afraid to tell
the woman about the blood. At first when she made me talk I

72

said I had my period but when the bleeding didn't stop I didn't tell her because a peace boy said I had a disease from sex and I was bleeding because of that and he didn't want me around because I was dirty and sick and I thought she'd throw me away too so I said I had called my parents. If you tell people in apartments that you called your parents they think you are fine then. My mother said I should be locked up like an animal for being a disgrace because of jail and she would lock me up like the animal I was. I ran away for good from all this place— home, Amerika, I can't think of no good name for it. I went far away to where they don't talk English and I never had to talk or listen or understand. No one talked so I had to answer. No one knew my name. It was a cocoon surrounded by cacophony. I liked not knowing anything. I was quiet outside, never trying. There was no talking anyway that could say I was raped more now and was broke for good. If it ain't broke don't fix it and if it is broke just leave it alone and someday it'll die. Here, Andreus is a man's name. Andrea doesn't exist at all, my momma's name, not at all, not one bit. It is monstrous to betray your child, bitch.

FIVE

In June 1966
(Age 19)

My name is Andrea but here in nightclubs they say *ma chère*.
My dear but more romantic. Sometimes they say it in a sullen
way, sometimes they are dismissive, sometimes it has a rough
edge or a cool indifference to it, a sexual callousness; sometimes they say it like they are talking to a pet dog, except
that the Greeks don't keep pets. Here on Crete they shoot cats.
They hate them. The men take rifles and shoot them off the
roofs and in the alleys. The cats are skeletal, starving; the
Cretans act as if the cats are cruel predators and slimy crawling
things at the same time. No one would dare befriend one here.
Every time I see a cat skulking across a roof, its bony, meager
body twisted for camouflage, I think I am seeing the Jews in
the ghettos of Eastern Europe sliding out of hiding to find
food. My *chère*. Doesn't it mean expensive? I don't know
French except for the few words I have had to pick up in the
bars. The high-class Greek men speak French, the peasants
only Greek, and it is very low-brow to speak English, vulgar.
No one asks my name or remembers it if I say it. In Europe
only boys are named it. It means manhood or courage. If they
hear my name they laugh; you're not a boy, they say. I don't
need a name, it's a burden of memory, a useless burden for a
woman. It doesn't seem to mean anything to anyone. There is
an Andreus here, a hero who was the captain of a ship that was
part of the resistance when the Nazis occupied the island. He
brought in guns and food and supplies and got people off the

island who needed to escape and brought people to Crete who needed to hide. He killed Nazis when he could; he killed some, for certain. No occupier has ever conquered the mountains here, rock made out of African desert and dust. Andreus is old and cunning and rich. He owns olive fields and is the official consul for the country of Norway; I don't know what that means but he has stationery and a seal and an office. He owns land. He is dirty and sweaty and fat. He drinks and says dirty things to women but one overlooks them. He says dirty words in English and makes up dirty limericks in broken English. He likes me because I am in love; he admires love. I am in love in a language I don't know. He likes this love because it is a rare kind to see. It has the fascination of fire; you can't stop looking. We're so much joined in the flesh that strangers feel the pain if we stop touching. Andreus is a failed old sensualist now but he is excited by passion, the life-and-death kind, the passion you have to have to wage a guerrilla war from the sea on an island occupied by Nazis; being near us, you feel the sea. I'm the sea for him now and he's waiting to see if his friend will drown. M venerates him for his role in the resistance. Andreus is maybe sixty, an old sixty, gritty, oiled, lined. M is thirty, old to me, an older man if I force myself to think of it but I never think, no category means anything, I can't think exactly or the thought gets cut short by the immense excitement of his presence or a memory of anything about him, any second of remembering him and I'm flushed and fevered; in delirium there's no thought. At night the bars are cool after the heat of the African sun; the men are young and hungry, lithe, they dance together frenetically, their arms stretched across each other's bodies as they make virile chorus lines or drunken circles. M is the bartender. I sit in a dark corner, a cool and pampered observer, drinking vermouth on ice, red vermouth, and watching; watching M, watching the men dance. Then sometimes he dances and they all leave the floor to watch because he is the great dancer of Crete, the magnificent dancer, a legend of grace and balance and speed. Usually the young men sing in Greek along with the records and dance showing off; before I was in love they sent over drinks but now no one would dare. A great tension falls over the room when sometimes one of them tries. There have been fist fights but I haven't understood until after what they were about. There was a tall blond boy, younger than M. M is short and dark. I couldn't keep my eyes off him and he took my breath away. I feel what I feel and I do what I want and everything shows in the heat coming off my skin. There are no lies in me; no language to be accountable in and also no lies. I am always in action being alive even if I am sitting quietly in a dark corner watching men dance. This room is not where I live but it is my home at night. We usually leave a few hours before dawn. The nightclub is a dark, square room. There is a bar, some tables, records; almost never any women, occasional tourists only. It is called The Dionysus. It is off a small, square-like park in the center of the city. The park is overwhelmingly green in the parched city and the vegetation casts shadows even in the night so that if I come here alone it is very dark and once a boy came up behind me and put his hand between my legs so fast that I barely understood what he had done. Then he ran. M and the owner of the club, Nikko, and some other man ran out when they saw me standing there, not coming in. I was so confused. They ran after him but didn't find him. I was relieved for him because they would have hit him. Women don't go out here but I do. *Ma chère* goes out. I've never been afraid of anything and I do what I want; I'm a free human being, why would I apologize? I argue with myself about my rights because who else would listen. The few foreign women who come here to live are all considered whores because they go out and because they take men as lovers, one, some, more. This means nothing to me. I've

76

always lived on my own, in freedom, not bound by people's
narrow minds or prejudices. It's not different now. The Greek
women never go out and the Greek men don't go home until
they are very old men and ready to die. I would like to be with
a woman but a foreign woman is a mortal enemy here.
Sometimes in the bar M and I dance together. They play
Amerikan music for slow dancing—"House of the Rising
Sun," "Heartbreak Hotel." The songs make me want to cry
and we hold each other the way fire holds what it burns; and
everyone looks because you don't often see people who have
to touch each other or they will die. It's true with us; a simple
fact. I have no sense of being a spectacle; only a sense of being
the absolute center of the world and what I feel is all the feeling
the world has in it, all of it concentrated in me. Later we drive
into the country to a restaurant for dinner and to dance more,
heart to heart, earth scorched by wind, the African wind that
touches every rock and hidden place on this island. There are
two main streets in this old city. One goes down a steep old
hill to the sea, a sea that seems painted in light and color,
purple and aqua and a shining silver, mercury all bubbling in
an irridescent sunlight, and there is a bright, bright green in
the sea that cools down as night comes becoming somber,
stony, a hard, gem-like surface, moving jade. The old Nazi
headquarters are down this old hill close to the sea. They keep
the building empty; it is considered foul, obscene. It is all
chained up, the great wrought iron doors with the great
swastika rusting and rotting and inside it is rubble. Piss on you
it says to the Nazis. The other main street crosses the hill at the
top. It crosses the whole city. The other streets in the city are
dirt paths or alleys made of stones. Nikko owns the club. He
and M are friends. M is lit up from inside, radiant with light;
he is the sea's only rival for radiance; is it Raphael who could
paint the sensuality of his face, or is it Titian? The painter of
this island is El Greco, born here, but there is no nightmare in

M's face, only a miracle of perfect beauty, too much beauty so that it can hurt to look at him and hurt more to turn away. Nikko is taller than anyone else on Crete and they tease him in the bar by saying he cannot be Cretan because he is so tall. The jokes are told to me by pointing and extravagant hand gestures and silly faces and laughing and broken syllables of English. You can say a lot without words and make many jokes. Nikko is dark with black hair and black eyes shaped a little like almonds, an Oriental cast to his face, and a black mustache that is big and wide and bushy; and his face is like an old photograph, a sculpted Russian face staring out of the nineteenth century, a young Dostoevsky in Siberia, an exotic Russian saint, without the suffering but with many secrets. I often wonder if he is a spy but I don't know why I think that or who he would spy for. I am sometimes afraid that M is not safe with him. M is a radical and these are dangerous times here. There are riots in Athens and on Crete the government is not popular. Cretans are famous for resistance and insurrection. The mountains have sheltered native fighters from Nazis, from Turks, but also from other Greeks. There was a civil war here; Greek communists and leftists were purged, slaughtered; in the mountains of Crete, fascists have never won. The mountains mean freedom to the Cretans; as Kazantzakis said, freedom or death. The government is afraid of Crete. These mountains have seen blood and death, slaughter and fear, but also urgent and stubborn resistance, the human who will not give in. It is the pride of people here not to give in. But Nikko is M's friend and he drives us to the country the nights we go or to my room the nights we go right there. My room is a tiny shack with a single bed, low, decrepit, old, and a table and a chair. I have a typewriter at the table and I write there. I'm writing a novel against the War and poems and theater pieces that are very avant-garde, more than Genet. I also have Greek grammar books and in the afternoons

78

I sit and copy the letters and try to learn the words. I love drawing the alphabet. The toilet is outside behind the chicken coops. The chickens are kept by an old man, Pappous, it means grandpa. There is my room, thin wood walls, un-finished wood, big sticks, and a concrete floor, no window, then the landlady's room, an old woman, then the old man's room, then the chickens, then the toilet. There is one mean, scrawny, angry rooster who sits on the toilet all the time. The old woman is a peasant who came to the city after all the men and boys in her village were lined up and shot by the Nazis. Two sons died. She is big and old and in mourning still, dressed from head to toe in black. One day she burns her hands using an iron that you fill with hot coals to use. I have never seen such an accident or such an iron. The only running water is outside. There is a pump. M's family is rich but he lives a vagabond life. He was a Communist who left the party. His family has a trucking business. He went to university for two years but there are so many books he hasn't read, so many books you can't get here. He was the first one on the island to wear bell-bottom pants, he showed up in them one day all puffed up with pride but he has never read Freud. He works behind the bar because he likes it and sometimes he carries bags for tourists down at the harbor. Or maybe it is political, I don't know. Crete is a hotbed of plots and plans. I never know if he will come back but not because I am afraid of him leaving me. He will never leave me. Maybe he flirts but he couldn't leave me; it'd kill him, I truly think. I'm afraid for him. I know there is intrigue and danger but I can't follow it or understand it or appraise it. I put my fears aside by saying to myself that he is vain, which he is; beautiful, smart, vain; he likes carrying the bags of the tourists; his beauty is riveting and he loves to see the effect, the tremor, the shock. He loves the millions of flirtations. In the summer there are women from everywhere. In the winter there are rich men from France who come on

79

yachts. I've seen the one he is with. I know he gets presents from him. His best friend is a handsome Frenchman, a *pied noir*, born in Algeria and he thinks it's his, right-wing; gunrunning from Crete for the outlawed O.A.S. I don't understand how they can be friends. O.A.S. is outright fascist, imperialist, racist. But M says it is a tie beyond politics and beyond betrayal. He is handsome and cold and keeps his eyes away from me. I don't know why I think Nikko looks Russian because all the Russians in the harbor have been blond and round-faced, bursting with good cheer. The Russians and the Israelis seem to send blond sailors, ingenues; they are blond and young and well-mannered and innocent, not aggressive, eternal virgins with disarming shyness, an ingenuity for having it seem always like the first time. I do what I want, I go where I want, in bed with anyone who catches my eye, a glimmer of light or a soupçon of romance. I'm not inside time or language or rules or society. It's minute to minute with a sense of being able to last forever like Crete itself. In my mind I am doing what I want and it is private and I don't understand that everyone sees, everyone looks, every-one knows, because I am outside the accountability of language and family and convention; what I feel is the only society I have or know; I don't see the million eyes and more to the point I don't hear the million tongues. I think I am alone living my life as I want. I think that when I am with someone I am with him. I don't understand that everyone sees and tells M he loves a whore but I would expect him to be above pettiness and malice and small minds. I've met men from all over, New Zealand, Australia, Israel, Nigeria, France, a Russian; only one Amerikan, not military, a thin, gentle black man who loved Nancy Wilson, the greatest jazz singer, he loved her and loved her and loved her and I felt bad after. I've met Greeks in Athens and in Piraeus and on Crete. It's not a matter of being faithful; I don't have the words or categories. It's being too alive to stop and living in the minute absolutely without a second thought because now is true. Everything I feel I feel absolutely. I have no fear, no ambivalence, no yesterday, no tomorrow; not even a name really. When I am with M there is nothing else on earth than us, an embrace past anything mortal, and when he is not with me I am still as alive, no less so, a rapture with no reason to wait or deny myself anything I feel. There are lots of Amerikans on Crete, military bases filled with soldiers, the permanent ones for the bases and then the ones sent here from Vietnam to rest and then sent back to Vietnam. Sometimes they come to the cafés in the afternoons to drink. I don't go near them except to tell them not to go to Vietnam. I say it quietly to tables full of them in the blazing sun that keeps them always a little blind so they hesitate and I leave fast. The Cretans hate Amerikans; I guess most Greeks do because the Amerikan government keeps interfering so there won't be a left-wing government. The C.I.A. is a strong and widely known presence. On Crete there are Air Force bases and the Amerikans treat the Cretans bad. The Cretans know the arrogance of occupying armies, the bilious arrogance. They recognize the condescension without speaking the literal language of the occupiers. Most of the Amerikans are from the Deep South, white boys, and they call the Cretans niggers. They laugh at them and shout at them and call them cunts, treat them like dirt, even the old mountain men whose faces surely would terrify anyone not a fool, the ones the Nazis didn't kill not because they were collaborators but because they were resisters. The Amerikans are young, eighteen, nineteen, twenty, and they have the arrogance of Napoleon, each and every one of them; they are the kings of the world all flatulent with white wealth and the darkies are meant to serve them. They make me ashamed. They hate anything not Amerikan and anyone with dark skin. They are pale, anemic boys with crew cuts; slight and tall and banal; filled with foul language that they fire at the natives instead of using guns. The words were dirty when they said them; mean words. I didn't believe any words were dirty until I heard the white boys say cunt. They live on the Amerikan bases and they keep everything Amerikan as if they aren't here but there. They have Amerikan radio and newspapers and food wrapped in plastic and frozen food and dishwashers and refrigerators and ranch-type houses for officers and trailers and supermarkets with Amerikan brands of everything. The wives and children never go off the bases; afraid of the darkies, afraid of food without plastic wrap, they don't see the ancient island, only Amerikan concrete and fences. The Amerikan military is always here; the bases are always manned and the culturally impoverished wives and children are always on them; and it is just convenient to let the Vietnam boys rest here for now, the white ones. The wives and the children are in the ranch-type houses and the trailers. They are in Greece, on the island of Crete, a place touched by whatever gods there ever were, anyone can see that, in fact Zeus rests here, one mountain is his profile, it is Crete, a place of sublime beauty and ancient heritage, unique in the world, older than anything they can imagine including their own God; but the wives and the children never see it because it is not Amerikan, not the suburbs, not pale white. The women never leave the bases. The men come off to drink ouzo and to say dirty words to the Greeks and to call them dirty names and laugh. Every other word is nigger or cunt or fucking and they pick fights. I know about the bases because an Amerikan doctor took me to one where he lived in a ranch-type house with an Amerikan kitchen with Formica cabinets and General Electric appliances. The Greeks barely have kitchens. On Crete the people in the mountains, mostly peasants, use bunsen burners to cook their food. A huge family will have one bunsen burner. Everything goes into one pot and it cooks on the one bunsen burner for ten

82

hours or twelve hours until late night when everyone eats. They have olive oil from the olive trees that grow everywhere and vegetables and fruit and small animals they kill and milk from goats. The family will sit at a wood table in the dark with one oil lamp or candle giving light but the natural light on Crete doesn't go away when it becomes night. There is no electricity in the mountains but the dark is luminous and you can see perfectly in it as if God is holding a candle above your head. In the city people use bunsen burners too. When Pappous makes a feast he takes some eggs from his chickens and some olive oil and some potatoes bought from the market for a few drachma and he makes an omelet over a bunsen burner. It takes a long time, first for the oil to get really hot, then to fry the potatoes, and the eggs cook slowly; he invites me and it is an afternoon's feast. If people are rich they have kitchens but the kitchens have nothing in them except running cold water in a stone sink. The sink is a basin cut out of a counter made of stone, as if a piece of hard rock was hauled in from the mountains. It's solid stone from top to bottom. There are no wood cabinets or shelves, just solid stone. If there is running hot water you are in the house of a millionaire. If you are just in a rich house, the people heat the water up in a kettle or pot. In the same way, there may be a bathtub somewhere but the woman has to heat up kettle after kettle to fill it. She will wash clothes and sheets and towels by hand in the bathtub with the water she has cooked the same way the peasant woman will wash clothes against rocks. There is no refrigerator ever anywhere and no General Electric but there may be two bunsen burners instead of one. You get food every day at open markets in the streets and that is the only time women get to go out; only married women. The Amerikans never go anywhere without refrigerators and frozen food and packaged food; I don't know how they can stay in Vietnam. The Amerikan doctor said he was writing a novel about the

Vietnam War like Norman Mailer's *The Naked and the Dead*.
He had a crew cut. He had a Deep South accent. He was blond
and very tanned. He had square shoulders and a square jaw.
Military, not civilian. White socks, slacks, a casual shirt. Not
young. Not a boy. Over thirty. Beefy. He is married and has
three children but his wife and children are away he says. He
sought me out and tried to talk to me about the War and
politics and writing; he began by invoking Mailer. It would
have been different if he had said Hemingway. He was a
Hemingway kind of guy. But Mailer was busy being hip and
against the Vietnam War and taking drugs so it didn't make
much sense to me; I know Hemingway had leftist politics in
the Spanish Civil War but, really, Mailer was being very loud
against Vietnam and I couldn't see someone who was happily
military appreciating it much, no matter how good *The Naked
and the Dead* was, if it was, which I myself didn't see. It was my
least favorite of his books. I said I missed Amerikan coffee so
he took me to his ranch-type house for some. I meant
percolated coffee but he made Nescafé. The Greeks make
Nescafé too but they just use tap water; he boiled the water.
He made me a martini. I have never had one. It sits on the
Formica. It's pretty but it looks like oily ethyl alcohol to me. I
never sit down. I ask him about his novel but he doesn't have
anything to say except that it is against the War. I ask to read it
but it isn't in the house. He asks me all these questions about
how I feel and what I think. I'm perplexed and I'm trying to
figure it out, standing right there; he's talking and my brain is
pulling in circles, questions; I'm asking myself if he wants to
fuck or what and what's wrong with this picture? Is it being in
a ranch-type house on an island of peasants? Is it Formica on an
ancient island of stone and sand? Is it the missing wife and
children and how ill at ease he is in this house where he says he
lives and why aren't there any photographs of the wife and
children? Why is it so empty, so not lived in, with everything

in place and no mess, no piles, no letters or notes or pens or old mail? Is it how old he is—he's a real adult, straight and narrow, from the 1950s unchanged until now. Is it that it is hard to believe he is a doctor? When he started talking to me on the street he said he was near where I live taking care of a Cretan child who was sick—with nothing no less, just a sore throat. He said it was good public relations for the military to help, for a doctor to help. Is it that he doesn't know anything about writing or about novels or about his own novel or even about *The Naked and the Dead* or even about Norman Mailer? Is it that he is in the military, must be career military, he certainly wasn't drafted, and keeps saying he is against the War but he doesn't seem to know what's wrong with it? Is it that he is an officer and why would such a person want to talk with me? Or is it that no man, ever, asks a woman what she thinks in detail, with insistence, systematically, concentrating on her answers, a checklist of political questions about the War and writing and what I am doing here on Crete now. Never. Not ever. Then I grasp that he is a cop. I was an Amerikan abroad in troubled times in a country the C.I.A. wanted to run and I'd been in jail against the War. I talked to soldiers and told them not to go to Vietnam. I told them it was wrong. I had written letters to the government telling them to stop. The F.B.I. had bothered me when they could find me, followed me, harassed me, interfered with me, and that's the honest truth; they'd threatened me. Now a tall man with a square face and a red neck and a crew cut and square shoulders, a quarterback with a Deep South accent, wants to know what I think. A girl could live her whole life and never have a man want to know so much. I love my country for giving me this unique experience. I try to leave it but it follows me. I try to disaffiliate but it affiliates. But I had learned to be quiet, a discipline of survival. I never volunteered anything or had any small talk. It was a way of life. I was never in danger of accidentally talking too much.

85

Living outside of language is freedom and chattering is stupid and I never talked to Amerikans except to tell them not to go to Vietnam; from my heart, I had nothing else to say to them. I would have liked to talk with a writer, or listen actually; that was the hook; I would have asked questions and listened and tried to understand what he was writing and how he was doing it and why and what it made him feel. I was trying to write myself and it would have been different from regular talk to talk with a writer who was trying to do something and maybe I could learn. But he wasn't a writer and I hadn't gibbered on about anything; perhaps he was surprised. Now I was alone with him in a ranch-type house and I couldn't get home without his help and I needed him to let me go; not keep me; not hurt me; not arrest me; not fuck me; and I felt some fear about how I would get away because it is always best to sleep with men before they force you; and I was confused, because it wasn't sex, it was answers to questions. And I thought about it, and I looked around the ranch-type house, and considered how strong he was and it was best not to make him angry; but I felt honor bound to tell my government not just about the War but about how they were fucking up the country, the U.S.A., and I couldn't act like I didn't know or didn't care or retreat. My name is Andrea I told him. It means manhood or courage. It is a European name but in Europe only boys are named it. I was born down the street from Walt Whitman's house, on Mickle Street in Camden in 1946. I'm from his street. I'm from his country, the country he wrote about in his poems, the country of freedom, the country of ecstasy, the country of joy of the body, the country of universal love of every kind of folk, no one unworthy or too low, the country of working men and working women with dignity; I'm from his country, not the Amerika run by war criminals, not the country that hates and kills anyone not white. I'm from his country, not yours. Do you know the map of his country? "I will not have a single person slighted or left away." "I am the poet of the Body and I am the poet of the Soul." "I am the poet of the woman the same as the man." "I too am not a bit tamed, I too am untranslatable, / I sound my barbaric yawp over the roofs of the world." "Do I contradict myself? / Very well then I contradict myself, / (I am large, I contain multitudes.)" He nursed soldiers in a different war and wrote poems to them. It was the war that freed the slaves. Who does this war free? He couldn't live in Amerika now; he would be crushed by how small it is, its mind, its heart. He would come to this island because it has his passion and his courage and the nobility of simple people and a shocking, brilliant, extreme beauty that keeps the blood boiling and the heart alive. Amerika is dead and filled with cruel people and ugly. Amerika is a dangerous country; it sends its police everywhere; why are you policing me? I loved his America; I hate my Amerika, I hate it. I was the first generation after the bomb. Didn't we kill enough yellow people then? My father told me the bomb saved him, his life, him, him; he put his life against the multitudes and thought it was worth more than all theirs; and I don't. Walt stood for the multitudes. Amerika was the country of the multitudes before it became a killing machine. In my mind I know I am leaving out the Indians; Amerika always was a killing machine; but this is my statement to the secret police and I like having a Golden Age rooted in Whitman. I put his patriotism against theirs. The War is wrong. I will tell anyone the War is wrong and suffer any consequence and if I could I would stop it right now by magic or by treason and pay any price. I don't think he knows who Walt Whitman is precisely, although Walt goes on the list, but he is genuinely immobilized by what I have said— because I say I hate Amerika. I've blasphemed and he doesn't recover easily though he is trained not to be stupid. He stands very still, the tension in his shoulders and fists making his body rigid, he needs his full musculature to support the tension. He asks me if I believe in God. I say I'm Jewish—a dangerous thing to say to a Deep South man who will think I killed Christ the same way he thinks I am killing Amerika—and it's hard to believe in a God who keeps murdering you. I want to say: you're like God, He watches like you do, and He lies; He says He is one thing but He is another. His eyes are cold like yours and He lies. He investigates like you do, with the same bad faith; and He lies. He uses up your trust and He lies. He wants blind loyalty like you do; and He lies. He kills, and He lies. He takes the very best in you, the part that wants to be good and pure and holy and simple, and He twists it with threats and pain; and He lies about it, He says He's not doing it, it's someone else somewhere else, evil or Satan or someone, not Him. I am quiet though, such a polite girl, because I don't want him to be able to say I am crazy so I must not say things about God and because I want to get away from this terrible place of his, this sterile, terrible Amerika that can show up anywhere because its cops can show up anywhere. He has a very Amerikan kind of charm—the casual but systematic ignorance that notes deviance and never forgets or forgives it; the pragmatic policing that cops learn from the movies—just figure out who the bad guys are and nail them; he's John Wayne posing as Norman Mailer while Norman Mailer is posing as Ernest Hemingway who wanted to be John Wayne. It's ridiculous to be an Amerikan. It's a grief too. He doesn't bother me again but a Greek cop does. He wants to see my passport. First a uniformed cop comes to where I live and then I have to go in for questioning and the higher-up cop who is wearing a silk suit asks me lewd questions and knows who I have been with and I don't want to have to leave here so I ask him, straight out, to leave me alone and he leaves it as a threat that maybe he will and maybe he won't. I tell him he shouldn't do what the Amerikans tell him and he flashes rage—at me but also at them; is this just another Amerikan colony, I ask him, and who does he work for, and I thought the people here had pride. He is flashfires of rage, outbursts of fury, but it is not just national pride. He is a dangerous man. His method of questioning starts out calm; then, he threatens, he seduces, he is enraged, all like quicksilver, no warning, no logic. He makes clear he decides here and unlike other officials I have seen he is no desk-bound functionary. He is a man of arbitrary lust and real power. He is corrupt and he enjoys being cruel. He says as much. I am straightforward because it is my only chance. I tell him I love it here and I want to stay and he plays with me, he lets me know that I can be punished—arrested, deported, or just jailed if he wants, when he wants, and the Amerikan government will be distinctly uninterested. I can't say I wasn't afraid but it didn't show and it wasn't bad. He made me afraid on purpose and he knew how. He is intensely sexual and I can feel him fucking and breaking fingers at the same time; he is a brilliant communicator. I'm rescued by the appearance of a beautiful woman in a fur coat of all things. He wants her now and I can go for now but he'll get back to me if he remembers; and, he reminds me, he always knows where I am, day or night, he can tell me better than I can keep track. I want him to want her for a long time. I'm almost wanting to kiss the ground. I've never loved somewhere before. I'm living on land that breathes. Even the city, cement and stone bathed in ancient light, breathes. Even the mountains, more stone than any man-made stone, breathe. The sea breathes and the sky breathes and there is light and color that breathe and the Amerikan government is smaller than this, smaller and meaner, grayer and deader, and I don't want them to lift me off it and hurt my life forever. I came from gray Amerika, broken, crumbling concrete, poor and stained with blood and some of it was my blood from when I was on my knees and the men came from behind and some of it was knife blood from

89

when the gangs fought and the houses seemed dipped in blood, bricks bathed in blood; why was there so much blood and what was it for—who was bleeding and why—was there some real reason or was it, as it seemed to me, just for fun, let's play cowboy. The cement desert I had lived on was the carapace of a new country, young, rich, all surging, tap-dancing toward death, doing handstands toward death, the tricks of vital young men all hastening to death. Crete is old, the stone is thousands of years old, with blood and tears and dying, invaders and resisters, birth and death, the mountains are old, the ruins are stone ruins and they are old; but it's not poor and dirty and dying and crumbling and broken into dirty dust and it hasn't got the pale stains of adolescent blood, sex blood, gang blood, on it, the fun blood of bad boys. It's living green and it's living light and living rock and you can't see the blood, old blood generation after generation for thousands of years, as old as the stone, because the light heats it up and burns it away and there is nothing dirty or ratty or stinking or despondent and the people are proud and you don't find them on their knees. Even I'm not on my knees, stupid girl who falls over for a shadow, who holds her breath excited to feel the steely ice of a knife on her breasts; Amerikan born and bred; even I'm not on my knees. Not even when entered from behind, not even bent over and waiting; not on my knees; not waiting for bad boys to spill blood; mine. And the light burns me clean too, the light and the heat, from the sun and from the sex. Could you fuck the sun? That's how I feel, like I'm fucking the sun. I'm right up on it, smashed on it, a great, brilliant body that is part of its landscape, the heat melts us together but it doesn't burn me away, I'm flat on it and it burns, my arms are flat up against it and it burns, I'm flung flat on it like it's the ground but it's the sun and it burns with me up against it, arms up and out to hold it but there is nothing to hold, the flames are never solid, never still, I'm solid, I'm still, and I'm on it, smashed up against it. I think it's the sun but it's M and he's on top of me and I'm burning but not to death, past death, immortal, an eternal burning up against him and there are waves of heat that are suffocating but I breathe and I drown but I don't die no matter how far I go under. You've seen a fire but have you ever been one—the red and blue and black and orange and yellow in waves, great tidal waves of heat, and if it comes toward you you run because the heat is in waves that can stop you from breathing, you'll suffocate, and you can see the waves because they come after you and they eat up the air behind you and it gets heavy and hard and tight and mean and you can feel the waves coming and they reach out and grab you and they take the air out of the air and it's tides of pain from heat, you melt, and the heat is a Frankenstein monster made by the fire, the fire's own heartbeat and dream, it's the monster the fire makes and sends out after you spreading bigger than the fire to overcome you and then burn you up. But I don't get burned up no matter how I burn. I'm indestructible, a new kind of flesh. Every night, hours before dawn, we make love until dawn or sunrise or late in the morning when there's a bright yellow glaze over everything, and I drift off into a coma of sleep, a perfect blackness, no fear, no memory, no dream, and when I open my eyes again he is in me and it is brute daylight, the naked sun, and I am on fire and there is nothing else, just this, burning, smashed up against him, outside time or anything anyone knows or thinks or wants and it's never enough. With Michalis before he left the island, before M, overlapping at the beginning, it was standing near the bed bent over it, waiting for when he would begin, barely breathing, living clay waiting for the first touch of this new Rodin, Rodin the lover of women. The hotel was behind stone walls, almost like a convent, the walls covered with vines and red and purple flowers. There was a double bed and a basin and a pitcher of water and two women sitting outside the stone wall watching when I walked in with Michalis and when I left with him a few hours later. The stone walls hid a courtyard thick with bushes and wild flowers and illuminated by scarlet lamps and across the courtyard was the room with the bed and I undressed and waited, a little afraid because I couldn't see him, waited the way he liked, and then his hands were under my skin, inside it, inside the skin on my back and under the muscles of my shoulders, his hands were buried in my body, not the orifices but the fleshy parts, the muscled parts, thighs and buttocks, until he came into me and I felt the pain. With Michel, before M, half Greek, half French, I screamed because he pressed me flat on my stomach and kept my legs together and came in hard and fast from the back and I thought he was killing me, murdering me, and he put his hand over my mouth and said not to scream and I bit into his hand and tore the skin and there was blood in my mouth and he bit into my back so blood ran down my back and he pulled my hair and gagged me with his fist until the pain itself stopped me from screaming. With G, a teenage boy, Greek, maybe fifteen, it was in the ruins under an ancient, cave-like arch, a tunnel you couldn't stand up in; it was outside at night on the old stone, on rubble, on garbage, fast, exuberant, defiant, thrilled, rough, skirt pulled up and torn on the rocks, skin ripped on the rocks, semen dripping down my legs. You could hear the sea against the old stone walls and the rats running in the rubble and then we kissed like teenagers and I walked away. With the Israeli sailor it was on a small bed in a tiny room with the full moon shining, a moon almost as huge as the whole sky, and I was mad about him. He was inept and sincere and I was mad about him, insane for his ignorance and fumbling and he sat on top of me, inside me, absolutely still, touching my face in long, gentle strokes, and there was a steely light from the moon, and I was mad for him. I wanted the moon to stay pinned in the sky forever, full, and the silly boy never to move. Once M and I went to the Venetian walls high above the sea. There was no moon and the only light was from the water underneath, the foam skipping on the waves. There was a ledge a few feet wide and then a sheer drop down to the sea. There was wind, fierce wind, lashing wind, angry wind, a cold wind, foreign, with freezing, cutting water in it from some other continent, wrathful, wanting to purge the ledge and own the sea. All night we fucked with the wind trying to push us down to death and I tore my fingers against the stone trying to hold on, the skin got stripped off my hands, and sometimes he was against the wall and my head fell backwards going down toward the sea and on the Roman walls we fucked for who was braver and who was stronger and who wasn't afraid to die. He wanted to find fear in me so he could leave me, so he could think I was less than him. He wanted to leave me. He was desperate for freedom from love. On the Roman wall we fucked so far past fear that I knew there was only me, it didn't matter where he went or what he did, it didn't matter who with or how many or how hard he tried. There was just me, the one they kept telling him was a whore, all his great friends, all the men who sat around scratching themselves, and no matter how long he lived there would be me and if he was dead and buried there would still be me, just me. I couldn't breathe without him but they expect that from a woman. I'd have so much pain without him I wouldn't live for a minute. But he wasn't supposed to need me so bad you could see him ripped up inside from a mile away. The pain wasn't supposed to rip through him; from wanting me; every second; now. He was supposed to come and go, where he wanted, when he wanted, get laid when he wanted, do this or that to me, what he wanted, sex acts, nice and neat, juicy and dirty but nice and neat picked from a catalogue of what men like or what men pay for, one sex act followed by another sex act and then he goes away to someone else or to somewhere else, a kiss if he condescends, I blow him, a fuck, twice if he has the time and likes it and feels so inclined; and I'm supposed to wait in between and when he shows up I'm supposed to suck and I'm supposed to rub, faster now, harder now, or he can rub, faster now, harder now, inside me if he wants; and there's some chat, or some money, or a cigarette, or maybe sometimes a fast dinner in a place where no one will see. But he's burning so bright it's no secret he's on fire; and it's me. Anyone near him is blinded, the heat hurts them, their skin melts, more than they ever feel when they fuck rubbing themselves in and out of a woman. He's burning but he's not indestructible. He's the sun; I'm smashed up against him; but the sun burns itself up; one day it will be cold and dead. He's burning towards death and a man's not supposed to. A dry fuck with a dry heart is being a man; a dry, heartless fuck with a dry, heartless heart. He's the great dancer, the most beautiful; he had all the women and all the men; and now he is self-immolating; he is torrential explosions of fire, pillars of flame, miles high; he is a force field of heat miles wide. The ground burns under him and anything he touches is seared. The heat spreads, a fever of discontent. The men are fevered, an epidemic of fury; they are hot but they can't burn. He's dying in front of them, torched, and I'm smashed up on him, whole, arms up and outstretched, on him, flat up against the flames, indestructible. The whore's killing him; she's a whore and she's killing you. He can't stay away but he tries. He enumerates for me my lovers. He misses some but I am discreet. He breaks down because I am not pregnant yet. I show him my birth control pills, which he has never seen; I explain that I won't be getting pregnant. He disappears for a day, two days, then suddenly he is in front of me, on his knees, his smile stopping my heart, he stoops with a dancer's swift grace, there is a gift in his hands but his hands don't touch mine, he drops the gift and I catch it and he is gone, I catch it before it hits the ground and when I look up he is gone, I could have dreamed it but I have the flowers or the bread or the book or the red-painted Easter egg or the drawing. He's gone and time takes his place, a knife slicing me into pieces; each second is a long, slow cut. Time can slow down so you can't outlast it. It can have a minute longer than your life. Time can stand still and you can feel yourself dying in it but you can't make it go faster and you can't die any faster and if it doesn't move you will never die at all and it won't move; you are caved in underground with time collapsed in on top of you. Time's the cruelest lover you'll ever have, merciless and thorough, wrapping itself right around your heart and choking it and never stopping because time is never over. Time turns your bed into a grave and you can't breathe because time pushes down on your heart to kill it. Time crawls with its legs spread out all over you. It's everywhere, a noxious poison, it's vapor and gas and air, it seeps, it spreads, you can't run away somewhere so it won't hurt you, it's there before you are, waiting. He's gone and he's left time behind to punish you; but why? Why isn't he here yet; or now; or now; or now; and not one second has passed yet. He doesn't want to burn; but why? Why should he want less, to be less, to feel less, to know less; why shouldn't he push himself as far as he can go; why shouldn't he burn until he dies? I have a certain ruthless objectivity not uncommon among those who live inside the senses; I love him without restraint, without limit, without respect to consequences, for me or for him; I am not sentimental; I want him; this is not dopey, stupid, sentimental love; nostalgia and lingering romance; this is it; all; everything. I don't care about his small stupid social life among stupid, mediocre men—I know him, self-immolating, torched, in me. His phony friends embarrass him, the men all around on the streets playing cards and drinking and gossiping, the stupid men who lust for how much he feels, can't imagine anything other than manipulating tourists into bed so they can brag or sex transactions for money or the duties of the marital bed, the roll-over fuck; and he's burning, consumed, dying; so what? He'd show up suddenly and then he'd be gone and he never touched me; how could he not touch me? He'd come in a burst and then he'd disappear and he'd never touch me and sometimes he brought someone with him so he couldn't touch me or be with me or stay near me or come near me to touch me; how could he not touch me? I went into a white hot rage, a delirium of rage; if I'd had his children I would have sliced their necks open. I used razor blades to cut delicate lines into my hands; physical pain was easy, a distraction. Keeping the blade on my hand, away from my wrist, took all my concentration, a game of nerves, a lover's game. I made fine lines that turned burgundy from blood the way artists etch lines in glass but the glass doesn't turn red for them and the red doesn't smear and drip. There was a man, I wanted it to be M but it wasn't M. He tied me up and hurt me and on my back there were marks where he used a whip he had for animals and I wanted M to see but he didn't come and he didn't see. I would have stayed there strung-up against the wall my back cut open forever for him to see but he didn't see. Then one day he came in the afternoon and knocked on the door and politely asked me to have dinner with him that night. Usually we talked in broken words in broken languages, messy, tripping over each other. This was a quiet, formal, aloof invitation with barely any words at all. He came in a car with a driver. We sat in the back. He was elaborately courteous. He didn't say anything. I thought he would explain things and say why. I sat quietly and waited. He was unfailingly polite. We ate dinner. He said nothing except do you like your dinner and would you like more wine and I nodded whatever he said and my eyes were open looking right at him asking him to tell me something that would rescue me, bring me back to being someone human with a human life.

Then he said he would take me home, formally, politely, and at my door he asked if he could come in and I said he could only if we could talk and he nodded his assent and the driver waited for him and we went in and he touched me to fuck me, his hands pushing me down on the bed, and I wanted him dead and I tried to kill him with my bare hands for touching me, for not saying one word to me, for pushing me to fuck me, and I hit his face with my fist and I hit his neck and I pushed his neck so hard I twisted it half around and he was stunned to feel the pain and he was enraged and he pushed me down to fuck me and he pinned me down with his hands and shoulders and chest and legs and he kept fucking me and he said now he was fucking me the way he fucked all whores, yes he went to brothels and fucked whores, what did I think, that he only fucked me, no man only fucked one woman, and I would find out how much he had loved me before because this was how he fucked whores and this was how he would fuck me from now on and it went on forever and I stopped fighting because my heart died and I lay still and I didn't move and it still kept going on and I stared at him and I hated him, I kept my eyes open and I stared, and it wasn't over for a long time but I had died during it so it didn't matter when it ended or when he stopped or when he pulled out of me finally or when he was gone from inside me and then it was over and there was numbness close to death throughout me and there was some man between my legs. I hadn't moved and I didn't move, I couldn't move, I was on my back and he had been on top of me to fuck me and then he slid down to where his head was between my legs and he turned over on his back and he rested the back of his head between my legs where he had fucked me and he rested there like some sweet, tired baby who had just been born only they put him between my legs instead of in my arms and he said we would get married now because there was nothing else left for either of us; pity the poor lover, it hurt him too. He was immensely sad and immensely bitter and he said we would get married now because married people did it like this and hated each other and felt dead, fucking was like being dead for them; pity the poor husband, he felt dead. He stayed between my legs, resting. I didn't move because there is an anguish that can stop you from moving and I couldn't kill him because there is an anguish that can stop you from killing. Something awful came, a suffering bigger than my life or your life or any life or God's life, the crucifixion God; the nails are hammered in but you don't get to die. It's the cross for ladies, a bed, and you don't get to die; the lucky boy, the favorite child, gets to die. You've been mowed down inside, slaughtered inside, a genocide happened in you, but you don't get to die. You're not God's son, you're His daughter, and He leaves you there nailed because you're some stupid piece of shit who loved someone and you will be there forever, in some bed somewhere for the rest of your life and He will make it a long time, He will make you get old, and He will see to it that you get fucked, and the skin around where you get fucked will be calloused and blistered and enraged and there will be someone climbing on you and getting in you and God your Father will watch; even when you're old He'll watch. M left at sunrise, sad boy, poor boy, immensely sad, tired boy, and time was back on top of me and I couldn't move and I waited on the bed to die but I didn't die because God hates me; it's hate. I couldn't move and I endured all the seconds in the day, every single second. A second stretches out past hell and when one is over another comes, longer, worse. It got dark and I dressed myself—that night, ten thousand years later, ten million years later; I dressed myself and I went to the club and M was serving drinks and his friend the *pied noir* was there, the handsome fascist, the gunrunner for the O.A.S., and this time he looked at me, now he looked at me, and it was hard to breathe, and I was transfixed by him; and the noisy room got quiet with danger and you could feel him and me and you could see him and me and we couldn't stop and the fuck we wanted filled the room even though we didn't go near each other and he was absolutely still and completely frightened because M might kill him or me and I didn't care but he was afraid, the great big man was afraid, and I wanted him and I didn't care what it cost just so I had him, and M said take her, I give her to you, he shouted, he spit, and I walked out in a rage, a modern rage that anyone would dare to give me to someone; me; a free woman. Outside there's an African wind blowing on the island, restless, violent, and there's perfume in the wind, a heavy poppy smell, intoxicating, sweet and heavy. The *pied noir* is deranged by it and he knows what M did and he is deranged by that, he wants me with M's nasty fuck on me, fresh like fresh-killed meat. God is the master of pain and He made it so you could love someone forever even if someone cut your heart open. I wait in my bed, I leave the front door open. I want the fascist; I want him bad. I am fresh-killed meat.

SIX

In June 1967
(Age 20)

One night I'm just there, where I live, alone, afraid, the men have been trying to come in. I'm for using men up as fast as you can; pulling them, grab, twist, put it here, so they dangle like twisted dough or you bend them all around like pretzels; you pull down, the asshole crawls. You need a firm, fast hand, a steady stare, calm nerve; grab, twist. First, fast; before they get to throw you down. You surprise them with your stance, warrior queen, quiet, mean, and once your hands are around their thing they're stupid, not tough; still mean but slow and you can get gone, it takes the edge off how mean he's going to be. Were you ever so alone as me? It doesn't matter what they do to you just so you get them first—it's your game and you get money; even if they shit on you it's your game; as long as it's your game you have freedom, you say it's fun but whatever you say you're in charge. Some people think being poor is the freedom or the game. It's being the one who says how and do it to me now; instead of just waiting until he does it and he's gone. You got to be mad at them perpetually and forever and fierce and you got to know that you got a cunt and that's it. You want philosophy and you're dumb and dead; you want true love and real romance, the same. You put your hand between them and your twat and you got a chance; you use it like it's a muscle, sinew and grease, a gun, a knife; you grab and twist and turn and stare him in the eye, smile, he's already losing because you got there first, between his legs; his

100

thing's in your fist and your fist is closing on him fast and he's got a failure of nerve for one second, a pause, a gulp, one second, disarmed, unsure, long enough so he doesn't know, can't remember, how mean he is; and then you have to take him into you, of course, you've given your word; there on the cement or in a shadow or some room; a shadow's warm and dark and consoling and no one can close the door on you and lock you in; you don't go with him somewhere unless you got a feeling for him because you never know what they'll do; you go for the edge, a feeling, it's worth the risk; you learn what they want, early, easy, it's not hard, you can ride the energy they give out or see it in how they move or read it off their hips; or you can guide them, there's never enough blow jobs they had to make them tired of it if worse comes to worse and you need to, it will make him stupid and weak but sometimes he's mean after because he's sure you're dirt, anyone who's had him in her mouth is dirt, how do they get by, these guys, so low and mean. It's you, him, midnight, cement; viscous dark, slate gray bed, light falling down from tarnished bulbs above you; neon somewhere rattling, shaking, static shocks to your eye, flash, zing, zip, winding words, a long poem in flickering light; what is neon and how did it get into the sky at night? The great gray poet talked it but he didn't have to do it. He was a shithead. I'm the real poet of everyone; the Amerikan democrat on cement, with everyone; it wears you down, Walt; I don't like poetry anymore; it's semen, you great gray clod, not some fraternal wave of democratic joy. I was born in 1946 down the street from where Walt Whitman lived; the girl he never wanted, I can face it now; in Camden, the great gray city; on great gray cement, broken, bleeding, the girls squashed down on it, the fuck weighing down on top, pushing in behind; blood staining the gravel, mine not his; bullshitter poet, great gray bullshitter; having all the men in the world, and all the women, hard, real, true, it wears you down, great gray virgin with fantastic dreams, you great gray fool. I was born in 1946 down the street from where Walt Whitman lived, in Camden, Andrea, it means manhood or courage but it was pink pussy anyway wrapped in a pink fuzzy blanket with big men's fingers going coochie coochie coo. Pappa said don't believe what's in books but if it was a poem I believed it; my first lyric poem was a street, cement, gray, lined with monuments, broken brick buildings, archaic, empty vessels, great, bloodstained walls, a winding road to nowhere, gray, hard, light falling on it from a tarnished moon so it was silver and brass in the dark and it went out straight into the gray sky where the moon was, one road of cement and silver and night stained red with real blood, you're down on your knees and he's pushing you from inside, God's heartbeat ramming into you and the skin is scraped loose and you bleed and stain the stone under you. Here's the poem you got. It's your flesh scraped until it's rubbed off and you got a mark, you got a burn, you got stains of blood, you got desolation on you. It's his mark on you and you've got his smell on you and his bruise inside you; the houses are monuments, brick, broken brick, red, blood red. There's a skyline, five floors high, three floors high, broken brick, chopped off brick, empty inside, with gravel lots and a winding cement road, Dorothy tap-dances to Oz, up the yellow brick road, the great gray road, he's on you, twisted on top of you, his arms twisted in your arms, his legs twisted in your legs, he's twisted in you, there's a great animal in the dark, him twisting draped over you, the sweat silver and slick; the houses are brick, monuments around you, you're laid out dead and they're the headstones, nothing written on them, they tower over your body put to rest. The only signs of existence are on you, you carry them on you, the marks, the bruises, the scars, your body gets marked where you exist, it's a history book with the signs of civilized life, communication, the city, the society, *belles lettres*, a primitive alphabet of blood and pain, the flesh poem, poem of the girl, when a girl says yes, what a girl says yes to, what happens to a girl who is poesy on cement, your body the paper and the poem, the press and the ink, the singer and the song; it's real, it's literal, this song of myself, you're what there is, the medium, the message, the sign, the signifier; an autistic poem. Tattooed boys are your friends, they write the words on their skin; but your skin gets used up, scraped away every time they push you down, you carry what you got and what you know, all your belongings, him on you through time, in the scars—your meanings, your lists, your items, your serial numbers and identification numbers, social security, registration, which one you are, your name in blood spread thin on your skin, spread out on porous skin, thin and stretched, a delicate shade of fear toughened by callouses of hate; and you learn to read your name on your body written in your blood, the book of signs, manhood or courage but it's different when pussy does it. You don't set up housekeeping, a room with things; instead you carry it all on you, not on your back tied down, or on your head piled up; it's in you, carved in, the cold on you, you on cement, sexy abrasions, sexy blood, sexy black and blue, the heat's on you, your sweat's a wet membrane between you and the weather, all there is, and you have burns, scars, there's gray cement, a silver gray under a tarnished, brassy moon, there's a cement graveyard, brick gravestones, the empty brick buildings; and you're laid out, for the fucking. Walt was a fool, a virgin fool; you would have been ground down, it's not love, it's slaughter, you fucking fool. I'm the field, they fall on me and bruise the ground, you don't hear the earth you fall on crying out but a poet should know. Prophets are fucking fools. What I figured out is that writers sit in rooms and make it up. Marx made it up. Walt made it up. Fucking fools like me believe it; do it; foot soldiers in hell. Sleep is the worst time, God puts you in a fuck-me position, you can't run, you can't fight, you can't stay alive without luck, you're in the dark and dead, they can get you, have you, use you; you manage to disappear, become invisible in the dark, or it's like being hung out to dry, you're under glass, in a museum, all laid out, on display, waiting for whatever gang passes by to piss on you; it's inside, they're not supposed to come inside but there is no inside where they can't come, it's only doors and windows to keep them out, open sesame and the doors and windows open or they bash them open and no one stops them and you're inside laid out for them, come, hurt me now, I'm lying flat, helpless, some fucking innocent naked baby, a sweet, helpless thing all curled up like a fetus as if I were safe, inside her; but there's nothing between you and them; she's not between you and them. Why did God make you have to sleep? I was born in Camden; I'm twenty; I can't remember the last time I heard my name. My name is and will the real one please stand up, do you remember that game show on television, from when it was easy. Women will whisper it to you, even dirty street women; even leather women; even mean women. You have to be careful if you want it from the street women; they might be harder than you, know where you're soft, see through you, you're all different with them because maybe they can see through you. Maybe you're not the hardest bitch. Maybe she's going to take from you. I don't give; I take. It's when she's on me I hear my name; doesn't matter who she is, I love her to death, women are generous this way, the meanest of us, I say her name, she says mine, kisses brushing inside the ear, she's wet all over me, it's all continuous, you're not in little pieces, I hear my name like the sound of the ocean in a shell; whether she's saying it or not. We're twisted around each other inside slime and sweat and tear drops, we're the wave and the surf, the undercurrent, the pounding of the tidal wave halfway around the world banging the beach on a bright, sunny day, the tide, high tide, low tide, under the moon or under a black sky, we're the sand wet and hard deserted by the water, the sand under the water, gravel and shell and moving claws crawling. I remember this one woman because I wanted her so bad but something was wrong, she was lying to me, telling me my lie but no woman lies to me. There's this woman at night I remember, in a restaurant I go when I'm taking a break, kosher restaurant with old men waiters, all night it's open, big room, plain tables, high ceilings, ballroom high and wide, big, empty feeling, old, old building, in New York, wide downtown street, gray street, fluorescent lights, a greenish light on green walls, oil paint, green, the old men have thick Jewish accents, they're slow moving, you can feel their bones aching, I sit alone over coffee and soup and she's there at the next table, the room's empty but she sits at the table next to me, black leather pants, she's got black hair, painted black, like I always wanted, and I want her but I'm her prey because she wants a bowl of fucking soup, she's picked me, she's coming for me, how did that happen, how did it get all fucked up, she sees me as the mark because I've got the food which means I've got the money and I can't go with her now because she has an underlying bad motive, she wants to eat, and what I feel for her is complete sex, so I'm the dope; and I don't do the dopey part; it's my game and she's playing it on me; she's got muscles and I want to see the insides of her thighs, I want to feel them, I want her undressed, I want her legs around my shoulders, she smiles, asks me how I am; be a fool, tell her how you are. I look right through her. I stare right through her while I'm deciding what to do. I ain't giving; I take. I want to be with her, I want to be between her legs and all over her and her thighs a vise around my neck; I want my teeth in her; I want her muscles squeezing me to death and I want to push down on her shoulders and I want my thighs crushing down on her, all my weight on her hips, my skin, bluish, on the inside of my thighs feeling her bones; but I'm the mark, that's how she sees it, and maybe she's meaner than me, or crazy, or harder, or feels less, or needs less, so she's on top and she takes; how many times have I done what she's doing now and did they want me the way I want her; well, they're stupid and I'm not; it hurts not to take her with me, I could put my hand on her and she'd come, I stare right through her, I look right through her but I'm devouring her at the same time which means she knows I'm a fool; she's acting harmless but maybe it's a lie, my instincts say it's a lie, there's no harmless women left alive this time of night, not on these streets. You risk too much if you go with a woman who needs less than you do; if you don't have to, if you have a choice, you don't take risks—you could lose your heart or your money or your speed; fucking fool who has a choice and doesn't use it; it's stupid middle-class girls you have to find or street women past wanting, past ambition, they live on bits of this and pieces of that, they're not looking for any heavy score, they live almost on air, it's pat, habit, they don't need you, but sometimes they like a taste; survival's an art, there are nuances, she's a dangerous piece of shit, stunning black eyes, and I'm smitten, and I walk out, look behind me, she came out, watched me, didn't follow, made me nervous, I don't often pass up what I want, I don't like doing it, it leaves an ache, don't like to ache too long without distracting myself by activity, anything to pass the time, and it makes me restless and careless, to want someone like that; I wanted her, she wanted food, money, most of what happens happens for food, all kinds of food, deep hungers that rock you in their everloving arms, rocked to eternal sleep by what you need, the song of myself, I need; need her; remember her; need women; need to hear my name; wanted her; she wanted food. What's inside you gets narrow and mean—it's an edge, it cuts, it's a slice of sharp, a line at the blade's end, no surface, no waste, no tease, a thin line where your meanest edge meets the air; an edge, no blade you can see. If you could stomp on me, this is what you'd see—a line, touch it, you're slivers. I'd be cut glass, you'd be feet. You'd dance blood. The edge of the blade, no surface, just what cuts, a thin line, touch it, draw blood. Inside, nothing else is alive. Where's the love I dream of. I hole up, like a bug in a rug. There's women who bore me; wasted time; the taste of death; junkie time; a junkie woman comes to me, long, languid afternoons making love but I didn't like it, she got beat up by her boyfriend, she's sincerely in love, black and blue, loving you, and he's her source; pure love; true romance. Don't like mixing women with obligation—in this case, the obligation to redeem her from pain. I want to want; I like wanting, just so it gets fulfilled and I don't have to wait too long; I like the ache just long enough to make what touches it appreciated a little more, a little drama, a little pain. I don't like no beat-up piece of shit; junkie stooge. You don't want the edge of the blade to get dull; then you got dullness inside and this you can't afford. The woman's got to be free; a beast of freedom; not a predator needing a bowl of fucking soup, not a fool needing a fucking fix; she's got to give freedom off, exude it, she's got to be grand with freedom, all swelled up with it, a Madame Curie of freedom, or she's Garbo, or more likely, she's Ché, she's got to be a monster of freedom, a hero of loveless love; Napoleon but they didn't lock her up or she got loose, now, for me; no beat up junkie fool; no beautiful piece looking for a hamburger. There's magnificent women out here. These lights light you up. You are on Broadway and there are stars of a high magnitude. There's the queen of them all who taught me—sweet name, Rebecca; ruthless crusher of a dyke; honest to God, she's wearing a gold lamé dress when I meet her in jail when I'm a kid, eighteen, a political prisoner as it were, as I saw myself, and she loves poetry and she sends me a pile of *New Yorker* magazines because, she says, I'm a poet; and I don't want her on me, not in jail, I'm too scared, too

107

hurt, but she protects me anyway, and I get out fast enough that I don't have to do her, and I see her later out here and I remember her kindness, which it was, real kindness, taking care of me in that place, which was why I was treated right by the other inmates as it were; I see her on the street, gold lamé against a window, I see her shimmering, and I go with her for thanks and because she is grand, and I find out you can be free in a gold lamé dress, in jail, whoring, in black skin, in hunger, in pain, in strife, the strife of the streets, perpetual war, gritty, gray, she's the wild one with freedom in her soul, it translates into how you touch, what's in your fingers, the silk in your hands, the freedom you take with who you got under you; you got your freedom and you take theirs for when you are with them, you are a caretaker of the fragile freedom in them, because most women don't got much, and you don't be afraid to take, you turn their skin to flames, you eat them raw, your name's all over them, you wrap them up in you, crush them in you, and what you give is ambition, the ambition to do it big, do it great, big gestures, free—girls do it big, girls soar, girls burn, girls take big not puny; stop giving, child, better to be stole from than to give—stop giving away the little that you got. I stay with her until she's finished with me, she's doing her art on me, she's practicing freedom on me; I'm shaking from it, her great daring, the audacity of her body on mine; she's free on me and I learn from it on me how to do it and how to be it; flamboyant lovemaking, no apology, dead serious, we could die right after this and this is the last thing we know and it's enough, the last minute, the last time, the last touch, God comes down through her on me, the good God, the divine God; master lovemaker, lightning in a girl, I've got a new theology, She's a rough Girl; and what's between my legs is a running river, She made it then She rested; a running river; so deep, so long, clear, bright, smart, racing, white foam over a cliff and then a dead drop and then it keeps on going, running, racing, then the smooth, silk calm, the deep calm, the long, silk body, smooth. I heard some man say I put it in her smooth, smooth was a noun, and I knew right away he liked children, he's after children, there are such men; but it's not what I mean; I mean that together we're smooth, it's smooth, we're smooth on each other, it's a smooth ride; and if I died right after I wouldn't feel cheated or sorry and every time I'm happy I had her one more second and I feel proud she wants me; and she'll disappear, she'll take someone else, but I'll sit here like a dumb little shit until she does, a student, sitting, waiting at her feet, let her touch me once, then once more, I'm happy near her, her freedom's holding me tight, her freedom's on me, around me, climbing inside me, her freedom's embracing me; wild woman; a wild woman's pussy that will not die for some junkie prick; nor songwriter; nor businessman; nor philosopher. The men are outside, they want to come in, I hear them rattling around, death threats, destruction isn't quiet or subtle, imagine those for whom it is, safe, blessedly safe; so in my last minutes on this earth, perhaps, I am remembering Rebecca who taught me freedom; I would sit down quiet next to her, wait for her, watch her; did you ever love a girl? I've loved several; loved. Not just wanted but loved in thought or action. Wasn't raped by any of them. I mean, rape's just a word, it doesn't mean anything, someone fucks you, so what? I can't see complaining about it. But I wasn't hurt by any of them. I don't mean I wasn't hurt by love; shit, that's what love does, it drags your heart over a bed of nails, I was hurt by love, lazy, desperate drinks through long nights of pain without her, hurting bad. Wasn't pushed around. Saw others who were. It's not that women don't. It's just that it had my name on it, men said pussy or dyke or whatever stupid distortion but I saw freedom, I heard Andrea, I found freedom under her, wrapped around her, her lips on me and her hands on me, in me, her thighs holding on to me; there's always men around waiting to break in, throw themselves on top, pull you down; but women's different, it's a fast, gorgeous trip out of hell, a hundred-mile-an-hour ride on a different road in the opposite direction, it's when you see an attitude that sets you free, the way she moves breaks you out, or you touch her shoulder and exhilaration shoots through you like a needle would do hanging from your vein if it's got something good in it; it's a gold rush; your life's telling you that if you're between her legs you're free—free's not peaceful and not always kind, it's fast, a shooting star you ride, if you're stupid it shakes you loose and hurls you somewhere in the sky, no gravity, no fall, just eternal drift to nowhere out past up and down. You can live forever on the curve of her hip, attached there in sweat and desire taking the full measure of your own human sorrow; you can have this tearing sorrow with your face pushing on the inside of her thigh; you can have her lips on you, her hands pushing on you as if you're marble she's turning into clay, an electricity running all over you carried in saliva and spit, you're cosseted in electric shock, peeing, your hair standing up on end, muscles stretched, lit up; there's her around you and in you everywhere, the rhythm of your dance and at the same time she's like the placenta, you breathe in her, surrounded; it's something men don't know or they'd do it, they could do it, but instead they want this push, shove, whatever it is they're doing for whatever reason, it's an ignorant meanness, but with a woman you're whole and you're free, it ain't pieces of you flying around like shit, it ain't being used up, you got scars bigger than the freedom you get in everyday life; do it the way you're supposed to, you got twenty-four hours a day down on your knees sucking dick; that's how girls do hard time. There's not many women around who have any freedom in them let alone some to spare, extravagant, on you, and it's when they're on

you you see it best and know it's real, now and all, there won't
be anything wilder or finer, it's pure and true, you see it, you
chase them, they're on you, you get enraptured in it, once you
got it on you, once you feel it moving through you, it's a
contagion of wanting more than you get being pussy for the
boys, you catch it like a fever, it puts you on a slow burn with
your skin aching and you want it more than you can find it
because most women are beggars and slaves in spirit and in life
and you don't ever give up wanting it. Otherwise you get
worn down to what they say you are, you get worn down to
pussy, bedraggled; not bewitched, bothered, bewildered; just
some wet, ratty, bedraggled thing, semen caked on you, his
piss running down your legs, worn out, old from what you're
sucking, I'm pretty fucking old and I have been loved by
freedom and I have loved freedom back. Did you ever have a
nightmare? Men coming in's my nightmare; entering; I'm in,
knock, knock. There's writers being assholes about outlaws;
outlaw this, outlaw that, I'm bad, I'm sitting here writing my
book and I'm bad, I'm typing and I'm bad, my secretary's
typing and I'm bad, I got laid, the boys say, like their novels
are letters home to mama, well, hell's bells, the boys got laid:
more than once. It's something to write home about, all right;
costs fifty bucks, too; they found dirty women they did it to,
dirty women too fucking poor to have a typewriter to stuff up
bad boy writer's ass. Shit. You follow his cock around the big,
bad city: New York, Paris, Rome—same city, same cock.
Big, bad cock. Wiping themselves on dirty women, then
writing home to mama by way of Grove Press, saying what
trash the dirty women are; how brave the bad boys are,
writing about it, doing it, putting their cocks in the big, bad,
dirty hole where all the other big, brave boys were; oh they say
dirty words about dirty women good. I read the books. I had a
typewriter but it was stolen when the men broke in. The men
broke in before when I wasn't here and they took everything,

my clothes, my typewriter. I wrote stories. Some were about life on other planets; I wrote once about a wild woman on a rock on Mars. I described the rock, the red planet, barren, and a woman with tangled hair, big, with muscles, sort of Ursula Andress on a rock. I couldn't think of what happened though. She was just there alone. I loved it. Never wanted it to end. I wrote about the country a lot, pastoral stuff, peaceful, I made up stories about the wind blowing through the trees and leaves falling and turning red. I wrote stories about teenagers feeling angst, not the ones I knew but regular ones with stereos. I couldn't think of details though. I wrote about men and women making love. I made it up; or took it from Nino, a boy I knew, except I made it real nice; as he said it would be; I left out the knife. The men writers make it as nasty as they can, it's like they're using a machine gun on her; they type with their fucking cocks—as Mailer admitted, right? Except he said balls, always a romancer. I can't think of getting a new typewriter, I need money for just staying alive, orange juice and coffee and cigarettes and milk, vodka and pills, they'll just smash it or take it anyway, I have to just learn to write with a pen and paper in handwriting so no one can steal it and so it don't take money. When I read the big men writers I'm them; careening around like they do; never paying a fucking price; days are long, their books are short compared to an hour on the street; but if you think about a book just saying I'm a prick and I fuck dirty girls, the books are pretty long; my cock, my cock, three volumes. They should just say: *I Can Fuck.* Norman Mailer's new novel. *I Can Be Fucked.* Jean Genet's new novel. *I'm Waiting To Be Fucked Or To Fuck, I Don't Know.* Samuel Beckett's new novel. *She Shit.* James Joyce's masterpiece. *Fuck Me, Fuck Her, Fuck It.* The Living Theatre's new play. *Paradise Fucked.* The sequel. *Mama, I Fucked a Jewish Girl.* The new Philip Roth. *Mama, I Fucked a Shiksa.* The new, new Philip Roth. It was a bad day they wouldn't let little boys say that word. I got to tell you, they get laid. They're up and down these streets, taking what they want; two hundred million little Henry Millers with hard pricks and a mean prose style; Pulitzer prizewinning assholes using cash. Looking for experience, which is what they call pussy afterward when they're back in their posh apartments trying to justify themselves. Experience is us, the ones they stick it in. Experience is when they put down the money, then they turn you around like you're a chicken they're roasting; they stick it in any hole they can find just to try it or because they're blind drunk and it ain't painted red so they can't find it; you get to be lab mice for them; they stick the famous Steel Rod into any Fleshy Hole they can find and they Ram the Rod In when they can manage it which thank God often enough they can't. The prose gets real purple then. You can't put it down to impotence though because they get laid and they had women and they fucked a lot; they just never seem to get over the miracle that it's them in a big man's body doing all the damage; Look, ma, it's me. Volume Twelve. They don't act like human beings and they're pretty proud of it so there's no point in pretending they are; though you want to—pretend. You'd like to think they could feel something—sad; or remorse; or something just simple, a minute of recognition. It's interesting that you're so dangerous to them but you fucking can't hurt them; how can you be dangerous if you can't do harm; I'd like to be able to level them, but you can't touch them except to be fucked by them; they get to do it and then they get to say what it is they're doing—you're what they're afraid of but the fear just keeps them coming, it doesn't shake them loose or get them off you; it's more like the glue that keeps them on you; sticky stuff, how afraid the pricks are. I mean, maybe they're not afraid. It sounds so stupid to say they are, so banal, like making them human anyway, like giving them the insides you wish they had. So what do you say; they're just so fucking filled with hate they can't do anything else or feel anything else or write anything else? I mean, do they ever look at the fucking moon? I think all the sperm they're spilling is going to have an effect; something's going to grow. It's like they're planting a whole next generation of themselves by sympathetic magic; not that they're fucking to have babies; it's more like they're rubbing and heaving and pushing and banging and shoving and ejaculating like some kind of voodoo rite so all the sperm will grow into more them, more boys with more books about how they got themselves into dirt and got out alive. It's a thrilling story, says the dirt they got themselves into. It's bitterness, being their filth; they don't even remember right, you're not distinct enough, an amoeba's more distinct, more individuated; they go home and make it up after they did it for real and suddenly they ain't parasites, they're heroes—big dicks in the big night taming some rich but underneath it all street dirty whore, some glamorous thing but underneath filth; I think even if you were with them all the time they wouldn't remember you day-to-day, it's like being null and void and fucked at the same time, I am fucked, therefore I am not. Maybe I'll write books about history—prior times, the War of 1812; not here and now, which is a heartbreaking time, place, situation, for someone. You're nothing to them. I don't think they're afraid. Maybe I'm afraid. The men want to come in; I hear them outside, banging; they're banging against the door with metal things, probably knives; the men around here have knives; they use knives; I'm familiar with knives; I grew up around knives; Nino used a knife; I'm not afraid of knives. Fear's a funny thing; you get fucked enough you lose it; or most of it; I don't know why that should be per se. It's all callouses, not fear, a hard heart, and inside a lot of death as if they put it there, delivered it in. And then out of nowhere you just drown in it, it's a million tons of water on you. If I was afraid of individual things, normal things—today, tomorrow, what's next, who's on top, what already has transpired that you can't quite reach down into to remember—I'd have to surrender; but it drowns you fast, then it's gone. I'd like to surrender; but to whom, where, or do you just put up a white flag and they take you to throw your body on a pile somewhere? I don't believe in it. I think you have to make them come get you, you don't volunteer, it's a matter of pride. Who do you turn yourself into and on what terms—hey, fellow, I'm done but that don't mean you get to hurt me more, you have to keep the deal, I made a deal, I get not to feel more pain, I'm finished, I'm not fighting you fucks anymore, I'll be dead if it's the way to accomplish this transformation from what I am into being nothing with no pain. But if you get dead and there's an afterlife and it's more of the same but worse—I would just die from that. You got all these same mean motherfuckers around after you're dead and you got the God who made it all still messing with you but now up close—He's around. You're listening to angels and you're not allowed to tell God He's one maggoty bastard; or you're running around in circles in hell, imprisoned by your fatal flaw, instead of being here on a leash with all your flaws, none fatal enough, making you a maggoty piece of meat. I want dead to mean dead; all done; finished; quiet; insensate; nothing; I want it to be peaceful, no me being pushed around or pushing, I don't want to feel the worms crawling on me or eating me or the cold of the wet ground or suffocating from being buried or smothering from being under the ground; or being stone cold from being dead; I don't want to feel cold; I don't want to be in eternal dark forever stone cold. Nothing by which I mean a pure void, true nonexistence, is different; it isn't filled with horror or dread or fear or punishment or pain; it's just an absence of being, especially so you don't have to think or know anything or figure out how you're going to eat or who's going to be on you next. It's not suffering. I don't have suffering in mind; not joy, not pain—no highs, no lows. Just not being; not being a citizen wandering around the universe in a body or loose, ethereal and invisible; or just not being a citizen here, now, under street lights, all illuminated, the light shining down. I hate the light shining down—display yourself, dear, show them; smile, spread your legs, make suggestive gestures, legs wide open—there's lots of ways to sit or stand with your legs wide open. Which day did God make light? You think He had the street lights in some big storeroom in the sky to send down to earth when women started crawling over sidewalks like cockroaches to stay alive? I think He did. I think it was part of the big plan—light those girls up, give them sallow light, covers pox marks, covers tracks, covers bruises, good light for covering them up and showing them at the same time, makes them look grotesque, just inhuman enough, same species but not really, you can stick it in but these aren't creatures that get to come home, not into a home, not home, not quite the same species, sallow light, makes them green and grotesque, creatures you put it in, not female ones of you, even a fucking rib of you; you got ones in good light for that. They stick it in boys too; anything under these lights is here to be used. You'd think they'd know boys was real, same species, with fists that work or will someday, but someday isn't their problem and they like the feel that the boy might turn mean on them—some of them like it, the ones that use the older ones. I read about this boy that was taken off the street and the man gave him hormones to make him grow breasts and lose his body hair or not get it, I'm not sure; it made me really sick because the boy was nothing to him, just some piece of something he could mess with, remake to what he wanted to play with, even something monstrous; I wanted to kill the guy; and I tried to figure out how to help the kid, but I just read it in *Time* or *Newsweek* so I wondered if I could find him or not. I guess it depends on how many boys there are being fed hormones by pedophiles. Once it's in *Newsweek*, I guess there are thousands. The kid's around here somewhere; it said Lower East Side; I hate it, what the man did to him. These Goddamn men would all be each other's meat if they weren't the butchers. They use fucking to slice you open. It's like they're hollow, there's nothing there, except they make big noise, this unbearable static, some screeching, high-pitched pain, and you can't see they're hollow because the noise diverts you to near madness; big lovemaker with fifty dollars to spend, seed to spill making mimetic magic, grind, bang, it's a boy, a big, bad boy who writes books, big, bad books. I see the future and it's a bunch of pricks making a literature of fucking, high art about sticking it in; I did it, ma; she was filth and I did it. Only you'll get a Mailer-Genet beast: I did it, ma, I did it to her, he did it to me. The cement will grow them; sympathetic magic works; the spilled seed, the grinding, bang bang, pushes the fuck out past the bounds of physical reality; it lurks in the biosphere; it will creep into weeping wombs; they'll be born, the next generation, out of what the assholes do to me; I've got enough semen dripping in me for a literary renaissance, an encyclopedia of novellas, a generation of genius; maybe some of them will paint or write songs. Mother earth, magic vessel, the altar where they worship, the sacred place; fifty dollars to burn a candle, or pills, or a meal and money; bang bang ain't never without consequences for the future of the race. No reason the race should be different from the people in it. There's no tomorrow I know of. I never seen one that ain't today. It's fine to be slut-mama to a literary movement; the corporeal altar of sympathetic motherhood to a generation; his loins; my ass. Immortal, anonymous means to his end. It's what the hippie girls all glittering, flecked, stardust, want: to be procreatrix with flowering hips and tea made from plants instead of

Lipton; they recline, posh and simple, all spread out draped in flowing cotton and color; they don't take money; well, they do, but they don't say so upfront—from my point of view they are mannerless in this regard; mostly they just hang on, like they have claws, it passes for spiritual, they just sit there until he comes back from wherever he's gone after coitus has made him triste, they say it's meditating but it's just waiting for some guy to show who's left; they ain't under the light, they are of it—luminescent fairy things from on high, just down for a fast, ethereal screw. I been to bed with them; usually a man and one of them, because they don't do women alone—too real for the nitrous oxide crowd, not Buddhistic enough—it's got an I want right between the legs and it's got your genitals leading your heart around or vice versa, who the hell knows, and it don't make the boy happy unless he gets to watch and the hippie girls do not irritate the love-boys by doing things that might not be directly and specifically for them. The hippie boys like bringing another woman into bed. You can shake some coke loose from them if you do it; or money, which they pretend is like nothing but they hold onto it pretty tight. Coke and orange juice is my favorite breakfast; they want you to do the coke with them because it makes them hard and high and ready but I like to take some off with me and do it alone or with someone I pick, not with someone in bed with some silly girl who ought to be a housewife but is seeing the big city and he's so hip he has to be able to roll over from one to another, dreaming it's another housewife, all girls are housewives to him; peace, flowers, love, clean my house, bake my bread. They try to tell you they see the real you, the sensitive you, inside, and the real you doesn't want money— she wants the good fucking he's got and to make strings of beads for him and sell them in flea markets for him; darling, it's sad. You convey to the guy that you're the real thing, what he never thought would be near him, street grime he won't be able to wash off, and he's so trembling and overwrought his prick starts shaking. There's some who do things real, don't spend their time posturing or preening; they just pull it out without philosophy. There's this one I had once, with a woman. I was on Demerol because I had an operation; my appendix came out but it had got all infected and it was a big slice in me and then they let me loose with a blood clot because there wasn't somewhere for me to stay and I didn't have money or no one to take care of me so they just let me out. My side didn't seem like it would stay sewed, it felt open, and there was a pain from the clot that was some evil drilling in my shoulder that they called reflexive pain which meant the pain was really somewhere else but I could only feel it in my shoulder. It hurt to breathe. You don't think about your shoulder or how it moves when you breathe unless some Nazi is putting a drill in it; I saw God the Nazi pushing His full weight on the drill and if I breathed it made more pressure from inside on where the drill was and there wasn't enough Demerol in the world. So I'm walking around, desperate and dreamy, in pain but liking the pills, and I see this shirt, fucking beautiful shirt, purple and turquoise and shades of blue all in flowers, silk, astonishing whirl of color; and the man's dark with long hair and a beard, some prototype, no face, just hair; and I take him back but there's this girl with him too, and she's all hippie, endlessly expressing herself and putting little pats on my hand, teeny weeny little pats, her hand to mine: expressing affection for another woman; heavy shit. I can barely believe this one's rubbing her hands on me. And the guy starts fucking, and he's some kind of monster of fuck, he lasts forever and a day, it's night, it's dark, and hours go by, and I see the light coming up, and she and me are next to each other, and he's in me, then he's in her, then me, then her, and my side is splitting open and I'm not supposed to be moving around with the clot but you can't keep your hips still the whole time although my interest comes and goes, at some point the boy takes off the shirt and I'm wondering who he is and why he's here, and I don't have to worry about her sentimentality because the boy isn't seeking variety and he don't want to watch, this is a boy who wants to fuck and he moves good but he's boring as hell, the same, the same, and when the pain hits me I am pretty sure I am really going to die, that the clot is loose in my blood somewhere and it's going to go to my brain, and I'm trying to think this is real glorious, dying with some Olympian fuck, but the pain is some vicious, choked up tangle of blades in my gut, and I try to choreograph the pain to his fuck, and I try to rest when he's not in me, and I am praying he will stop, and I am at the same time trying to savor every second of my last minutes on earth, or last hours as it turns out, but intellectual honesty forced me to acknowledge I was bored, I was spending my last time bored to death, I could have been a housewife after all; and the light comes up and I think, well, dawn will surely stop him; but he fucks well into daylight, it's bright morning now with a disagreeably bright sun, profoundly intrusive, and suddenly there's a spasm, thank the Lord, and the boy is spent, it's the seventh day and this man who fucks must rest. And I thank God. I do. I say, thank you, Lord. I say, I owe You one. I say, I appear still to be alive, I know I was doing something proscribed and maybe I shouldn't address You before he even moves off me but I am grateful to You for stopping him, for making him tired, for wearing him out, for creating him in Your image so that, eventually, he had to rest. I can't move because my insides are messed up. My incision is burning as if there are lighted coals there and I'm afraid to see if it is open or if it will bleed now and my shoulder has stones crushed into it as if some demolition team was crushing granite, reflexive pain from some dead spot, I don't know where, and I truly think I might not ever move again and I truly think I might have opened up and I truly think I might still die; and I want to be alone; die alone or bleed alone or endure the pain alone; and I'm lying there thinking they will go now when the girl starts pawing me and says stupid, nice things and starts being all lovey dovey like we're both Gidget and she wants now to have the experience, if you will, of making love with a woman; this is in the too-little-too-late category at best; and I am fairly outraged and astonished because I hurt so much and my little sister in sensitivity thinks we should start dating. So I tell them to go; and she says but he doesn't like me better, maybe he needs you to be there—needs you, can you imagine—and I'm trying to figure out what it has to do with him, why it's what he wants when I want them to go; it's what I want; I never understand why it's always with these girls what he wants—if he's there and even if he ain't in sight or in the vicinity; he had his hours doing what he wants; and she tells me she's disappointed with me for not being loving and we could all share and this is some dream come true, the most amazing thing that's ever happened, to her or ever on earth, it's the proof that everything is possible, and the pain I'm in is keeping me from moving because I can't even sit up but I'm saying very quiet, get out now. And she's saying it's her first time with a woman and she didn't really get to do anything—tourist didn't get to see the Eiffel Tower—and I say yes, that's right, you didn't get nothing. So she's sad like some lover who was real left her and she's handling me like she read in some book, being a tender person, saying everything bland and stupid, all her ideals about life, everything she's hoped for, and she's preachy with the morality of sharing and unity and harmony and I expect her to shake her finger at me and hit my knuckles with a ruler and make me stand in a corner for not being some loving bitch. There's a code of love you have to learn by heart, which I never took to, and I'm thinking that if she don't take her treacle to another planet I'm going to stand up, no matter what the pain, and physically carry her out, a new little bride, over the threshold to outside. She's some sobbing ingenue with a delicate smile perpetually on her face shining through tears which are probably always with her and she's talking about universal love when all the boy did was fuck us to death as best he could, which in my case was close but no cigar and I couldn't bring myself to think it was all that friendly; and I had a short fuse because I needed another pill, I was a few behind and I was looking forward to making them up now in the immediate present, I could talk real nice to Demerol and I didn't want them there for when I got high again; so I said, you go, because he really likes you and you should stay with him and be with him and be good to him, so the dumb bitch leaves with the prince of peace over there, the boy's already smoking dope so he's already on another plane taking care of himself which is what he's really good at; and she's uncomprehending and she's mournful that I couldn't get the love part right but they went, I saw the boy's turquoise and purple silk shirt float by me and the drippy, sentimental girl in cotton floated out still soliciting love. I never understood why she thought you could ask for it. No one can ask it from me. I never can remember his face; peculiar, since his head was right above me for so long, his tongue in my mouth, he kissed the whole time he fucked, a nice touch, he was in her kissing me or in me kissing her so no one'd get away from him or decide to do something else; I just can't remember his face, as if I never saw it. He was a Taurus. I stayed away from them after that if I knew a man was one because they stay too long, slow, steady, forever. I never saw such longevity. She was Ellen, some flower child girl; doomed for housework. I'm not. I ain't cleaning up after them. I keep things as clean as I can; but you can't really stay clean; there's too much heat and dirt. It's a sweltering night. The little nymphs, imps, and pimps of summer flitter about like it's tea time at the Ritz. There's been uprisings on the streets, riots, lootings, burning; the air is crackling with violence, a blue white fire eating up the oxygen, it's tiny, sharp explosions that go off in the air around your head, firecrackers you can't see that go off in front of you when you walk, in front of your face, and you don't know when the air itself will become some white hot tornado, just enough to crack your head open and boil your brains. That's outside, the world. Summertime and the living is easy. You just walk through the fires between the flames or crawl on your belly under them; rough on your knees and elbows. You can be in the street and have a steaming mass, hot heat, kinetic, come at you, a crowd, men at the top of their energy, men spinning propelled by butane, and they bear down on you on the sidewalk, they come at you, martial chaos; they will march over you, you'll be crushed, bone marrow ground into a paste with your own blood, a smear left on a sidewalk. The crowd's a monster animal, a giant wolf, huge and frantic, tall as the sky, blood pulsing and rushing through it, one predator, bearing down, a hairy, freaky, hungry thing, bared teeth, ugly, hungry thing, it springs through the air, light and lethal, and you will fucking cringe, hide, run, disappear, to be safe— you will fucking hide in a hole, like some roachy thing you will crawl into a crack. You can hear the sound of them coming, there's a buzz coming up from the cement, it vibrates and kicks up dust, and somewhere a fire starts, somewhere close, and somewhere police in helmets with nightsticks are bearing down on the carnivorous beast, somewhere close and you can hear the skulls cracking open, and the blood comes, somewhere close there's blood, and you can hear guns, there's guns somewhere close because you smell the burning smell, it's heat rising off someone's open chest, the singed skin still smoking where the bullet went through; the wolf's being beat down—shot over and over, wounded, torn open—it's big manly cops doing it, steel faces, lead boots—they ain't harassing whores tonight. It looks like foreplay, the way the cops bear down on the undulating mass; I stroke your face with my nightstick; the lover tames the beloved; death does quiet you down. But a pig can't kill a wolf. The wolf's the monster prick, then the pigs come and turn the wolf into a girl, then it's payback time and the wolf rises again. In the day when the wolf sleeps there are still fires; anything can suddenly go up in flames and you can't tell the difference at first between a fire and a summer day, the sun on the garbage, the hot air making the ghetto buildings swell, the brick bulging, deformed and in places melting, all the solid brick wavy in the heat. At night the crowd rises, the wolf rises, the great predator starts a long, slow walk toward the bullets waiting for it. The violence is in the air; not symbol; not metaphor; it's thick and tasty; the air's charged with it; it crackles around your head; then you stay in or go out, depending on—can you stand being trapped inside or do you like the open street? I sleep days. It's safer. I sleep in daylight. I stay awake nights. I keep an eye out. I don't like to be unconscious. I don't like the way you get limp. I don't like how you can't hear what goes on around you. I don't like that you can't see. I don't like to be waiting. I don't like that you get no warning. I don't like not to know where I am. I don't like not to know my name. I sleep in the day because it's safer; at night, I face the streets, the crowd, the predator, any predator, head on. I'd rather be there. I want to see it coming at me, the crowd or anything else or anyone. I want it to look at me and I want a chance. There's gangs everywhere. There's arson or fires or wolf packs or packs of men; men and gangs. The men outside my door are banging; they want to come in; big group fuck; they tear me apart; boys' night out. It's about eight or nine at night and I'm going out soon, it's a little too early yet, I hear them banging on the door with knives and fists, I can't get out past them, there's only one way out; I can't get past them. Once night comes it's easy to seal you in. Night comes and you have the rules of the grave, different rules from daylight, they can do things at night, everyone can, they can't do in the day; they will break the door down, no one here calls the police, I don't have a gun, I have one knife, a pathetic thing, I sleep with it under my pillow. I figure if someone's right on top of me I can split him apart with it. I figure if he's already on top of me because I didn't hear him and didn't see him because I was unconscious and I wake up and he's there I can stick it in him or I can cut his throat. I figure it gives me time to come to, then I try for his throat, but if I'm too late, if I can't get it, if he's somehow so I can't get his throat, then I can get his back. Or I can finish myself off if there's no other way; I think about it each time I lie down to sleep, if I can do it, draw the knife across my throat, fast, I try to prepare myself to do it, in my mind I make a vow and I practice the stroke before I sleep. I think it's better to kill him but I just can't bear them no longer, really, and it's unknown if I could do it to me; so fast; but I keep practicing in my mind so if the time comes I won't even think. It would be the right thing. I don't really believe in hurting him or anyone. I have the knife; I can't stand to think about using it, what it would be like, or going to jail for hurting him, I never wanted to kill anybody and I'd do almost anything not to. I know the men outside, they're neighborhood, this block, they broke in before, in daylight, smashed everything, took everything, they ran riot in here, they tell me they're coming to fuck me, they say so out on the street, hanging on the stoop; they say so. They've broken in here before, that's when I started sleeping with the knife. Inside there's too many hours to dawn; too many hours of dark to hold them off; they'll get in; I know this small world as well as they do, I know what they can do and what they can't do and once it's night they can break the door down and no one will stop them; and the police don't come here; you never see a cop here; there's no way to keep them out and my blood's running cold from the banging, from the noise of them, fists, knives, I don't know what, sticks, I guess, maybe baseball bats, the arsenal of the streets. The telephone's worthless, they cut the wire when they broke in; but no one would come. This is the loneliest I ever knew existed; now; them banging. There's things you learn, tricks; no one can hurt me. I'm not some stupid piece of shit. You got a gang outside, banging, making threats. They want to come in; fuck. They'll kill me; fuck me dead or kill me after. It's like anything, you have to face what's true, you don't get to say if you want to handle it or not, you handle it to stay alive. So what's it to me; if I can just get through it; minimum damage, minimum pain, the goal of all women all the time and it's not different now. If you're ever attacked by a gang you have to get the leader. If you get him, disable him, pull him away from the others, kill him, render him harmless, the others are nothing. If you miss him, attack him but miss, wound him, irritate him, aggravate him, rile him, humiliate him without taking him out, you are human waste, excreta. So it's clear; there's one way. There's him. I have to get him. If I can pull him away from them, to me, I have a chance; a chance. I open the door. I think if I grab him between the legs I'm in charge; if I pull his thing. I learn the limits of my philosophy. Every philosophy's got them. I ain't in charge. It's fast. It's simple. I open the door. It's a negotiation. The agreement is he comes in, they stay out; he doesn't bring the big knife he has in with him; it stays outside; if I mess with him, he will hurt me with it and turn me over to them; if anything bad happens to him or if I don't make him happy, he will turn me over to them. This is consent, right? I opened the door myself. I picked him. I just got to survive him; and tomorrow find a way out; away from here. He comes in; he's Pedro or Joe or Juan; he swaggers, touches everything, there's not much left he notes with humor; he wants me to cook him dinner; he finds my knife; he

keeps it; he keeps saying what he'll do to me with it; I cook; he
drinks; he eats; he keeps talking; he brags; he talks about the
gang, keeps threatening me, what he'll do to me, what they'll
do to me, aspects of lovemaking the gang would also enjoy
and maybe he'll just let them in now or there's time after,
they're waiting, right outside, maybe he'll call them in but
they can come back tomorrow night too, there's time, no need
to worry, nice boys in the gang, a little rough but I'll enjoy
them, won't I? Then he's ready; he's excited himself; he's even
fingered himself and rubbed himself. Like the peace boys he
talks with his legs spread wide open, his fingers lightly
caressing his cock, the denim pulled tight, exerting its own
pressure. He goes to the bed and starts to undress and he runs
one hand through the hair on his chest and he holds the knife in
the other hand, he fingers the knife, he rubs his thumb over it
and he caresses it and he keeps talking, seductive talk about
how good he is and how good the knife is and I'm going to like
them both and he's got a cross on a chain around his neck and it
glistens in his hair, it's silver and his skin is tawny and his hair
on his chest is black and curly and thick and it shines and I'm
staring at it thinking it shouldn't be there, the shiny cross, I am
having these highly moral thoughts against the blasphemy of
the cross on his chest, I think it is wrong and concentrate on
the immorality of wearing it now, doing this, why does he
wear it, what does it mean, his shirt is off and his pants are
coming off and he is rapturous with the knife in his hand and I
look at the cross and I look at the knife and I think they are both
for me, he will hold the knife, maybe I can touch the cross, I
will try to touch it all through and maybe it will be something
or mean something or I won't feel so frightened, so alone in
this life now, and I think I will just touch it, and there's him,
there's the cross, there's the knife, and I'm under them and I
don't know, I will never remember, the hours are gone, blank,
a tunnel of nothing, and I'm naked, the bell rings, it's light

outside so it's been five hours, six, there's a knock on the door, insistent knocking, he says don't answer it, he says don't move, he holds the knife against me, just under my skin, the tip just under it, and I try to fight for my life, I say it's a friend who expects me to be here and will not go away and I will have to answer the door and I won't say anything and I won't tell or say anything bad, I will just go to the door to tell my friend to go away, to convince him everything's fine, and someone's knocking and he has a deep voice and I don't know what I will do when I reach the door or who it is on the outside or what will happen; but I'm hurt; dizzy; reeling; can't feel anything but some obscure pain somewhere next to me or across the room and I don't know what he's done, I don't look at any part of me, I cover myself a little with a sheet, I pull it over me and I don't look down, I have trouble keeping my head steady on my shoulders, I don't know if I can walk from the bed to the door, and I think I can open the door maybe and just keep walking but I am barely covered at all and maybe the gang's outside and you can't walk naked in a sheet, they'll just hurt you more; anyone will. I can't remember and I can barely carry my head up and I have this one chance; because I can't have him do more; you see? I got up, I put something around me, over me, a sheet or something, just held it together where I could, and I took some steps and I kept whispering to the man with the knife in my bed that I would just get rid of the man at the door because he wouldn't go away if I didn't come to the door and really I would just make him go away and I kept walking to the door to open it, not knowing if I would fall or if the man in the bed would stick the knife in me before I got there, or who was on the other side of the door and what he would do; would he run or laugh or walk away; or was it a member of the gang, wanting some. It was cool and clear and light outside and it was a man I didn't know except a little, a big man, so tall, so big, such a big man, and I whispered to him to help me, please help me, and I talked out loud that I couldn't come out now for breakfast like we had planned and I whispered to say that I was hurt and that the man inside was a leader of a gang and I indicated the big knife on the window ledge, out of my reach, a huge dagger, almost a sword, that I had got the man to leave outside and I whispered that he was in my bed now with a knife and out loud I tried to say normal things very loud but I was dizzy and I wasn't sure I could keep standing and the big man caught on quick and said normal things loud, questions so I could answer them and didn't have to think of new things because I'm shaking and I say the man's in my bed with a knife and please help me he was with a gang and I don't know where they are and maybe they're around and they'll show up and it's dangerous but please help me and the big man strides in, he doesn't take the big knife, I almost die from fear but he just does it, I used my chance and there's none left, he has long legs and they cover the distance to the bed in a second and the man in my bed is fumbling with the knife and the big man, so big, with long legs, says I'm his; his girl; his; this is an insult to him; an outrage to him; and the man in the bed with the knife says nothing, he grovels, he sweats, he asks forgiveness, he didn't mean no harm, you know how it is man; and hey they agree it's just a misunderstanding and they talk and the man in my bed with the knife is sweating and the man who saved me is known to be dangerous, he is known, a known very serious man, a quiet man, a major man, and he says he's my man and I'm his woman and he don't want me having no trouble with sniveling assholes and any insult he throws makes the man in my bed with the knife sweat more and grovel more and the big man, the man with the long legs, he speaks very soft, and he says that now the man in the bed with the knife will leave and the man in the bed with the knife fumbles to put his pants on and fumbles to put his shirt on and fumbles to get his shoes on and the big man, the man with the

129

long legs, says quietly, politely, that nobody had ever better mess with me anymore and the man who was in my bed with the knife says yeah and sure and please and thank you and I am some kind of prom queen, bedecked, bejeweled, crowned princess, because the man with the long legs says I am his, and Pedro or Juan or Joe is obsequious and he says he is sorry and he says he didn't understand and he says he made a mistake and they chat and I'm shaking bad, I'm there covered a little, I'm shaking and I'm not really covered and I'm covered in sweat and I'm trying not to fall down faint and I'm shaking so much I'm nearly naked, I'm hurt, my head falls down and I see my skin, all bruised anywhere you can see as if I turned blue or someone painted me blue, and there's blood on me but I can't look or keep my eyes open, I'm just this side of dead but I'm holding on, I'm shaking but I got something covering me somewhere and I'm just not quite dead, I'm keeping something covering me somewhere, and Pedro or Juan or Joe leaves, he leaves mumbling an apology to the big man and I'm saying thank you to the big man with serious formality, quiet and serious and concentrating, and I'm something that ain't fresh and new, I'm something that ain't clean, and I don't know anything except he's got to go now because I have to curl up by myself to die now, it's time, I'm just going to put myself down on the bed, very careful, very slow, on my side with my knees raised a little, curled up a little, and I'm going to God, I am going to ask God to take me in now, I am going to forgive Him and I am going to put aside all my grudges against Him for all what He did wrong and for all the pain I ever had or saw and I am going to ask Him to take me away now from here and to somewhere else where I don't have to move ever again, where I can be curled up a little and nothing hurts and whatever hurts don't have to move and that I don't have to wake up no more but the big man ain't through and I say later or tomorrow or come back and he says I have to pay my debts

and he talks and he threatens and he has a deep voice and he is
big and he has long arms and he isn't leaving, he says, and he is
strong and he pulls me down and gets on top of me and says I
owe him and he fucks me and I say God You must stop him
now but God don't stop him, God don't have no problem
with this, God rides on the back of the man and I see Him there
doing it and the man uses his teeth on me where men fuck and
God's for him and I'm wondering why He likes people being
hurt and I'm past hating Him and past Him and I can't beg
Him no more for respite or help or death and the big man has
his teeth, between my legs, inside me and on the flesh all
around, he's biting, not a little, deep bites, he's using his teeth
and biting into the lips of my labia and I'm thinking this is not
happening and it is not possible and it is not true and I am
thinking it will stop soon because it must stop soon but it does
not stop soon because the man has fucked but it means nothing
to him except he had to do it so he did it but this is why he is
here, the real reason, this biting in this place, he is wanting to
do this other awful thing that is not like anything anyone ever
did before and I say this is not happening and even You are not
so cruel to let this man do this and keep doing it and not
making him stop but the man has long arms and he's driven, a
passionate man, and he holds me down and he has long legs
and he uses his arms and legs to keep me pinned down and he is
so big, so tall, he can have his face down there and still he
covers me to hold me down, my shoulders, my breasts; but
my head twists back and forth, side to side, like some loose
head of a doll screwed on wrong. He is cutting me open with
his teeth, he looks up at me, he bites more, he says lovers'
things, he is the great lover and he is going slow, with his
mouth, with his teeth, and then watching my head try to
screw itself off my neck; and he gets in a frenzy and there's no
words for this because pain is littler and sweeter and someday
it ends but this doesn't end, will not end, it will never end, it's

dull, dirty, rusty knives cutting my labial lips or the edge of a
rusty tin can and it's inside me, his teeth reaching inside me
turning me inside out, the skin, he is pulling me open and he is
biting inside me and I'm thinking that pain is a river going
through me but there's no words and pain isn't a river, there's
just one great scream past sound and my mind moves over, it
moves out of my head, I feel it escape, it runs away, it says no,
not this, no and it says you cannot but the man does and my
mind just fucking falls out of my brains and I am past being
anything God can help anyway and He's making the man
stronger, He's making the man happy, the man likes this, he is
liking this, and he is proud to be doing it so good like a good
lover, slow, one who lasts, one who takes time; and this is real;
this happened and this will last forever, because I am just
someone like anyone and there's things too bad for me and I
didn't know you could be lying flat, blue skin with blood from
the man with the knife, to find love again, someone cutting his
way into you; and I'm just someone and it's just flesh down
there, tender flesh, somewhere you barely touch and you
wouldn't cut it or wound it; no one would; and I have pain all
over me but pain ain't the word because there's no word, I
have pain on me like it's my skin but pain ain't the word and it
isn't my skin, blue with red. I'm just some bleeding thing cut
up on the floor, a pile of something someone left like garbage,
some slaughtered animal that got sliced and sucked and a man
put his dick in it and then it didn't matter if the thing was still
warm or not because the essential killing had been done and it
was just a matter of time; the thing would die; the longer it
took the worse it would be; which is true. He had a good time.
He did. He got up. He was friendly. He got dressed. I wasn't
barely alive. I barely moaned or whispered or cried. I didn't
move. He left. The gang was somewhere outside. He left the
door open, wide open, and it was going to be a hundred years
before I could crawl enough to close it. There was daylight

streaming in. It was tomorrow. Tomorrow had finally come, a long tomorrow, an eternal tomorrow, I'm always here, the girl lying here, can't run, can't crawl, where's freedom now, can't move, can't crawl, dear God, help me, someone, help me, this is real, help me; please, help me. I hate God; for making the pain; and making the man; and putting me here; under them all; anyone that wants.

SEVEN

In 1969, 1970, 1971

(Age 22, 23, 24, 25)

Yeah, I go somewhere else, a new country, not the fucking U.S.A., somewhere I never been, and I'm such a sweet genius of a girl that I marry a boy. Not some trash bourgie; a sweet boy who'd done time; I rescued him from jail once, I took all my money and I gave it to some uniformed pig for him; a hostage, they had kidnapped him, taken him out of his bed and out of where he lived in handcuffs in the middle of the night and they kept him; I mean, he just fucking disappeared and it was that he was locked up. They let me in the prison, the great gray walls that are built so high and so cold you can't help but feel anyone in them is a tragic victim buried alive. You wouldn't be right but that's what you'd feel. Cold stone, a washed-out gray. I was a child standing there, just a girl, money in my hand, love in my heart, telling the guard I wanted my friend loose and had come to pay for him to go now, with me; I felt like a child because the prison was so big and so cold, it was the gray of the Camden streets, only it was standing up instead of all spread out flat to the horizon, it was the streets I grew up on rising high into the sky, with sharp right angles, an angry rectangle of pale gray stone, a washed-out gray, opaque, hard, solid, cold, except it wasn't broken or crumbling—each wall was gray concrete, thick, the thickness of your forearm—well, if you see someone's forearm up someone's ass you know how long, how thick it is, and I seen these things, I traveled a hard road until now; not how a gentleman's forearm seems draped in a shirt but what it is if it's in you—a human sense of size, chilling enough to remember precisely, a measurement of space and pain; once the body testifies, you know. It was cold gray stone, an austere monument; not a castle or a palace or an old monastery or a stone winery in cool hills or archaic remains of Druids or Romans or anything like that; it was cold; stone cold; just a stone cold prison outside of time, high and nasty; and a girl stands outside it holding all her money that she will ever have in her cute little clenched fist, she's giving it to the pigs for a man; not her man; a man; a hero; a rebel; a resister; a revolutionary; a boy against authority, against all shit. He's all sweet inside, delicate, a tender one, and on the outside he is a fighting boy with speed and wit, a street fighting boy, a subversive; resourceful, ruthless, a paragon, not of virtue but of freedom. Bombs here and there, which I admire, property not people; blowing up symbols of oppression, monuments to greed and exploitation, statues of imperialists and war-mongers; a boy brave enough to strike terror in the heart of business as usual. I'm Andrea, I say to the guard as if it matters; I have the money, see, here, I've come to get him out, he's my friend, a kind, gentle, and decent boy, I say showing a moral nature; I am trying to be a human being to the guard, I'm always a pacifist at war with myself, I want to ignore the uniform, the gun, inside there's someone human, I want to act human, be human, but how? I think about these things and I find myself trying; trying at strange times, in strange places, for reconciliation, for recognition; I decide reciprocity must be possible *now*, for instance, now standing at a guard booth at the outermost concrete wall of the concrete prison. Later, when I am waiting for his release, I will be inside the concrete building and all the guards and police and guns will disappear as if it's magic or a hallucination and I will wander the halls, just wander, down in the cell blocks, all painted an oily brazen white, the bars to the cells painted the same bright white—I will wander; wander in the halls like a tourist looking around at the bars, the cells, the men in the cages, the neat bunk beds; the men will call things out in a language I don't understand, grinning and gesticulating, and I will grin back—I'm lost and I walk around and I walk quite a long way in the halls and I wonder if the police will shoot me if they find me and I hope I can find my way back to the room where they left me and I think about what strange lapses there are in reality, ellipses really, or little bumps and grinds, so that there are no police in the halls anywhere and I can just walk around: loaded down with anxiety, because in Amerika they would shoot me if I was wandering through; it's like a dream but it's no dream, the clean white prison without police. Now, outside, with the guard, at the first barricade, I act nice with both fear and utopia in my heart. Who is the guard? Human, like me. I came for my friend, I say, and I say his name, many times, in the strange language as best I can, I spell it, I write it out carefully. I don't say: my friend you Nazis grabbed because he's political—my friend who makes bombs, not to hurt anyone but to show what's important, people not property—my friend who's afraid of nothing and no one and he has a boisterous laugh and a shy smile—my friend who disappeared from his home three nights ago, disappeared, and no one knew where he was, disappeared, gone, and you had come in the middle of the night and handcuffed him and brought him here, you had hauled him out of bed and taken him away, you had kidnapped him from regular life, you had pushed him around, and you didn't have a reason, not a lawful one, not one you knew about, not a real crime with a real indictment, it was harassment, it was intimidation, but he's not some timid boy, he's not some tepid, tame fool; he's the real thing. He's beyond your law. He's past your reach. He's beyond your understanding. He's risk and freedom outside all restraint. I never quite knew what they arrested him for, a way he had of disappearing inside a narrative, you never could exactly pin down a fact but you knew he was innocent. He was the pure present, a whirling dervish of innocence, a minute-to-minute boy incarnating innocence, no burden of memory or law, untouched by convention. And I came looking for him, because he was kind. He said Andrea, whispered it; he said Andrea shy and quiet and just a little giddy and there was a rush of whisper across my ear, a little whirlwind of whisper, and a chill up and down my spine. It was raining; we were outside, wet, touching just barely, maybe not even that. He lived with his family, a boarder in a house of strangers, cold, acquisitive conformers who wanted money and furniture, people with rules that passed for manners, robots wanting things, more things, stupid things. He had to pay them money to live there. I never heard of such a thing: a son. I couldn't go there with him, of course. I had no place to stay. I was outside all night. It rained the whole night. I didn't have anywhere to go or anywhere to live. I had gone with a few different men, had places to stay for a few weeks, but now I was alone, didn't want no one, didn't have a bed or a room. He came to find me and he stayed with me; outside; the long night; in rain; not in a bed; not for the fuck; not. Rain is so hard. It stops but you stay wet for so long after and you get cold always no matter what the weather because you are swathed in wet cloth and time goes by and you feel like a baby someone left in ice water and even if it's warm outside and the air around you heats up you get colder anyway because the wet's up against you, wrapped around you and it don't breathe, it stays heavy, intractable, on you; and so rain is very hard and when it rains you get sad in a frightened way and you feel a loneliness and a desolation that is very big. This is always so once you been out there long enough. If you're inside it don't matter—you still get cold and lonely; afraid; sad. So when the boy came to stay with me in the rain I took him to my heart. I made him my friend in my heart. I pledged friendship, a whisper of intention. I made a promise. I didn't say nothing; it was a minute of honor and affection. About four in the morning we found a café. It's a long way to dawn when you're cold and tired. We scraped up money for coffee, pulled change out of our pockets, a rush of silver and slugs, and we pooled it on the table which is like running blood together because nothing was held back and so we were like blood brothers and when my blood brother disappeared I went looking for him, I went to the address where he lived, a cold, awful place, I asked his terrible mother where he was, I asked, I waited for an answer, I demanded an answer, I went to the local precinct, I made them tell me, where he was, how to find him, how much money it took to spring him, I went to get him, he was far away, hidden away like Rapunzel or something, a long bus ride followed by another long bus ride, he was in a real prison, not some funky little jail, not some county piss hole, a great gray concrete prison in the middle of nowhere so they can find you if you run, nail you, and I took all my money, my blood, my life for today and tomorrow and the next day and for as long as there was, as far ahead as I can count, and I gave it like a donor for his life so he could be free, so the piglets couldn't put him in a cage, couldn't keep him there; so he could be what he was, this very great thing, a free man, a poor boy who had become a revolutionary man; he was pure—courage and action, a wild boy, so wild no one had ever got near him before, I wish I was so brave as him; he was manic, dizzying, moving every second, a frenzy, frenetic and intense with a mask of joviality, loud stories, vulgar jokes; and then, with me, quiet, shy, so shy. I met him when he had just come back from driving an illegal car two times in the last month into Eastern Europe, crossing the borders illegally into Stalinist Eastern bloc countries—I never understood exactly which side he was

138

on—he said both—he said he took illegal things in and illegal people out—borders didn't stop him, armies didn't stop him, I crossed borders with him later, he could cross any border; he wore a red star he said the Soviets had given him, a star of honor from the government that only some party insiders ever got, and then he fucked them over by delivering anarchy in his forays in and out of their fortressed imperial possessions. He had a Russian nickname, his *nom de guerre*, and since his life was subversion, an assault on society, war against all shit and all authority, his *nom de guerre* was his name, the only name anyone knew he had; no one could trace him to his family, his origins, where he slept: a son paying rent. Except me. In fact the cops arrested him for not paying traffic tickets, thousands of dollars, under the conventional birth name; he ended in the real prison resisting arrest. Even in jail he was still safely underground, the *nom de guerre* unconnected to him, the body in custody. When I married him I got his real name planted on me by law and I knew his secrets, this one and then others, slowly all of them, the revolutionary ones and the ones that went with being a boy of his time, his class, his parents, a boy raised to conform, a boy given a dull, stupid name so he would be dull and stupid, a boy named to become a man who would live to collect a pension. I was Mrs. him, the female one of him by law, a legal incarnation of what he fucking hated, an actual legal entity, because there is no Mrs. *nom de guerre* and no girl's name ever mattered on the streets or underground, not her own real name anyway, only if she was some fox to him, a legendary fox. I was one: yeah, a great one. I had my time. But it was nasty to become Mrs. his Christian names and his daddy's last name, the way they say Mrs. Edward James Fred Smith, as if she's not Sally or Jane; the wedding was my baptism, my naming, Mrs. what he hates, the one who needs furniture and money, the one you come home to which means you got to be somewhere, a rule, a law, Mrs. the law, the one who says get the mud off your shoes because it's dirtying the floor, the one who just cleaned the fucking floor after all. I never thought about mud in my whole fucking life but when you clean the floor you want to be showed respect. I lived with him before we got married; we were great street fighters; we were great. No one could follow the chaos we made, the disruptions, the lightning-fast transgressions of law; passports, borders, taking people or things here or there; street actions, explosions, provocations, property destruction, sand in gas tanks, hiding deserters from Vietnam, the occasional deal. We had a politics of making well-defined chaos, strategically brilliant chaos; then we made love. We did the love because we had run our blood together; it was fraternal love but between us, a carnal expression of brotherhood in the revolutionary sense, a long, fraternal embrace for hours or days, in hiding, in the hours after when we wanted to disappear, be gone from the world of public accountability; and he whispered Andrea, he whispered it urgently, he was urgent and frantic, an intense embrace. He taught me to cook; in rented rooms all over Europe he taught me to cook; a bed, a hot plate, he taught me to make soup and macaroni and sausages and cabbage; and I thought it meant he was specially taking care of me, he was my friend, he loved me, we'd make love and he'd cook. He'd learned in the Navy, mass meals enhanced by his private sense of humor and freedom, the jokes he would tell in the private anarchy of the relatively private kitchen, more personal freedom than anywhere else, doing anything else. He got thrown out; they tried to order him around, especially one vicious officer, he didn't take shit from officers, he poured a bowl of hot soup over the officer's head, he was in the brig, you get treated bad and you toughen up or break and his rebellion took on aspects of deadly force, he lost his boyish charm although he always liked to play but inside it was a life-or-death hate of authority, he made it look like fun but it was very dark; a psychiatrist rescued him, got him discharged. His parents were ashamed. He joined real young to get away from them; he didn't have much education except what he learned there—some about cooking and explosives; some about how to do hard time. He learned some about assault and authority; you could assault anyone; rules said you couldn't; in real life you could. Mommy and daddy were ashamed of him when he came home; they got colder, more remote. Oh, she was cold. Ignorant and cold. Daddy too, but he hid himself behind a patriarchal lethargy; head of the clan's all tuckered out now from a life of real work, daily service, for money, for food, tired for life, too tired to say anything, too tired to do anything, has to just sit there now on his special chair only he can sit on, a vinyl chair, and read the newspaper now, only he gets to read the newspaper, which seems to take all day and all night because he ponders, he addresses issues of state in his head, he's the daddy. Day and night he sits in the chair, all tuckered out. He's cold, a cold man whose wife took the rap for being mean because she did things—raised the kids, cleaned the floor, said eat now, said sleep now, said it's cold so where's the coal, said we need money for clothes, terrible bitch of a woman, a tyrant making such demands, keeping track of the details of shelter; and she got what she needed if she had to make it or barter for it or steal it; she was one of them evil geniuses of a mother that kept her eye open to get what was needed, including when the Nazis were there, occupying, when some didn't get fed and everyone was hungry. Daddy got to sit in the special chair, all for him. Of course, when he was younger he worked. On boats. Including for the Nazis. He had no choice, he is quick to say. Well, not that quick. He says it after a long, rude silence questioning why is it self-evident that there was no choice or questioning his seeming indifference to anything going on around him at the time. Well, you see, of course, I had no choice. No, well, they didn't have to threaten, you see, I simply did what they asked; yes, they were fine to me; yes, I had no trouble with them; of course, I only worked on a boat, a ship, you know. Oh, no, of course, I didn't hurt anyone; no, we never saw any Jews; no, of course not, no. Mommy did, of course; saw a Jew; yes, hid a Jew in a closet for several days, yes. Out of the kindness of her heart. Out of her goodness. Yes, they would have killed her but she said what did the Jews ever do to me and she hid one, yes. Little Jew girl became his daughter-in-law—times have changed, he would note and then he would nod ponderously—but it was the hero, mommy-in-law, who'd say things like "jew it down" because she did the work of maintaining the family values: fed the family materially and spiritually. But my husband wasn't one of them; the worse they were, the purer, the more miraculous, he was. He wasn't of them; he was of me; of what I was and knew; of what I thought and hoped; of the courage I wanted to have; of the will I did have; of the life I was leading, all risk and no tomorrow; and he was born after the war like me; a child of after. So there was this legal thing; the law decrees; it made me their daughter-in-law more than it made me his wife. There was it and them on the one hand and then there was us: him in exile from them—I thought he was as orphaned as I was; and braver; I thought he was braver. I embraced him, and he embraced me, and neither of us knew nothing about tomorrow and I never had. I didn't wait for him like some middle-class girl wanting a date or something in ruffles or someone wanting a husband; I wasn't one of them and I didn't want a husband; I wanted a friend through day and night. I didn't ask him what he liked so I could bow and scrape and my idea wasn't to make him into someone safe, denatured. He was an anarchist of spirit and act and I didn't want no burden of law on him. I just wanted to run with him, be his pal in his game, and hold him; hold him. I indulged an affection for him, a fraternal affection that was real and warm and robust and sort of interesting on its own, always sort of reaching out towards him, and I felt tender towards him, tender near him, next to him, lying next to him; and we were intense, a little on edge, when we holed up together, carnal; our home was the bed we were in, a bed, an empty room, the floor, an empty room, maybe not a regular home like you see on television but we wasn't like them on television, there wasn't two people like us anywhere, so fragile and so reckless and so strong, we were with each other and for each other, we didn't hide where we had been before, what we had done, we had secrets but not from each other and there wasn't anything that made us dirty to each other and we embraced each other and we were going to hole up together, kind of a home, us against them, I guess, and we didn't have no money or *ideas*, you know, pictures in your head from magazines about how things should be—plates, detergents, how them crazy women smile in advertisements. It's all around you but you don't pick it up unless you got some time and money and neither of us had ever been a citizen in that sense. We were revolutionaries, not consumers—not little boy-girl dolls all polished and smiling with little tea sets playing house. We were us, unto ourselves. We found a small place without any floor at all, you had to walk on the beams, and he built the floor so the landlord let us stay there. We planned the political acts there, the chaos we delivered to the status quo, the acts of disruption, rebellion. We hid out there, kept low, kept out of sight; you turn where you are into a friendly darkness that hides you. We embraced there, a carnal embrace—after an action or during the long weeks of planning or in the interstices where we drenched ourselves in hashish and opium until a paralysis overtook us and the smoke stopped all the time. I liked that; how everything slowed down; and I liked fucking after a strike, a proper climax to the real act—I liked how everything got fast and urgent; fast, hard, life or death; I liked bed then, after, when we was drenched in perspiration from what came before; I liked revolution as foreplay; I liked how it made you supersensitive so the hairs on your skin were standing up and hurt before you touched them, could feel a breeze a mile away, it hurt, there was this reddish pain, a soreness parallel to your skin before anything touched you; I liked how you was tired before you began, a fatigue that came because the danger was over, a strained, taut fatigue, an ache from discipline and attentiveness and from the imposition of a superhuman quietness on the body; I liked it. I liked it when the embrace was quiet like the strike itself, a subterranean quiet, disciplined, with exposed nerve endings that hurt but you don't say nothing. Then you sleep. Then you fuck more; hardy; rowdy; long; slow; now side by side or with me on top and then side by side; I liked to be on top and I moved real slow, real deliberate, using every muscle in me, so I could feel him hurting—you know that melancholy ache inside that deepens into a frisson of pain?—and I could tease every bone in his body until it was ready to break open, split and the marrow'd spread like semen. I could split him open inside and he never had enough. I had an appetite for him; anything, I'd do anything, hours or days. In my mind, I wasn't there for him so much as I was the same as him. I could feel every muscle in his body as if it were mine and I'd taunt each muscle, I'd make it bend and ache and stretch and tear, I'd pull it slow, I'd make it move toward me so much it would've come through his skin except I'd make him come before his skin'd burst open. I didn't have no shyness around him and I didn't have to act ignorant or stupid because he wasn't that kind of man who wanted you to overlay everything with the words of a fool like you don't know nothing. Some was perverse according to how these things are seen but that's a concept, not a fact, it's a concept over people's eyes so much you wish they would go blind to

get rid of the concept once and for all. It's how the law makes
you see things but we were different. We were inside each
other; a fact; wasn't perverse; couldn't be. We turned each
other inside out and it binds you and there wasn't nothing he
did to me that I didn't do to him and we'd talk and cook and
roam around and drink and smoke and we'd visit his friends,
which wasn't always so good because to them I was this
something, I didn't understand it but I hated it, I was this
something that came into a room and changed everything.
There were these guys, mostly fighters, anarchists, some
intellectuals, and when I came into the room everything was
different. I was his blood and that's how we acted, not giggly
or amorous, but I think I was just this monstrous thing, this
girlfriend or wife, that is completely different from them and
cannot talk without making them mad or crazy, that cannot
do anything but just must sit quiet, that does not have any
reason to be in the room at all, not this room where they are,
only some other room somewhere else to be fucked, sort of
kept like a pet animal and the man goes there when he's done
with the real stuff, the real talk, the real politics, the real work,
the real getting high, even the real fucking—they go somewhere together and get women together to do the real
fucking, they hunt down women together or buy women
together or pick up women together to do the real fucking;
and then in some one room somewhere hidden away is the
wife or girlfriend and she's in this sort of vacuum, sealed
away, vacuum packed, and when she comes out to be
somewhere or to say something there is an embarrassment and
they avert their eyes—the man failed because she's outside—
she got out—like his pee's showing on his pants. We'd go to
these meetings late at night. These guys would be there; they
were famous revolutionaries, famous to their time and place,
criminals according to the law; brilliant, shrewd, tough guys,
detached, with formal politeness to me. One was a junkie, a

flamboyant junkie with long, silken, rolling brown curls, great pools of sadness in his moist eyes, small and elegant, a beauty, soft-spoken, always nodding out or so sick and wretched that he'd be throwing up a few times a night and they'd expect me to clean it up and I wouldn't, I'd just sit there waiting for the next thing we were all going to discuss, and someone would eventually look me in the eye, a rare event, and say meaningfully, "he just threw up," and time would pass and I'd wait and eventually someone would start talking about something; I didn't get how the junkie was more real than me or how his vomit was mine, you know. When the junkie'd come to where we lived he would vomit and sort of challenge me to leave it there, as he had fouled my very own nest, and he'd ask for a cup of tea and I'd clean it up but I wouldn't get him the tea and I tried to convey to my husband that my hospitality was being abused, *our* hospitality, of course, that I wasn't being treated fair, not that some rule was being broke but that the boy was being rude to me; I told my husband to clean it up finally but he never did it too good. I told my husband who I still thought was my brother that I didn't want the junkie to come anymore because he didn't treat me in an honorable way and I said I wasn't born for this. So there were these fissures coming between us because the fraternal affection was with him and the junkie from the old days together, not him and me from now, and I was shocked by this, I couldn't grasp it. I went into the rooms with him but it came down on him how bad it was from the men and it came down on me that I wasn't supposed to be anywhere near where they were. I kept going to the rooms because we kept hitting targets all over the city and we'd need to get off the streets fast and he'd know some place he wanted to be, one friend or another, and they'd all be there; it would contradict the plan but he'd say it was necessary. Some were on the run for recent crimes but most were burned out, living in times past, not fighting no more, most stopped long ago and far away and they were just burned out to hell. Yeah, they were tired, I respected that; I mean, I fucking loved these heroes; I knew they were tired, tired from living on their nerves, from hiding, from jail, from smoke, from fucking, which came first for some but last for others. Some had children they had deserted; some lived in the past, remembering stray girls in cities they were passing through. They were older than me but not by a lot. I wanted their respect. I hadn't given up and I did anything anybody else did and I wasn't afraid of nothing so how come it was like I wasn't there? I mean, I was too honorable to be anything other than strong and silent, I tell you; but I thought silence made its own sound, you count on revolutionaries to hear the silence, otherwise how can the oppressed count on them? Every lunatic was someone we knew that we dropped in on or stayed with while we were running—or moving just for the sake of speed, the fun of flight. We went to other cities, hitchhiking; we lived in small rented rooms, slept on floors. We went to other countries— we begged, we borrowed, yeah, we stole, me more than him, stealing's easy, I been stealing all my life, not a routine or some fixed act, just here and there as needed, from stores when I was a kid, when I was hungry or when there was something I wanted real bad that I couldn't have because it cost money I didn't have—I never minded putting money out if I had it in my pocket—I mean, I remember taking a chocolate Easter egg when I was a kid or my proudest, most treasured acquisition, a blues record by Dave Van Ronk, the first man I ever saw with a full beard like a beatnik or a prophet; I took money when I needed it and could get it easy enough; pills; clothes. Money's what's useful. He began dealing some shit, it wasn't too hard or dangerous compared to running borders with other contraband but it got so he did it without me more and more; he spent more and more time with these lowlife gangster types, not political revolutionaries at all but these vulgar guys who packed guns and just did business; he said it's just for money, what's it got to do with you or with us, I'll just do it fast, get the money, it's nothing; and it was nothing, I didn't have no interest in money per se, but it got so he did the running, he was free, freedom and flight were his, he'd pick up and go, I didn't know where he was or who with or when I'd meet them they'd be lowlife I had no interest in, just toadies as much as some corporate businessmen were and I'd feel very bored with them and they'd treat me like I was a skirt and I'd feel superior and because I didn't want no part of them I didn't challenge it, I'd just put up with it and be relieved when he did his shit for money elsewhere; he hunted money down, he hunted dope down, he drove the secret highways of Europe at a hundred miles an hour, without me, increasingly without me, and I stayed home and dusted walls, waiting, I waited, while I waited I cleaned, I dusted, I washed things, I made things nice, I put something here or there, little touches, but especially I washed things—I washed floors, dishes, clothes, anything could be washed I fucking washed it; and I would of course keep thinking; I'd be doing laundry but I'd think I was thinking—housework wasn't what *I* was doing, not me, no, I was thinking. I shared the fruits of all this labor with him, clean clothes, clean dishes, clean floors, my thinking, which has always been first-rate in some senses, and I saw him put the thinking I had done into action so I felt like some pretty major player, running dope and making money all over Europe, and I kept thinking, and I saw the thinking go into political actions, so I felt pretty major, and I just kept washing and thinking; washing, ironing, and thinking; washing, shopping, and thinking; washing, cooking, and thinking; washing, scrubbing, and thinking; washing, folding, and thinking. I saw the consequences of my thinking; it was us out there, not just him. I was important; he knew; you don't need recognition in a revolutionary life. Increasingly he incarnated freedom, I dreamed it; especially he was the one who got to be free outside the four walls, and I got to be what he rolled over on when he got home, dead tired and mean as madness. He did—he got on top, he fucked me, he went to sleep. I was incredulous. In the aftershock I ironed, I washed, I scrubbed, I cooked. I'd lie there awake after he rolled off me, on my back, not moving, for hours—outraged, a pristine innocence, stunned in disbelief; this was me; *me*. We'd entertain too, the revolutionary couple, the subversives—I learned to do it. It's like you see in all those films where the bourgie wife slinks around and makes the perfect martini amidst the glittering furniture; well, shit, honey, I made the most magnificent joint a boy could sit down to on a beanbag chair. I mean, I made a joint so gorgeous, so classic and yet so full of savagery and bite, so smooth and so deadly, so big and so right, you'd leave your wife and family and kill your fucking mother just to sit on the floor *near* it. I was the perfect wife, illegally speaking; I mean, I learned how to be a stoned sweet bitch, the new good housekeeping. Your man comes to visit my man and he don't walk home; I am dressed fine and mostly I am quiet except for an occasional ironic remark which establishes me, at least in my own mind, as smart, and I roll a fine joint, and in this way I've done my man proud; he's got the best dope and a fine woman—and a clean house, I mean, a fucking clean house; and I ain't somebody's dumb wife except in the eyes of the law because I defy society—I defy society—I roll joints, I have barely seen a martini, there's nothing I ain't done in bed, including with him, except anal intercourse, I won't have it, not from him, I don't know why but I just won't, I don't want him in me that way, I think it's how I said he's my husband; husband. But I don't think he even knew about it. I'd be as perfect as I could according to his demands, gradually expressed, over time. Everything escalates. Didn't matter how brilliant my joints were once he started using a chellum, a Turkish pipe for hash, rare in Europe, not used because you had to be so fucking aggressive to use it, the hashish and tobacco went in it, it was like a funnel, and you pulled it fast and hard into your lungs through a kind of wind tunnel made by your hands clasped at the bottom of the funnel and the bitter smoke hit your lungs with a burning punch, with the force óf an explosion, and your bloodstream was oxygenated with hash and nicotine. I didn't like the chellum but I had to do it, keeping up with Mr. Jones as it were. Can't find yourself being too delicate, too demure, unable to take the violence of the hit; not if you are Mrs. Jones; have to run *with* the boy or the boy runs without you, he don't slow down to wait, he don't say, Andrea doesn't like this, she likes that, so let's do that. Same with sex. He pushes you down and does it. You solicit his personal recognition. You ask his indulgence. You beg: remember me; me. It changes slow. He tied me up to fuck me more and more; tied me up to this nice little modern brass bed we got, we had a little money; he had from the beginning, in rented rooms, on mattresses, on floors, it doesn't take much, but it was only sometimes; now he tied me up to fuck me invariably and I was bored, tired and bored, irritated and bored; but he wanted it which had to mean he needed it and I want him to do what he needs, I think every man should have what he needs, I think if he has it maybe he won't need it in a bad way; and I love him—not in love but I love him; *him*; I'm with him because it's him; him; I want him to want me; me. I said no or not now or let's just make love and don't tie me up, we don't need it, or even I don't want it now, I don't like it, or trying to say that I didn't want to anymore and it had to matter to him that I didn't want to because this is me; me. I said in all kindness and with all tenderness that I didn't want to but he did want to and so we did because it was easier to than not to and it wasn't like we hadn't before so it wasn't like I had any grounds for saying no or any right and it was so fucking dull and stupid and I'd want it to be over and I'd wait for it to be over, especially to be untied; I learned how to wait, not just when he was doing things to me but after when he'd leave me there while he'd putter around or watch television or do something, I'd never know what exactly. I'd get bad pains in my side from the fucking or really from every time he tied me to fuck me and I was so fucking bored it was like being back on the streets but still easier frankly, just awful in some tedious way: when will he be done, when's he going, when's it going to be over. I know I'm saying I was bored, not morally repelled, and you don't have a right to nothing if you ain't morally repelled, and I know I don't deserve nothing, but I wanted us back being us, the wild us outside and free or stretched out together body to body and carnal, mutual; not this fucking tame stupid boring tie me up then fuck me. I don't have some moral view. My view was that I was on his side; that's what being married meant to me; I was on his side the way a friend on the street, that rarest creature, is on your side; anything, any time, you need it, you got it, I don't ask why, I don't ask any Goddamn thing, I do it, I take any pain that comes with it or any consequences and I don't blab about it or complain or be halfhearted, I just take it. That was it fundamentally for me. I'd think, when's he going, except he wasn't going; the husband gets to stay. I started having this very bad pain in my left side and I felt frustrated and upset because I hated this, it wasn't anything for me; it was banal. I hated having to go through these routines and I'd see the rope coming out, or the movement toward the bed, or the belts, I'd see the shadow of something that meant he wanted this now and I'd try to divert him to something else, anything else, football, sports, anything, or if I saw it was going to happen I'd try to seduce him to be with me; with me. More and more it was pretend, I had to pretend—the sooner he'd come, the

151

sooner it'd be over, but he liked it, he really liked it, and it went on and on; afternoons, fading to dusk. After he'd be jubilant, so fucking high and full of energy, jumping and dancing around, and I'd have this pain in my left side, acute and dreadful, and I wanted to crawl into a corner like some sick animal and he'd want to go visit this one and that one, married couples, his friends, his family; we'd go somewhere and he'd be ebullient and shining and fine and dancing on air, he'd be golden and sparkling, and I'd be trying to stand the pain in my side, I'd be quiet, finally quiet, a quiet girl, not thinking at all, finally not thinking, eyes glazed over, nothing to say, didn't think nothing, just sit there, pale, a fine pallor, they like white girls pale, unwashed, he wouldn't let me wash, dressed, oh yes, very well-dressed, long skirts, demure, some velvet, beautifully made, hippie style but finer, better, simpler, tailored, the one who'd been naked and tied, and he'd look over and he'd see me fucked and tied and I'd feel sticky and dirty and crazy and I'd feel the bruises between my legs because he left them there and I'd feel the sweat, his sweat, and I'd be polite and refined and quiet while he strutted. The men would know; they could see. They'd fuck me with their eyes, smile, smirk, they'd watch me. He liked ropes, belt, sticks, wooden sticks, a walking stick or a cane; cloth gags some-times. I didn't feel annihilated; I felt sick and bored. He'd always do it to me but sometimes he'd have me do it to him as a kind of prologue, a short prologue, and I hated it but I'd try to keep him occupied, excited, I'd try to get him to come, he'd want to get hard but I'd want to make him come, I'd do anything to make him come so the next part wouldn't happen but it always did, you put your heart into staying alive, acting like you're in charge; married, a married woman, with what we been to each other, this is just a hard stretch, he's having some trouble, it will change, I'll love him enough, give him what he needs, it will change, I can do anything, absolutely anything. I'd go through the motions, tying him, doing what he wanted, mostly light strokes of a cotton wrap-around belt and fellating him and then he was ready and he'd tie my wrists to the bed and I'd start waiting and soon the pain in my side would come and I'd know it was going to last for hours and he'd use a leather belt, a heavy belt, with a big buckle, a silver buckle, or sticks, or he'd begin with his open hand, or he'd use a brush, and he'd do what he wanted and he'd take his time and then sometime he'd fuck me and I'd hope it was over and sometimes it was and sometimes he'd do more and after he would untie me and he wanted to visit folks and party, didn't matter who or where, even his terrible family, he'd play cards, the men would play cards, or if it was real late at night he'd want an after midnight movie, a cowboy movie, an edge of night crowd where there were always people he knew and deals he could make and he'd strut by them, circle around them, regale them, touch and poke them, tell vulgar jokes, sell hash or score and always, always he'd smoke; or we'd go to an after-hours club and he'd deal and strut; and I'd sit there, the quiet, used thing; the pale, used thing. I'd moan and do everything you're supposed to; I'd egg him on to try to get him to finish; I just hate the fucking feel of rope around my wrists; I hate it. We didn't use mechanical things; you can use anything; you can do anything any time with anything. The bed was in a tiny middle room, a passageway really, no windows, and I'd lay there, my wrists tied to the headboard, and the walls would be nearer each time, the room would get smaller each time; and sometimes, more and more, he'd leave me spread-eagle on the bed, my ankles tied to the base of the bed, and he'd be done, and he'd get up, he'd fuck me with my legs tied spread apart and then he'd be dead weight on top of me, he'd be done, and sometime he'd get up, when he wanted, and he'd stand there, his back to me, and he'd putter around, he'd find his pants, he'd pick out a new shirt to wear, he'd hum, and I'd

153

want to reach out like this was still us, not just him, and he'd be only a few feet away, but I couldn't and I'd say his name and he'd keep his back to me and I'd ask him to untie me and he'd keep his back to me and I'd tell him my side hurt and he'd putter around and I'd see his back and then I'd close my eyes and wait. Then, sometimes, he'd say we were going out, and I'd say I'm sick and I don't want to, and then I'd get scared that he'd leave me there tied up and I'd say I wanted to go, I really did, and he'd sit down on the bed and he'd untie one rope around my wrist and then he'd make it tighter to hurt me and then he'd untie it because I was shaking from fear that he'd leave me there and I'd put on clothes, what he liked, and I'd follow him, quiet. I never thought there was anything I couldn't walk away from; not me. If I didn't like being married I'd just leave. I didn't care about the law. I wasn't someone like that. This was a few fucking ropes; so what? I was getting nervous all the time; anxious; and he'd keep waking me up to do something to me; to fuck me; to tie me; I'd be sleeping, he'd be gone, he'd come in out of nowhere, he'd be on me in the bed where I was sleeping, I just could never get enough sleep. It was ordinary life; just how every day went; I'd think I could do it one more day, I could last one more day, he'll leave, he'll change, he will go somewhere with someone, a girl, he'll find a girl, he'll go away to buy or sell drugs and he'll get caught, he'll go to jail, he'll go back to running with his pack of boys; a man will always leave, you can count on it, wait long enough, he's gone, how long will long enough be? I'd be counting seconds, on the bed, waiting. He painted the bedroom a dark, shocking blue, all the walls and the ceiling; I screamed, I cried, I begged, I can't stand it, the walls will close in on me, it makes the ceiling feel like it's on top of me, I'll smother, I can't bear it, I screamed obscenities and I called him names and I could barely breathe from the tears and he hit me, hard, in the face, over and over; and I ran away; and I was outside in the cold a long time; I didn't have my coat; I was crying uncontrollably; I went to the park; men tried to pick me up; I was freezing; my face was swelling; I couldn't stop crying; I felt ashamed; I got scared; I went back; he wanted to make love; I was tied in the room. I knew he was capable of frenzies of rage; but not at me—he broke furniture, he punched his fist into walls, once he tore up a pile of money, tore it into a million pieces—it was rage at things; not me; I don't care about things. It was an internal agony, he was tormented, he was so distraught, and I thought I'd love him and it would help that I did. When the violence possessed him, it didn't have anything to do with me; it didn't; I was terrified by the magnitude of it, like the way you're frightened of a big storm with thunder that cracks the earth open and lightning that looks like the sky's exploding, you feel small and helpless and the drama of it renders you passive, waiting for it to be over, hoping it won't hurt you by accident. The first time his frenzy landed on me—landed on me, a shower of his fists pummeling me—I just didn't believe it. It wasn't something he would really do; not to me; me. It was some awful mistake; a mistake. I didn't clean the refrigerator. I had never seen anyone clean one before—I mean, I never had, however stupid I am I hadn't—and I didn't see why I should do it and I didn't want to do it and he told me to do it and I said no and he went mad, it was some seizure, something happened to him, something got inside him and took him over, and he beat me nearly to death, it's a saying but I think it's true, it means that some part of you that is truly you does die, and I crawled into a corner, I crawled on the floor down low so he wouldn't kick me, I crawled, and I was sick in the corner but I didn't move, and he was sorry, and he helped me, he washed my face and he put me in bed and he covered me up and he let me sleep and it just wasn't something you could imagine happening again. Or I didn't do the laundry right. I didn't separate the clothes right.

I washed his favorite T-shirt in with the colored clothes and some colors ran in it and he held it up and he berated me for how stupid I was and how I did this to hurt him on purpose because it was his favorite T-shirt and I was trying to placate him so I was trying to smile and be very nice and I said it was just a mistake and I was sorry and he said you always have some fucking smart answer and he hit me until I was wet stuff on the floor. Everything just keeps happening. You do the laundry, you think you are free, you get waked up by someone on you fucking you or he ties you up and you get a pain in your side and then you go to the movies and time slows down so that a day is almost never over, it never exactly ends, nothing exactly ever stops or starts, I'd sit in the movie wondering what would happen if I just stood up and started begging for help, I wanted to, I wanted to just stand up and say help me; help me; he's hurting me; he, this one here, he hurt me so bad just before; help me; take me somewhere; help me; take me somewhere safe; and I knew they'd laugh, he'd make them laugh, some jokes about women or how crazy I was and the stoned assholes would just laugh and he'd keep me there through the movie and then life would just go on; then or later, that night or tomorrow, he would hurt me so bad; like Himmler. There's normal life going on all around you and you have your own ordinary days and it is true that they are ordinary because doing the laundry is ordinary and being fucked by your husband is ordinary and if you are unhappy that is ordinary too, as everyone will tell you if you ask for help. Old ladies in the neighborhood will pat your hand and say yes, dear, but someday they get sick and die. You can't remember if there was a prior time and you get so nervous and so worried and you just keep trying to do everything better, the cleaning, bed, whatever he wants, you concentrate on doing it good, the way he likes it, and you just squeeze your mind into a certain shape so you can concentrate on not making mistakes and some days you can't and you talk back or are slow or say something sarcastic and you will be hurt. Did you provoke it, did you want it, or are you just a fucking human being who's tired of the little king? If you tell anyone or ask for help they blame you for it. Everyone's got a reason it's your fault. I didn't clean the refrigerator, I did mess up the laundry, I wasn't in the right, I'm supposed to do those things, I'm the wife after all, whoever heard of one who didn't know how to do those things, he has rights too; I'm supposed to make him happy. And I let him tie me up so it's on me what happened and if I say I didn't like it people just say it's a lie, you can't face it, you can't face how you liked it; and I can't explain that I'm not like them, I'm not someone virginal in the world like them, I been facing what I liked since I was born and being tied up isn't what they think, the words they use like "sadomasochism" or "bondage," three-dollar words for getting a trick to come, and they get all excited just to say them because they read about them in books and they are all philosophers from the books and I hate them, I hate the middle-class goons who have so much to say but never spent one fucking day trying to stay alive. And when you are a fucking piece of ground meat, hamburger he left on the floor, and he fucks you or he fucking leaves you there for dead, whichever is his pleasure that day, it's what you wanted, what you are, what's inside of you, like you planned it all along, like you're General Westmoreland or something instead of messed up, bleeding trash, and if you're running away they send you back for more, and they don't give you money to help you, and they tell you that you like it; fucking middle-class hypocrite farts. I have a list. I remember you ones. You try to pull the wool over someone else's eyes about how smart you are and what humanitarians you all are on the side of whoever's hurting. Nelson Mandela provoked it. What do you think about that, assholes? We all of us got the consolation that nobody remembers the worst things. They're gone; brain just burns them away. And there's no words for the worst things so ain't no one going to tell you the worst things; they can't. You can pick up any book and know for sure the worst things ain't in it. It's almost funny reading Holocaust literature. The person's trying so hard to be calm and rational, controlled, clear, not to exaggerate, never to exaggerate, to remember ordinary details so that the story will have a narrative line that will make sense to you; you—whoever the fuck you are. The person's trying so hard to create a twenty-four-hour day. The person picks words carefully, sculpts them into paragraphs, selects details, the victim's selection, selects details and tries to make them credible—selects from what can be remembered, because no one remembers the worst. They don't dare scream at you. They are so polite, so quiet, so civil, to make it a story you can read. I am telling you, you have never read the worst. It has never been uttered by anyone ever. Not the Russians, not the Jews; never, not ever. You get numb, you forget, you don't believe it even when it's happening to you, your mind caves in, just collapses, for a minute or a day or a week or a year until the worst is over, the center caves in, whoever you were leaves, just leaves; if you try to force your mind to remember it leaves, just fucking empties out of you, it might as well be a puddle on the ground. Anything I can say isn't the worst; I don't remember the worst. It's the only thing God did right in everything I seen on earth: made the mind like scorched earth. The mind shows you mercy. Freud didn't understand mercy. The mind gets blank and bare. There's nothing there. You got what you remember and what you don't and the very great thing is that you can't remember almost anything compared to what happened day in and day out. You can count how many days there were but it is a long stretch of nothing in your mind; there is nothing; there are blazing episodes of horror in a great stretch of nothing. You thank God for the nothing. You get on your fucking knees. We are doing some construction in our apartment and we had a pile of wood beams piled up and he got so mad at me—for what?—something about a locked door; I didn't lock the door or he didn't lock the door and I asked him why not—and he picked up one of the wood beams and he beat me with it across my legs like he was a trained torturer and knew how to do it, between the knees and the ankle, not busting the knees, not smashing the ankles, he just hammered it down on my legs, and I don't remember anything before or after, I don't know what month it was or what year; but I know it was worse, the before and the after were worse; the weeks I can't remember were worse; I remember where it happened, every detail, we had the bed in the hall near the wood beams and we were sleeping there temporarily and it was early on because it wasn't the brass bed yet, it was just a dumpy old bed, an old mattress, and everything was dull and brown, there was a hall closet, and there was a toilet at one end of the hall and a foyer leading to the entrance to the apartment at the other end of the hall, and there wasn't much room, and it was brown and small and had a feeling of being enclosed and I know I was sitting on the bed when he began to hit me with the beam, when he hit me with it the first time, it was so fast or I didn't expect it because I didn't believe it was possible, I didn't understand what happened, or how it could; but I remember it and the only thing that means is that it isn't the worst. I know how to calibrate torture—how to measure what's worse, what's better, what's more, what's less. You take the great morbid dark blank days and you have located the worst. You pray it ain't buried like Freud says; you pray God burned it out like I say. Some weeks later he wanted to have dinner with his sister and brother-in-law. I could limp with a great deal of pain. I was wearing dark glasses because my eyes had cuts all around them and were discolored from bruises and swollen out of shape; I don't know when my eyes got that way; the time of the wood beam or in the weeks I can't remember after; but I had to wear the glasses so no one would see my eyes. Them kinds of bruises don't heal fast like in the movies. They all played cards and we had cheese fondue which I never saw before. I walked with a bad limp, I concealed the pain as best I could, I wore the dark glasses, I had a smile pasted on my face from ear-to-ear, an indelible smile, and brother-in-law brought up the limp and I said smiling with utter charm that I had tripped over the beams and hurt myself. Don't worry, I whispered urgently to my husband, I would never tell. I would never tell. What you did (hoping he doesn't hear the accusation in saying he did it, but he does of course and he bristles). I'm on your side. I wouldn't tell. Brother-in-law, a man of the world, smiles. He knows that a lot of stupid women keep falling down mountains. He's a major in the military; we say a fascist. He knew. He seemed to like it; he flushed, a warm, sexy flush; he liked it that I lied and smiled. There's no what happened next. Nightmares don't have a linear logic with narrative development, each detail expanding the expressive dimensions of the text. Terror ain't esthetic. It don't work itself out in perfect details picked by an elegant intelligence and organized so a voyeur can follow it. It smothers and you don't get no air. It's oceanic and you drown, you are trapped underneath and you ain't going to surface and you ain't going to swim and you ain't dead yet. It destroys and you cease to exist while your body endures anyway to be hurt more and your mind, the ineffable, bleeds inside your head and still your brain don't blow. It's an anguish that implodes leaving pieces of you on the wall. It's remorse for living; it's pulling-your-heart-apart grief for every second you spent alive. It is all them cruel things you can't remember that went to make up your days, ordinary days. I was in the bedroom. It was dark blue, the ceiling too. I'd be doing what he wanted, or trying to. He fucked me a lot. I'd be crying or waiting. I'd be staring. I'd stare. I was like some idiot, staring. After he fucked me I'd just be there, a breathing cadaver. You just wait, finally, for him to kill you; you hope it won't take too long, you won't have to grow old. Hope, as they say, never dies. Time's disappearing altogether, it doesn't seem to exist at all, you wait, he comes, he hurts you this way or that, long or short, an enormous brutality, physical injury or psychological torture, he doesn't let you sleep, he keeps you up, he fucking tortures you, you're in a prison camp, you're tied up or not, it's like being in a cell, he tortures you, he hurts you, he fucks you, he doesn't let you sleep, it doesn't stop so it can start again, there's no such thing as a twenty-four-hour day. I don't know. I can't say. I didn't go out anymore. I couldn't walk, really, couldn't move, either because physically I couldn't or because I couldn't. There's one afternoon he dragged me from the bed and he kept punching me. He pulled me with one hand and punched me with the other, open hand, closed fist, closed fist, to my face, to my breasts, closed fists, both fists, I am on the kitchen floor and he is kneeling down so he can hit me, kneeling near me, over me, and he takes my head in his hands and he keeps banging my head in his hands and he keeps banging my head against the floor. He punches my breasts. He burns my breasts with a lit cigarette. He didn't need to hold me down no more. He could do what he wanted. He was punching me and burning me and I was wondering if he was going to fuck me, because then it would be over; did I want it? He was shouting at me, I never knew what. I was crying and screaming. I think he was crying too. I felt the burning. I saw the cigarette and I felt the burning and I got quiet, there was this incredible calm, it was as if all sound stopped. Everything continued—he was punching me and burning me; but there was this perfect quiet, a single second of absolute calm; and then I passed out. You see how kind the mind is. I just stopped existing. You go blank, it's dark, it's a deep, wonderful dark, blank, it's close to dying, you could be dead or maybe you are dead for a while and God lets you rest. You don't know anything and you don't have to feel anything; not the burns; not the punches; you don't feel none of it. I am grateful for every minute I cannot remember. I thank You, God, for every second of forgetfulness You have given me. I thank You for burning my brain out to ashes and hell, wiping it out so it is scorched earth that don't have no life; I am grateful for an amnesia so deep it resembles peace. I will not mind being dead. I am waiting for it. I have breasts that burst into flames, only it's blood. Suddenly there's a hole in my breast, in the flesh, a deep hole that goes down into my breast, I can be anywhere, or just sitting talking somewhere, and blood starts coming out of my breast, a hole opens up as if the Red Sea were splitting apart but in a second, half a second, it wasn't there and then suddenly it is there, and I know because I feel the blood running down my breast, there's a deep hole in my breast, no infection, it never gets infected, no pus, no blood poisoning ever, no cyst, completely clean, a hole down into the breast, you see the layers of skin and fat inside, and blood pours out, clean blood, just comes out, it hurts when the hole comes, a clean hurt, a simple, transparent pain, the skin splitting fast and clean, opening up, and I'm not in any danger at all though it takes me some years to realize this, it's completely normal, completely normal for me, I am sitting there talking and suddenly the skin on a breast has opened up and there is a deep, clean hole in my breast and blood is pouring down my chest and I'm fine, just fine, and the hole will stay some days and the blood will come and go. They're my stigmata. I know it but I can't tell anyone. They come from where the burns were, the skin bursts open and the blood washes me clean, it heals me, the skin closes up new, bathed in the blood: clean. Because I suffered enough. Even God knows it so He sent the sign. I've

162

seen all the movies about stigmata and it's just like in the
movies when someone explains what real stigmata is so we
can tell it from a trick; it's real stigmata on me; it's God saying
He went too far. He loves me. It's Him saying I'm the best
time He ever had. They asked in the camps, they asked where
is God; but they didn't answer: omnipotent, omniscient,
omnipresent, He's right here, having a good time. When you
get married, it's you, the man, and God, just like is always
said. God was there. The film unrolled. The live sex show
took place. I'm filthy all over. The worst thing was I'd just
crawl into bed and wait for him to fuck me and he'd fuck me. I
couldn't barely breathe. His long hair'd be all over me in my
face, in my eyes, in my nose, in my mouth, and it was so hot I
couldn't breathe so I went to a barber and I got my hair cut off,
almost shaved like at Dachau so I'd be able to breathe, so my
hair wouldn't mix with his, so there'd be less hair, I got
dressed, I found some change, I was scared, I didn't know
what would happen to me, I told the man to take all my hair
off, keep cutting, keep cutting, shorter, less, keep cutting,
shave it shorter, I just couldn't stand all the hair in my face; but
it didn't get no cooler and I'd lie still, perfectly still, on my
back, my eyes open, and he'd fuck me. He didn't need no
rope. You understand—he didn't need no rope. You understand the dishonor in that—he didn't need no rope and God
just watched and it was your standard issue porn, just another
stag film with a man fucking a woman too stupid or too near
dead to be somewhere else; a little ripe, a little bruised; eyes
glazed over, open but empty; I would just lie there for him and
he didn't need no rope. We was married. I don't think rape
exists. What would it be? Do you count each time separate;
and the blank days, they do count or they don't?

EIGHT

In March 1973
(Age 26)

I was born in 1946 in Camden, New Jersey, down the street from Walt Whitman's house, Mickle Street, but my true point of origin, where I came into existence as a sentient being, is Birkenau, sometimes called Auschwitz II or The Women's Camp, where we died, my family and I, I don't know what year. I have a sense memory of the place, I've always had it although of course when I was young I didn't know what it was, where it was, why it was in my mind, the place, the geography, the real place, the way it was, it's partial in my mind but solid, the things I see in my mind were there, they're pushed back in my mind, hard to get at, behind a wall of time and death. Everything that matters about me begins there. I remember it, not like a dream and it's not something I made up out of books—when I looked at the books I saw what I already had seen in my mind, I saw what I already knew was there. It's the old neighborhood, familiar, a far-back memory, back before speech or rationality or self-justification, it's way back in my mind but it's whole, it's deep down where no one can touch it or change it, it can't be altered by information or events or by wishful thinking on my part. It's my hidden heart that keeps beating, my real heart, the invisible one that no physician can find and death can't either. Not everyone was burned. At first, they didn't have crematoria. They pushed all the bodies into huge mass graves and put earth on top of them but the bodies exploded from the gases that come when bodies decompose; the earth actually heaved and pulled apart, it swelled and rose up and burst open, and the soil turned red. I read that in a book and I knew right away that it was true, I recognized it as if I had seen it, I thought, yes, that seems more familiar to me than the crematoria, it was as if my soul had stayed above and watched and I saw the earth buckle and the red come up through the soil. I always knew what Birkenau was like from the parts of it I have in my mind. I knew it was gray and isolated and I knew there were low, gray huts, and I knew the ground was gray and flat, and it was winter, and I knew there were pine trees and birch trees, I see them in the distance, upright, indifferent, a monstrous provocation, God's beauty, He spits in your face, and there were huge piles of things, so big you thought they were hills of earth but they were shoes, you can see from currently published photos that they were shoes—the piles were higher than the buildings, and there was a huge, high arch. I have never liked seeing pictures of the Arc de Triomphe in Paris, because they always make me feel sad and scared, because at Birkenau there was a high arch that looked like a sculpture against that desolate sky. You think in your mind the yellow star is one thing—you make it decorous and ornamental, you give it esthetic balance and refinement, a fineness, a delicacy, maybe in your mind you model it on silver Stars of David you have seen—but it was really a big, ugly thing and you couldn't make it look nice. I think I was only waist-high. You don't know much if you're a kid. I remember the women around me, masses of women, I held someone's hand but I don't think it was someone I even knew, I can't see any faces really because they are all taller and they were covered, heavy coats, kerchiefs on their heads, layers of clothes fouled by dirt, but if you're a child you're like a little cub, a puppy, and you think you're safe if you're huddled with women. They're warm. They keep you warm. You want to be near them and you believe in them without thinking. I wasn't there too long. We walked somewhere, we waited, we walked, it was over. I've seen birch trees here in the United States in the mountains but I have always transposed them in my mind to a different landscape: that low, flat, swampy ground past the huts. Birch trees make me feel sad and lonely and afraid. There's astrologers who say that if you were born when Pluto and Saturn were traveling together in Leo, from 1946 to about the middle of 1949, you died in one of the concentration camps and you came right back because you had to, you had an urgency stronger than death could ever be, you had to come back and set it right. Justice pushed you into a new womb and outrage, a blind fury, pushed you out of it onto this earth, this place, this zoo of sickies and sadists. You are an avenging angel; you have a debt to settle; you have a headstart on suffering. I consider Birkenau my birthplace. I consider that I am a living remnant. I consider that in 1946 I emerged, I burst out, I was looking for trouble and ready for pain, I wanted to kill Nazis, I was born to kill Nazis, I wasn't some innocent born to play true love and real romance, the parlor games that pass for life. I got these fucked-up compassionate parents who believed in law and kindness and blah blah. I got these fucked-up peaceful Jews. I got these fucked-up civilized parents. I was born a girl. I have so many planets in Libra that I try to be fair to flies and I turn dog shit into an esthetic experience. Even my mother knew it was wrong. She named me Andrea for "manhood" or "courage." It's a boy's name; the root, *andros*, means "man" in Greek. It's "man" in the universal sense, too. Man. She and God joined hands to tease me almost to death. He put brains, great hearts, great spirits, into women's bodies, to fuck us up. It's some kind of sick joke. Let's see them aspire in vain. Let's see them fucked into triviality and insignificance. Let's see them try to lose at checkers and tic-tac-toe to boys, year in, year out, to boys so stupid He barely remembered to give them an I.Q. at all, He forgot their hearts, He forgot their souls, they have no warrior spirit or sense of honor, they are bullies and fools; let's make each one of the boys imperial louts, let's see these girls banged and bruised and bullied; let's see them forced to act stupid so long and so much that they learn to be stupid even when they sleep and dream. And mother, handmaiden to the Lord, says wear this, do that, don't do that, don't say that, sit, close your legs, wear white gloves and don't get them dirty, girls don't climb trees, girls don't run, girls don't, girls don't, girls don't; wasn't nothing girls actually did do of any interest whatsoever. It's when they get you a doll that pees that you recognize the dimensions of the conspiracy, its institutional reach, its metaphysical ambition. Then God caps it all off with Leviticus. I have to say, I was not amused. But the meanest was my daddy: be kind, be smart, read, think, care, be excellent, be serious, be committed, be honest, be someone, be, be, be; he was the cruelest joker alive. There'd be "Meet the Press" on television every Sunday and they'd interview the Secretary of State or Defense or a labor leader or some foreign head of state and we'd discuss the topic, my daddy and me: labor, Suez, integration, law, literacy, racism, poverty; and I'd try to solve them. We would discuss what the President should do and what I would do if I were Secretary of State. He would listen to me, at eight, at ten, at twelve, attentively, with respect. The cruelty of the man knew no bounds. You have a right to hate liberals; they make promises they cannot keep. They make you believe certain things are possible: dignity in the world, and freedom; but especially equality. They make equality seem as if it's real. It's a great sorrow to grow up. The world ain't liberal. I always wanted excellence. I wanted to attain it. I didn't start out with apologies. I thought: I am. I wanted to mix with the world, hands on, me and it, and I'd have courage. I wasn't born nice necessarily but nurture triumphed over nature and I wanted to be the good citizen

who could go from my father's living room out into the
world. I got all fucked up with this peace stuff—how you can
make it better, anything better, if you care, if you try. I didn't
want to kill Nazis, or anyone. In this sense I knew right from
wrong; it was an immutable sense of right and wrong; that
killing killed the one doing the killing and that killing killed
something precious and good at the center of life itself. I knew
it was wrong to take an individual life, mine, and turn it into a
weapon of destruction; I knew I could and I said no I won't; I
could have; I was born with the capacity to kill; but my father
changed my heart. I said, it's Nazism you have to kill, not
Nazis. People die pretty easy but cruelty doesn't. So you got
to find a way to go up against the big thing, the menace; you
have to stop it from being necessary—you have to change the
world so no one needs it. You have to start with the love you
have to give, the love that comes from your own heart; and
you can't accept any terror of the body, restrictions or
inhibitions or totalitarian limits set by authoritarian types or
institutions; there's nothing that can't be love, there's nothing
that has to be mean; you take the body, the divine body, that
their hate disfigures and destroys, and you let it triumph over
murder and rage and hate through physical love and it is the
purest democracy, there is no exclusion in it. Anything,
everything, is or can be communion, I-Thou. Anything,
everything, can be transformed, transcended, opened up,
turned from opaque to translucent; everything's luminous,
lambent, poignant, sweet, filled with nuance and grace,
potentially ecstatic. I thought I had the power and the passion
and the will to transform anything, me, now, with the simple
openness of my own heart, a heart pretty free of fear and
without prejudice against life; a heart loving life. I didn't have
a fascist heart or a bourgeois heart; I just had this heart that
wanted freedom. I wanted to love. I wanted; to love. I never
grasped the passive part where if you were a girl you were

supposed to be loved; he picks you; you sit, wait, hope, pray, don't perspire, pluck your eyebrows, be good meaning you fucking sit still; then the boy comes along and says give me that one and you respond to being picked with desire, sort of like an apple leaping from the tree into the basket. I was me, however, not her, whomever; some fragile, impotent, mentally absent person perpetually on hold, then the boy presses the button and suddenly the line is alive and you get to say yes and thank you. In Birkenau it didn't matter what was in your gorgeous heart, did it; but I didn't learn, did I? I wanted to love past couples and individuals and the phoney baloney of neurotic affairs. I didn't want small personalities doing fetishized carnal acts. I thought adultery was the stupidest thing alive. John Updike made me want to puke. I didn't think adultery could survive one day of real freedom. I didn't think it was bad—I thought it was moronic. I wanted a grand sensuality that encompassed everyone, didn't leave anyone out. I wanted it dense and real and full-blooded and part of the fabric of every day, every single ordinary day, all the time; I wanted it in all things great and small. I wanted the world to tremble with sexual feeling, all stirred up, on the edge of a thrill, riding a tremor, and I wanted a tender embrace to dissolve alienation and end war. I wanted the world's colors to deepen and shine and shimmer and leap out, I didn't want limits or boundaries, not on me, not on anyone else either; I didn't want life flat and dull, a line drawing done by some sophomore student at the Art League. I thought we'd fuck power to death, because sexual passion was the enemy of power, and I thought that every fuck was an act of passion and compassion, beauty and faith, empathy and an impersonal ecstasy; and the cruel ones, the mean ones, were throwbacks, the old order intransigent and refusing to die, but still, the fuck, any fuck, brought someone closer to freedom and power closer to dying. And yes, the edge is harrowing and poverty is

not kind and power ain't moved around so easy, especially not
by some adolescent girl in heat, and I fell very low over time,
very low, but I had devotion to freedom and I loved life. I
wasn't brought low in the inner sanctum of my belief; until
after being married, when I was destroyed. I remembered
Birkenau. I wished I could find my way back to the line, you
wait, you walk, you wait, you walk some more, it's over. I
know that's ignorant; I am ignorant. I wanted peace and I had
love in my heart and being hurt didn't mean anything except I
wasn't dead yet, still alive, still having to live today and right
now; being hurt didn't change anything, you can't let fear
enter in. According to the way I saw life, I incarnated peace.
Maybe not so some understand it but in my heart I was peace;
and I never thought any kind of making love was war; make
love, not war; and when it was war on me I didn't see it as such
per se; war was Vietnam. I never thought peace was bland; or I
should be insipid or just wait. Peace has its own drive and its
own sense of time; you need backbone; and it wants to win—
not to have the last word but to be the last word; it's fierce,
peace is; not coy, not pure, not simpering or whimpering, and
maybe it's not always nice either; and I was a real peace girl
who got a lot of it wrong maybe because staying alive was
hard and I did some bad things and it made me hard and I got
tough and tired, so tired, and nasty, sometimes, mean:
unworthy. Why'd Gandhi put those young girls in his bed and
make them sleep there so he could prove he wouldn't touch
them and he could resist? I never got nasty like that, where I
used somebody else up to brag I was someone good. There's
no purity on this earth from ego or greed and I never set out to
be a saint. I like everything being all mixed up in me; I don't
have quarrels with life like that; I accept we're tangled. In my
heart, I was peace. Once I saw a cartoon in *The New Yorker*,
maybe I was eighteen. It showed a bunch of people carrying
picket signs that said "Peace." And it showed one buxom

woman carrying a sign that said "Piece." I hated that. I hated it. But you either had to be cowed, give in to the pig shit behind that cartoon, or you had to disown it, disown the dumb shit behind it. I disowned it all. I disowned it without exception. I kept none of it. I pushed it off me. I purged my world of it. I disavowed anyone who tried to put it on me. There couldn't be this garbage between me and life; like some huge smelly dump you had to trudge through or crawl through to slide up against someone else who was also real. And by the time you got to them you smelled like the garbage. I said no. I said I will not. I said it is not on me. I said I may be poor but I am not afraid. I said I want. I said I am not afraid to pay. I said I will not shield myself. I said I will not pretend to live life; I will live it. I said I will not apologize and I will not lie. I said, if I die, I die. I was never afraid to die. I got tough in some ways but I stayed soft inside the core of my belief where there was tenderness for others, sometimes. I kept a caring eye. I kept a caring heart. Over the injury I still believed there was love; not the love of two but the love of many. I still believed in us, all of us, us, if we could get free from rules and obedience and being robots. I liked doing sabotage, I'm not saying I had a pretty heart, I wasn't a nice girl and I'm not claiming it. I had some ruthlessness. I wasn't easy to kill. I could keep going. I wanted to live. I'm just saying I cared. Why didn't I kill him? Why didn't I? I'm the most ardent pacifist the world ever saw. And fuck meant all kinds of making love—it was a new word. It was fucking if you got inside each other, or so near you couldn't be pulled apart. It was joy and risk and fun and orgasm; not faking it; I never have. It didn't have to do with who put what where. It was all kinds of wet and all kinds of urgent and all kinds of here and now, with him or her. It was you tangled up with someone, raw. It wasn't this one genital act, in out in out, that someone could package and sell or that there was an etiquette for. It wasn't some imitation of something you saw somewhere, in porn or your favorite movie star saying how he did it. It was something vast, filled with risk and feeling; feeling; personal love ain't the only feeling—there's feelings of adventure and newness and excitement and Goddamn pure happiness— there's need and sorrow and loneliness and certain kinds of grief that turn easy into touching someone, wild, agitated, everywhere—there's just liking whoever it is and wanting to pull them down right on you, they make you giddy, their mere existence tickles you to death, you giggle and cheer them on and you touch them—and there's sensation, just that, no morality, no higher good, no justification, just how it feels. There's uncharted waters, you ain't acting out a script and there's no way past the present, you are right there in the middle of your own real life riding a wave a mile high with speed and grace and then you are pulled under to the bottom of the world. The whole world's alive, everything moves and wants and loves, the whole world's alive with promise, with possibility; and I wanted to live, I said yes I want to live. There's not something new about wanting love in spite of knowing terror; or feeling love and having it push against your thighs from inside and then those thighs carry you out past safety into hell. There's nothing new about wanting to love a multitude. I was born on Mickle Street in Camden in 1946, down the street from Walt Whitman's house. I grew up an orphan sheltered by the passion of his great heart. He wanted everyone. He wanted them, to touch. He was forced, by his time and place, into metaphor. He put it in poems, this physicalized love that was universal, he named the kinds and categories he wanted, men and women, he said they were worthy, all, without exception, he said he wanted to be on them and in them and he wanted them in him, he said it was love, he said *I am*, he said *I am* and then he enumerated the ones he wanted, he made *I am* synonymous with *you are* and *we are*.

172

Leaves of Grass is his lists of lovers, us, the people, all of us; he used grandiose language but it was also common, vulgar; he says *I am* you and you and you, you exist, I touch you, I know you, I see you, I recognize you, I want you, I love you, *I am*. In the Civil War he was devoted to wounded soldiers. He faced the maiming and the mutilation, and he loved those boys: "(Many a soldier's loving arms about this neck have cross'd and rested, / Many a soldier's kiss dwells on these bearded lips.)" It was before surgeons washed their hands, before Lister, and legs were sawed off, sutures were moistened with saliva, gangrene was commonplace. He visited the wounded soldiers day in and day out. He didn't eroticize suffering, no; it was the communion of being near, of touching, of a tender intimacy inside a vale of tears. He saw them suffer and he saw them die and he wrote: "(Come sweet death! be persuaded O beautiful death! / In mercy come quickly.)" I got to say, I don't think a three-minute fuck was his meaning. I don't. It's an oceanic feeling inside and you push it outward and once you start loving humanity there is no reason to make distinctions of beauty or kind, there's something basic in everyone that asks love, forgiveness, an honorable tenderness, a manly tenderness, you know, strong. He was generous. Call him a slut. If a war happens, it marks you for life, it's your war. Walt's was the Civil War, North against South, feuding brothers, a terrible slaughter, no one remembers how bloody and murderous it was. Mine was Vietnam; I didn't love the soldiers but I loved the boys who didn't go. My daddy's war was World War II. Everyone had their own piece of that war. There's Iwo Jima, Pearl Harbor, Hiroshima; Vichy and the French Resistance; sadists, soldier boys, S.S., in Europe. My daddy was in the Army. My daddy was being sent to the Pacific when Truman dropped the bomb; the bomb. He says it saved his life. Hiroshima and Nagasaki saved his life. I never saw him wish anyone harm, except maybe Strom Thurman and

Jesse Helms and Bull Connor, but he thought it was okay, hell, necessary, for all those Japanese to die so he could live. He thought he was worth it, even if it was just a chance he would die. I felt otherwise. He had an unreasonable anger against me. *I* would have died, he said, I would have *died*. He was peace-loving but nothing could shake his faith that Hiroshima was right, not the mass death, not the radiation, not the pollution, not the suffering later, not the people burned, their skin burned right off them; not the children, then or later. The mushroom cloud didn't make him afraid. To him it always meant he wasn't dead. I was ashamed of him for not caring, or for caring so much about himself, but I found what I thought was common ground. I said it was proved Truman didn't have to do it. In other words, I could think it was wrong to drop the bomb and still love my father but he thought I had insufficient respect and he had good intuition because I couldn't see why his life was worth more than all those millions. I couldn't reconcile it, how this very patient, very kind, quite meek guy could think he was more important than all the people. It wasn't that he thought the bomb would stop Jews from being massacred in Europe; it was that he, from New Jersey, would live. He didn't understand that I was born in the shadow of the crime, a shadow that covered the whole earth every day from then on. We just were born into knowing we'd be totally erased; someday; inevitably. My daddy used to be beat up by other boys at school when he was growing up. He was a bookworm, a Jew, and the other boys beat the shit out of him; he didn't want to fight; he got called a sissie and a kike and a faggot, sheenie, all the names; they beat the shit out of him, and yes, one did become the chief of police in the Amerikan way; and then, somehow, an adult man, he knows he's worth all the Japanese who died; and I wondered how he learned it, because I have never learned anything like it yet. He was humble and patient and I learned a kind of personal pacifism from him; he went into the Army, he was a soldier, but all his life he hated fighting and conflict and he would not fight with arms or support any violence in word or deed, he tried persuasion and listening and he'd avoid conflict even if it made him look weak and he was gentle, even with fools; and I learned from him that you are supposed to take it, as a person, and not give back what you got; give back something kinder, better, subtler, more elevated, something deeper and kinder and more human. So when he didn't mind the bomb, when he liked it because it saved his life, his, I was dumb with surprise and a kind of fascinated revulsion. Was it just wanting to stay alive at any cost or was it something inside that said *me, I am*; it got sort of big and said *me*. It got angry, beyond his apparent personality, a humble, patient person, tender and sensitive; it went *me, I am*, and it said that whatever stood between him and existence had to be annihilated. *I* would have died. *I* might have died. As a child I was horrified but later I tried to understand why I didn't have it—I was blank there, it was as if the tape was erased or something was just missing. If someone stood between me and existence, how come I didn't think I mattered more; why didn't I kill them; I never would put me above someone else; I never did; I never thought that because they were doing something to annihilate me I could annihilate them; I figured I would just be wounded or killed or whatever, because life and death were random events; like I tried to tell my father, maybe he would have lived. When someone pushes you down on the ground and puts himself in you, he pushes himself between you and existence—you do die or you will die or you can die, it's the luck of the draw really, not unlike maybe you'll get killed or maybe you won't in a war; except you don't get to be proud of it if you don't die. I never thought anyone should be killed just because he endangered my existence or corrupted it altogether or just because I was left a shadow haunting my own life; I mean really killed. I never thought anyone should really die just because one day he was actually going to kill me, fucking render me dead: inevitably, absolutely; no doubt. I didn't think any one of them should really die. It was outside what I could think of. Is there anything in me, any *I am*, anything that says I will stop you or anything that says I am too valuable and this bad thing you are doing to me will cost you too much or anything that says you cannot destroy me; cannot; me. If someone tortures you and you will die from it eventually, someday, for sure, one way or another, and you can't make the day come soon enough because the suffering is immense, then maybe he should die because he pushed himself between you and existence; maybe you should kill him to push him out of the way. Do you think Truman would have bought it? My daddy wouldn't have either. At best he'd say why did this tragic thing happen to you—it would never be possible to pin down which tragic thing he meant—and he'd be bitter and mad, not at the bad one but at me; I'd be the bad one for him. At worst I'd be plain filth in his eyes. I don't know why I can't think all the Japanese should die so I can stay alive or why I can't think some man should die. I'll never be a Christian, that's for sure. I can't stand thinking Christ died for me; it makes me sick. I got some idea of how much it hurt. I can't stand the thought. *I am*; but so what? I've actually been willing to die so none of them would get hurt, even if they're inside me against what I want. Now I started thinking they're the Nazis, the real Nazis of our time and place, the brownshirts, they don't put you on a train, they come to where you are, they get you one by one but they do get you, most of you, nearly all, and they destroy your heart and the sovereignty of your body and they kill your freedom and they make you ashen and humiliate you and they tear you apart and it ain't metaphor and they injure you beyond repair or redemption, they injure your body past any known suffering, and you die, not them, you; they kill you some-

176

times, slow or fast, with mutilation or not; and you are more likely to murder yourself than them; and that's wrong, child of God, that's wrong. I can never think someone should die instead of me; but they should if they came to do the harm in the first place; objectively speaking, they should. I think perhaps they should. My reason says so; but I can't face it. I run instead; run or give in; run or open my legs; run or get hit; run, hide, do it, do it for them, do whatever they want, do it before they can hurt me more, anticipate what they want, do it, keep them cooled out, keep them okay, keep them quiet or more quiet than they would be if I made them mad; give in or run; capitulate or run; hide or run; hide; run; escape; do what they say; I used to say I wanted to do it, what they wanted, whatever it was, I used to say it was me, I was deciding, I wanted, I was ready, it was my idea, I did the taking, I decided, I initiated, hey I was as tough as them; but it was fuck before they get mad—it was lower the risk of making them mad; you use your will to make less pain for yourself; you say *I am* as if there is an I and then you do what pleases them, girl, what they like, what you already learned they like, and there ain't no I, because if there was it wouldn't have accepted the destruction or annihilation, it wouldn't have accepted all the little Hitler fiends, all the little Goering fiends, all the little Himmler fiends, being right on you and turning you inside out and leaving injury on you and liking it, they liked seeing you hurt, and then you say it's me, I chose it, I want it, it's fine—you say it for pride so you can stay alive through the hours after and so it won't hit you in the face that you're just some piece of trash who ain't worth nothing on this earth. No one can't kill someone; how'd I become no one; and why's he someone; and how come there's no I inside me; how come I can't think he should die if that's what it takes to blow him loose? I'm a pilgrim searching for understanding; because there's nothing left, I'm empty and there's nothing and it takes a lot of pride to lie. I wanted; what did I want? I wanted: freedom. So they are ripping me apart and I smile I say I have freedom. Freedom is semen all over you and some kinky bruises, a lot of men in you and the certainty of more, there's always more; freedom and abundance—my cup ran over. There's a special freedom for girls; it doesn't get written down in constitutions; there's this freedom where they use you how they want and you say *I am*, *I choose*, *I decide*, *I want*—after or before, when you're young or when you're a hundred—it's the liturgy of the free woman—I choose, I decide, I want, I am—and you have to be a devout follower of the faith, a fanatic of freedom, to be able to say the words and remember the acts at the same time; devout. You really have to love freedom, darling; be a little Buddha girl, no I, free from the chain of being because you are empty inside, no ego, Freud couldn't even find you under a microscope. It's a cold night, one of them unusual ones in New York, under zero with a piercing wind about fifteen miles an hour. There's no coat warm enough. I lived in someone's room, slept on the floor. It was Christmas and she said to meet her at Macy's. I followed the directions she gave me and went to the right floor. I never saw anything so big or so much. There's hundreds of kinds of sausages all wrapped up and millions of different boxes of cookies all wrapped up and bottles of vinegar and kinds of oil and millions of things; I couldn't get used to it and I got dizzy and upset and I ran out. I lived with the woman who helped me when I was just a kid out of jail—she still had the same apartment and she fed me but I couldn't sleep in my old room, her husband slept in it now, a new husband, so I slept on a sofa in the room right outside the kitchen and there were no doors. There was the old sofa, foam rubber covered with plaid cloth, and books, and the door to the apartment was a few feet away. When you came in you could turn right or left. If you turned left you went to the bathroom or the living room. The living room had a big double bed in it where she slept, my friend. If you turned right you came to the small room that was the husband's and past that you came to the open space where I slept and you came to the kitchen. The husband didn't like me being there but he didn't come home enough for it to matter. He was hard and nasty and arrogant but politically he was a pacifist. He looked like a bum but he was rich. He ordered everyone around and wrote poems. He was an anarchist. My old room had to stay empty for him, even though he had his own apartment, or studio as he called it, and never told her when he was showing up. A friend of hers gave me a room for a few months in a brownstone on West 14th Street—pretty place, civilized, Italian neighborhood, old, with Greenwich Village charm. The room belonged to some man in a mental institution in Massachusetts. It was a nutty room all right. Two rooms really. The first wasn't wider than both your arms outstretched. There was a cot, a hot plate, a tiny toilet, a teeny tiny table that tipped over if you put too much on it. The second was bigger and had windows but he filled it up so there wasn't any room left at all: a baby grand piano and humongous plants taller than me, as tall as some trees, with great wide thick leaves stretched out in the air. It was pure menace, especially how the plants seemed to stretch out over everything at night. They got bigger and they seemed to move. You could believe they were coming toward you and sometimes you had to check. The difference between people who have something and me is in how long a night is. I have listened to every beat of my heart waiting for a night to end; I have heard every second tick on by; I've heard the long pauses between the seconds, enough time to die in, and I've waited, barely able to breathe, for them to end. Daylight's safer. The big brown bugs disappear; they only come out at night and at night you're always afraid they'll be there so you can't help but see them, you don't really always know whether they're real or not, you see them in your mind or out of the corner of your eye, you're always afraid they'll be there so if you see one slip past the corner of your eye in the dark you will start waiting in fear for morning, for the light, because it chases them away and you can't; nothing you can do will. Same for burglars; same for the ones who come in to get you; daylight; you wait for daylight; you sit in the night, you light up the room with phony light, it's fake and dim and there's never enough, the glare only underlines the menace, you can see you're beseiged but there's not enough light to vaporize the danger, make it dissolve, the way sunlight does when finally it comes. You can sleep for a minute or two, or maybe twenty. You don't want to be out any longer than that. You don't get undressed. You stay dressed always, all the time, your boots on and a knife right near you or in your hand. You get boots with metal reinforced tips, no matter what. You don't get under the covers. You don't do all those silly things—milk and cookies, Johnny Carson, now I lay me down to sleep. You sit absolutely still or lie down rigid and ready for attack and you listen to the night moving over the earth and you understand that you are buried alive in it and by the grace of random luck you will be alive in the morning—or won't be—you will die or you won't and you wait to find out, you wait for the light and when it comes you know you made it. You hear things break outside—windows, you can hear sheets of glass collapsing, or windows being broke on a smaller scale, or bottles dashed on cement, thrown hard, or trash cans emptied out and hurled against a cement wall, or you hear yelling, a man's voice, threat, a woman's voice, pain, or you hear screams, and you hear sirens, there are explosions, maybe they are gun shots, maybe not—and you hope it's not coming after you or too near you but you don't know and so you wait, you just wait, through every second of the night, you wait for the night to end. I spend the change I can find on cigarettes and orange juice. I think as long as I am drinking orange juice I am healthy. I think orange juice is the key to life. I drink a quart at a time. It has all these millions of vitamins. I like vodka in my orange juice but I can't get it; only a drink at a time from a man here and there, but then I leave out the orange juice because I can do that myself, I just get the vodka straight up, nothing else in the glass taking up room but it's greed because I like rocks. I never had enough money at one time to buy a bottle. I love looking at vodka bottles, especially the foreign ones—I feel excited and distinguished and sophisticated and part of a real big world when I have the bottle near me. I think the bottles are really beautiful, and the liquid is so clear, so transparent, to me it's like liquid diamonds, I think it's beautiful. I feel it connects me with Russia and all the Russians and there is a dark melancholy as well as absolute joy when I drink it. It brings me near Chekhov and Dostoevsky. I like how it burns the first drink and after that it's just this splendid warmth, as if hot coals were silk sliding down inside me and I get warm, my throat, my chest, my lungs, the skin inside my skin, whatever the inside of my skin is; it clings inside me. My grandparents came from Russia, my daddy's parents, and I try to think they drank it but I'm pretty sure they wouldn't have, they were just ghetto Jews, it was probably the drink of the ones who persecuted them and drove them into running away, but I don't mind that anyway, because now I'm in Amerika and I can drink the drink of Cossacks and peasants if I want; it soothes me, I feel triumphant and warm, happy too. I have this idea about vodka, that it is perfect. I think it is perfect. I think it is beautiful and pure and filled with absolute power—the power of something absolutely pure. It's completely rare, this perfection. It's more than that the pain dies or it makes you magic; yeah, you soar on it and you get wise and strong by drinking it and it's a magnificent lover, taking you whole. But I love just being near it in any way, shape, or form.

I would like to be pure like it is and I'd like to have only pure things around me; I wish everything I'm near or I touch could be as perfect. I feel it's very beautiful and if I ever die I wouldn't mind having a bottle of it buried with me, if someone would spring for it: one bottle of Stoli hundred proof in honor of me and my times, forever. I'd drink it slow, over time. It'd make the maggots easier to take, that's for sure. It does that now. They ain't all maggots, of course. I been with people who matter. I been with people who achieved something in life. I want excellence myself. I want to attain it. There's this woman married to a movie star, they are damned nice and damned rich, they take me places, to parties and dinners, and I eat dinner with them at their house sometimes and she calls me and gets me in a cab and I go with her. I met her because I was working against the Vietnam War some more. I got back to New York in November 1972. It was a cold winter. I had nothing; was nothing; I had some stories I was writing; I slept on the floor near someone's bed in a rented room. Nixon bombed a hospital in North Vietnam. All these civilians died. I couldn't really stand it. I went to my old peace friends and I started helping out: demonstrations, phone calls, leaflets, newspaper ads, the tricks of the trade don't change. I had this idea that important Amerikans—artists, writers, movie stars, all the glitz against the War—should go to North Vietnam sort of as voluntary hostages so either Nixon would have to stop the bombing or risk killing all them. It would show how venal the bombings were; and that they killed Vietnamese because Vietnamese were nothing to them, just nothing; and it was morally right to put yourself with the people being hurt. Inside yourself you felt you had to stop the War. Inside yourself you felt the War turned you into a murderer. Inside yourself you couldn't stand the Vietnamese dying because this government was so fucking arrogant and out of control. There was a lot of us who never stopped thinking about the

War, despite our personal troubles; sometimes it was hard not to have it drive you completely out of your mind—if you let it sink in, how horrible it was, you really could go mad and do terrible things. So I got hooked up with some famous people who wanted to stop the War; some had been in the peace movement before, some just came because of the bombings. We wanted to stop the bombing; we wanted to pay for the hospital; we wanted to be innocent of the murders. The U.S. government was an outlaw to us. The famous people gave press conferences, signed ads, signed petitions, and some even did civil disobedience; I typed, made phone calls, the usual; shit work; but I also tried to push my ideas in. The idea was to use their fame to get out anti-War messages and to get more mainstream opposition to the War. Hey, I was home; only in Amerika. One day this woman came in to where we were working—to help, she said; was there anything she could do to help, she asked—and she was as disreputable looking as me or more so—she looked sort of like a gypsy boy or some street waif—and they treated her like dirt, so condescending, which was how they treated me, exactly, and it turned out she was the wife of this mega-star, so they got all humble and started sucking. I had just talked to her like a person from the beginning so she invited me to their house that night for dinner—it turned out it was her birthday party but she didn't tell me that. I got there on time and no one else came for an hour so her and me and her husband talked a lot and they were nice even though it was clear I didn't understand I wasn't supposed to show up yet. She took me places, all over, and we caroused and talked and drank and once when he wasn't home she let me take this elaborate bath and she brought me a beautiful glass of champagne in the tub, then he came in, and I don't know if he was mad or not, but he was always real nice to me, and nothing was going on, and there wasn't no bath or shower where I lived, though I was ashamed to say so, I had to make an appointment with someone in the building to use theirs. They kept me alive for a while, though they couldn't have known it. I ate when I was with them; otherwise I didn't. My world got so big: parties, clubs, people; it was like a tour of a hidden world. Once she even took me to the opera. I never was there before. She bought me a glass of champagne and we stood among ladies in gowns on red velvet carpets. But then they left. And I knew some painters, real rich and famous. One of them was the lover of a girl I knew. He befriended me, like a chum, like a sort of brother in some ways. He just acted nice and invited me places where he was where there were a lot of people. He didn't mind that I was shy. He talked to me a lot. He seemed to see that I was overwhelmed and he didn't take it wrong. He tried to make me feel at ease. He tried to draw me out. I sort of wanted to stay away from places but he just tried to get me to come forward a little. In some ways he seemed like a camp counselor organizing events: now we hike, now we make purses. I'd go drinking with all these painters in their downtown bars and they had plenty of money and it wasn't a matter of tit for tat, they just kept the drinks coming, never seemed to occur to them to stop drinking. I knew his girlfriend who was a painter. At first when I met him I had just got back. I was sleeping on floors. I slept on her floor some nights when he wasn't there. She was all tortured about him, she was just all twisted up inside, but I never understood why, she was pretty incoherent. We drank, we talked about him, or she did; she didn't have any other subject. There wasn't no sexual feeling between him and me and he acted cordial and agreeable. We went on a bus with some other people they knew to New Hampshire for Thanksgiving. I think he paid but I wasn't sure. I didn't have any money to go but they wanted me to go; they had friends there. We went on the Greyhound bus and it let us off somewhere in Vermont and someone, another painter from up there, was supposed to pick us up, but he didn't come all night, so we were in the parking lot of the bus station, locked out of the depot, deserted and freezing through the whole night; and in the morning we got a bus the rest of the way. It was like being on a camping trip in the Arctic without any provisions—we'd pass around the ugly coffee from the machine outside. We got cold and hungry and angry and people's tempers flared, but he sort of held it all together. His name was Paul, she was Jill. They fought a lot that night but hell it was cold and awful. He was gregarious but sort of opaque, at least to me; I couldn't figure out anything about him really. He wasn't interesting, he wasn't real intelligent, and then suddenly, mentally, he'd be right on top of you, staring past your eyes into you, then he'd see whatever he saw and he'd move on. He had a cold streak right down the middle of him. He wasn't someone you wanted to get close with and at the same time he held you on his margin, he kept you in sight, he had this sort of peripheral vision so he always knew where you were and what you needed. He kept you as near as he wanted you. He had a strong will and a lot of insistence that you were going to be in his scout troop sitting around the fire toasting marshmallows. He had opinions on everything, including who took too many drugs and who was really gay. We got to New Hampshire and there was this big house a woman built with a tree right up the center of it going out the roof and all the walls were windows and it was in the middle of the woods and I never saw anything so imposing, so grand. It wasn't rich so much as handsome from hard work and talent. The two women who lived there had built it themselves. One was a painter, one a filmmaker; and it was real beautiful. There was a lot of people around. Then the food came, a real Thanksgiving, with everything, including things I never saw before and I didn't know what they were, it was just beyond anything I had ever seen, and it was warm and fine and it was just people saying this and that. I'd been away a long time. I didn't know what mostly they were talking about. Someone tried to explain who Archie Bunker was to me but I couldn't understand what was funny about it or how such a thing could be on television and I don't like jokes against faggots. I sat quiet and drank Stoli all I wanted, day and night. We all bunked down in different parts of the huge room. I made love with a real young guy who reminded me of a girl I used to know; and some woman too who I liked. Then somehow this guy Paul got us all back to New York. He had been in the loft bed with Jill. It was the only real bed and it was private because it was up so high and behind a structural beam. They just kept fighting all night so he was aggravated and he was angry anybody else made love, he said the noise kept him up. So he wanted to leave and it was follow the leader. It was a nice Thanksgiving, a real one in a way, as if I lived here, on this earth, in ways that were congenial to me. The people had furniture and books and music and food and a big fire and they talked about all sorts of things, books, music, everyday things, and the filmmaker showed her film. I got back to New York, slept where I could, mostly on floors, it could get harrowing, I would get pretty tired, I wasn't really understanding how to put an end to it, I felt just perpetually exhausted and stupid, I didn't see how you get to be one of these people who seemed plugged in—food, money, apartment, that stuff. I'd get warm in the bars with the painters. I'd go downtown and they'd be there and we'd drink. Sometimes one of the guys would hit on me but mostly I said no. I don't like painters. They seem very cold to me, the men; and the women were all tormented like Jill, talked about men all the time, suffered, drank. I don't know. I made love with some of the women but they were just sort of servants to the men; drunk, servile. I fucked some of the men but they were so self-involved, so completely cold, in love with themselves, so used to being mean to whoever was with them. They put this

shit on a canvas and they make it thick or thin and it's blobs or
something and then they're known for doing that and they just
do it over and over and then they're very crass in bed, they're
just fucking-machines, I never knew men who just wanted to
fuck and that's it, I mean, you couldn't even say it was a power
trip because it was too cold and narrow for that, greedy and
cold; they really should have just masturbated but they wanted
to do it in a girl. Paul kept making social events and he and Jill
invited me. Then New Year's came and Paul had me to this
big dinner; Jill too but it was at his loft, his building I guess, I
couldn't really grasp that part of it. I was afraid to go but he
said it would be fine and I didn't have to do anything or say
anything; I didn't believe it because usually you had to cook or
clean or something but it was true because this was some
elegant sit-down dinner and there was people serving dinner
and he hadn't cooked it but someone, some real cook, had. It
was New Year's Eve. It made me feel special to be there, even
though I was scared. I felt like someone, not someone famous
or someone rich, just someone who could be somewhere
inside with people and nice things, I felt warm and in the midst
of grace and abundance. It made me feel that there were people
in the world who were vibrant, who talked, who laughed. It
was not just some place to be—it was fine, a fine place. I was
almost shaking to see it, the table, the candles, the china, the
silverware, vigorous, jubilant people, warm and ruddy and
with this physical vitality that almost bounced off the walls. I
was so lonely that winter. I came back in November 1972, all
broke down. It was a bitter cold winter. I went to Paul's loft on
New Year's Eve for dinner; a formal dinner; except no one
was dressed formal or acted formal. It was shimmering. It was
dazzling. There was plates and beautiful glasses and there was
food after food, all cooked, all served, first one thing, then
another, then another, it went on and on, it was like a hundred
meals all at once, and no one seemed to find it surprising like I

did; I was like a little child, I guess; I couldn't believe it was real. There were candles and music but not just candles, the candleholders were so beautiful, silver, crafted, antique, old, so old, I thought they must have come right from Jerusalem. There were about twenty people altogether. The men were mostly painters, mostly famous, pretty old. They talked and told jokes. The girls were painters too but they didn't say much except for one or two who talked sometimes and they were real young, mostly. There was a man and a girl and a man and a girl all around the table. There was all these wines and all these famous men asking you if you wanted more. You had the feeling you could ask for anything and these great men, one of them or all of them, would turn heaven and earth to get it for you. I was shy, I didn't know what to say; I certainly wasn't no great artist *yet* and I wanted to keep my dreams private in my heart. I said I was writing stories. I said I was against the War. The men said, one by one, that you couldn't be political and an artist at the same time but they didn't argue or get mad at me; it was more like how you would correct a child who had made an embarrassing mistake. One of them took me aside and asked me if I remembered him. He looked so familiar, as if I should reach out and touch his face. I said hadn't we seen a movie together once. He said we had made love and I was on mescaline and hadn't I liked it and didn't I remember him. He was real nice about it and I said oh yes, of course, and it was nice, and there were a lot of colors. He didn't seem to get mad. I smiled all night, because I was nearly awed. The men had this vitality, they were sort of glowing. I never knew such a thing could happen. You listened to them, because they might say something about art. One talked to me about death. He was a real famous painter. He said that both him and me were artists. He said artists were the only people who faced death without lying. He said that was the reason to make love—because you had looked death in

188

the face and then you defied it. He said the others didn't understand that but he did and I did and so would I come with him. And I laughed. I didn't go with him but I laughed, he made me happy, I laughed, I felt it was such beautiful bullshit and I laughed. I thought it was a real nice thing for him to say. It was a new year. I was drinking champagne. I wasn't alone. I wasn't outside. I was safe. It was so much—beauty and life and gracious ease; it was so surprising, so completely wonderful and new; it was glittering and sparkling, it was small and warm, it was new and scary and exciting and real fine. I started having this dream over and over. It was New York, streets I knew, usually down in the Village, around Washington Square, sometimes on Fifth Avenue above the Square. It was very dark. The dark was almost a person, a character in the dream. The dark had a kind of depth, almost a smell, and it was scary and dense and it was over everything, you almost couldn't see anything through it. The dream was somewhere in the Village, sometimes near those big impersonal buildings on Fifth Avenue, but even if it's deeper in the Village the buildings are stone, big, impersonal, not the town houses or brownstones of the Village, but the impersonal Fifth Avenue buildings, a cold rich city made of cold stone. Somehow I go into one and it opens into this huge feast, this giant party in this giant ballroom, physically it's almost underground as if you are going down inside the ground but there is this grand ballroom and the women have gowns and jewels and the men are shiny and pretty in black suits and ruffled silk shirts but no one makes me leave, at first I'm afraid but no one makes me leave, there's lots of noise and there's music and there's food, all sorts of weird kinds of food, cocktail food and real food and drinks and it's warm and friendly and in the dream I say yes, I've been here before, it's waiting, it's always here, it's just part of New York, you don't have to ever be afraid, hidden away there's always something like this, you just have to find it, and it fades, the dream fades, and I wake up feeling flushed and tired and happy and I think it's out there if only I can remember where it is and it's not until I'm out on the streets that I understand I just dreamed it, I wasn't really there, not just last night but ever, but still I think New York is full of such places, only I don't know where they are. But after New Year it just was colder and harder; there's not a lot of magic in the world, no beautiful fairy godmother to wave her wand so you can stop sifting through ashes and go to the ball. I slept outside the kitchen in my old friend's apartment; I wrote stories, slow, real slow, over and over, a sentence again and again, I did peace stuff against the War, I got food from bars mostly. You go during happy hour and you only need one drink. You can get a man to get it for you or if you have the change you can do it and then there's warm food and you can eat; they make it real fatty usually but it's good, heavy and warm and they bring out more and more until happy hour's over. I met the actor and his wife and she took me everywhere, all around. Sometime I moved into the loony's room with the carnivorous plants and I wrote stories, slow, real slow, word by word, then starting over. I had nothing and I was nothing and I couldn't tell no one how I was hurt from being married. And I kept drinking with the painters. I liked the noisy bars and the people all excited with drinking and art and all the love affairs going on all around, with all the torment, because it wasn't my torment, it didn't come near my torment. It was distracting, a kind of static that interrupted the pain I was carrying. I got the peace group to give me seventy-five dollars a week and I worked every morning for them, making phone calls, writing leaflets, mimeographing, typing, doing shit. I said I was a writer if someone asked. I worked on my stories, slow; I stayed alive as best I could; I waited through long nights, I waited. Now it's bitter cold; a bitter cold night; unusual in New York; with the temperature under zero; with the wind blowing about fifteen miles an hour, trying to kill you, cutting you in half and then in half again, you can't withstand it, there's nothing can keep it from running through you like a knife. I'm in my little room, the loony's room; I'm staying calm; I don't like being alone, it's hard, but I'm thinking I'm okay, I'm inside, I'm okay; I'm thinking I will take out my notebook and work, sit with the words, make sentences, cross words out, you hear a kind of music in your head and you transpose it into words but the words sit there, block letters, just words, they don't sing back, so you have to keep making them better until they do, until they sing back to you, you look at it and it moves like a song. You hear it moving, there's a buzz on it and the buzz is music, not noise; it can be percussive but it's still lyrical, it sings. It's a delicate thing, knowing when it's right. At the same time it's like being in first grade where you had to write the words down careful in block letters and you had to make them perfect; because you keep trying like some six-year-old to make the words perfect so they look back at you and they are right, as if there's this one right way and it sits there, pure and clear, when you're smart enough, finally, to put it on the page in front of you. I always want to run away from it: putting the words down, because they're always wrong at first and for a long time they stay wrong, but now the cold night keeps me in, the wind, the killer wind, I sit on the cot, I move my papers to the tiny table, I get out a pencil and I find some empty paper, and I start again, I begin again, I have started again over and over and tonight I start again, and I hear the words in my heart. I came back with two laundry bags, like canvas shopping bags. I carried them on the plane. They were my laundry bags from when I was a housewife. One has manuscripts and a couple of books. The other has a sweater and some underwear and a pair of pants. I don't have anything else, except a fairly ragged skirt that I'm wearing, I made it myself with some cheap cloth, it has clumps and bulges and I've got a couple of T-shirts. I think the manuscripts are precious. I think you can do anything if you must. I think I can write some stories and I think it doesn't matter how hard it is. I'm usually pretty tired by night but the nights are long and if you can write the time isn't the same kind of burden; the words, like oxen, pull the dark faster through time. I think it is good to write; I think perhaps someday I might write something beautiful like *Death in Venice*, something just that lovely and perfect, and I think it would be worth a person's whole life to write one such thing. I have an invitation to go to Jill's art opening, her first show ever. It is a big event for her. Girls don't get to have shows very easy, and some people say it is because of Paul; she's resentful of him; I tell her it doesn't matter one way or the other, the point is to do it, just do it. I feel I should go but I don't have clothes warm enough for this particular night. I walk everywhere because I don't have money for subways, I walk long distances, I took my husband's warm coat when I left—it's the least you can give me, I said, he was surprised enough when I grabbed it that he didn't take it away—it's a sheepskin coat from Afghanistan but it doesn't have any buttons so you can't stay warm in bad wind—it's heavy and stiff and it doesn't close right and if there's bad wind it rips through the opening; I was running away and I wanted the warm coat, I knew it would last longer than money, I was thinking about the streets, I was remembering. And he gave me some money too, took some change out of his pocket, some bills he was carrying, handed it to me, said yeah, take this too. It was maybe what you'd spend on a cheap dinner. I wanted his coat. I was leaving and there was my coat and I thought about having to get through one fucking night in my coat, a ladies' coat, my wife coat, tailored, pretty, gray, with style and a little phony fur collar, a waist, it had a waist, it showed off that you had breasts, and I thought, shit, I won't live through one night in that piece of shit, I thought, I'd better have a real coat, I thought, the bastard has a real coat and yes I will risk my life to get it so I grabbed it and at first he didn't want me to have it but I said shit boy it's a real cheap way to end a marriage and he could've smashed me but he didn't because he wanted me out and he looked at me and said yeah take it and you don't wait a second, you grab it and you get out. I never was sorry I took it. I slept on it, I slept under it, I wrapped it around me like it was my real skin, my shelter, my house, my home, I didn't need to buy other stuff for staying warm, I wore a cheap T-shirt under it, nothing else, I didn't have to worry about clothes or nothing like that; but tonight's too cold for it, there's nights like that, wind too bad, too strong, no respite; tonight's too cold. I think I'm going to sit still, sit quiet and calm, inside, in a room, in this quiet room, work on my story, cross out, put new words down, try to make it sing for me, for me now, here and now, in my head now. They say Mann was a bourgeois writer. I never saw it myself. I think he was outside them and I wondered how he knew when it was beautiful enough and when it was right. It seemed you had to have this calm. You had to be still. I think it's this funny thing inside that I'm just getting close to, this way of listening, you can sort of vaguely hear something, you have to concentrate and get real still but then you hear this thin thread of something inside, and the words ride on it right or they don't but if you get the words perfect they are just right on that thread, balanced just right. I can't really do it though because I'm always tired and I'm always afraid. I shake. I can't quiet down enough. The fear's new. I wasn't some frightened girl. I'm afraid to sit still. I'm afraid to be alone. I'm afraid when it's quiet. Any time I remember I'm afraid. Any time I dream I'm afraid. Any time I have to sit still alone I'm afraid. I just got this shake in me, this terror; it's like the room ain't empty except it's hollow, worse than empty, like some kind of tunnel in hell, all dark with nothing, a perfect void, I'm part of the void and the air I'm breathing is part of it and the walls of the room are the tunnel and I'm trapped in a nothing so damned real it's fixed forever. I shake bad when I'm alone. I work on the stories barely able to hold the pencil in my hand. I don't have no dope to calm me down. The shake gets less if I smoke some dope, even a small joint. Mentally I concentrate on calming myself down so the shake's inside but I ain't trembling so bad in my body, I'm more normal. So I sit for as long as I can, writing words down and saying the sentences out loud to myself and then I start speeding up inside with fear and there's no reason and so I have to start calming myself all over again, I concentrate on it until I'm sitting still, not shaking. Then he just came right inside. The door opened and he was in. I heard the locks unlocking— New York locks, real locks, I heard the cylinders turning, but I didn't grasp it, it was just a noise I couldn't associate with anything, and the door opened before I could register the sound and he's there, the guy's there, short, dark, wiry, sort of bent but from rage, a kind of twisted anger in his muscles, he's tied in knots and it twists him all up and he's raging all over the apartment touching things and screaming and it's him, they told me he was locked up, it's the guy, paranoid schizophrenic they said, a very smart guy they said, but out of control, locked up, smart they said, a very smart guy but really fucked up in the head, hears things, sees things, paranoid, has delusions, and the landlady's not here and no one's here to calm him down who knows him or to say who I am and he's screaming and I am saying who I am and saying the names of the landlady and his neighbors and saying, oh, they didn't know he'd be back, and I was just here for this second, a few hours, a day, and I was just leaving, just now, and he's screaming and he's hitting the table and he's suddenly silent and staring and he's between me and my stuff and I say I'll be back for it and he shouldn't worry and it's all okay and of course it's his place and I haven't touched a thing, and I'm trying to get my coat but he's in the way and he's between me and my laundry bags, and me and my papers, and I grab the coat in a fast jump and swoop and I say the landlady will come back for my stuff or he can put it outside and he's standing there rigid and I run, I have the coat, I keep talking, I get out, out of the apartment, out of the building, down the steps in the hall, down the stoop, out, and I've got the keys to my old friend's apartment, my old peace friend, for the sofa outside the kitchen and she got me the loony's room and she said to come back anytime so I turn to her, I'm pretty scared and I'm shaking and I'm running and I don't know if he's calling the police because there's no one in the building to say who I am or that they said I could stay there and I'm running to my old friend's place and it's a bitter cold night with the wind at about fifteen miles an hour, under zero, the streets are deserted, they are bare, and I think well okay, I'm safe, I got out, anybody'd be shaking, I took everyone's word that he wouldn't be back without enough warning, I relaxed, I took things out of my laundry bags, I was there a couple of months nearly, I mean, I never completely relax and I never completely unpack; and I wasn't asleep, thank God, but now I have to figure out where to go, and I run to my old friend's apartment and I have the keys in my hand but I knock first because maybe she is there and she is inside and she asks who it is and I say I am me and I say what happened, that the guy came back, showed up, opened the door, was in, and I ran and I need a place to sleep tonight and it's, ah, freezing out there, and she says there's someone with her and she doesn't want me to come in because he's with her and I say okay, fine, yeah, it's fine, yeah, it's okay, yeah, okay, because you don't press yourself on someone even if they told you always to come to them and they gave you keys, they have freedom and if they say no then you ain't wanted there, and I think about saying to her you have to do this because I have nowhere to go and nothing and I will die out there, this ain't no joke, tonight's a dying night, but you can't push yourself on someone and I figure she knows that anyway and you can't count on no one, they will let you die and that's just the truth, and she don't even open the door to see my face or pass me money, she keeps it locked and I hear her fasten the chain, and I'm in the hall of her building and I think I can go to Jill's art opening, it's all I can think of, a bar's more uncertain, more dangerous, and I can spend at least a few hours there inside and there's people there I know and I can find a place to sleep maybe on someone's floor, I don't want to fuck anyone, I just know I don't, but maybe I can find somewhere, I only got a couple of dollars and it don't last long and you can't stay warm through a whole night on it and I don't know anything past I have to find a place to sleep tonight and get out of the cold and I will worry about the rest tomorrow, where to go and what to do, I will think about it tomorrow, and I say to myself that I ain't scared and so what and this is nothing, absolutely nothing, piece of cake, no problem, I'll just go and have a drink or something at the opening and I'll ask around and the art opening will last maybe until two a.m., and then there's only four hours or maybe five until dawn, five really, and I can do that; I can do it; if I think four hours I can do it and then after it's only a little more time and there'll be light; I can do it; it ain't new and I can do it; and probably I can find somewhere to sleep and if I have to fuck I will but I don't want to but so what if I do but I won't; I can last through tonight. I'm walking in the wind, it's like swimming in the ocean against a deep and deadly tide, I'm walking down to Soho, the streets are bare and the wind is cruel, just fucking brutal cruel, I get about half a block at a time and I try to find a doorway, warm up, walk as much more as I can stand, the wind just freezes you, your chest, your blood, your bones; it fucking hurts; it ain't some moderate pain, it's desperate like some anguish possessing you. Soho's industrial lofts and galleries and a couple of bars, there's long streets with nowhere to go, it's as if the doorways disappeared because the buildings are industrial buildings and there's elevators you have to use to get inside, not normal doors, the painters living there are illegal and there's no shops or stores to step into and Jill's gallery is way downtown, near Canal Street, a long walk, and the cold's hurting me and I'm afraid. My mind is rocking back and forth from I can find someone and if I have to I'll fuck them even no matter what and I can make it from two to six if I have to, I can. There's no bums out, there's no whores, everyone's folded inside some crease somewhere and anyone who ain't might not live until morning; there's nights like that; and I get there and I take the warehouse elevator up and it's white, it's a huge warehouse room painted a glossy white and there's all these people dressed in real clothes, you know, outfits, for style, and the women's all acting nice and flirty with the men and it's warm and the men's all acting smart and polite and civilized and there's wine, white wine, and there's Stoli and bourbon and ice, and there's cheese and some little pieces of food, some little sandwiches, tender little things you can eat in one bite, you'd be hard pressed to take two, you know those funny little sandwiches that are always wet and sort of wilted, and the room's so shiny and white and big the people almost disappear in it, the ceiling's so high you feel like a little ant, and it seems the people are sparse though there's a lot of them, they don't look like the wind got to them but rather they're all polished up, all shined, and there's paintings on the walls, Jill's paintings, and in the middle of the room there's Jill but she's not looking all polished up, she's sort of gray and miserable, and I say hi and I congratulate her and she's mad and sad and I say well it's a big deal, really, and your nerves are bound to get frayed, aren't they, and she gets darker and stranger, and Paul comes over, and she glowers, and he says some pleasant things, and she and he seem to agree that the paintings are on the wall and the people are in the room, and there's a certain amount of tension over this, and Paul's saying normal things like hey have something to drink and there's food, take some, or have some, and I'm saying the sort of foolish things people say about paintings, aren't they strong, aren't they interesting, haven't they grown, don't they dominate the room, and it works kind of like Valium because Jill evens out and there's a small smile out of one side of her mouth at least and I think I should just walk around and see about finding someone I can ask for a place to sleep, and I walk around, and I have one drink to warm up because I can't drink because I don't know what the rest of the night will be and relaxing isn't in the picture until there's shelter and I have a wet sandwich and I chat with this woman and this man and they're mostly painters and they really all want to say something about the relationship, Paul and Jill, not the paintings, so there's this catty, gossipy quality to everything and also it's all secretive because no one wants to be accidentally overheard by Jill or Paul and while Jill is staying one place, dead center in the room, just standing there by a particularly big painting, Paul is all over, behind people, in conversations, introducing people, the real host, the scout leader; and he chats with me awhile too. But I'm scared, because I know this will end and real life will come back. I know the trick's not to look desperate. I know the trick's to seem as if there's nothing wrong; why the hell do you need to sleep on someone's floor if nothing's wrong? I can't think of any plausible reason but I figure it's not rational as such, you know, reasons, it's attitude, you have to have a kind of calm as if it's just normal so no one thinks they'll have to give you anything; or care for you. So I make myself steady and I think this is normal and I ain't so scared as actually I am and I think well Jill knows everyone here and she's my friend so I'll ask her and I take her aside, meaning just a little off her mark, and I say I need a place to sleep and is there anyone here who might put me up just for one night, and she says she'll think about it, and I smile and act as if it's okay one way or another and I drift off and more time passes, and I'm drinking soda and thinking, every second thinking, my heart beating too fast in fear, but outside I'm calm and simple, and Jill comes up and says, listen, I'm going home with Paul so why don't you stay at my loft, and I say that's great, because it is, and I am fucking happy, I think even it will be nice, it's a big place, it's sort of dark but it's fine, you know, with a bed on a kind of platform, a mattress really, and it's really nice, you know, so I'm at ease, I mean I am really happy, and I pour myself a stiff drink, a real fine drink, and I'm chatting away like a real person, you know, I can't emphasize enough how my heart slows down and how my blood stops racing and how inside my head calms down and I'm just a person, not so shiny as the others but not scared no more, more like a happy girl of the regular kind, and then, once the adrenaline has subsided altogether, I feel how tired I am, I feel how it's worn me out, I feel how cold I got and how I'm just dragged out and enervated, weary, and it's midnight by now, I been at the opening a long time, and I think it's decent to leave, so I go to Jill, and she and Paul are holding hands and they are looking happy and I am glad there's a truce and I ask if I could go to her loft now, and she's upset or confused or something, and my heart sinks, but he says, look, I'm going to stay at Jill's loft with her, it's just easier, so why don't you go to my place, it's empty, there's no problem, I'll give you the keys, okay? I say things like I don't want to put you out and are you sure it's okay and he says what is obvious, I ain't putting him out because it's a big night for Jill and he's staying with her at her place because it's just better for her that way; and I say fine; and everyone says fine; and he's going to give me the keys and directions because I'm not sure where it is from here and I'm waiting for him to come tell me these things, he said he'd write them down, and fatigue is dragging me down, and I get my coat and he comes and says hell I'll just walk you there, it's no big deal, Jill's going to be here for a couple of hours yet, I'll walk you and come back, it's just a few blocks away; and I was glad because I didn't want to get lost and I don't know it around here so good and it's late and the streets are a little scary down here, it's not a regular neighborhood, and the wind has made the streets bare and menacing as if it's blowing dark shadows in your face to smother you, and we go out, and it's colder than before, you are turned half to ice and the streets are empty, just this naked cement with tides of wind sweeping over it like a sandstorm in the desert, and he says shit let's get a drink, and we step into a bar, we fucking dive into it, grateful it's there, and we're at the bar and I'm drinking my Stoli straight up and I don't have no money and I say so because I'm planning to pay half because that's fair and also I don't want wrong ideas communicated or to take advantage because he's a famous painter and he's saying shit it doesn't matter, it's so fucking cold we won't make it if we don't take care of ourselves, and we talk about Hemingway or something, and we take off again, and we get a little further and there's another bar and we dive in, grateful, and we sit at the bar and there's another Stoli in front of me and we're talking about some actor he knows who's shooting cocaine and he's saying it's a tragedy and I'm thinking yeah it is; and I'm saying Jill will worry and he's saying there's plenty of time and I'm saying we should just brave it and walk to his place and he's saying it's Jill's opening and she's the center of attention and that's how it should be and it's good for her, she needs to stand more on her own, and he's proud of her, and it'll be fine, and there's another Stoli and another and another bar and another and he's putting down ten dollar bills for the bartender and I see the vodka in front of me and I drink it, and we talk about

Hemingway, and Ginsberg, and Whitman, and we duck into another bar, and it's almost empty, they all are, the weather makes everything deserted and quiet and we seem like the only people on earth, really, and the streets get darker, and the wind gets colder, and the Stoli goes down smoother, easier, faster, and he unrolls the bills faster, easier, more, and I'm saying shit I'm tired and I'm telling him my sad story of this night and how I didn't have anywhere to go and how I don't have no money and how things are and he's concerned, he's listening, I'm saying how frightened I was and he's taking it all in; and shit I can drink like any man, you know, I mean, I can drink, I don't fold, and I say I can outdrink him and he don't think so but I fucking do because he stops but he keeps ordering them for me and I know I'm going to be crashing soon so I'm not concerned, there's nothing I have to do but sleep, alone, warm, inside, and we get to his place and I ask for his keys and he says he'll open it because it's hard and he opens it, it's a lot of locks, it's locks that slip and slide and look like they have jaws, they move and slide and spring and jump, and the door finally gets open and he says he'll take me up and inside the door there's steps but first he locks the locks from inside, he locks them with his keys and he says see this is how you do it when you come in, don't forget now, and he pockets the keys and I think I have to remember to get them so when he leaves I'll be able to lock the door behind him, it's unfamiliar to me and I don't want to forget, and then there's the steps, these huge, wood steps, these towering flights, these creaky, knotted steps, these splintery steps, there's maybe a hundred of them, it's so high up you can't see the top, so you go up the first twenty or something and there's a big, empty room, more like a baseball field, it's not like an apartment building where there's other people on the first landing, there's no one there and it's empty, and there's another twenty or thirty steps and it's knottier and there's holes in the middle of the steps and you're trying to get up them without looking like a fool or falling and there's another floor that's some cavernous room with canvases and boxes and it's brown, all brown, stretched canvases and paintings wrapped in brown paper for shipping and huge standing spirals of brown twine like statues and brown masking tape and these vast rolls of heavy brown tape, the kind of tape you have to wet and you use it to reinforce heavy boxes, and there's brown boxes, cartons, unfolded and folded and there's brown crates, it's a kind of dead brown room, the air's brown, not just dark but brown as if it's colored brown, as if the air itself is brown, and the walls and the floor and everything in it is dull brown and it's not a room in the normal sense, in the human sense, it's more like an airstrip, and you keep climbing and then there's this next floor, it's big like a fucking commercial garage or something and it's completely covered in paint, oil paint, you could park a hundred cars in it but the whole floor is thick with dried red paint, oil paint or acrylics you know, like the blob's all dead and it died in here, the paint's fucking deep on the floor, it's shocking pinks and royal blues and yellows so bright they hurt your eyes, I don't mean the floor is painted like someone put paint on a brush and used the brush to paint the floor or a wall or something, it's more like the paint is spilled on gallon after gallon, heaps and heaps of it, it's inches thick or feet thick, it dries hard and sticky, you walk on it with trepidation thinking you will sink but it's firm, it gives a little but it's firm, it's dry, it's like an artist's palette like you see in the movies but it's a whole real floor of a room as big as a city block and you walk on it like you're outside in the hills walking on real ground that's uneven and it's been wet and you sink in some places or at least you expect to, the earth's higher and lower by inches and you got boots to help you find your footing, your feet sink in but not really, the ground just gives a little and it ain't even, you don't fall but your footing ain't sure, but it's paint, not

202

earth, paint, it must be a million paint stores all emptied out on the floor and then rising from the paint, from the thick, dried, uneven, shocking paint, there's canvases and there's paint on them, beautiful paint, measured, delicate by contrast, esthetic, organized into colors and shapes that have to do with each other, they touch, you see right away that there is meaning in their touch, there's something in it, it's not random, it's too fine, almost emotionally austere, your heart sort of skips a beat to see how intelligent the paint is, you look up from the chaos of the paint on the floor to the delicacy of the paint on the canvas and I at least almost want to cry, I just feel such sorrow for how frail we are. I just had never seen it so clear how art is about mortality, finding the one thin strain of significance, a line of sorrow, the thread of a meaning, an idea against death, an assertion with color or shape as if you could draw a perfect line to stand against it, you know, so it would break death's heart or something. I can see why he wanted to walk me through this because it's his paintings, precious to his soul. You wouldn't want some stranger rooting around in it; or even touching it. You have to go through the whole room, the whole distance of it, its full length, to get to the stairs that take you to the top floor where he lives. I keep being afraid I'll sink in the paint but I get to the stairs and they're normal, just wood stairs, even, sanded, finished, with a bannister, and I climb up after him; it was different New Year's Eve, soft and glowing, with grand tables and linen and crystal. Now it's pretty empty, big, vast really; there's a big blow heater hanging from the ceiling and he turns it on and it blows hot air out at you, it's like being in a hot wind, it dries the air out, it's a musky, lukewarm, smelly draft, and he puts it on higher and it's like being in a hot wind, warm but unpleasant, an awful August day with a wind so steady and stale that the air pushes past you, old air, used already. At one end of the huge room is a single wood chair. At the other end is a sort of kitchen, a sink, running water, a refrigerator, and in front there's a kitchen counter and in front of that there's a single bed to sleep on, a sort of sofa maybe, flat, no headboard, no cushions, no back, nondescript, covered with cloth, it's a couch or an old mattress on springs or something. Way in the back, to the left of the kitchen, hard to see, extending behind the kitchen but you can't really see how far, there's a kind of cage, it's chicken wire, it goes from the floor to the ceiling, and there's a double bed behind the chicken wire, and I ask what it is, and he says he sleeps there with girls, some girls like it, it's his bedroom, he's got cuffs for it that fasten on the chicken wire but it's got nothing to do with me, I can sleep on the sofa, and I'm feeling a chill, my blood goes cold and I feel a certain fear I can't define and do not want to think about, and I've tried to shake him all night but there's the fact he's sort of stuck on, I can't shake him loose, and I'm feeling like I've been traveling a long time in a foreign place, the land's strange, the natives are strange, it's been a long way up the mountain and you don't know if the way down's booby-trapped and you know the sidewalks are roads of windswept death, they're not harboring no lost souls tonight, you ain't going to make it some hours out there. I am fucking blind drunk, asshole drunk, dumb bitch drunk, and I'm figuring he's Jill's lover who's got to be back because it's her opening night and he'll go back soon, it's just a matter of time, and I don't look at the cage, like he said it's got nothing to do with me and I try not to think about the cuffs and I stay way on the other side of the place, near the single wood chair, my solace, my home, the place I pick out where I'm staying as long as he's here and I can sit here the whole night, just sit, and he says hey it's no problem you sleep on the sofa here see and he makes some tea and we take the tea downstairs to where the paintings are and I think this is the right direction, at least he's on his way out, and he shows me the paintings, one by one, he shows them to me, it's sort of amazing, it's like being scraped up off the street and suddenly the Museum of Modern Art's open to you, a special honored guest, he shows them to me one by one and I'm pretty awed and pretty quiet except he asks me questions, what do I think of this and what do I think of this and I try to say something, I say things about poems they remind me of because I don't know how to say things about paintings and there's one a little different, it's an emotional upheaval, not intellectual like most of the others, and I like it a lot, it's brazen and aggressive and real romantic and I say so and he says well, it's named after me then, and I think it's probably because he's drunk and he'll change it back tomorrow but tonight it is named for me; *Andy* he calls it, a nickname I hate. I say I'll lock him out and he says he's going to call Jill to say he's on his way and we walk upstairs and I sit on the single wood chair but he doesn't go near any phone which I don't even know where it is, I sit on the wood chair and I dig my nails into it and he pours me another drink and I'm saying I've had enough but once it's in my hands I'm nervous so I drink it and it's pretty much like I'm submerged in a tank of alcohol, the fumes are drowning out any air, I'm close to asphyxiation. I sit real still on the chair, I down the drink like it's water, I hold onto the chair for dear life, I see the chicken wire and it scares me, I think about outside and it scares me, and he's just standing there, real benign, there's not a hint of sex, there's not a spark I can see, it's Jill's art opening, he's her lover and these facts have only one outcome which is he's going to her now or soon and I just have to sit here still until he does and I ask where Jill sleeps and he says behind the chicken wire and I feel out of my fucking mind, I feel insane, and he's totally level; and his eyes change, I never looked at his eyes before but now they're cold, they are real cold, they have a steel quality, you might say they are mean and you might say they are cruel and you might say they have my blood smeared on them and he's saying he'll just tuck me in, I should just lie

down and he'll cover me with a blanket and then he'll leave
and I'm saying he should leave now and I'm Jill's friend and he
says he just wants me to sit next to him on the single bed just
for a minute, just sit there next to him, and I am some falling
down drunk stupid bitch but I am not going near him, I am
sitting on the chair, I have got my fingernails dug in, and he's
saying, totally level, totally calm, you can leave if you want,
quiet voice he has, you can just leave, quiet voice, soft voice,
cold eyes, not brown, yellow eyes, ochre eyes, dirty yellow
eyes, quiet voice, you can leave or you can just come here and
sit with me, sit next to me, just for a minute, or you can leave,
or you can leave, or you can sit here, next to me or you can
leave; and I thought, can I?—the door's locked from inside,
you can't stay on the streets, the bars are closed, there's no
strangers outside you can find, even if you was going to risk it,
and you can barely put one foot in front of another, everything
in front of your eyes is streaked and moving, everything's got
a tail like a comet racing through the sky, everything's a shiny
streak whirling past you and you are standing still unless you
are falling, you fall and stop, fall and stop; and he's saying you
can leave and you're wondering if he'd let you anyway,
because finally it occurs to you he is more than a liar, or why
would he be so calm? He's so quiet; quiet voice; you can leave;
or come right here, sit near me, just near me; and then there's
whatever's past the fucking sunset, you know, the ocean
pounds the shore or something, there's a hurricane, many die,
it breaks apart the beach, shacks, houses, stone walls, they're
wrecked, Atlanta burns, you know, metaphor, I'd rather talk
in metaphor than say the things he did, God made metaphor
for girls like me, you know, life is nasty, short, brutish, short,
you can be snuffed out, it's so fast, so mean, so easy,
someone's eyes go cold, they go mean, they say sit near me
and you say no and they say sit near me and you say no and
they say sit near me and you say no and it's like a boy and a girl

and some courtly dance except he is saying you can leave, a
death threat, you can leave, with his cold eyes gleaming a
devil's yellow from the meanness of it, a dirty yellow, as if his
eyeballs changed from brown to some supernatural ochre and
he puts his hands on my shoulders and his hands are strong and
he lifts me up from the single wood chair and there's this kind
of long waltz the length of the great ballroom where his arms
are around me and I am going one, two, three, four, against
him, in the opposite direction from him trying to get past him
and he is using my own motion to push me back to where he
wants and he sits me down on the single bed and we just sit there
like chaste kids, teenagers, side by side, we each look straight
ahead except he's got his hand on my neck, we're Norman
Rockwell except his fingers are spread the width of my neck,
his fingers are around my neck, circling my neck and I turn my
head to face him, my body's staring outwards but I turn my
face toward him and I say to him I don't want to do this, I get
him to face me and I look him in the eye and I say I don't want
to do this and his hand tightens on my neck and I feel his
fingers down under my skin and into the muscle of my neck
and he says quiet, totally level, totally calm: it doesn't matter,
darling, it doesn't matter at all. I'm thinking he means it
doesn't matter to him to fuck and I smile in a kind of gratitude
but it's not what he means and he takes his other hand and he
puts it up at the neck of my T-shirt and he pulls, one hand's
holding my neck from behind and the other's pulling off my
T-shirt, pulling it half off, ripping it, it burns against my skin
like whiplash, and he pushes me down on the bed and I see my
breast, it's beautiful and perfect and kind of cascading, there's
no drawing can show how it's a living part of me, human, and
when he puts his mouth on it I cry, not so he can tell, inside I'm
turned to tears, I see his face now up against my breast, he's
suckling and I hate him, I feel the inside of his mouth, clammy
and toothy and gummy, the cavity of his mouth and the sharp

porcelain of his teeth, there's the edge of his teeth on my nipple, and he's got my underpants torn off me and my legs pushed up and spread and he's in me and I think I will count to a hundred and it will be over but it isn't, he's different, I try to push him off and he raises himself above me and he smiles at me and he pushes me back, he holds me down, and I give up, I do, I stay still, my body dies as much as it can, hate distilled, a perfect hate expressed in a perfect physical passivity, a perfect attentiveness to dying, he's going to say I'm a bad lay because I won't move but I hate him and I won't move. I just wait now for him to come but he's different, he won't come, he pushes my neck to hurt it and he kisses me, I feel his mouth on me, he's in me, sudden, brutal, unpleasant; vomitous; then he's out of me, he's kissing me, he kisses me everywhere, he rams into me then he's out, he's kissing, he's kissing my stomach, he's kissing my legs, then he's in me and my thighs are pushed back past my shoulders, then he's kissing me, he's kissing my anus and licking it and he's kissing my legs and he's talking to me, your skin reminds me of Bridget's, he says, Bridget has beautiful skin, some whispering bullshit like I'm his lover or his friend or something, conspiring with him, and then he's ramming himself in me and then he's kissing me and I am confused and afraid and I am paralyzed, I don't move, I don't want to move, I won't move but also I can't move, hate pins me there flat, still, a perfect passivity, I think I am physically real but my body's incoherent to my own mind because I can't follow what he's doing to me or what he wants, he's doing it to me but I don't know what it is, there's no organizing principle, there's no momentum or logic, I'm desperate for an end but there's no end, he's brutal and cold and chaotic and I say this will end but it doesn't end, he rams, he kisses, I say this is real, I am real, surely I am real, the physical reality is overwhelmingly brutal and nasty, he tempers it, he thinks, with these kisses, each one must be washed off, gotten off, later, the skin must be gotten off later, gotten rid of, the cells must be scraped off, I will need new skin, clean skin, because he is expectorating all over me, I will need to rub and scrape, I can use a knife or a stone, I'll scrape it off, he's in me, then he withdraws, then he kisses, he kisses my stomach, he kisses my feet—my feet; he kisses my legs, I feel a searing pain in my leg, I feel a terrible bad pain, I feel sharp shots of pain, then he rams, he kisses, he pushes, he pushes my legs apart, he pushes them back, he rams, he kisses, he must of read a book, girls like this, girls like that, you kiss girls, you kiss them; you kiss them; he's kissing me and saying things as if we are friends or I know him or something and then he rams in, brutal bastard, and then he's a lover, kissing; and this is my body but it ain't, I say it ain't, I say it ain't, I say I ain't here and it ain't me; but time's real—*time is real*—time's real; there's a long time until dawn, there's a couple of hours until six and then there's maybe an hour after that until there's real light, you know, sun, sun coming down from the sky, sun filtering down through the cold, sun traveling down; heating up, even a little, the streets, stone cold, steel-like daggers, the slab they lay you out on; my slab, a stone cold street; and a girl who wants to live, such a girl, a girl who fucking wants to live doesn't go out until dawn, can't go out until dawn; girls don't go out at night; girls who want to live don't go out at night; you need light to go out; you need sun; you need daylight; you need it to be a little warmer, you need the edge off the cold, you need the wind warmed up a little, you need it pale out, not dark, you need it yellow or yellowish or even a flat silver or gray, a dull gray, you need it gray or grayish or a dirty white at least, you need it ash or a pale, pale blue as if it's got a wash over it, a watercolor wash, a greenish hue, or you need it to be pink, a pinkish color, you need it pink, a little pink and a little warm, pinkish and warmish, you need light, you need light that's fresh and new, wholesome, washed in a subtle pastel color, a pale hue, you need real light, honest light, well-established light, not half dark, not stained by dark, not transitory or illusory, you need it yellow from sun or even silver or gray, you need it heated up, cozy, as if someone lit a match and burned it to heat up the air, you need the sun mixing with the wind, a touch of heat, you need it to be daytime if you're a girl so you can be safe and warm and at night you have to stay inside so you won't get hurt; you don't go out after dark; you stay inside at night, you don't be stupid and fuck up or some stranger could hurt you, some bad man, a Nazi or some ghoul. You got to stay inside and if there's a boy who likes you he'll sit next to you and he'll kiss you and you can just stay with him. Paul's asleep. He's pinning me down, half on top of me, a lover but slightly displaced, half on me, half on the bed, it's a single bed, it's been light a long time, two hours, three hours, I watched the light come, it's slow at first, then it's sudden, it's pale today, a delicate yellow, a pale cold tone, I'm a student of light and time; my eyes are swollen open as if I saw something that fixed them in place but I didn't see nothing special, I always wait with my eyes open, I had them open, I didn't close them, it doesn't help to close them, I waited for light but he didn't stop just because there was light, sometimes something's important to you but it doesn't matter to someone else but you don't know that, you don't understand it, he lasted well past the light and then he fell asleep without moving much, I wouldn't have minded turning into a pumpkin but the lovely lady had to stay at the ball, the beautiful princess loved by the boy, he liked her so much; then he fell asleep without moving much, his body the full length of mine, half on me, half off, his arms holding onto me, one spread over me, dead weight, one leg was spread over me, dead weight; and I was completely still, I stayed completely still, except my eyes wander, and I decide I'm never going to lie down again, I'm never going to lie down on my back, I'm going to sit or I'm going to stand up always from now on, in alleys or in apartments or anywhere, and I try to move but I hurt, I am filled with aches under my skin, in my bones, in my joints, in my muscles, I'm stiff and I'm sore and then my head's separate, it's very big and there's a thud in it, a bang, a buzz, and there's polka dots in the air, painted on, in the whole vast room, dancing dots, black and navy blue, and he's watching me, I move slowly and finally I am sitting, sitting on the edge of the bed, the single bed, sitting, chaste, just sitting, and my right leg is split open, the skin on it is split open in two places, above my knee and under my knee, the skin's torn, there's big jagged pieces of skin, there's gashes, it's deep tears, deep cuts, blood, dried blood and wet blood, my leg's torn open in two places, his kisses, his lover's kisses opened the skin, inside it's all angry looking as if it's turning to a yellow or greenish pus, it's running with dirty, angry blood, I think it needs stitches but I can't get stitches and I'm scared of gangrene, old ladies get it on the street, winos get it when there's sores, and I go to wash it at the sink but it hurts too much and I think his water's dirty, I'm sure he has dirty water, it looks dirty, and the skin's splitting apart more, as if it's a river running over land, and I concentrate on getting out, finding my clothes, putting on my clothes, they're torn and fucked up, and I ask for the keys to get out and he says something chatty and he smiles, it's English but I can't exactly understand it so I nod or smile in a neutral way and I think I'd better get out and he says see you or see you again or see you soon, it's English but it's hard to understand, I can't make out the separate words, and I say yeah, yeah, of course, sure, and it doesn't seem to be enough so I say I'll call, it seems better, it's affirmative, he relaxes, he smiles, he's relaxed back into the bed, and I move, slowly, not to alarm him, not to stir him, not to call attention to myself, I try to move the way they tell you with a book on your head, smooth and calm and quiet, firm and fast and sure, ladylike,

self-abnegating, to disappear, and I take the keys and I go
down the steps, very slow, it's hard, the blood from the gashes
is dripping down and the leg's opening more and it hurts, it
hurts very much—if you spread your arms out full, that much,
or even more maybe. If it was a knife you could put the skin
back together and there wouldn't be so many diseases, knives
are cleaner, this won't go back together, it's ripped, it's too
torn, it's dirty, some special dirt, it's named after him, this
dirt, it's called *Paulie*, I named it after him; and I leave the keys
like he told me inside the door in the hall on the floor, it's
unlocked now, the door's open, I walk out and it's deserted,
cold, bare, bare city streets, calm, no wind, a perfect, pure,
clean cold, cold enough to kill the germs on my leg, it'll freeze
them and they'll die, I think it must be the case, if you can kill
them through heat, sterilization, you must be able to kill them
through cold, I think the damaged tissue's already freezing and
the germs are dying or they will and it's good there's no wind
because if anything moves my leg screams, the skin screams,
it's like a flashfire ignited up my leg, a napalm exploding on
me; and he's sleeping upstairs, he's in bed, he didn't get out of
bed, he's asleep, he was back asleep almost before I left, he
seemed to be waiting for me to kiss him goodbye or good
morning or hello, I said I'll call and he relaxed back into bed, I
stared, I made myself move, I moved fast, quiet, which is why
they teach you to walk with a book on your head, you walk
quiet, with poise, you have a straight back, you take firm,
quiet steps, and I wish someone would go up now while he's
asleep and kill him or rob him, I wish I could put a sign on the
door—it's open, kill him, rob him, I think there's some
chance, it's a bad neighborhood, maybe somebody'll find
him. I'm dirty; all my clothes are torn and fucked up as if they
were urinated on or wrapped in a ball and used to wipe
someone's ass. I call Jill from a pay phone. He raped me, I say.
He's not the milk of human kindness she says and hangs up; is

raped me worse than cheated on you? I got some change, some quarters, some dimes, my favorite, half dollars, they're pretty like silver, I like them. She knew it was bad; raped me. The earth's round but the streets are flat. There's rain forests but the streets are cold. I can't really say I understand. It's ten a.m. I'm twenty-six years old. I got a wound on my leg, a nasty sore, dirty fucking sore from a rabid dog, slobbering mangy cur, an old bag lady's sore, ugly fucking sore; maybe the A.S.P.C.A.'d come and get him. I could use a drink. I got to sleep before there's night, it comes fast in winter, you lose track. It's ten a.m.; and soon it will be ten-o-five; soon. You have to count fast, keep counting, to keep track. Ugly, fucking, stupid bitch, got to sleep, can't lie down. There's fleas.

NINE

In October 1973
(Age 27)

There's a basketball court next to where I live, not a court exactly, a hoop high up, and broken cement, rocks, broken glass; there's boys that play, the game ain't ballet like on television, it's malice, they smash the ball like they're smashing heads and you don't want to distract them, you want their eyes on the ball, always on the ball, you want them playing ball; so you get small and quiet walking by, you don't let nothing rattle or shake, you just blend, into the sidewalk, into the air, get gray like the fence, it's wire, shaky, partly walling the place in, you walk quiet and soft and hope your heart don't beat too loud; and there's a parking lot for cops right next to the basketball, not the official vehicles but the cars they come to work in, the banged up Chevys and Fords they drive in from the suburbs because most of them don't live here no more but still, even though they got more money than they make you don't see nothing smart and sleek, there's just this old metal, bulky, heavy, discolored. The young cops are tight and you don't want to see them spring loose, their muscles are all screwed together real tight and their lips are tight, sewed tight, and they stand straight and tight and they look ahead, not around, their pupils are tight in the dead center of their eyes staring straight ahead; and the older ones wear cheap sports jackets too big for them, gray, brown, sort of plaid, nearly tweed, wrinkled, and their shoulders sag, and they are morose men, and their cars can barely hold them, their legs fall out loose and disorganized and then they move their bodies around to be in the same direction as the legs that fell down, they move the trunks of their bodies from behind the steering wheels against gravity and disregarding common sense and the air moves out of the way, sluggish and slow, displaced by their hanging bellies, and they are tired men, and they see everything, they have eyes that circle the globe, insect eyes and third eyes, they see in front and behind and on each side, their eyes spin without moving, and they see you no matter how blank and quiet you are, they see you sneaking by, and they wonder why you are sneaking and what you have to hide, they note that you are trash, they have the view that anything female on this street is a piece of gash, an open wound inviting you in for a few pennies, and that you especially who are walking by them now have committed innumerable evils for which you must pay and you want to argue except for the fact that they are not far from wrong, it is not an argument you can win, and that makes you angrier against them and fearful, and you try to disappear but they see you, they always see you; and you learn not to think they are fools; they will get around to you; today, tomorrow, someday soon; and they see the boys playing basketball and they want to smash them, smash their fucking heads in, but they're too old to smash them and they can't use their guns, not yet, not now; even the young cops couldn't smash them fair, they're too rigid, too slow up against the driving rage of the boys with the ball; so you see them noting it, noting that they got a grudge, and the cars are parked on gravel and broken glass and rocks and they should have better and they know it but they don't and they won't and later they get to use the guns, somewhere, the city's full of fast black boys who get separated from the pack; and you hear the fuck, shit, asshole, of the basketball players as a counterpoint to the solitary fuck, shit, asshole, of the lone cops as they emerge from their cars, they put down their heavy legs and their heavy feet in their bad old shoes, all worn, chewed leather, and they pull themselves out of their old cars, and they're tired men, overweight, there ain't many young ones at all, and there's a peculiar sadness to them, the fascists are melancholy in Gotham, they say fuck, shit, asshole, like it's soliloquies, like it's prayers, like it's amen, like it's exegesis on existence, like it's unanswered questions, urgent, eloquent, articulated to God; lonely, tired old Nazis, more like Hamlet, though, than like Lear, introspective from exhaustion, not grand or arrogant or merciless in delusion; and the boys hurl the ball like it's bombs, like it's rocks and stones, like it's bullets and they're the machines of delivery, the weapons of death, machine guns of flesh, bang bang bang, each round so fast, so hard, as the ball hits the ground and the boy moves with it, a weapon with speed up its ass; and they're a choir of fuck, shit, asshole, voices still on the far edge of an adolescent high, not the raspy, cigarette-ruined voices of the lonely, sad men; the boys run, the boys sing the three words they know, a percussive lyric, they breathe deep, skin and viscera breathe, everything inside and outside breathes, there's a convulsion, then another one, they exhale as if it's some sublime soprano aria at the Met, supreme art, simple, new each time, the air comes out urgent and organized and with enough volume to fill a concert hall, it's exhilarating, a human voice, all the words they don't know; and the cops, old, young, it don't matter, barely breathe at all, they breathe so high up in the throat that the air barely gets out, it's thin and depressed and somber, it's old and it's stale and it's pale and it's flat, there's no words to it and no music, it's a thin, empty sound, a flat despair, Hamlet so old and dead and tired he can't even get up a stage whisper. The cops look at the boys, each cop does, and there's this second when the cop wants to explode, he'd unleash a grenade in his own hand if he had one, he'd take himself with it if it meant offing them, fuck them black boys' heads off, there's this tangible second, and then they turn away, each one, young, old, tight, sagging, each one, every day, and they pull themselves up, and they kick the rocks, the broken glass, the gravel, and they got a hand folded into a fist, and they leave the parking lot, they walk big, they walk heavy, they walk like John Wayne, young John, old John, big John, they walk slow and heavy and wide, deliberate, like they got six-shooters riding on each hip; while the boys move fast, mad, mean, speeding, cold fury in hot motion. You want them on each other; not on you. It ain't honorable but it's real. You want them caught up in the urban hate of generations, in wild west battles on city streets, you want them so manly against each other they don't have time for girlish trash like you, you want them fighting each other cock to cock so it all gets used up on each other. You take the view that women are for recreation, fun, when the battle's over; and this battle has about another hundred years to go. You figure they can dig you up out of the ground when they're ready. You figure they probably will. You figure it don't matter to them one way or the other. You figure it don't matter to you either; just so it ain't today, now, tonight, tomorrow; just so you ain't conscious; just so you ain't alive the next time; just so you are good and dead; just so you don't know what it is and who's doing it. If you're buying milk or bread or things you have to go past them, walk down them streets, go in front of them, the boys, the cops, and you practice disappearing; you practice pulling the air over you like a blanket; you practice being nothing and no one; you practice not making a sound and barely breathing; you practice making your eyes go blank and never looking at anyone but seeing where they are, hearing a shadow move; you practice being a ghost on cement; and you don't let nothing rattle or make noise, not the groceries, not your shoes hitting the ground, not your arms, you don't let them move or rub, you don't make no spontaneous gestures, you don't even raise your arm to scratch your nose, you keep your arms still and you put the milk in the bag so it stays still and you go so far as to make sure the bag ain't a stupid bag, one of them plastic ones that makes sounds every time something touches it; you have to get a quiet bag; if it's a brown paper bag you have to perfect the skill of carrying it so nothing moves inside it and so you don't have to change arms or hands, acts which can catch the eye of someone, acts which can call attention to you, you don't shift the bag because your hand gets tired or your arm, you just let it hurt because it hurts quiet, and if it's a plastic bag it's got to be laminated good so it don't make any rustling noise or scratching sound, and you have to walk faster, silent, fast, because plastic bags stand out more, sometimes they have bright colors and the flash of color going by can catch someone's attention, the bag's real money, it costs a dime, it's a luxury item, you got change to spare, you're a classy shopper so who knows what else you got; and if it's not colorful it's likely to be a shiny white, a bright white, the kind light flashes off of like it's a mirror sending signals and there's only one signal widely comprehended on cement: get me. The light can catch someone's eye so you have to walk like Zen himself, walk and not walk, you are a master in the urban Olympics for girls, an athlete of girlish survival, it's a survival game for the world's best. You get past them and you celebrate, you celebrate in your heart, you thank the Lord, in your heart you say a prayer of gratitude and forgiveness, you forgive Him, it's sincere, and you hope He don't take it as a challenge, razor-sharp temper He's got, no do unto others for Him; and if you hear someone behind you you beg, in half a second you are on your knees in your heart begging Him to let you off, you promise a humility this time that will last, it will begin right now and last a long, long time, you promise no more liturgical sacrilege, and your prayer stops and your heart stops and you wait and the most joyous sound on God's earth is that

the man's feet just stomp by. Either he will hurt you or he will
not; either He will hurt you or He will not. Truth's so simple
and so severe, you don't be stupid enough to embellish it. I
myself live inside now. I don't take my chances resting only in
the arms of God. I put myself inside four walls and then I let
Him rock me, rock me, baby, rock me. I lived outside a lot;
and this last summer I was tired, disoriented. I was too tired,
really, to find a bed, too nervous, maybe too old, maybe I got
old, it happens pretty fast past eighteen like they always
warned; get yourself one boy when you're eighteen and get
yourself one bed. It got on my nerves to think about it every
night, I don't really like to be in a bed per se. I stayed in the lot
behind where the police park their cars, there's a big, big dirt
lot, there's a fence behind the police cars and then there's
empty dirt, trash, some rats, we made fires, there's broken
glass, there's liquor to stay warm, I never once saw what it
was, it's bottles in bags with hands on the bags that tilt in your
direction, new love, anti-genital love, polymorphous perverse, a bottle in a bag. You got to lift your skirt sometimes
but it doesn't matter and I have sores on me, my legs is so dirty
I just really don't look. You don't have to look. There's many
mirrors to be used but you need not use them. I got too worn
out to find some bed each new night, it got on my nerves so I
was edgy and anxious in anticipation, a dread that it would be
hard to find or hard to stay or hard to pay, if I just stayed on the
dirt lot I didn't have to worry so much, there's nothing
trapping you in. Life's a long, quiet rumble, and you just shake
as even as you can so you don't get too worn out. When I lifted
up my skirt there was blood and dirt in drips, all dried, down
my legs, and I had sores. I felt quiet inside. I felt okay. I didn't
worry too much. I didn't go see movies or go on dates. I just
curled up to sleep and I'd drink whatever there was that
someone give me because there's generous men too; I see
saliva; I see it close up; if I was an artist I would paint it except I

don't know how you make it glisten, the brown and the gold in it; I saw many a face close up and I saw many a man close up and I'd lift my skirt and it was dirty, my legs, and there was dried blood. I was pretty dirty. I didn't worry too much. Then I got money because my friend thought I should go inside. I had this friend. I knew her when I was young. She was a pacifist. She hated war and she held signs against the Vietnam War and I did too. She let me sleep in her apartment but enough's enough; there's places you don't go back to. So now I was too dirty and she gave me money to go inside definitively; which I had wanted, except it was hard to express. I thought about walls all the time. I thought about how easy they should be, really, to have; how you could fit them almost anywhere, on a street corner, in an alley, on a patch of dirt, you must make walls and a person can go inside with a bed, a small cot, just to lie down and it's a house, as much of a house as any other house. I thought about walls pretty much all the time. You should be able to just put up walls, it should be possible. There's literally no end to the places walls could go without inconveniencing anyone, except they would have to walk around. They say a roof over your head but it's walls really that are the issue; you can just think about them, all their corners touching or all lined up thin like pancakes, painted a pretty color, a light color because you don't want it to look too small, or you can make it more than one color but you run the risk of looking busy, somewhat vulgar, and you don't want it to look gray or brown like outside or you could get sad. There's got to be some place in heaven where God stores walls, there's just walls, stacked or standing up straight like the pages of a book, miles high and miles wide running in pale colors above the clouds, a storage place, and God sees someone lost and He just sends them down four at a time. Guess He don't. There's people take them for granted and people who dream about them—literally, dream how nice they would be, pretty and painted, serene. I wouldn't mind living outside all the time if it didn't get cold or wet and there wasn't men. A roof over your head is more conceptual in a sense; it's sort of an advanced idea. In life you can cover your head with a piece of wood or with cardboard or newspapers or a side of a crate you pull apart, but walls aren't really spontaneous in any sense; they need to be built, with purpose, with intention. Someone has to plan it if you want them to come together the right way, the whole four of them with edges so delicate, it has to be balanced and solid and upright and it's very delicate because if it's not right it falls, you can't take it for granted; and there's wind that can knock it down; and you will feel sad, remorseful, you will feel full of grief. You can't sustain the loss. A roof over your head is a sort of suburban idea, I think; like that if you have some long, flat, big house with furniture in it that's all matching you surely also will have a roof so they make it a synonym for all the rest but it's walls that make the difference between outside and not. It's a well-kept secret, arcane knowledge, a mystery not often explained. You don't see it written down but initiates know. I type and sometimes I steal but I'm stopping as much as I can. I live inside now. I have an apartment in a building. It's a genuine building, a tenement, which is a famous kind of building in which many have lived in history. Maybe not Trotsky but Emma Goldman for certain. I don't go near men really. Sometimes I do. I get a certain forgetfulness that comes on me, a dark shadow over my brain, I get took up in a certain feeling, a wandering feeling to run from existence, all restless, perpetual motion. It drives me with an ache and I go find one. I get a smile on my face and my hips move a little back and forth and I turn into a greedy little fool; I want the glass all empty. I grab some change and I hit the cement and I get one. I am writing a certain very serious book about life itself. I go to bars for food during happy hours when my nerves aren't too bad, too loaded down with pain, but I keep to myself so I can't get enough to eat because bartenders and managers keep watch and you are supposed to be there for the men which is why they let you in, there ain't no such thing as a solitary woman brooding poetically to be left alone, it don't happen or she don't eat, and mostly I don't want men so I'm hungry most of the time, I'm almost always hungry, I eat potatoes, you can buy a bag of potatoes that is almost too heavy to carry and you can just boil them one at a time and you can eat them and they fill you up for a while. My book is a very big book about existence but I can't find any plot for it. It's going to be a very big book once I get past the initial slow beginning. I want to get it published but you get afraid you will die before it's finished, not after when it can be found and it's testimony and then they say you were a great one; you don't want to die before you wrote it so you have to learn to sustain your writing, you take it serious, you do it every day and you don't fail to write words down and to think sentences. It's hard to find words. It's about some woman but I can't think of what happens. I can say where she is. It's pretty barren. I always see a woman on a rock, calling out. But that's not a story per se. You could have someone dying of tuberculosis like Mann or someone who is suffering—for instance, someone who is lovesick like Mann. Or there's best-sellers, all these stories where women do all these things and say all these things but I don't think I can write about that because I only seen it in the movies. There's marriage stories but it's so boring, a couple in the suburbs and the man on the train becoming unfaithful and how bored she is because she's too intelligent or something about how angry she is but I can't remember why. A love story's so stupid in these modern times. I can't have it be about my life because number one I don't remember very much and number two it's against the rules, you're supposed to make things up. The best thing that ever happened to me is these walls and I don't think you could turn that into a story per se or even a novel of ideas that people would grasp as philosophical: for instance, that you can just sit and they provide a framework of dignity because no one's watching and I have had too many see too much, they see you when they do things to you that you don't want, they look, and the problem is there's no walls keeping you sacred; nor that if you stand up they are solid which makes you seem real too, a real figure in a room with real walls, a touchstone of authenticity, a standard for real existence, you are real or you feel real, you don't have to touch them to feel real, you just have to be able to touch them. My pacifist friend gave me money to live here. She saw me on the street one day, I guess, after I didn't go back to her apartment no more. She said come with me and she got a newspaper and she found an apartment and she called the landlord and she put the money in my hand and she sent me to the landlord which scared me because I never met one before, a real one, but also she wasn't going to let the cash go elsewhere which there was a fair chance it would, because I would have liked some coke or something or some dinner or some drinks and a movie and a book or something more real than being inside which seemed impossible—it seemed not really available and it seemed impossible to sustain so it made more sense to me to use the cash for something real that I knew I could get, something I knew how to use. I started sending her money back as soon as I got some, I'd put some in an envelope and mail it back even if it was just five dollars but she said I was stupid because she only said it was a loan but it wasn't and I didn't need to pay it back and everyone knew that which is my weakness, how everyone got to know things but I don't know them. I can't think of any stories about pacifists that aren't true. There's nothing imaginary about walls, or eating, nothing fictive as it were, but more especially there's nothing imaginary about them when they're missing. My walls are thin; yeah I wish they were mine. Nothing's yours. God hurts you if you think they're yours. In one second of a bad thought you can bring evil down on you. The walls are thin. I dream there's holes in them and I get scared as if it's not really inside. There's not much food and I know it ain't mine in any meaningful sense. You're supposed to make things up, not just write down true things, or sincere things, or some things that happened. My mother who you can't make up either because there's nothing so real as one named me Andrea as if I was someone: distinct, in particular. She made a fiction. I'm her book, a made-up story written down on a birth certificate. You could also say she's a liar on such a deep level she should be shot by all that's fair; deep justice. If I was famous and my name was published all over the world, in Italy and in Israel and in Africa and in India, on continents and subcontinents, in deserts, in ancient cities, it would still be cunt to every fucking asshole drunk on every street in the world; and to them that's not drunk too, the sober ones who say it to you like they're calling a dog: fetch, cunt. If I won the Nobel Prize and walked to the corner for milk it would still be cunt. And when you got someone inside you who is loving you it's still cunt and the ones who'd die if they wasn't in you, you, you in particular, at least that night, at least then, that time, that place, to them it's still cunt and they whisper it up close and chill the blood that's burning in you; and if you love them it's still cunt and you can love them so strong you'd die for them and it's still cunt; and your heartbeat and his heartbeat can be the same heartbeat and it's still cunt. It's behind your back and it's to your face; the ones you know, the ones you don't. It's like as if nigger was a term of intimate endearment, not just used in lynching and insult but whispered in lovemaking, the truth under the truth, the name under the name, love's name for you and it's the same as what hate calls you; he's in you whispering nigger. It's thugs, it's citizens, it's cops, it's strangers, it's the ones you want and the ones you deplore, you ain't allowed indifference, you have to decide on a relationship then and there on the spot because each one that passes pisses on you to let you know he's there. There's some few you made love with and you're still breathing tight with them, you can still feel their muscles swelling through their skin and bearing down on you and you can still feel their weight on you, an urgent concentration of blood and bone, hot muscle, spread over you, the burden of it sinking into you, a stone cliff into a wet shore, and you're still tangled up in them, good judgment aside, and it's physical, it's a physical memory, in the body, not just in the brain, barely in the brain at all, you got their sweat on you as part of your sweat and their smell's part of your smell and you have an ache for them that's deep and gnawing and hurtful in more than your heart and you still feel as if it's real and current, now: how his body moves against you in convulsions that are awesome like mountains moving, slow, burdensome, big, and how you move against him as if you could move through him, he's the ocean, you're the tide, and it's still cunt, he says cunt. He's indelibly in you and you don't want redemption so much as you want him and still it's cunt. It's what's true; Andrea's the lie. It's a lie we got to tell, Jane and Judith and Ellen and whomever. It's our most desperate lie. My mother named me Andrea. It means manhood or courage. It means not-cunt. She specifically said: not-cunt. This one ain't cunt, she declared, after blood spilled and there was the pain of labor so intense that God couldn't live through it and wouldn't which is why all the pain's with us and still she brought herself to a point of concentration and she said: not-cunt. This one's someone, she probably had in mind; a wish; a hope; let her, let her, something. Something. Let her something. Don't, not with this one. Just let this one through. Just don't do it to this one. She wrote: not-cunt, a fiction, and it failed, and the failure defeated her and turned her cold to me, because before I was

even ten some man had wrote "this one's cunt," he took his
fingers and he wrote it down on me and inside me, his fingers
carved it in me with a pain that stayed half buried and there
wasn't words I had for what he did, he wrote I was cunt, this
sweet little one who was what's called a child but a female one
which changes it all. My mama showed that fiction was
delusion, hallucination, it was a long, deranged lie designed to
last past your own lifetime. The man, on the other hand, was a
pragmatist, a maker of reality, a shaper of history, an
orchestrator of events. He used life, not paper, bodies, not ink.
The Nazis, of course, synthesized the two: bodies and ink.
You can't even say it would solve the problem to have
numbers on us, inked on. Numbers is as singular as names
unless we are all zero, 0, we could all be 0; Pauline Réage
already suggested it, of course, but she's a demagogue and a
utopian, a kind of Stalinist of female equality, she wants us all
equal on the bottom of anything that's mean enough to be on
top; it has a certain documentary quality. Unlike Réage, my
mother just made it up, and her fiction was a lie, almost
without precedent, not recognized as original or great, a
voyage of imagination; it was just a fucking lie. I don't want to
tell lies, not for moral reasons but it's my idea of pride, you
name it, I can take it. I was born in a city where the walls were
falling down; I didn't see many solid walls. The streets were
right next to you it seemed because you could always hear the
buzz, the hum, the call, as if drums were beckoning you to the
tribal dance; you could see the freedom. Inside was small and
constrained with rules designed to make you some kind of
trained cockroach and outside was forever, a path straight to
the heart of the world; there were no limits, it spread out in
front of you to anywhere, with anyone. Limits were another
lie, a social fiction all the zombies got together to tell. The
destination was always the street because the destination was
always freedom; out from under; no rule on top of you. You

could almost look through the brick, which was crumbling, and you had this sense that every building had holes in it, a transparency, and that no walls were ever finished or ever lasted; and the cement outside was gray, cracked, streaked with blood from where they threw you down to have fun with you on hot nights and cold nights, the boys with their cars and knives; I knew some of those boys; I loved Nino who said "make love" as if it was something real special and real nice and so fine, so precious and kind and urgent, his eyes burned and his voice was low and soft and silk, it wrapped itself around you, he didn't reach out, he didn't move towards you, you had to let him know, you had to; I could still fucking die for what he promised with his brilliant seduction, a poor, uneducated boy, but when he did it I got used to being hurt from behind, he used his knife, he made fine lines of blood, delicate, and you didn't dare move except for your ass as he wanted and you didn't know if you'd die and you got to love danger if you loved the boy and danger never forsakes you; the boy leaves but danger is faithful. You knew the cement under you and the brick around you and the sound of the boys speeding by in their cars and the sudden silence, which meant they were stalking you. I was born in Camden down the street from where Walt Whitman lived, Mickle Street, he was the great gray poet, the prophetic hero of oceanic verse; also not-cunt. Great poet; not-cunt. It's like a mathematical equation but no one learns it in school by heart; it ain't written down plain on the blackboard. It's algebra for girls but no one's going to teach you. You get brought down or throwed down and you learn for yourself. There's no mother on earth can bear to explain it. I can't write down what happened and I can't tell lies. There's no words for what happened and there's barely words for the lies. If I was a man I would say something about fishing and it would be a story, a perfectly fine one too; the bait, the hook, the lake, the wind, the shore, and then everything else is the manly stuff. If I was a man at least I'd know what to say, or I'd say it so grand it wouldn't matter if it was true or not; anyone'd recognize it and say it was art. I could think of something important, probably; recognizably so. If I was a man and something happened I could write it down and probably it would pass as a story even if it was true. Of course, that's just speculation. I'd swagger, too, if I was a man; I'm not proud to say it but I'm sure it's true. I would take big steps, loud ones, down the street; I could be the Zen master of fuck you. I would spread myself out and take up all the space and spread my legs wide open in the subway to take up three seats with just my knees like they do. I would be very bold and very cool. I'd be smarter than I am now, I'm sure, because what I knew might matter and I'd remember more, I'm sure. I don't think I'd go near women though because I wouldn't want to hurt them. I know how everything feels. I think if I was a man my heart would not hurt so much and I wouldn't have this terror I am driven by but cannot name. I think I could write a poem about it, perhaps. I think it could probably make a very long poem and I could keep rewriting it to get every nuance right and chart it as it changed over time; song of himself, perhaps, a sequel. Ginsberg says he chased Whitman through supermarkets; I fucking was him; I embraced all the generations without distinctions and it failed because of this awfulness that there is no name for, this great meanness at the heart of what they mean when they stick it in; I just don't know a remedy, because it is a sick and hostile thing. Even if there were no wars I think I could say some perceptions I had about life, I wouldn't need the Civil War or the Vietnam War to hang my literary hat on as it were, and I could be loud, which I would try, I'm sure, I could call attention to myself as if I mattered or what happened did or as if I knew something, even about suffering or even about life; and, frankly, then it might count. I could stop thinking every minute about where each sound is coming from and where the shadows are each minute. I can't even close my eyes now frankly but I think it's because I'm this whatever it is, you can have sophisticated words for it but the fact is you can be sleeping inside with everything locked and they get in and do it to you no matter how bad it hurts. In magazines they say women's got allure, or so they call it, but it's more like being some dumb wriggling thing that God holds out before them on a stick with a string, a fisher of men. The allure's there even if you got open sores on you; I know. The formal writing problem, frankly, is that the bait can't write the story. The bait ain't even barely alive. There's a weird German tradition that the fish turned the tables and rewrote the story to punish the fisherman but you know it's a lie and it's some writer of fiction being what became known as a modernist but before that was called outright a smartass; and the fish still ain't bait unless it's eviscerated and bleeding. I just can't risk it now but if I was a man I could close my eyes, I'm sure; at night, I'd close them, I'm sure. I don't think my hands would shake. I don't think so; or not so much; or not all the time; or not without reason; there's no reason now anyone can see. My breasts wouldn't bleed as if God put a sign on me; blessing or curse, it draws flies. Tears of blood fall from them; they weep blood for me, because I'm whatever it is: the girl, as they say politely; the girl. You're supposed to make things up for books but I am afraid to make things up because in life everything evaporates, it's gone in mist, just disappears, there's no sign left, except on you, and you are a fucking invisible ghost, they look right through you, you can have bruises so bad the skin's pulled off you and they don't see nothing; you bet women had the vapors, still fucking do, it means it all goes away in the air, whatever happened, whatever he did and however he did it, and you're left feeling sick and weak and no one's going to say why; it's just women, they faint all the time, they're sick all the time, fragile things, delicate things, delicate like the best punching bags you ever seen. They say it's lies even if they just did it, or maybe especially then. I don't know really. There's nothing to it, no one ever heard of it before or ever saw it or not here or not now; in all history it never happened, or if it happened it was the Nazis, the exact, particular Nazis in Germany in the thirties and forties, the literal Nazis in uniform; when they were out of uniform they were just guys, you know, they loved their families, they paid off their whores, just regular guys. No one else ever did anything, certainly no one now in this fine world we have here; certainly not the things I think happened, although I don't know what to call them in any serious way. You just crawl into a cave of silence and die; why are there no great women artists? Some people got nerve. Blood on cement, which is all we got in my experience, ain't esthetic, although I think boys some day will do very well with it; they'll put it in museums and get a fine price. Won't be their blood. It would be some cunt's they whispered to the night before; a girl; and then it'd be art, you see; or you could put it on walls, make murals, be political, a democratic art outside the museums for the people, Diego Rivera without any conscience whatsoever instead of the very tenuous one he had with respect to women, and then it'd be extremely major for all the radicals who would discover the expressive value of someone else's blood and I want to tell you they'd stop making paint but such things do not happen and such things cannot occur, any more than the rape so-called can happen or occur or the being beaten so bad can happen or occur and there are no words for what cannot happen or occur and if you think something happened or occurred and there are no words for it you are at a dead end. There's nothing where they force you; there's nothing where you hurt so much; there's nothing where it matters, there's nothing like it anywhere. So it doesn't feel right to make things up, as you must do to write fiction, to lie, to elaborate, to elongate, to exaggerate, to distort, to get tangled up in moderations or modifications or deviations or compromises of mixing this with that or combining this one with that one because the problem is finding words for the truth, especially if no one will believe it, and they will not. I can't make things up because I wouldn't know after a while what's blood, what's ink. I barely know any words for what happened to me yesterday, which doesn't make tomorrow something I can conceive of in my mind; I mean words I say to myself in my own head; not social words you use to explain to someone else. I barely know anything and if I deviate I am lost; I have to be literal, if I can remember, which mostly I cannot. No one will acknowledge that some things happen and probably at this point in time there is no way to say they do in a broad sweep; you describe the man forcing you but you can't say he forced you. If I was a man I could probably say it; I could say I did it and everyone would think I made it up even though I'd just be remembering what I did last night or twenty minutes ago or once, long ago, but it probably wouldn't matter. The rapist has words, even though there's no rapist, he just keeps inventing rape; in his mind; sure. He remembers, even though it never happened; it's fine fiction when he writes it down. Whereas my mind is getting worn away; it's being eroded, experience keeps washing over it and there's no sea wall of words to keep it intact, to keep it from being washed away, carried out to sea, layer by layer, fine grains washed away, a thin surface washed away, then some more, washed away. I am fairly worn away in my mind, washed out to sea. It probably doesn't matter anyway. People lead their little lives. There's not much dignity to go around. There's lies in abundance, and silence for girls who don't tell them. I don't want to tell them. A lie's for when he's on top of you and you got to survive him being there until he goes; Malcolm X tried to stop saying a certain lie, and maybe I should change from Andrea because it's a lie. It's just that it's a precious thing from my mother that she tried to give me; she didn't want it to be such an awful lie, I don't think. So I have to be the writer she tried to be—Andrea; not-cunt—only I have to do it so it ain't a lie. I ain't fabricating stories. I'm making a different kind of story. I'm writing as truthful as the man with his fingers, if only I can remember and say; but I ain't on his side. I'm on some different side. I'm telling the truth but from a different angle. I'm the one he done it to. The bait's talking, honey, if she can find the words and stay even barely alive, or even just keep the blood running; it can't dry up, it can't rot. The bait's spilling the beans. The bait's going to transcend the material conditions of her situation, fuck you very much, Mr. Marx. The bait's going way past Marx. The bait's taking her eviscerated, bleeding self and she ain't putting it back together, darling, because, frankly, she don't know how; the bait's a realist, babe, the bait's no fool, she's just going to bleed all over you and you are going to have to find the words to describe the stain, a stain as big as her real life, boy; a big, nasty stain; a stain all over you, all the blood you ever spilled; that's the esthetic dimension, through art she replicates the others you done it to, gets the stain to incorporate them too. It's coming right back on you, sink or swim; fucking drown your head in it; give in, darling; go down. That's the plan, in formal terms. The bait's got a theory; the bait's finding a practice, working it out; the bait's going to write it down and she don't have to use words, she'll make signs, in blood, she's good at bleeding, boys, the vein's open, boys, the bait's got plenty, each month more and more without dying for a certain long period of her life, she can lose it or use it, she works in broad strokes, she makes big gestures, big signs; oh and honey there's so much bait around that there's going to be a bloodbath in the old town tonight, when the new art gets its start. You are going to be sitting in it; the

232

new novel; participation, it's called; I'm smearing it all over you. It ain't going to be made up; it ain't going to be a lie; and you are going to pay attention, directly, even though it's by a girl, because this time it's on you. If I find a word, I'll use it; but I ain't waiting, darling, I already waited too long. If you was raised a boy you don't know how to get blood off, you're shocked, surprised, in Vietnam when you see it for the first time and I been bleeding since I was nine, I'm used to putting my hands in it and I *live*. You don't give us no words for what's true so now there's signs, a new civilization just starting now: her name's not-cunt and she's just got to express herself, say some this and that, use what's there, take what's hers: her blood's hers; your blood's hers. Here's the difference between us, sweet ass: I'm using blood you already spilled; mine; hers; cunt's. I ain't so dirty as to take yours. I don't confuse this new manifesto with being Artaud; he was on the other side. There are sides. If he spills my blood, it's art. If I put mine on him, it's deeply not nice or good or, as they say, interesting; it's not interesting. There's a certain—shall we understate?—distaste. It's bad manners but not rude in an artistically valid sense. It's just not being the right kind of girl. It's deranged but not in the Rimbaud sense. It's just not being Marjorie Morningstar, which is the height to which you may aspire, failed artist but eventually fine homemaker. It's loony, yes, it's got some hate in it somewhere, but it ain't revolutionary like Sade who spilled blood with style; perhaps they think a girl can't have style but since a girl can't really have anything else I think I can pull it off; me and the other bait; there's many styles of allure around. Huey Newton's my friend and I send ten percent of any money I have to the Black Panthers instead of paying taxes because they're still bombing the fucking Vietnamese, if you can believe it. He sends me poems and letters of encouragement. I write him letters of encouragement. I'm afraid to show him any of my pages I wrote because perhaps he's not entirely cognizant of the problems, esthetic and political, I face. I look for signs in the press for if he's decent to women but there's not too much to see; except you have to feel some distrust. He's leading the revolution right now and I think the bait's got to have a place in it. I am saying to him that women too got to be whole; and old people cared for; and children educated and fed; and women not raped; I say, not raped; I say it to him, not raped. He's saying the same thing back to me in his letters, except for the women part. He is very Mao in his poem style, because it helps him to say what he knows and gives him authority, I can see that, it makes his simple language look strong and purposeful, not as if he's not too educated. It's brilliant for that whereas I am more lost; I can't cover up that I don't have words. I can't tell if *raped* is a word he knows or not; if he thinks I am stupid to use it or not; if he thinks it exists or not; because we are polite and formal and encouraging to each other and he doesn't say. I am working my part out. He is taking care of the big, overall picture, the big needs, the great thrust forward. I am in a fine fit of rebellion and melancholy and I think there's a lot that's possible so I am in a passion of revolutionary fire with a new esthetic boiling in me, except for my terrible times. The new esthetic started out in ignorance and ignominy, in sadness, in forgetting; it pushed past sadness into an overt rebellion—tear this down, tear this apart—and it went on to create: it said, we'll learn to write without words and if it happened we will find a way to say so and if it happened to us it happened. For instance, if it happened to me it happened; but I don't have enough confidence for that, really, because maybe I'm wrong, or maybe it's not true, or how do you say it, but if it happened to us, to us, you know, the ones of us that's the bait, then it happened. It happened. And if it happened, it happened. We will say so. We will find a way to say so. We will take the blood that was spilled and smear it in public ways so it's art and politics and science; the fisherman won't like the book so what's new; he'll say it ain't art or he'll say it's bullshit; but here's the startling part; the bait's got a secret system of communication, not because it's hidden but because the fisherman's fucking stupid; so arrogant; so sure of forever and a day; so sure he don't listen and he don't look and he says it ain't anything and he thinks that means it ain't anything whereas what it means is that we finally can invent: a new alphabet first, big letters, proud, new letters from which will come new words for old things, real things, and the bait says what they are and what they mean, and then we get new novels in which the goal is to tell the truth: deep truth. So make it all up, the whole new thing, to be able to say what's there; because they are keeping it hidden now. You're not supposed to write something down that happened; you're supposed to invent. We'll write down what happened and invent the personhood of who it happened to; we'll make a language for her so we can tell a story for her in which she will see what happened and know for sure it happened and it mattered; and the boys will have to confront a new esthetic that tells them to go suck eggs. I am for this idea; energized by it. It's clear that if you need the fisherman to read the book— his critical appreciation as it were—this new art ain't for you. If he's got what he did to you written on him or close enough to him, rude enough near him, is he different, will he know? I say he'll have to know; it's the brilliance of the medium—he's it, the vehicle of political and cultural transcendence as it were. It's a new, forthright communication—they took the words but they left your arm, your hand, so far at least; it could change, but for now; he's the living canvas; he can refuse to understand but he cannot avoid knowing; it's your blood, he spilled it, you've used it: on him. It's a simplicity Artaud failed, frankly, to achieve. We'll make it new; *épater* the fuckers. Then he can be human or not; he's got a choice, which is more than he ever gave; he can put on the uniform, honest, literal Nazi, or not. The clue is to see what you don't have as the starting place and you look at it straight and you say what does it give me, not what does it take; you say what do I have and what don't I have and am I making certain presumptions about what I need that are in fact their presumptions, so much garbage in my way, and if I got rid of the garbage what then would I see and could I use it and how; and when. I got hope. I got faith. I see it falling. I see it ending. I see it bent over and hitting the ground. And, what's even better is that because the fisherman ain't going to listen as if his life depended on it we got a system of secret communication so foolproof no scoundrel could imagine it, so perfect, so pure; the less we are, the more we have; the less we matter, the more chance we get; the less they care, the more freedom is ours; the less, the more, you see, is the basic principle, it's like psychological jujitsu except applied to politics through a shocking esthetic; you use their fucking ignorance against them; ignorance is a synonym in such a situation for arrogance and arrogance is tonnage and in jujitsu you use your opponent's weight against him and you do it if you're weak or poor too, because it's all you have; and if someone doesn't know you're human they're a Goddamn fool and they got a load of ignorance to tip them over with. You ain't got *literature* but you got a chance; a chance; you understand—a chance; you got a chance because the bait's going to get it, and there's going to be a lot of wriggling things jumping off God's stick. I live in this real fine, sturdy tenement building made out of old stone. They used to have immigrants sleeping in the hallways for a few pennies a night so all the toilets are out there in the halls. They had them stacked at night; men sleeping on top of each other and women selling it or not having a choice; tenement prostitution they call it in books, how the men piled in the halls to sleep but the women

236

had to keep putting out for money for food. They did it standing up. Now you walk through the hall hoping there's no motherfucker with a knife waiting for you, especially in the toilets, and if you have to pee, you are scared, and if you have to shit, it is fully frightening. I go with a knife in my hand always and I sleep with a knife under my pillow, always. I have not had a shit not carrying a knife since I came here. I got a bank account. I am doing typing for stupid people. I don't like to make margins but they want margins. I think it's better if each line's different, if it flows like a poem, if it's uneven and surprising and esthetically nice. But they want it like it's for soldiers or zombies, everything lined up, left and right, with hyphens breaking words open in just the right places, which I don't know where they are. I type, I steal but less now, really as little as possible though I will go to waitress hell for stealing tips, I know that, I will be a prisoner in a circle of hell and they will put the faces of all the waitresses around me and all their shabby, hard lives that I made worse, but stealing tips is easy and I am good at it as I have been since childhood and when I have any money in my pocket I do truly leave great chunks of it and when I am older and rich I will be profligate and if I ever go broke in my old days it will be from making it up to every waitress alive in the world then, but this generation's getting fucked unavoidably. Someday I will write a great book with the lines moving like waves in the sea, flowing as much as I want them. I'm Andrea is what I will find a deep way to express in honor of my mama who thought it up; a visionary, though the vision couldn't withstand what the man did to me early; or later, the man, in the political sense. I make little amounts of money and I put them in the bank and each day I go to the bank for five dollars, except sometimes I go for two days on seven dollars. I wait in line and the tellers are very disturbed that I have come for my money. It's a long walk to the bank, it's far away because there aren't any banks in the neighborhood where I live, and it's a good check on me because it keeps me from getting money for frivolous things; I have to make a decision and execute it. When an emergency occurs, I am in some trouble; but if I have five dollars in my pocket I feel I can master most situations. My astrology said that Mercury was doing some shit and Saturn and things would break and fall apart and I went to unlock the two locks on my door to my apartment and the first lock just crumbled, little metal pieces fell as if it was spiders giving birth, all the little ones falling out of it, it just seemed pulverized into grains and it just was crushed to sand, the whole cylinder of the lock just collapsed almost into molecules; and the second lock just kept turning around and around but absolutely nothing locked or unlocked and then there was this sound of something falling and it had fallen through the door to the other side, it just fell out of the door. It was night, and even putting the chain on didn't help. I sat with my knife and stared at it all night to keep anyone from breaking in. The crisis of getting new locks made me destitute and desperate and on such occasions I had to steal. I always considered it more honorable to myself than fucking; less honorable to who I did it to; it was new to pick me over them. I just knew I'd live longer stealing than fucking. Of course I stole from the weak; who doesn't? I had thought fucking for money was stealing from the strong but it only robbed me, although I can't say of what, because there's more wordlessness there, more what's never been said; I'm not formulated enough to get at it. I had a dog someone dumped on me saying they were going to have it killed. It was so fine; you can weave affirmation back, there can be a sudden miracle of happiness; my dog was a smiling, happy creature; I thought of her as the quintessential all-Amerikan, someone wholly extroverted with no haunted insides, just this cheerful, big, brilliant creature filled with licks and bounces; and I loved what made her happy, a stick, a stone, I mean, things I could actually provide. I think making her happy was my happiest time on earth. She was big, she bounced, she was brown and black, she was a German shepherd, and she didn't have any meanness in her, just play, just jump, just this joy. She didn't have a streak of savagery. If there was a cockroach in the apartment, a small one because we didn't have the monsters, she'd stand up over it and she'd study it awhile and then she'd pick it up in her mouth and she'd carry it to her corner of the room and she'd put it down and sit on top of it. She'd be proud and she'd sit with her head held high while the awful little thing would crawl out from under her and get lost in some crack in the wall. You ever seen a proud dog? They have this look of pride that could break your heart like they done something for you the equivalent of getting you out from under an avalanche and they are asking nothing in return, just that you look at the aquiline dignity of their snouts. I got to say I loved her more than my heart could bear and we'd go on walks and to the park but the park near me was full of broken glass and winos and junkies and I was afraid for her, that she'd hurt her feet. You couldn't really let her run or anything. She ate a lot, and I didn't, but I felt she had certain rights, because she depended on me or someone, she had to; so I felt I had to feed her and I felt I had to have enough money and I felt her life was in my hands and I felt her life was important and I felt she was the nicest, most kind creature I ever knew. She'd sit with me and watch the door when the locks fell apart but she didn't grasp it and I couldn't count on her sense of danger, because it wasn't attuned to the realities of a woman's life. Someone might be afraid of her or not. Someone might hurt her. I'd die if they hurted her. I'd probably have throwed myself on her to protect her. I just couldn't bear the thought of someone hurting her. Her name was Gringo, because the man who had her and who named her wasn't a fine, upstanding citizen, he was degenerate, and I was afraid he would hurt her, and I was afraid she would die, and I think there is nothing worse than knowing an animal is being hurt, except for a child, for which I thank God I don't have one, even though my husband would have taken it away from me, I know. If something's in your charge and it must love you then for something cruel to happen to it must shatter your heart into pieces, by which I mean the pain is real and it is not made better by time because the creature was innocent and you are not; or I am not. I kept her fine. I kept her safe. I kept her sleek and beautiful and without any sores or any illnesses or any bad things on her skin or any marks; I kept her gleaming and proud and fine and fed; I kept her healthy and I kept her strong and I kept her happy; and she loved me, she did. It was a little beyond an ignorant love, I truly believe. She knew me by my reverence for her; I was the one that lit up inside every time my eyes beheld her. I never could train her to do anything but sit; usually I said sit a second after she had done it, for my own self-respect; and she pulled me about one hundred miles an hour down the street; I loved her exuberance and could not condemn it as bad behavior; I loved that she was sweet and extrovert and unhaunted and I didn't want any shadows forming on her mind from me shouting or pulling or being an asshole in general; I couldn't romp but my heart jumped when she bounced and wagged and waved and flew like some giant sparrow heading toward spring; and I counted on the respect pricks have for big dogs to keep me safe but it didn't always, there was always ones that wanted to fight because she was big, because they thought she was more male than them, bigger than them, stronger than them, especially drunks or mean men, and there was men in the park with bigger dogs who wanted their dogs to hurt her or fight with her or mount her or bite her or scare her or who made me move by threatening to set their dog on her to show their dog was bigger or meaner or to make me move because I was gash according to them and they was men. It's simple and always the same. I moved with a deep sense of being wronged. I shouldn't have had to move but I couldn't risk them hurting her—more real life with a girl and her dog who are hurting no one. The toilet was too small to take her into and I couldn't leave her loose in the hall because some man upstairs, a completely sour person, hated her and kept threatening to call all these different city agencies with cops for animals that would take her away; but probably I wouldn't have left her there anyway because I'd be afraid something unexpected would happen and she'd be helpless; so she had to stay in the apartment when I went to the toilet and I locked the door to protect her. It's unimaginable, how much I loved her. She was so deep in my heart I would've died for her, to keep her safe. Every single piece of love I had left in me was love for her; except for revolutionary love. You become the guardian of a creature and it becomes your soul and it brings joy back to you, as if you was pure and young and there was nothing rough or mean and you had tomorrow, really. She made me happy by being happy and she loved me, a perfect love, and I was necessary, beyond the impersonal demands of the revolution per se. I had always admired the Black Panthers, with a certain amount of skepticism, because I been on the streets they walked and there's no saints there, Mao's long march didn't go through Camden or Oakland or Detroit or Chicago. I didn't get close with Huey until I saw a certain picture. I think it will be in my brain until I die. I had admired him; how he created a certain political reality; how he stood up to police violence, how he faced them down, then the Survival Program, free food for children, free shoes, some health care, teaching reading and writing; it was real brilliant; and he just didn't die, I mean, you fucking could not kill him, and I admire them that will not die. I knew he had run women but I also been low; I couldn't hold it against him; I couldn't hold anything against him, really, because it's rough to stay alive and reach for dignity at the same time; you can fucking feed children on top of that and you got my respect. I stayed aloof, also because I wasn't some liberal white girl, middle-class by skin, I had to take his measure and I couldn't do it through public perceptions or media or propaganda or the persona that floated through the air waves. I saw him do fucking brilliant things; I mean, you got to know how hard it is to do fucking anything; and I saw him survive shootings, the police were trying to assassinate him, no doubt; and I saw him transcend it; and I saw him build, not just carry a fucking gun. Then there's this picture. He's been shot by the police and he's cuffed to a gurney in an emergency room at Kaiser Hospital, October 1967. His chest is bare and raised; it's raised because his arms are cuffed to the legs of the gurney, pulled back towards his head; he's wounded but they pulled his arms back so his chest couldn't rest on the gurney, so he's stretched by the manacles, his chest is sticking up because of the strain caused by how his arms are pulled back and restrained, it would hurt anyone, I have been tied that way, it hurts, you don't need a bullet in you for it to give you pain, there's a white cop in front of him, fully dressed, fully armed, looking with surprise at the camera, and there's this look on Huey's face, half smile, half pain, defiant, his eyes are open, he ain't going to close them and he ain't going to die and he ain't going to beg and he ain't going to give in and he ain't thinking of cutting his losses and he ain't no slobbering, frightened fool, and behind him there's a white nurse doing something and a sign that says "Dirty Needles And Syringes Only," and she ain't looking at him at all, even though he's right next to her, right against her side almost. I have been cuffed that way, physically restrained. I have been lying there. I have memories when I see this picture, I see my life in some of its aspects, I see a hundred thousand porn magazines too in which the woman, some woman, is cuffed the same way, and the cop is or isn't in the photograph, and the cuffed woman is white or black, and I see on Huey's face a defiance I have never seen on her face or on my own, not that I have seen mine but I know what the photo would show, a vapid pain, a blank, hooded stare, eyes that been dead a long, long time, eyes that never stared back let alone said fuck you. I see that he is defiant and that the cop is scared and that the cop has not won. I see that even though Huey's chest is raised because his arms are stretched back and he is cuffed there is pride in that raised chest. I see that his eyes are open and I see that there is a clearness in his eyes, a willfulness, they are not fogged or doped or droopy. I see that he is looking directly at the camera, he's saying I am here, this is me, I am, and the camera can't take his picture without making his statement. I see that there is no look of shame or coyness on his face, he ain't saying fuck me. I see that his nakedness is different from mine, that his pride is unknown to me. I see that the cop and the nurse are barely existing and that Huey is vivid and real and alive, he's jumping off the page and they are robots, ciphers, automatons, functionaries, he's bursting with defiance, the raised chest, however painful, is bursting with pride. I wonder if anyone would ever jerk off to the picture; you know, black boy in chains; but I don't believe they would, I don't, he's nobody's piece of meat, his eyes wouldn't let you and you'd worry what he'd do when he's uncuffed later, his eyes would see you and he'd come to get you and you'd know it in your heart and in your hand. He's oppressed. He didn't learn to read really until he was eighteen. He's been low; he knows. He's put together a grassroots organization that's defying the cops; he's made it international in scope, in reach, in importance. He's poor. He was born socially invisible but darling look at him now; manacled on that gurney he is fully vivid and alive and the white nurse and the white cop are simply factotums of power with nothing that is their own; the life's with him. They got nothing that does express *I am*; whereas Huey, shot,

243

manacled, naked down to his waist, says *I am* with his strange, proud smile that shows the pain and his clear, wide-open eyes that don't look away but look right through you, they see you front to back; and I've been on that bed, it's the bed of the oppressed, the same cuffs, the same physical pain, as bad, I think as bad, the same jeopardy, I have been on that bed; and they want him to give in and fade away and yet he has endured and in the picture he is declaring that he will endure, it is in every aspect of his demeanor and the camera shows it, he's wounded but he's not afraid, he's manacled but he's not surrendering; he ain't fucked; he just ain't fucked; there's no other way to say it. Even if he's been fucked in his life, by which I mean literally, because I don't know what he's done or not done and there's not too many strangers to being fucked on the street, he ain't been fucked; it ain't what he is. I love him for it. I fucking love him for it. He's spectacular and there is a deep humanism in him that expresses itself precisely in surviving, not going under, standing up; even tied down, he's standing up; and he's gone beyond the first steps, the original Black Panther idea that had to do with arming against police violence, now he's an apostle of social equality and he is fucking feeding the children; he's been physically hurt and he's been laid out on the bed of pain and his idea of what's human has gotten broader and kinder and more inclusive, and that's revolutionary love, and I know it, and I got it, and while there's many reasons he can't trust me, nor me him, we have been on the same bed of pain, cuffed, and I didn't have his pride, and I need him to teach me; I need to learn it—defiance, the kind a bullet can't stop. I don't know if he's kind to women or not and it worries me but I put it aside because there's what I know about that bed of pain he's cuffed to; I think I'm annihilated inside by it; I think I'm shot to hell inside, with nothing but gangrene everywhere there was a wound; I see, I feel, an inner collapse that comes from the humiliation of how they do you on the bed of pain; bang bang. I tell him I know the man; but I don't know if he knows what I mean. I know the man. He acts to me with respect as if he grasps my meaning. I am trying to say, without saying, that the man fucked me too; but I don't know how to say I became it and he didn't and now I'm refusing to be it or I'm in the process and that there's profound injustice in making someone it, in crushing them down so their insides are fucked in perpetuity. I die for men to admire, from a stance of parity; I admire Huey; I am struggling for parity, what I see as his revolutionary dignity and self-definition, his bravery—not in defying authority, I been through that, but in upending the reality that said what he was and what was on top of him. He sends me poems and maxims, and I am thinking whether to send him some. I love him. I think maybe he could be for women. In some speeches he says so. He says men have been arrogant over women and there's new freedoms women need to have. During the days I type for four dollars an hour, which means that if I am prepared to go ape-shit or stir crazy I could certainly make up to thirty-two dollars a day, on some days; but I can only stand to do it four hours or maybe three, and I really couldn't stand to do it every day, although I have tried to for the money, I have tried; if I could do three hours every day I would be fine, unless something happened. It's just that I do it and I do it and I do it and not much time has elapsed it turns out and I get bored and restless as if my mind is physically lifting itself out of my head and hitting the walls like some trapped fly. I feel a profound distaste for it, sitting there and doing this stupid shit. I feel a bitterness, almost guilt or remorse, it's unbearable in the minute or at that time as if I'm betraying being alive, there's too much moving in me and I cannot fucking waste it in this chickenshit way. It's not a matter of having an idea of a picture of life, or taking exception to the idea of typing or being a secretary or doing something of the sort, I don't have some prior idea of how I should be or how life should be, a magazine picture in my head, you know, or from television, or from the romances other people say they want. It ain't a thought in any sense at all. It's that I am not her and I cannot be her, I fucking am not her, I can't do it, I can't sit still and type the shit. It's just that I want what I want, which is throughout me, not just my brain, and it's to feel and move and fuck. I don't try to resolve it. I figure you have to be humble before life. Life tells you, you don't tell it, and you can't argue with what won't sit still long enough to be argued with. I have to break loose one way or another, drink or fuck, find some real noise, you know, a fucking stream of real noise and messing around to jump right in; that's my way. If it's tepid I don't want it and I don't do it from habit or just because it's there to be done, it's a big change I made in myself, I have to feel it bad, I don't do nothing on automatic; people think if it's on the bad side it ain't bourgeois but I don't; I think if it's tepid it don't matter what it is class-wise or style-wise. I don't solve things in my mind to impose it on reality, because it ain't worth much to do so; for instance, to say you don't want to be some fucked thing so don't fuck. Fucking never feels like you will end up some fucked thing anyway; it pushes you out so fast and so far it ain't a matter of what you think and it's stupid to misidentify it, the problem. You're some poor, fragile person in the middle of an ocean you never seen the whole of; you don't know where it starts or where it stops or how deep down it goes and what you got to do is swim and hope, hope and swim; you learn everything you know from it, it don't learn a fucking thing from you. You can make promises to yourself in your mind but your mind is so small up against the world; you got to have some respect for the world; or so I see and that's my way; but, then, I ain't holding out for a pension. I type my hours, however many I can make it through, putting as much pressure on myself as I can stand, which isn't making a lot of progress, and I keep a time sheet, which I make as honest as possible but it is hard not because I want to lie but because I just fucking cannot keep track, I can't pay enough attention to it to keep track, so I just approximate sort of combining what I need with what seems plausible and I come up with something. I cannot write every fucking thing down to keep track of my time as if I'm some asshole and I find it profoundly unbearable to do robot stuff. Sometimes I work for a writer, a poet, and I deliver packages, which at least means I go on subways and taxis and see places, and I file papers away alphabetically and I type, except she says you have to put a space before the colon and a space after it, one space after it instead of just no space before it and two spaces after it as every typist does. In theory I am for defying convention but typing is something you do automatic like you're the machine, not it, and you learn to put two spaces after the colon and none before it and your hands do that and your brain ain't fast enough to stop them and I spend half my time correcting the stupid thing with white Liquid Paper and eraser stuff and trying to align it right when I'm typing the colon back in and I just really want her to drop dead because of it. Passions can be monumental. I can barely keep my ass on the typing chair at her desk; I mean, she owns the desk; she has her desk, a big desk, and then the desk where I sit, a little desk and her desk is in her big room and my desk is in a little anteroom right off her big room so she can always see me but I'm off to the side, relegated to being help in a clear way; it has its own eloquence and I feel it acutely and it gets me mad. I try to take the typing home with me so I don't have to sit at the little desk in the little room with her watching but she wants me to do it there and there's this tug of war. She's real seductive and I am too fucking bored to care because if I give in to it then I will have to be there more and if I am there more I will have to type more and if I have to type more I will die.

247

There's apparently some edge she sees; she thinks I'm turbulent, she says; I think I'm calm and patient in a world of endless and chaotic bullshit, which I say but it falls on deaf ears; I smile and I'm nice and completely calm except for when I have to bolt but she sees some street tough or something wild and gets all excited and I don't have a lot of respect for it; she says I'm pure. I just smile because I don't know what bullshit it is exactly. Even if I don't type she keeps me around. I can barely keep myself under wraps sometimes, frankly; I want to bolt. I smile, I'm nice, I'm calm, but she treats me careful, as if I'm volatile or dangerous somehow, which I am not, because in my soul I am a real sweetheart which is the truth, a deep truth, an honest truth, I don't yell or shout or think how to hurt people and I feel dedicated to peace as she is too. I just get bored so deep it hurts the pits of me, stomach and groin precisely, I feel a long pain and I can't sit still through it; it's hit-the-road pain. She tells me how to be a writer and I listen because as long as I am listening I don't have to type; I listen, though often I'm bored, and I haven't mastered the art of inner stillness, though I will, I am sure. Then there's the lovemaking part, a moment comes, and I slide out from under, with a certain newfound grace, I must say, and if I can't slide, I bolt, and it's abrupt. She keeps me on, even though I never exactly get the typing done or the filing done and she never nails me; never. It's a long walk to her place to type and I walk it often, because I fucking love to walk, even though it's stupid and not safe and you have to be a prophet who can look down a street and know what it's got in store for you, and I do it happy and proud and I fucking love the long walks. I go there and back early and late and sometimes I get there and I just can't bear to stay so I leave right away, I take some cup of coffee or food, fast, with her, she'll always make me something as if it's natural, and the typing doesn't get done but I don't have some money either. Other times she gives me a cash advance and I

248

have it burning in my hand and if I'm feeling slow and
stringent with myself I get it to the bank and if I'm feeling
restless, all speeded up, wanting to spit in the eye of God, out
drink Him, out fuck Him, I keep it on me. I type, I walk long
walks across town, ballets on cement, jumping and hopping
and then a slow, melancholy step, solemn or arms swinging,
in the face of the wind or in drizzle or rain or in sun, in calm,
cool sun. I walk my sweet and jubilant dog in the neighborhood protecting the pads of her feet from the stupid glass the
winos leave all broken all over and the fucking junkie shit
that's all over, and then there's the time each day I sit down in
purposeful concentration to write in a notebook, some
sentences on a buried truth, an unnamed reality, things that
happened but are denied. It is hard to describe the stillness it
takes, the difficulty of this act. It requires an almost perfect
concentration which I am trying to learn and there is no way to
learn it that is spelled out anywhere or so I can understand it
but I have a sense that it's completely simple, on the order of
being able to sit still and keep your mind dead center in you
without apology or fear. I squirm after some time but it ain't
boredom, it's fear of what's possible, how much you can
know if you can be quiet enough and simple enough. I move
around, my mind wanders, I lose the ability to take words and
roll them through my brain, move with them into their
interiors, feel their colors, touch what's under them, where
they come from long ago and way back. I get frightened
seeing what's in my own mind if words get put to it. There's a
light there, it's bright, it's wide, it could make you blind if you
look direct into it and so I turn away, afraid; I get frightened
and I run and the only way to run is to abandon the process
altogether or compromise it beyond recognition. I think about
Céline sitting with his shit, for instance; I don't know why he
didn't run, he should've. It's a quality you have to have of
being near mad and at the same time so quiet in your heart that

you could pass for a spiritual warrior; you could probably break things with the power in your mind. You got to be able to stand it, because it's a powerful and disturbing light, not something easy and kind, it comes through your head to make its way onto the page and you get fucking scared so your mind runs away, it wanders, it gets distracted, it buckles, it deserts, it takes a Goddamn freight train if it can find one, it wants calming agents and soporifics, and you mask that you are betraying the brightest and best light you will ever see, you are betraying the mind that can be host to it; Blake's light, which he was not afraid of and did not betray; Whitman's light which he degraded into some fucking singsong song like he was Dinah Shore or Patti Page, how much is that doggie in the window; the words didn't rise up from the light, only from a sentimental wish, he had a shadow life and in words he piled shadow on shadow so there's this tumult, a chaos of dreams running amok; dreams are only shadows; whereas Blake's light is perfect and pure, inside the words, so lucid, so simple, so plain; never a cartoonish lie. Of course it's different for me because I turned tricks and been fucked nearly to death and I have been made weary with dirt and my mind's been buried alive, really, smashed down right into the ground, pushed under deep; but something ain't different if I could conquer the fear of seeing and knowing, if I wasn't so afraid of the light burning right through my stupid brain. You want to smoke a joint or something to make it calmer and duller; not brighter; it ain't brighter; it calms you right down or it frenzies you up but so you are distracted, mentally moving here and there, you want something between you and the light, a shield, a permeable barrier, you want to defuse it or deflect it, to mellow it out, to make it softer, not so deadly to your own soul, not so likely to blow all your own circuits, you can't really stand too much light in a world where you got to get used to crawling around like an insect in the dark, because it's like mining coal in that if you don't get out of the mine what goes through you will collapse you. Your mind does stupid tricks to mask that you are betraying something of grave importance. It wanders so you won't notice that you are deserting your own life, abandoning it to triviality and garbage, how you are too fucking afraid to use your own brain for what it's for, which is to be a host to the light, to use it, to focus it; let it shine and carry the burden of what is illuminated, everything buried there; the light's scarier than anything it shows, the pure, direct experience of it in you as if your mind ain't the vegetable thing it's generally conceived to be or the nightmare thing you know it to be but a capacity you barely imagined, real; overwhelming and real, pushing you out to the edge of ecstasy and knowing and then do you fall or do you jump or do you fly? Life can concentrate itself right in your head and you get scared; it is cowardice. I notice that my eyes start to wander across the wall, back and forth, keep wandering across nothing, or looking at the fucking paint, I notice that my feet are moving and I'm shifting on the chair, a straight-back wood chair you have to sit still on, there's no license to move but I'm moving, rattling my feet, rocking, rocking on my heels, and then there's an urgent sensation in my thighs and in my hips and wherever sex is down there, whatever you want to call it, there's only bad names for it but it isn't bad and it is real and it sends you out, it sends you away, it makes you impatient and distracted, and I feel like busting out, and some nights I do, I bust out. I take all the money I got on me, and if it's ten dollars I'm flush, and I just bolt, I get out and drink, I find a man, sometimes a woman, sometimes both, I like both at once, I like being drunk, or I start out just for a drink and I end up with someone, drunk; fucking happy drunk; no light but everything glistens; no illumination but everything shines. Sometimes I just walk, I can walk it off, aimlessly. It's as dangerous as fucking, takes nearly the same adrenaline, just to take a walk at night, even if you walk towards the neon and not towards the dark park; ain't a woman in Amerika walks towards the park. If I can calm myself I go home. But there's times if I was a man I'd kill someone. I feel wild and mean and I'm tired of being messed with, I got invisible bars all around me and I have blame in my heart to them that put them there and I want to fucking tear them apart, I want my insides turned out in bruising them, I don't want no skin left on me that ain't roughed them up, I want them bloodied, I want to dance in men's blood, the cha-cha, the polka, the tango, the rhumba, hard, fast, angular dances or stomping dances or slow killing dances, the murder waltz, I want to mix it up with killing right next to me, on my side; it's hot in my heart and cold in my brain and I ain't ever going to feel sorry; or I'd take one of them boys and I'd turn him inside out and put something up his ass and I'd hear him howl and I'd expect a thank-you and a yes ma'am; and I would get it. Don't matter how dangerous you feel, all the danger's to you, so it's best to settle down and end up back inside your stupid fucking walls that you wanted so much; alone, inside the walls, a Valium maybe or a 'lude so you don't do no damage to yourself; love your walls, citizen. I want them bruised and bloodied but I don't get what I want as my mama used to tell me but I didn't believe her; besides I wanted something different then; her point was that I had to learn the principle that I wasn't supposed to get what I wanted; and my point was that I wasn't going to learn it. You don't name someone not-cunt and then betray the meaning and make them fit in cages; I didn't learn it, fucking bitch of a mother. It's a rainy night. The rain is slick over the cement and on the buildings like diamonds dripping; a liquid dazzle all soft and rolling and swelled up, like a teardrop. It's one of them magic nights where the rain glows and the neon is dull next to it; like God lit a silver flame in the water, it's a warm, silver, glassy shine, it sparkles, it's a night but it ain't dark because it's a slick light you could skate on and everything looks translucent and as if it's moving, it slides, it shines. It's beckoning to me as if God took a paint brush and covered the world in crystal and champagne. It's wet diamonds out there, lush and liquid, I never could pass up the sparkle, it's a wet, shimmering night, a wet, dazzling night; but warm, as if it's breathing all over you, as if it's wrapped around you, a cocoon, that wispy stuff. If there's acid in your brain everything's fluid and monstrous bright; this is as if the acid's out there, spread over the city, the sidewalks are drenched in it and the buildings are bathed in it and the air is saturated with it, nothing's standing still and it is monstrous bright and I love the fucking city when it's stoned. Inside it's dull and dry and I'm not in a constructive mood and there is a pain that runs down me like a river, a nasty, surging river, a hard river, a river that starts up high and races down to below falling more than flowing, falling and breaking, shattering; it's a river that goes through me top to bottom; the pain's intractable and I can barely stand it; it's not all joie de vivre when a girl goes dancing; the pain's a force of nature beyond my ability to bear and I can't take the edge off it very easy and I can't stand needles and I can't sit still with it and I can't rip it out, although if it was located right precisely in my heart I would try, I would take my fucking hands and I would take my fucking fingers and I would rip my chest open and I would try. It's raining and the rain makes me all steamy and damp inside and out and it ain't a man I want, it's a drink, a dozen fucking drinks to blot out the hard pain and the hard time, each and every dick I ever sucked, and the bottle ain't enough because I can't stand the quiet, a quiet bottle in a quiet room; I can't stand the quiet, lonely bottle in the quiet, lonely room. Lonely ain't a state of mind, it's a place of being; a room with no one else in it, a street with no one else on it; a city abandoned in the rain; empty, wet streets; cement that stretches uptown, downtown, empty, warm, wet, until the sky starts, a perspiring sky; empty cars parked on empty streets, damp, deserted streets lined with dark, quiet buildings, civilized, quiet stone, decorous, a sterile urban formalism; the windows are closed, they're sleeping or dead inside, you won't know until morning really, a gas could have seeped in and killed them in the night; or invaders from outer space; or some lethal virus. I need noise; real noise; honest, bad noise; not random sounds or a few loud voices or the electronic drone of someone's television seeping out of a cracked window; not some dignified singer or some meaningful lyric; not something small or fine or good or right; I need music so loud you can't hear it, as when all the trees in the forest fall; and I need noise so real it eats up the air because it can't live on nothing; I need noise that's like steak, just so thick and just so tough and just so immoral, thick and tough and dead but bloody, on a plate, for the users, for the fucking killers, to still their hearts, to numb anything still left churning; a percussive ambience for the users. It's got to be brute so it blocks out anything subtle or nuanced or kind, even, and it's got to be unceasing so you can't hear a human breath and it's got to stomp on you so your heart almost stops beating and it's got to be lunatic, unorganized, perpetual, and it has to be in a crowded room where there's gristle and muscle and cold, mean men and you can't hear the timbre of their voices and you don't need to see them or touch them because the noise has you, it's air, it's water, you breathe, you swim; I need noise, and it's too late to buy a bottle anyway, even if I had enough money, because it is very dear, it would be like buying a diamond tiara for a princess or some fine clothes, a fine jewel, it is out of my reach, I have not had one of my own ever and I don't count the bottles you can't see in the paper bags because that is a different thing altogether, more like gasoline or like someone took matches and lit up your throat or you're pouring kerosene down it or some sharp-edged thing scrapes it raw. I need enough bills to keep drinking so no one's going to chase me away or say I can't pay rent on the stool or so I don't have to smile at no one or so no bartender don't have me thrown out; I am fearful about that; they always treat you so illegitimate but if you can show enough money they will tolerate you sitting there. There's not enough money for me to eat even if they'd let me so I put that out of my mind, I would like lobster of course with the biggest amount of drawn butter, just drenched in it, just so much it drips down and you can feel it spreading out inside your mouth all rich and glorious, it's like some divine silky stuff but there's never enough of it and I have to ask for more and they act parsimonious and shocked. If you sit at a table you have to buy dinner, they don't have some idea that you could just sit there and be cool and watch or have a little of this and a little of that; they only have the idea that everyone's lying, you know, everyone's pretending, everyone's trying to rip them off, everyone's pretending to be rich so they have to see the money or everyone's pretending they're going to eat so they have to see the money or everyone's pretending they can pay for the drinks so they have to see the money and if you're a woman you don't get a table even if you got money; my idea is if I have enough money and I put it out in front of me on the bar and I keep drinking and drinking I can stay there and then I don't have to look to my right or to my left at a man for a fucking thing; I can if I want but I am not obliged. I'm usually too shy to push my way in and I've never tried it, I just know you're not supposed to be there alone, but tonight I want to drink, it's what I want like some people want to win the Indy 500 or there's some that want to walk on the moon; I want to drink; pure. I want to sit there and have my own stool and I don't want to have to be worried about being asked to leave or made to leave because I'm just some impoverished girl or gash that's loose. I will stare at the clear liquid, crystal, in the glass, and I will contemplate it as a beautiful thing and I will feel the pain that is monumentally a part of me and I will keep drinking and I will feel it lessen and I will feel the warmth spread out all over me inside and I will feel the surging, hard, nasty river go warmer and smoother and silkier as the Stoli runs with it, as it falls from top to bottom inside me, first it's on the surface of the river, then it's deeper down in it, then it's a silk, burning stream, a great, warm stream, and it will gentle the terrible river of pain. I will think deeply; about art; about life; I will keep thoughts pouring through me as inside I get warmer and calmer and it hurts less, the hurt dims and fades or hides under a fucking rock, I don't care; and my brow will curl, you know, sullen, troubled, melancholy, as if I'm some artist in my own right myself; and the noise will be beautiful to me, part of a new esthetic I am cultivating, and I will hear in it the tumult of bare existence and the fierce resonance of personal pain as if it's a riff from Charlie Parker to God and I will hear in it the anarchic triumph of my own individual soul over the deep evil that has maimed me. I take the bills and crush them into my pocket and I walk, I run, I light down the stairs and out the building, I leave my quiet room, and I hit the streets and I walk, fast, dedicated, determined, stubborn, filled with fury, spraying piss and vinegar, to Max's, about twelve blocks from where I live, an artists' restaurant and bar, because I know it will be filled with ramrod hard noise and heat, a crush of hard, noisy men, artists and poseurs and I don't know the difference, poseurs and the famous and I don't know the difference, it's a modern crime but I can't concentrate on it enough to remember the ones you're supposed to know, except Warhol because he's so strange and he'd stand out anywhere and I don't want to go near him; but the difference mostly is that I think I am the artist, not them, but you can't say that and it's hard even to keep thinking it though I don't know why it's so hard, maybe because girls aren't ever it; but all the poseurs and

all the famous will be at the tables where I can't go, even if I
had money to eat they wouldn't let me eat there, not alone,
and I won't be one of the pleading girls who is begging to be
allowed to go to the tables, I will just get a stool at the bar if the
guy at the door lets me in, he might not and usually I am too
shy to defy him and I hang tight with a man but tonight I want
in myself, I want the noise and the hard edge and the crush and
I want to drink, I want to find a place at the bar for myself and
it's got my name on it even though I don't got no name for the
purposes of the man at the door but the stool's mine and I will
drink and I will stay as long as I have bills in front of me and it's
an unwritten law about girls, that they don't let you sit
anywhere, so you never quite understand why you can be
somewhere sometimes and not the same place the next time
and you figure out you got to hang on to a man and you are his
shadow, like Wendy sewing Peter Pan's shadow back on. It
sure insures a steady flow of affection woman to man if you
can't even sit down without one. Tonight I have a singular
distaste for a man. I'm not starting out with any interest
whatsoever. He'd have to catch my eye like starlight or it'd
have to be like fairy dust where you want some and you need a
taste, it's something that tickles you deep down but you can't
reach it to scratch, like the cut of a record you listen to a
thousand times or you got a taste you can't get rid of so you're
like some fucking hamster on one of them wheels just running
and running or you're skimming coke off the top of something or smack off the top of something, you just get smitten,
lightly but completely, stuck in the moment but also riveted
so you can't shake it loose, infatuated now, freedom now,
there's some special charge coming from him and you're
plugged in and it's sparking, it's not like you want to get laid
and you're looking for someone who's going to be good, it's
more like some trait you can't identify strikes you wham, it's
got an obsession lurking under it, it's a light feeling but under

it is a burning habit, a habit you ain't got yet but you just want to play with it once, like skinpopping heroin or something, you know, it ain't serious but you want it. I take an energetic walk with the city all glowing wet, all sparkling, for me, as if it's for me, the light's for me and the rain's for me and it's stoned out of its fucking mind for me; and the buildings are just pure glitter and the light's coming down from heaven luscious and wet; for me. The boy at the door can't keep me out because I stride in and I am aglow; he's a mandarin standing there with his little list and his leather jacket and his pretensions and his snobbish good looks and I mumble words I know he can't hear and I never yet met a man who wasn't stupider than me and he's trying to decide am I someone or not and I am not fucking anyone but I am striding in my motorcycle boots and I am wet and I am bound for glory at the bar and I push my way through the crowd and fuck him and he's watching me, he sees that I ain't headed for a table which would transgress the laws of the universe, and it ain't a girl's trick to sit somewhere she ain't entitled because a man didn't pick her out already; he sees I want the bar and I suppose it's faintly plausible that a girl might want a drink on her own or it confuses him enough that he hesitates and he who hesitates is lost. I take out all the bills I have and he's watching me do it and I put it down in front of me, a nice pile, substantial, and I am firmly sitting on a stool and I have spread my elbows out on the bar to take up enough space to declare I am alone and here to drink and he don't know I don't have more money and I order my Stoli on the rocks and I ain't making no move to take my change or move my money so he relaxes as if letting me there will not do monumental harm to the system that is in place and that it is his job to protect and the bodies close in around me to protect me from his scrutiny and the noise closes in around me and I am swallowed up and I disappear and I am completely cosseted and private and safe and I feel like some new thing, just newly alive, and there's the placenta hugging me and I'm wet with fucking life and I stare into my fucking drink, my triumphal drink, I stare into it as if it's tea leaves and I'm the world's oldest, wisest gypsy, I got gold earrings down to my knees and I got foresight and hindsight and I am a reader of history, there's layers of history, vulgar and occult, in the stuff and if you lit a fire to it you'd burn history up. And shit I love it; a solitary human being covered all over by noise, a dense noise that bubbles and burns and cracks all over you like fire, small fire, a million tiny, exploding fires; or a super-human embrace by some green, slimy, scaly monster, it's big and all over you and messy, it's turbulent and dramatic and ever so much bigger than a man and its embrace is over-whelming, a descent, an invasion that covers the terrain, a crush of locusts but you aren't repelled, only exhilarated at how awesome it is, how biblical, how spectacular; like as if it took you back to ancient Egypt and you saw something sublime in the desert and you had to walk across it but you could; it wraps itself around you like some spectacular excess of nature not man, you're crawling with it but it ain't bad and it ain't loathsome and there's no fear, it's just exactly extreme enough and wild enough and it says it's nighttime in human history now in Amerika and Moses has his story and you have yours and each of you gets the whole universe to roll around in because everything was made to converge at the point where you are amidst all the rest of life of whatever kind, composi-tion, or characteristics, it's a great mass all around you, the blob, a loud blob, Jell-O, loud Jell-O, and you're some frail, simple thing at the center and what you are to them doesn't matter because the noise protects you from knowing what you are to them; noise has a beauty and noise has a function and a quiet girl sometimes needs it because the night is long and life is hard and pain is real and you stare into the glass and you drink, darling, you drink, and you contemplate and you drink; you go slow and you speed up and you drink; and you are a deep thinker and you drink; and you have some hazy, romantic thoughts and some vague philosophical leanings and you drink; and you remember some pictures that flash by in your mind and you drink; and there's sad feelings for a fleeting minute and you drink; and you choreograph an uprising, the lumpen rise up, and you drink; and there's Camden reaching right out for you, it's taking you back, and you drink; a man nudges you from the right and you drink; he puts his face right up close to yours and you drink; he's talking about something or other and you drink; you don't look left or right, you just drink, it's worship, it's celebration, you'd kneel down except for that you might not be able to synchronize your movements, in your heart you kneel; and you drink; you taste it and you roll it around your tongue and down on into your throat and down on into your chest and you get fiery and warm and you drink it down hard and fast and you sit stone still in solemn concentration and you drink; the noise holds you there, it's almost physical, the noise, it's a superhuman embrace, bigger than a man's, it's swamp but not swampy, it's dry and dark and hot and popping, it's dense and down and dirty and you drink; the noise keeps you propped up, your back upright and your legs bent and your feet firmly balanced on the stool, except the stool's higher now, and you drink; and you're like Alice, you're getting smaller and it's getting bigger, and then you remember Humpty Dumpty was a fucking eggshell and you could fall and break and Dorothy got lost in Oz and Cinderella was made into a pumpkin or nearly such and there's a terrible decline and fall awaiting you, fear and travail, because the money's gone, you been handing it over to the big man behind the bar and you been drinking and you been contemplating and the pile's gone and there's terrible challenges ahead, like physically getting off the stool and physically getting out of the room and physically getting home; it hardly seems possible that you could actually have so many legs and none of them have any bones that stand up straight and you break it down into smaller parts; pay up so the bartender don't break your fingers; get off the stool; stand up; walk, try not to lean on anyone, you can't use the men as leaning posts, you can't volley yourself to the front sort of springing off one after the other, because one or another will consider it affection; get to the door; don't fall on the mandarin with the list, don't trip in front of him, don't throw up; open the door on your own steam; get out the door fully clothed, jacket, T-shirt, keys; once outside, you make another plan. These are hard things; some of them may actually be impossible. It may be impossible to pay the bartender because you may have drunk too much and it may be impossible to get off the stool and it may be impossible to walk and it may be impossible to stand up and it may be impossible to find the door. It's sad, you're an orphan and it's hard to concentrate, what with poor nutrition and a bad education; but sociology will not save your ass if you drank more money than you got because a citizen has to pay their bar bills. There's two dollars sitting on the bar in front of you, the remains of your pile like old bones, fragments of an archaic skeleton, little remnants of a big civilization dug up and you're eyeing it like it's the grail but with dishonorable intent and profane desire. It's rightly the bartender's. He's been taking the money as it's been due with righteous discipline, which is why you ain't overdrawn on the account; you asked him in a tiny mouse voice afraid of the answer, you squeaked in the male din, a frightened whisper, you asked him if you owed, you got up the nerve, and you're straight with him as far as it goes but these extra bills are rightly his; or you could have another drink; but you had wanted to end it well, with some honor; and also he ain't a waitress, dear, and the money's got his mark on it; and he ain't cracked a smile or said a tender word all night, which a girl ain't used to, he don't like girl drinkers as a matter of principle you assume, he's fast, he's quiet, he's got a hard, cold face with a square jaw and long, oily hair and a shirt half open and a long earring and bad teeth and he's aloof and cold to you; and then suddenly, so fast it didn't happen, there's a big, warm hand on your hand, a big, hairy hand, and he's squeezing your fingers around the two dollars and he's half smiling, one half of his face is smiling, and he says darling take a fucking cab. You stare at him but you can't exactly see him; his face ain't all in one piece; it's sort of split and moving; and before you exactly see his mouth move and hook it up with his words he's gone, way to a foreign country, the other end of the bar where they're having bourbon, some cowboys with beards and hats. Life's always kind in a pinch. The universe opens up with a gift. There's generosity, someone gives you something special you need; two dollars and you don't have to suck nothing, you are saved and the man in his generosity stirs you deeply. You're inspired to succeed with the rest of the plan—move, stand, walk, execute each detail of the plan with a military precision, although you wish you could take off your T-shirt because it's very hot but you follow the plan you made in your mind and although your legs buckle and the ground isn't solid, it's swelling and heaving, you make it past the strange, wavy creatures with the deep baritone voices and the erections and you get out, you get out the door even though it's hard and you're afraid because you can see outside that it's raining, it's raining very hard, it's pouring down, it's so wet, you really have an aversion to it because all your clothes will be drenched and soaking and your lungs will be wet and your bones will get all damp and wet and you can't really see very well and the rain's too heavy and everything looks different from before and you can't really see through the rain and it's getting in your eyes as if your eyes are under water and burning, all drowned in water, they hurt, and everything's blurred and your hair's all wet as if it won't ever be dry again and there's water in your ears deep down and it hurts and everything's chilly and wet. The world's wet and watery and without definition and without any fixed places of reference or fixed signs and it's as if the city's floating by you, like some flood uprooted everything and it's loose on the rapids and everywhere you step you are in a flood of racing cold water. Your feet are all wet and your legs are all wet and you squoosh in your boots and all your clothes are soaked through and you are dripping so much that it is as if you yourself are raining, water's flooding off you and it's useless to be a person with legs who counts on solid ground because here you have to walk through water, which isn't easy, you're supposed to swim through it but there's not enough to swim through and there's too much to walk through, it's as if you're glued and gummy and loose and the ground's loose and the water's loose and you're breathing in water as much as air and you feel like some fucking turkey that's going to drown in the rain; which probably you will. You're trying to walk home and it's been a long time, the old trick of putting one foot in front of the other doesn't seem to be working and you don't seem to have got very far but it's hard to tell since nothing looks right or familiar and everything's under water and blurry and you're cold and sort of fixed in place because the water's weighing you down, kind of making you so heavy you can't really move as if you're an earthbound person moving effortlessly through air as is the case with normal people on normal days because it ain't air, it's water. You're all wet as if you was naked and your clothes are wet and heavy as if they was lead and your breasts are sore from the wet and the cold and your pubic hair's all wet and rubbing up against the wet stuff all bunched up in your crotch and there's rain rolling down your legs and coming out the bottom of your pants and you'd be happier naked, wet and naked, because the clothes feel very bad on you, wet and bad. They're heavy and nasty and cold. The money's in your hand and it's all wet, all rained out, soaking wet, and your hand's clutched, and you try proceeding through the wet blur, you need to stay on the sidewalks and you need to avoid oncoming cars and turning cars and crazy cars that can't see any better than you and you need to see the traffic lights and you need to see what's in front of you and what's on the side of you and what's behind you, just as on any regular day, and at night even more; but you can't see and the rain keeps you from hearing as well and you proceed slowly and you don't get too far; it's been a long time you been out here and you haven't gone but half a block and you are drenched in water and breathing too fast and breathing too hard and your legs aren't carrying you right and the ground's not staying still and the water's pushing you from behind and it'd like to flatten you out and roll over you, and it ain't nice lapping against the calves of your legs; and a cab stops; which you have barely ever ridden in before, not on your own; it stops; you've been in them when someone's given you money to deliver packages and said where to go and exactly what to do and how much it would cost and still you were scared it would cost too much and you wouldn't have it and something terrible would happen; a cab stops and you don't know if two dollars is enough or if he thinks you're turning tricks, a dumb wet whore, or if he just wants to fuck or if you could get inside and he'd just take you home, a passenger; a cab stops and you're afraid to get in because you're not a person who rides in cabs even in extremis even though you have two dollars and it's for taking a cab as the bartender said if you didn't dream it and probably he knows how much everything costs; a cab stops; and you're wet; and you want to go home; and if you got in the cab you could be home almost right away, very close to right away, you could be home in just some few minutes instead of a very long time, because if you walk you don't know how long it will take or how tired you'll be and you could get so tired you just stop somewhere to give up, a doorway, an abandoned car, or even if you keep going it will take a long time; and if you got in the cab you could sit still for a few minutes in perfect dignity and it would be dry and quiet and you would be in the back, a passenger, and you could jump if he pulled shit, if he started driving wild or going somewhere strange, and you'd give him the two dollars and he'd take you home, and you get in the cab, it's dark and leather and you're scared about the money so you say upfront that you only got two dollars and he asks where you're going and you say and he says fine, it's fine, it's okay, it's no problem, and he says it's raining and you say yeah, it is; and he says some quiet, simple things, like sometimes it rains too hard, and you say yes; he's quiet and softspoken and there's long, curly hair cascading down his back and he says that I'm wet with some sympathy and I say yes I am; and he asks me what I do in a quiet and sympathetic way and I say I'm a writer; and he says he's a musician, very quiet, nice; and I say I drank too much, I was writing and I got restless and I got drunk and he says yes he knows what that's like, very quiet, very nice, he's done it too, everyone does it sometimes, but he doesn't keep talking, he's very quiet, he talks soft, not a lot, and there's quiet moments and I think he's pretty nice and I'm trying to watch the streets to see where we are and we're going towards where I live but up and down blocks, it doesn't seem direct but I don't know because I don't drive and I don't know if there's one-way streets and the meter's off anyway and he's English like in films with a distinguished accent, sort of tough like Albert Finney but he talks quiet and nice, a little dissonant; he's sort of slim and delicate, you know how pretty a man can be when he's got fine features, chiseled, and curls, and he's sort of waif-like, kind of like a child in Dickens, appealing with a pull to the heart, street pretty but softspoken, not quite hard, not

apparently cynical, not a regular New York taxi driver as I've
seen them, all squat and old, but graceful, lithe, slight, young,
younger than me probably, new, not quite used but not
untouched, virginal but available, you can have him but it isn't
quite right to touch him, he's withdrawn and aloof and it
appears as a form of refinement, he's delicate and finely made,
you wonder what it would be like to touch him or if he'd be
charmed enough to touch you back, it's a beauty without
prettiness except this one's pretty too, too pretty for me, I
think, I never had such a pretty, delicate boy put together so
fine, pale, the face of an old, inbred race, now decadent,
fragile, bloodless, with the heartrending beauty of fine old
bones put together delicately, reconstructed under glass, it
wouldn't really be right to touch it but still you want to, just
touch it; and you couldn't really stop looking at him in the
mirror of the taxi, all the parts of his face barely hang together,
all the parts are fragile and thin, it's delicate features and an
attitude, charm and insouciance but with reserve, he puts out
and he holds back, he decides, he's used to being wanted, he's
aloof, or is it polite, or is it gentle? He turns around and smiles
and it's like angel dust; I'm dusted. I get all girlish and
embarrassed and I think, really, he's too pretty, he doesn't
mean it, and there's a real tense quiet and we drive and then he
stops and we're there and I hand him the two dollars because
we agreed and he says real quiet, maybe I could come in, and I
say yes, and I'm thinking he's so pretty, it's like being in a
movie with some movie star you have a crush on only he's
coming with you and it's not in a movie but you know how a
crush on someone in a film makes you crazy, so weird, as if
you could really touch him even though he's flat and on film
and the strange need you think you have for him and the things
you think you would do with him, those are the feelings,
because I have a stupid crush, an insane crush, a boy-crazy
crush, and I am thinking this is a gorgeous night with the

visitation of this fine boy but I am so fucking drunk I can barely get up the steps and I think he'll turn around and go because it can't be nice for him and now he can see how drunk; smashed; as if I got Stoli pumping through my heart and it's fumes I'm inhaling, fumes rising out of my own veins or rising from my chest, like a fog rising out of my chest, and I am falling down drunk and such a fool, in my heart I am romantic for him, all desire and affection verging on an impolite hunger, raw, greedy, now, now, but there's my beautiful dog, my very gorgeous and fine dog, my heart, my beast of joy and love, my heart and soul, my friend on romps and good times around the block, and she's jumping up and down and she's licking me and she's jumping all over me and it makes me fall and I say I have to walk her because I do, I must, she's got rights, I explain, I have this idea she's got rights, and I think he will leave now but he says, very quiet and nice, oh I'll walk her, you just lie here, and I am flat out drunk, laid out drunk, flat and drunk on my bed, a mattress on the floor, barely a mattress, a cut piece of foam rubber, hard and flat, it's an austere bed for serious solitude or serious sex and I am fucking stretched out and the walls move, a fast circle dance, and he takes her leash and they leave and I'm smiling but time goes by and I get scared, I start waiting, I start feeling time brushing by me, I start thinking I will never see my dog again and I think what have I done and I think I will die from losing her if he doesn't bring her back and I think I have to call the police or I have to follow him and find him or I have to get up and get out and call to her and I think about life without her if she were gone and I'd die and I try to move an arm but I can't move it and there's a pain coming into my heart which says I am a pale shadow of what you will feel the rest of your life if she's gone, it says you'll mourn the rest of your life and there's a grief that will burn up your insides and leave them just bare and burned and empty, burned ugly and barren, obliterated; and I know that if she's gone I'm going to pull myself to pieces, pull my mind apart, tear myself open, rend my breast, turn my heart to sackcloth, make ashes out of my heart; if she's gone I'm lost; a wanderer in madness and pain; despondent; a vagabond turned loose one last time, sad enough to turn the world to hell; I'll touch it, anything before me, and make it hell. I will rage on these streets a lifetime and I will build fires from garbage in buildings and I will hurt men; for the rest of my time here on earth, I will hurt them. I will wander and I will wail and I will break bottles to have shards of glass I can hold in my hand so they cut both ways, instead of knives, I'll bleed they will bleed both at the same time, the famous two-edged sword, I will use them on curly-haired boys and I will keep on after death and I will never stop because the pain will never stop and you won't be able to erase me from these streets, I will sweep down like lightning except it will be a streak of blood from the shard of glass that cuts both ways, and I will find one and he will bleed. I've got this living brain but my body's dead, won't move, it's inert, paralyzed, couldn't move to save me or her but once I can move I will begin the search, I will find her, my dog; without her, there's no love. It's as if I drank some poison that's killed my muscles so they can't move and time's going by and I'm counting it, the minutes, and I'm waiting, and my heart is filling up with pain, suffering is coming upon me; and remorse; because I did it, this awful thing that made this awful loss. Then they're there, him and her, and she's laughing and playing with her leash and he's smiling and happy and I'm thinking he's beautiful, inside too, in spirit, and I am near dying to touch him, I want to make real love, arduous, infatuated love touched by his grace, and I'm wondering what he will be like, naked and fine, intense, first slow, now; and I reach for him and he pulls me up so I'm on my knees in front of him and he's standing on the mattress and he takes his cock out and I'm thinking I'll hold it and he wants it in my mouth and I'm thinking I will kiss it and lick it and hold it in my mouth and undress him as I do it and I'm thinking how happy and fine this will be, slow, how stopped in time and tender, he holds my head still by my hair and he pushes his cock to the bottom of my throat, rams it in, past my throat, under it, deeper than the bottom, I feel this fracturing pain as if my neck shattered from inside and my muscles were torn apart ragged and fast, an explosion that ripped them like a bomb went off or someone pushed a fist down my throat but fast, just rammed it down, and I feel surprise, this one second of complete surprise in which, without words, I want to know the meaning of this, his intention; there's one second of awesome, shocking surprise and then I go under, it's black, there's nothing, coma, death, complete black under the ground or past life altogether in a region of nothing without shadows of life or memory or dreams or fear or time, there's nothing, it's perfect, cold, absolute nothing. When I wake up I think I am dead. I begin to see the walls, barely, I barely see them, and I see I'm in a room like the room I was in when I was alive and I think this is what death is like, the same but you're dead, the same but you stay here forever alone, the same walls but you barely see them and the same place where you died, the same body, but it's not real, it's not alive, it doesn't feel real, it's cold and shadowy and you're there alone for all the rest of time cut off from the living and it's empty, your dog's not here in the room in death, in the cold, shaky, shadowy room, it's an imitation in shadows of where you were but it's empty of her and you will be here alone forever, lonely for her, there's no puppies with the dead, no solace; you wake up and you know you're dead; and alone. Only my eyes move but they barely see, the walls look the same but I barely see them; time's nothing here; it stands still; it's not changing, never; you're like a mummy but with moving eyes scanning the shadowy walls, but barely seeing them; and then the pain comes; the astonishing pain, like someone skinned the inside of your throat, took a knife and lifted the skin off inside so it's raw, all blood, all torn, the muscles are ripped open, ragged, stretched and pulled, you're all ripped up inside as if you had been torn apart inside and under your throat there's a deep pain as if it's been deep cut, deep sliced, as if there's some deadly sickness down there, a contagion of long-suffering death, an awful illness, a soreness that verges on having all the nerves in your body up under your throat and someone's crushed broken glass into them and there's a physical anguish as if someone poured gasoline down your throat and lit it; an eternal fire; deep fire; deep pain. I felt the pain, and as the pain got sharper and deeper and stronger and meaner, the walls got clearer, I saw them clearer and they stayed still, and as the pain got worse, crueler, I could feel the bed under me and my old drunk body and I figured out that I was probably alive and time had passed and I must of been out, in a coma, unconscious, suspended in nothing except whatever's cold and black past actual life, and I couldn't move and I wanted my dog but I couldn't call out for her or make any sound, even a rasping sound, and I couldn't raise myself up to see where she was although in my mind I could see her all curled up in her corner of the room at the foot of the mattress, being good, being quiet, how she curled her head around to her tail and the sweet, sad look on her face, how she'd just sit thinking with her sweet, melancholy look and I hoped she'd come and lick me and I wondered if she needed to be walked again yet but if she did she'd be around me and I'd manage it, I swear I would, and I wondered if she was hungry yet and I made a promise in my heart never to put her in danger with a stranger again, with an unknown person, never to take a chance with her again, I couldn't understand what kind of a man it was because it wasn't on my map of the world and I ain't got a child's map, did he like it, to ram it down to kill me, a half second brutality of something off the map that didn't even exist anywhere even between men and women or with Nazis; and I don't know if he did other things, I can't feel nothing or smell nothing, he could have done anything, I don't feel nothing near my vagina, I try to feel with my fingers, if it's wet, if it's dirty, if it hurts, but everything's numb except my throat, the hurt of it, I'm thinking he could have done anything, fucked me or masturbated on me or peed on me, I wouldn't know, I'm feeling for semen or wet places with my fingers but I can't move because my throat can't move or the pain implodes, there can't be a single tremor even, I can't lift myself up and I know I'll never know and I push it out of my mind, that I will never know; I push it out and I am pulled under by the pain because my throat's crushed into broken bits and it's lit with kerosene and the fire's spreading up my neck to my brain, a spreading field of fire going up into my cranial cavity and it's real fire, and probably the pain's seeping out onto the floor and spreading, it's red and bloody or it's orange and hot; penis smashed me up; I fall back into the cold, black nothing, grateful; and later I wake up, it's night but I don't know of what day except my dog would've come by me, I'd remember her by me, but I wake up and it's hollow, my life's hollow, I got an empty life, I'm alive and it's empty, she's gone, I raise myself up on my elbow and I look, I keep looking, there's a desolation beyond the burdens of history, a sadness deeper than any shame. I'll take the physical pain, Lord, I deserve it, double it, triple it, make it more, but bring her back, don't let him hurt her, don't make her gone. I look, I keep looking, I keep expecting her, that she will be there if I look hard enough or God will hear me and the boy will walk through the door saying he just walked her and I pray to just let him bring her back, just let him walk in the door; just this; days could go by and I wouldn't know; he'll be innocent in my eyes, I swear. I hallucinate her and I think she's with me and I reach out and she's not real and then I fall back into the deep blackness and when I wake up I look for her, I wait for her; I'm waiting for her now. My throat's like some small animal nearly killed, maimed for religious slaughter, a small, nearly killed beast, a poor warm-blooded thing hurt by some ritual but I never heard of the religion, there's deep sacrifice, deep pain. I can't move because the poor thing'd shake near to torture; it's got to stay still, the maimed thing. I couldn't shout and I couldn't cry and I couldn't whisper or moan or call her name, in sighs, I couldn't whisper to myself in sighs. I couldn't swallow or breathe. I sat still in my own shit for some long time, many, many days, some months of days, and I rocked, I rocked back and forth on my heels, I rocked and I held myself in my arms, I didn't move more than to rock and I didn't wash and I didn't say nothing. I swallowed down some water as I could stand it, I breathed when I could, not too much, not too soon, not too hard. If he put semen on me it's still there, I wear it, whatever he did, if he did it I carry it whatever it is, I don't know, I won't ever know, whatever he did stays done, anything he tore stays torn, anything he took stays gone. I look for her; I scan the walls; I stare; I see; I know; I will make myself into a weapon; I will turn myself into a new kind of death, for them; I got a new revolutionary love filling my heart; the real passion; the real thing. Ché didn't know nothing, he was ruling class. Huey killed a girl, a young prostitute, seventeen; he was pimping but she wasn't one of his. He was cruising, slow, in a car. Baby, she called out, baby, oh babe. He shot her; *no one calls me baby*. She said baby; he said cunt. Some of them whisper, a term of endearment; some of them shout. There's gestures more eloquent than words. She said something, he said something, she died. Sister child, lost heart, poor girl, I'll avenge you, sister of my heart. Did it hurt or was death the easy part? I don't know what my one did, except for taking her; but it don't matter, really, does it? Not what; nor why; nor who; nor how.

TEN

April 30, 1974
(Age 27)

Ma. Ssa. Da. Ma. Ssa. Da. Ma. Ssa. Da. Hear my heart beat.
Massada. I was born there and I died there. There was time;
seventy years. The Jews were there, the last ones, the last free
ones, seventy years. The zealots, they were called; my folks,
my tribe; how I love them in my heart. Never give in. Never
surrender. Slavery is obscene. Die first. By your own hand; if
that's what it takes; rather than be conquered; die free. No
shame for the women, they used to say; conquered women;
shame. Massada. I used to see this picture in my mind, a
woman on a rock. I wrote about her all the time. Every time I
tried to write a story I wrote there is a woman on a rock, even
in the eighth grade, there's a woman, a strong woman, a fierce
woman, on a rock. I didn't know what happened in the story. I
couldn't think of a plot. I just saw her. She was proud. She was
strong. She was wild by our standards or so it seemed, as if
there was no other word; but she didn't seem wild; because she
was calm; upright; with square shoulders, muscled; her eyes
were big and fearless and looked straight ahead; not like
women today, looking down. She was ancient, from an old
time, simple and stark, dirty and dark, austere, a proud,
unconquerable woman on a rock. The rock towers. The rock
is barren; nothing grows, nothing erodes, nothing changes; it
is hard and old and massive. The rock is vast. The rock is
majestic, high and bare and alone; so alone the sun nearly
weeps for it; isolated from man and God; unbreachable; a

towering wall of bare rock, alone in a desert where the sun makes the sand bleed. The sun is hot, pure, unmediated by clouds or sky, a white sun; blinding white; no yellow; there's a naked rock under a steaming, naked sun, surrounded by molten, naked sand. It's a rock made to outlast the desert, a bare and brazen rock; and the Dead Sea spreads out near it, below it, touching the edge of the desert that touches the edge of the rock. Dead rock; dead water; a hard land; for a hard people; God kept killing us, of course, to make us hard enough; genocide and slavery and rape were paternal kindnesses designed to build character, to rip pity out of you, to destroy sentimentality, your heart will be as barren as this rock when I'm done with you, He said; stern Father, a nasty Daddy, He made history an incest on His children, slow, continuous, generation after generation, a sadistic pedagogy, love and pain, what recourse does a child have? He loves you with pain, by inflicting it on you, a slow, ardent lover, and you love back with suffering because you are helpless and human, an imprisoned child of Him caged in the world of His making; it's a worshipful response, filled with awe and fear and dread, bewildered, why me, why now, why this, why aren't You merciful, why aren't You kind; and because it's all there is, this love of His, it's the only love He made, the only love He lets us know, ignorant children shut up in Daddy's house, we yearn for Him and adore Him and wait for Him, awake, afraid, shivering; we submit to Him, part fear, part infatuation, helpless against Him, and we thank Him for the punishment and the pain and say how it shows He loves us, we say Daddy, Daddy, please, begging Him to stop but He takes it as seduction, it eggs Him on, He sticks it in; please, Daddy. He didn't rest on the seventh day but He didn't write it down either, He made love, annihilation is how I will love them. You might say He had this thought. It was outside the plan. The six days were the plan. On the seventh He stretched

Himself out to take a big snooze and a picture flashed through His mind, a dirty picture, annihilation is how I will love them, and it made everything work, it made everything hang together: everything moved. It was like putting the tide in the ocean. Instead of a stagnant mass, a big puddle, there was this monstrous, ruthless thing gliding backwards and forwards at the same time and underneath the planet broke, there were fissures and hurricanes and tornadoes and storms of wind, great, carnivorous storms; everything moved; moved and died; moved, killed, and died. On the seventh day He made love; annihilation is how I will love them; it was perfect and Creation came alive animated by the nightmare of His perfect love; and He loved us best; of all His children, we were the chosen; Daddy liked fucking us best. That Christ boy found out; where are You, why have You forsaken me; common questions asked by all the fucked children loved to death by Daddy. At Massada we already knew what He wanted and how He wanted it, He gloried in blood. We were His perfect children; we made our hearts as bare and hard and empty as the rock itself; good students, emblematic Jews; pride was prophecy. Nearly two thousand years later we'd take Palestine back, our hearts burned bare, a collective heart chastened by the fire of the crematoria; empty, hard. Pride, the euphemism for the emotions that drove us to kill ourselves in a mass suicide at Massada, the nationalist euphemism, was simple obedience. We knew the meaning of the Holy Books, the stories of His love, the narrative details of His omnipresent embrace; His wrath, orgasmic, a graphic, calculating treachery. Freedom meant escape from Him; bolting into death; a desperate, determined run from His tormenting love; the Romans were His surrogates, the agents of slavery and rape, puppets on the divine string. It was the play within the play; they too suffered; He loved them too; they too were children of God; He toyed with them too; but we were

275

Daddy's favorite girl. We had the holy scrolls; and a synagogue that faced towards Jerusalem, His city, cruel as is befitting; perpetual murder, as is befitting. The suicide at Massada was us, His best children, formed by His perfect love, surrendering: to Him. Annihilation is how I will love them; He loved loving; the freedom for us was the end of the affair, finally dead. Yeah, we defied the Romans, a righteous suicide it seemed; but that was barely the point; we weren't prepared to have them on top, we belonged to Him. Everything was hidden under the floor of a cell that we had sealed off; to protect the holy scrolls from Roman desecration; to protect the synagogue from Roman desecration; we kept His artifacts pure and hidden, the signs and symbols of His love; we died, staying faithful; only Daddy gets to hurt us bad; only Daddy gets to put His thing there. First we burned everything we had, food, clothes, everything; we gathered it all and we burned it. Then ten men were picked by lot and they slit the throats of everyone else. Then one man was chosen by lot and he slit the throats of the other nine, then his own. I have no doubt that he did. There were nearly a thousand of us; nine hundred and sixty; men, women, children; proud; obedient to God. There was discipline and calm, a sadness, a quiet patience, a tense but quiet waiting for slaughter, like at night, how a child stays awake, waiting, there is a stunning courage, she does not run, she does not die of fear. Some were afraid and they were held down and forced, of course; it had to be. It was by family, mostly. A husband lay with his wife and children, restrained them, their throats were slit first, then his, he held them down, tenderly or not, and then he bared his throat, deluded, thinking it was manly, and there was blood, the way God likes it. There were some widows, some orphans, some lone folks you didn't especially notice on a regular day; but that night they stood out; the men with the swords did them first. It took a long time, it's hard to kill nearly

276

a thousand people one by one, by hand, and they had to hurry because it had to be done before dawn, you can do anything in the dark but dawn comes and it's hard to look at love in the light. We loved God and we loved freedom, we were all God's girls you might say and freedom, then as now, was in getting sliced; a perfect penetration, then death; a voluptuous compliance, blood, death. If you're God's girl you do it the way He likes it and He's got special tastes; the naked throat and the thing that tears it open, He likes one clean cut, a sharp, clean blade; you lay yourself down and the blade cuts into you and there's blood and pain; and the eyes, there's a naked terror in the eyes and death freezes it there, you've seen the eyes. The blood is warm and it spreads down over you and you feel its heat, you feel the heat spreading. Freedom isn't abstract, an idea, it's concrete, in life, a sliced throat, a clean blade, freedom now. God's girl surrenders and finds freedom where the men always bragged it was; in blood and death; only they didn't expect it to be this way, them on their backs too, supine, girlish; God's the man here. There's an esthetic to it too, of course: the bodies in voluntary repose, waiting; the big knife, slicing; the rich, textured beauty of the anguish against the amorphous simplicity of the blood; the emotions disciplined to submission as murder comes nearer, the blood of someone covers your arm or your shoulder or your hand and the glint of the blade passes in front of your eyes and you push your head back to bare your throat, slowly so that you will live longer but it looks sensual and lewd and filled with longing, and he cuts and you feel the heat spreading, your body cools fast, before you die, and you feel the heat of your own blood spreading. Was Sade God? Maybe I was just seventy; I was born on the rock but the adults who raised me were new to it and awkward, not native to the rock, still with roots down below, on softer ground; I died there, a tough one, old, tough skin from the awful sun, thick and leathery, with deep furrows

277

like dried up streams going up my legs and up my arms and creasing my face, scarified you might say from the sun eating up my skin, cutting into it with white hot light, ritual scars or a surgeon's knife, terrible, deep rivers in my skin, dried out rivers; and maybe I'd had all the men, religion notwithstanding, men are always the same, filled with God and Law but still sticking it in so long as it's dark and fast; no place on earth darker than Massada at night; no boys on earth faster than the Jews; nice boys they were, too, scholars with the hearts of assassins. Beware of religious scholars who learn to fight. They've been studying the morals of a genocidal God. Shrewd and ruthless, smart and cruel, they will win; tell me, did Massada ever die and where are the Romans now; profiles on coins in museums. A scholar who kills considers the long view; will the dead survive in every tear the living shed? A scholar knows how it will look in writing; beyond the death count of the moment. Regular soldiers who fight to kill don't stand a chance. The corpses of all sides get maggots and turn to dust; but some stories live forever, pristine, in the hidden heart. They prayed, the Jewish boys, they made forays down the rock to fight the Romans until the military strength of the Romans around the rock was unassailable, they took a little extra on the side when they could get it, like all men. I probably had my eye on the younger ones, twenty, virile, new, they had no memory of being Jews down on the low ground, they had only this austere existence, they were born here of parents who were born here of parents who either were born here or came here young and lived their adult years on this rock. Sometimes Jews escaped the Romans and got here, made it to the top; but they didn't bring profane ideas; they stripped themselves of the foreign culture, the habits of the invaders; they told us stories of Roman barbarism, which convinced us even more; down below the Romans were pigs rolling in shit, above we were the people of God. No one here doubted it, especially not the young men; they were pure, glowing, vibrant animals lit up by a nationalism that enhanced their physical beauty, it was a single-minded strength. There were no distracting, tantalizing memories of before, below. We lived without the tumult of social heterodoxy, there was no cultural relativism as it were. The young men were hard, cold animals, full of self-referential pride; they had no ambivalence, no doubt; they had true grit and were incapable of remorse; they lived in a small, contained world, geographically limited, flat, all the same, barren, culturally dogmatic, they had a few facts, they learned dogma by rote, it was a closed system, they had no need for introspection, there were no moral dilemmas that confronted them, troubled them, pulled them apart inside; they were strong, they fought, they prayed but it was a form of nationalism, they learned racial pride, they had the thighs of warriors, not scholars, and they used them on women, not Romans, it was the common kind of killing, man on girl, as if by being Jews alone on this desolate rock, isolated here, they were, finally, like everyone else, all the other men, ordinary, like Romans, for instance; making war on us, brutal and quick if not violent, but they beat women too, the truth, finally, they did. The sacred was remote from them except as a source of national pride; pure Jews on a purely Jewish rock they had a pure God of the Jews, His laws, Holy Books, the artifacts of a pure and superior nation. The rock was barren and empty and soon it would be a cemetery and the bloodletting would become a story; nearly fiction, nearly a lie; abridged, condensed, cleaned up; as if killing nine hundred and sixty people, men, women, and children, by slicing their throats was an easy thing, neat and clean, simple and quiet; as if there was no sex in it and no meanness; as if no one was forced, held down, shut up; well, frankly, murdered; as if no one was murdered; as if it was noble and perfect, a bloodless death, a murderless murder, a mass suicide with universal consent, except for the women and the children; except for them. You get sad, if you understand. The men were purely male, noble and perfect, in behalf of all the Jews; the young ones especially, strong animals, real men, prideful men, physically perfect specimens dark and icy with glistening thighs, ideologically pure, racially proud, idealists with racial pride; pure, perfect, uncorrupted nationalists; beautiful fascists; cold killing boys; until God, ever wise, ever vicious, turned them into girls. I was probably an old woman making a fool of herself with memories and desires, all the natural grace and learned artifice of young women burned away by wear and tear and the awful, hot sun. Still, sometimes you'd like to feel one of the young ones against you, a last time, one last time; nasty, brutish, short. It's a dumb nostalgia. They never were very good, not the fathers, not the sons. Or maybe I was some sentimental old fool who'd always been a faithful wife, except once, I was lonely and he was urgent, and I had a dozen grandchildren so this rock knew my blood already, I had labored here, and now I sat, old, under the sun, and my brain got heated with foresight and grief and I saw them as they soon would be, corpses with their throats slit, and maybe I howled in pain, an animal sound, or I denounced them in real words, and the young men said she's an old fool, she's an old idiot, she's loony, ignore her, it's nonsense, and I tried to tell the girls and the children how they'd be killed soon, with the awful slice across the throat; these are fanatic boys, I said, driven by an idea, I said, it is murder, not suicide, what they will do to you; and they asked if it was the will of God and of course now I see why you must lie but I said yes, it's His will, always, that we should suffer and die, the will of God is wrong, I said, we have to defy the will of God, we have to defy the Romans and the Jews and the will of God, we have to find a way to live, us, you see, us; she's loony, they said; you'll be stretched out, I said, beautiful and young, too soon, dressed and ornamented, and your throats will be naked as if your husbands are going to use your mouths but it will be a sword this time, a real one, not his obscene bragging, one clean cut, and there will be blood, the way God likes. I didn't want to see the children die and I was tired of God. Enough, I said to Him; enough. I didn't want to see the women die either, the girls who came after me, you get old and you see them different, you see how sad their obedience is, how pitiful; you see them whole and human, how they could be; you see them chipped away at, broken bit by bit, slowed down, constrained; tamed; docile; bearing the weight of invisible chains; you see it is terrible that they obey these men, love these men, serve these men, who, like their God, ruin whatever they touch; don't believe, I say, don't obey, don't love, let him put the sword in your hand, little sister, let Him put the sword in your hand; then see. Let him bare his throat to you; then see. The day before it happened I quieted down, I didn't howl, I didn't rant or rave, I didn't want them to lock me up, I wanted to stay out on the rock, under the hot sun, the hot, white sun; my companion, the burning sun. I was an old woman, wild, tough, proud, strong, illiterate, ah, yes, the people of the Book, except for the women and girls, God says it's forbidden for us, the Book, illiterate but I wanted to write it down today, quiet, in silence, not to have to howl but to curl up and make the signs on the page, to say this is what I know, this is what has happened here, but I couldn't write, or read; I was an old woman, tough, proud, strong, fierce, quiet now as if dumb, a thick quiet, an intense, disciplined quiet; I was an old woman, wild, tough, proud, with square shoulders muscled from carrying, from hard labor, sitting on a rock, a hard, barren rock, a terrible rock; there was a woman sitting on a rock, she was strong, she was fierce, she was wild, she wasn't afraid, she looked straight ahead, not down like women now, she was dark and dirty, maybe mad, maybe just old, near naked with rags covering her, her hair was long and shining and dirty, a gleaming silver under the hot, white sun; but wild is perhaps not the right word because she was calm, upright, quiet, in intentional solitude, her eyes were big and fearless and she faced the world head-on not averting her eyes the way women do now; she could see; she didn't turn her eyes away. She was sitting on a hard, barren rock under a hot, white sun, and then the sun went down, got lower in the sky, lower and lower yet, a little lower; the sun got lower and the light got paler, then duller; the sun got low and she took a piece of rock, a sharp piece of rock, and she cut her throat; I cut my throat. No Romans; no fascist Jewish boys however splendid their thighs or pristine their ideals; no. Mine was a righteous suicide; a political refusal to sanction the current order; to say black was white. Theirs was mass murder. A child can't commit suicide. You have to murder a child. I couldn't watch the children killed; I couldn't watch the women taken one last time; throats bared; heads thrown back, or pushed back, or pulled back; a man gets on top, who knows what happens next, any time can be the last time, slow murder or fast, slow rape or fast, eventual death, a surprise or you are waiting with a welcome, an open invitation; rape leading, inexorably, to death; on a bare rock, invasion, blood, and death. Massada; hear my heart beat; hear me; the women and children were murdered, except me, I was not, when you say Massada you say my name, I discovered pride there, I outlined freedom, out from under, Him and him and him; let him put the sword in your hand, little sister, then see; don't love them; don't obey. It wasn't delirium; or fear; I saw freedom. Does Massada thrill you, do you weep with pride and sorrow for the honor of the heroes, the so-called suicides? Then you weep for me, I make you proud, the woman on the rock; a pioneer of freedom; a beginning; for those who had no say but their throats were ripped open; for the illiterate in invisible chains; a righteous suicide; a resistance suicide; mad woman; mad–dog suicide; this girl here's got a ripped throat, Andrea, the zealot, freedom is the theory, suicide the practice; my story begins at Massada, I begin there, I see a woman on a rock and I was born in blood, the blood from her throat carried by time; I was born in blood, the slit between the legs, the one God did Himself so it bleeds forever, one clean cut, a perfect penetration, the memory of Massada marked on me, my covenant with her; God sliced me, a perfect penetration, then left me like carrion for the others, the ones He made like Him, in His own image as they always say, as they claim with pride, or vanity I would say, or greed; pride is me, deciding at Massada, not Him or him or him. You're born in blood, washed in it, you swim out in it, immersed in it, it's your first skin, warm, hot on fragile, wrinkled, discolored flesh; we're born to bleed, the ones He sliced Himself; when the boys come out, the toy boys, tiny figurines made like Him, He has it done to them, symbolically, the penis is sliced so they're girls to Him; and the toy boy'll grow up pushing the cut thing in girls who are born cut open big, he'll need to stick it in and stick it in and stick it in, he doesn't like being one of God's girls even a little; and it's a memory, isn't it, you were girls to Me at Massada; a humiliation; think of the last ten, nine of them on their big knees, throats bared, one slice, the tenth sticks it up himself, there's a woman I saw in a porn magazine, she did that to herself, she smiled; did number ten, the big hero, smile, a coy look at God, heavy mascara around the eyes, a wide smile, the sword going in and somehow he fingers his crotch at the same time? The Christians wouldn't stand for it; they said Christ's the last one, he died for us so we don't need to be cut but God wants them sliced and they know it so they do it for health or sanitation as if it's secular garbage removal but in their hearts they know, God wants them cut, you don't get away with not being a girl for Him except you won't be His favorite girl. They take it out on us, all of them, sliced or threatened, sliced or evading it, enlisted or the equivalent of draft dodgers; manly men; fucking the hole God already made; He was there first; there are no virgin girls; the toy boys always get used goods. Their thing, little next to His, aspires to omnipresence; and Daddy watches; a perpetual pornography; blood-and-guts scenes of pushing and hitting and humiliation, the girl on the bed, the girl on the floor, the girl in the kitchen, the girl in the car, the girl down by the river, the girl in the woods, the girls in cities and towns, prairies and deserts, mountains and plains, all colors, a rainbow of suffering, rich and poor, sick and well, young and old, infants even, a man sticks it in the mouths of infants, I know such a man; oh, he's real; an uncle of mine; an adult; look up to him, listen to him, obey him, love him, he's your uncle; he was born in Camden but he left, smart, a big man, he got rich and prominent, an outstanding citizen; five infants, in the throat, men like the throat, his own children, it was a daddy's love, he did that, a loving daddy in the dark, and God watched, they like the throat, the smooth cavity of an infant's mouth and the tiny throat, a tight passage, men like it tight, so tiny; and the suction, because an infant sucks, it pulls and it sucks, it wants food but this food's too big, too monstrous, it sucks, it pulls it in, and daddy says to himself it wouldn't suck if it didn't like it; and Daddy watches; and the infant gags, and the infant retches, and the infant chokes; and daddy comes; and Daddy comes; the child vomits, chokes, panics, can't breathe, forever, a lifetime on the verge of suffocation. I don't have much of a family, I prefer the streets frankly to various pieties but sometimes there are these shrieks in the night, a child quaking from a crime against humanity, and she calls out, sister she says, he sliced my throat with a sword, I remember it but I don't, it happened but it didn't, he's there in the dark all the time, watching, waiting, he's a ghost but he isn't, it's a secret but why doesn't everyone know? How does an infant get out from under, Him and him; him; oh, he does it for a long time, it begins in the crib, then she crawls, a baby girl and all the relatives go ooh and ah and the proud papa beams, every night, for years, until the next one is born, two years, three years, four years, he abandons the child for the next infant, he likes infants, tiny throat, tight suction, helpless, tiny, cute thing that seems to spasm whole, you know how infants crinkle all up, their tiny arms and their tiny legs, they just all bunch up, one moving sex part in spasm with a tight, smooth, warm cavity for his penis, it's a tiny throat, and the infant sucks hard, pulls the thing in. Years later there are small suicides, a long, desperate series of small suicides, she's empty inside except for shadows and dread, sick with debilitating illnesses, no one knows the cause or the cure, she chokes, she gags, she vomits, she can't swallow; there's asthma, anxiety, the nights are saturated with a menace that feels real, specific, concrete, but you can't find it when you turn on the light; and eventually, one day or some day, none of us can swallow; we choke; we gag; we can't stop them; they get in the throat, deep enough in, artists of torment; a manly invasion; taking a part God didn't use first. If you're adult before they rape you there you've got all the luck; all the luck there is. The infants; are haunted; by familiar rapists; someone close; someone known; but who; and there's the disquieting certainty that one loves him; loves him. There are these women—such fine women—such beautiful women—smart women, fine women, quiet, compassionate women—and they want to die; all their lives they have wanted to die; death would solve it; numb the pain that comes from nowhere but somewhere; they live in rooms; haunted; by a familiar rapist; they whisper daddy; daddy, daddy, please; asleep or awake they want to die, there's a rapist in the room, the figure of a man invading, spectral, supernatural, real but not real, present but not there; he's invading; he's a crushing, smothering adversary; it's some fucking middle-class bedroom in some fucking suburb, there aren't invading armies here but there's invasion, a man advancing on sleeping children, his own; annihilation is how I will love them; they die in pieces inside; usually their bodies survive; not always, of course; you want God to help them but God won't help them, He's on the other side; there are sides; the suicides are long and slow, not righteous, not mass but so lonely, so alone; could we gather up all the women who were the little girls who were the infants and say do it now, end it now, one time, here; say it was you; say it happened to you; name names; say his name; we will have a Massada for girls, a righteous mass suicide, we could have it on any street corner, cement, bare, hard, empty; but they're alone, prisoners in the room with the rapist even after he's gone; five infants, uncle; it makes Auschwitz look small, uncle; deep throat, my uncle invented deep throat, a fine, upstanding man. I can do the arithmetic; five equals six million; uncle pig; uncle good Jew; uncle upstanding citizen; uncle killer fucking pig; but we have a heroic tradition of slaughtering children in the throat; feel the pride. I'll gather them up and show you a righteous suicide; in Camden; home; bare, hard, empty cement, hard, gray cement, cement spread out like desert rock, cement under a darker sun, a brooding sun, a bloody sun, covered over, burgundy melting, a wash of blood over it; even the sun can't watch anymore. There were brick houses the color of blood; on hard, gray rock; we come from there, uncle, you and I, you before me, the adult; you raped your babies in pretty houses, rich rooms; escaped the cement; they threw me down on the cement and took me from behind; but I'll bet you never touched a girl when you were a homeboy, slob; too big for you, even then, near your own size; we'll have Massada in Camden, a desolate city, empty and bare and hard as a rock; and I will have the sword in my hand and I will kill you myself; you will get down on your big knees and you will bare your throat and I will slice it; a suicide; he killed himself, the way they did at Massada; only this time a girl had the sword; and it was against God, not to placate Him. Every bare, empty, hard place spawns a you, uncle, and a me; homeboy, there's me and you. The shit escaped; into death; the shit ran away; died; escaped to the safe place for bandits, the final hideaway where God the Father protects His gang; they watch together now, Father and His boy, a prodigal son, known in the world of business for being inventive, a genius of sorts, known among infants as a genius; of torment; destruction; and I'm the avenging angel, they picked me, the infants grew up and they picked me; they knew it would take a Camden girl to beat a homeboy; you had to know the cement, the bare, empty rock; he was a skeleton when he died, illness devoured him but it wasn't enough, how could it be enough, what's enough for the Himmler of the throat? I know how to kill them; I think them dead for a long time; I make them waste away; for a long time; I don't have to touch them; I just have to know who they are; uncle, the infants told me; I knew. I was born in Camden in 1946 down the street from Walt Whitman, an innocent boy, a dreamer, one of God's sillier creatures, put on earth as a diversion, a kind of decoy, kind of a lyrical phony front in a covert war, a clever trick by rape's best strategist, he had God-given talent for God-given propaganda; the poet says love; as command; the way others say sit to a dog; love, children, love; or love children; the poet advocates universal passion; as command; no limits; no rightful disdain; humanity itself surges, there is a sweep of humanity, we are waves of ecstasy, the common man, and woman, when he remembers to add her; embrace the common man; we are a human family consecrated to love, each individual an imperial presence in the climactic collective, a sovereign unto himself; touch each other, without fear, and he, Walt, will touch everyone; every one of us; we all get loved by him, rolled up in him, rolled over by him; his thighs embrace us; he births us and he fucks us, a patriarch's vision, we take him in our mouths, grateful; he used words to paint great dreams, visionary wet dreams, democracy's wet dreams; for the worker and the whore; each and all loved by him; and in his stead, as he's busy writing poems, all these others, the common men, push it in and come; I loved him, the words, the dreams; don't believe them, don't love them, don't obey the program written into the poem, a series of orders from the high commander of pain; bare the throat, spread the legs, suck the thing; only he was shy, a nineteenth-century man, they didn't say it outright then; he said he wanted everyone, to have them, in the poems; he wanted to stick it in everywhere; and be held too, the lover who needs you, your compassion, a hint of recognition from you, a tenderness from your heart, personal and singular; the pitiful readers celebrate the lyric and practice the program, the underlying communication, the orders couched in language as orgasmic as the acts he didn't specifically say; he was lover, demanding lover, and father; he spread his seed everywhere, over continents; as if his ejaculation were the essence of love; as if he reproduced himself each time; with his hand he made giants; as if we all were his creatures; as if his sperm had washed over the whole world and he begat us, and now he'd take us; another maniac patriarch, a chip off the old block; the epic drama of a vast possession as if it were an orgy of brotherly love, kind, tender, *fraternité*; as if taking everyone were gentle, virile but magnanimous, a charity from body to body, soul to soul; none were exempt, he was the poet of inclusion; you could learn there were no limits, though you might not know the meaning until after they had touched you, all of them, his magnificent masses, each one; you could stay as innocent, or nearly, as the great, gray poet himself, until you'd done the program; then you'd be garbage somewhere, your body literal trash, without the dignity of a body bag, something thrown out, dumped somewhere, sticky from sperm, ripped inside, a torn anus, vaginal bruises and tears, a ripped throat; the tissue is torn; there's trauma to the tissue, says the doctor, detached, not particularly interested; but the tissue is flesh, of a human, and the trauma is injury, of a human, the delicate lining of the vagina is flesh, the interior lining of the throat is flesh, not meant for invasion, assault; flesh lines the anus; it's already limned with cracks and bleeding sores; mortal fools bleed there, we are dying all the time; love's intense and there will be great, jagged rips, a searing pain, it burns, it bleeds, there are fistfuls of blood, valleys of injury too wide and too deep to heal, and the shit comes out, like a child, bathed in blood, and there's fire, the penis pushed in hard all at once for the sake of the pain, because the lover, he likes it; annihilation is how I will love them. You'll just be loved to death, tears, like cuts, and tears, the watery things; it wasn't called the Civil War, or Vietnam; it wasn't a war poets decried in lyrics apocalyptic or austere, they couldn't ever see the death, or the wounded soldier, or the evil of invasion, a genocidal policy if I remember right, it's hard to remember; love's celebrated; it's party time; hang them from the rafters, the loved ones, pieces of meat, nice and raw, after the dogs have had them, clawed them to pieces, chewed on their bones; bloody, dirty pieces strung out on street corners or locked up in the rapist's house. One whole human being was never lost in all of history or all of time; or not so a poet could see it or use fine words to say it. Walt sings; to cover up the crimes; say it's love enough; enough. And art's an alibi; I didn't do it, I'm an artist; or I did do it but it's art, because I'm an artist, we do art, not rape, I did it beautiful, I arranged the pieces so esthetic, so divine; and them that love art also did not do it; *I support art*. Walt could sing, all right; obscuring a formal truth; as if a woman had an analogous throat; for song; then they stuff it down; sing then darling.

The poems were formal lies; lies of form; bedrock lies; as if the throat, pure but incarnate, was for singing in this universal humanity we have here, this democracy of love, for one and all; but they stuff it down; then try singing; sing, Amerika, sing. I saw this Lovelace girl. I'm walking in Times Square, going through the trash cans for food; I roam now, every day, all the time, days, nights, I don't need sleep, I don't ever sleep; I'm there, digging through the slop for some edible things but not vegetables because I never liked vegetables and there's standards you have to keep, as to your own particular tastes. I am searching for my dog, my precious friend, on every city street, in every alley, in every hole they got here where usually there's people, in every shooting gallery, in every pimp's hallway, in every abandoned building in this city, I am searching, because she is my precious friend; but so far I have not found her; it's a quest I am on, like in fables and stories, seeking her; and if my heart is pure I will find her; I remember Gawain and Galahad and I try to survive the many trials necessary before finding her and I am hoping she wasn't taken to wicked, evil ones; that she's protected by some good magic so she won't be hurt or malnourished or used bad, treated mean, locked up or starved or kicked; I'm hoping there's a person, half magic, who will have regard for her; and after I've done all the trials and tribulations she will come to me in a dark wood. I've got pain, in my throat, some boy tore it up, I rasp, I barely talk, it's an ugly sound, some boy killed it, as if it were some small animal he had to maim to death, an enemy he had to kill by a special method, you rip it up and it bleeds and the small thing dies slow. It's a small, tight passage, good for fun, they like it because it's tight, it hugs the penis, there's no give, the muscles don't stretch, at some point the muscles tear, and it must be spectacular, when they rip; then he'd come; then he'd run. You couldn't push a baby through, like with the vagina; though they'd probably think it'd be good for a laugh;

have some slasher do a cesarean; like with this Lovelace girl, where they made a joke with her, as if the clit is in her throat and they keep pushing penises in to find it so she can have an orgasm; it's for her, of course; always for her; a joke; but a friendly one; for her; so she can have a good time; I went in, and I saw them ram it down; big men; banging; you know, mean shoving; I don't know why she ain't dead. They kept her smiling; if it's a film you have to smile; I wanted to see if it hurt, like with me; she smiled; but with film they edit, you know, like in Hollywood. She had black and blue marks all over her legs and her thighs, big ones, and she smiled; I don't know why we always smile; I myself smile; I can remember smiling, like the smile on a skeleton; you don't ever want them to think they did nothing wrong so you smile or you don't want them to think there's something wrong with you so you smile, because there's likely to be some kind of pain coming after you if there's something wrong with you, they hit you to make it right, or you want them to be pleased so you smile or you want them to leave so you smile or you just are crapping in your pants afraid so you smile and even after you shit from fear you keep smiling; they film it, you smile. Sometimes a man still offers me money, I laugh, a hoarse, ugly laugh, quite mad, my throat's in ribbons, just hanging streaks of meat, you can feel it all loose, all cut loose or ripped loose in pieces as if it's kind of like pieces of steak cut to be sautéed but someone forgot and left it out so there's maggots on it and it's green, rotted out, all crawling. Some one of them offers me money and I make him sorry, I prefer the garbage in the trash cans, frankly, it's cleaner, this walking human stuff I don't have no room in my heart for, they're not hygenic. I'm old, pretty old, I can't take the chance of getting cancer or something from them; I think they give it to you with how they look at you; so I hide the best I can, under newspapers or under coats or under trash I pick up; my hair's silver, dirty; I remember when I was different and these legs were silk; and my breasts were silk; but now there's sores; and blood; and scars; and I'm green inside sometimes, if I cut myself something green comes out, as if I'm getting green blood which I never heard of before but they keep things from you; it could be that if you get so many bad cuts body and soul your blood changes; from scarlet to a dank green, an awful green; some chartreuse, some Irish, but mostly it is morbid, a rotting green; it's a sad story as I am an old-fashioned human being who had a few dreams; I liked books and I would have enjoyed a cup of coffee with Camus in my younger days, at a café in Paris, outside, we'd watch the people walk by, and I would have explained that his ideas about suicide were in some sense naive, ahistorical, that no philosopher could afford to ignore incest, or, as I would have it, the story of man, and remain credible; I wanted a pretty whisper, by which I mean a lover's whisper, by which I mean that I could say sweet things in a man's ear and he'd be thrilled and kind, I'd whisper and it'd be like making love, an embrace that would chill his blood and boil it, his skin'd be wild, all nerves, all smitten, it'd be my mark on him, a gentle mark but no one'd match it, just one whisper, the kind that makes you shiver body and soul, and it'd just brush over his ear. I wanted hips you could balance the weight of the world on, and I'd shake and it'd move; in Tanzania it'd rumble. I wanted some words; of beauty; of power; of truth; simple words; ones you could write down; to say some things that happened, in a simple way; but the words didn't exist, and I couldn't make them up, or I wasn't smart enough to find them, or the parts of them I had or I found got tangled up, because I couldn't remember, a lot disappeared, you'd figure it would be impressed on you if it was bad enough or hard enough but if there's nothing but fire it's hard to remember some particular flame on some particular day; and I lived in fire, the element; a Dresden, metaphysically speaking; a condition; a circumstance; in time, tangential to space; I stepped out, into fire. Fire burns memory clean; or the heart; it burns the heart clean; or there's scorched earth, a dead geography, burned bare; I stepped out, into fire, or its aftermath; burnt earth; a dry, hard place. I was born in blood and I stepped out, into fire; and I burned; a girl, burning; the flesh becomes translucent and the bones show through the fire. The cement was hot, as if flames grew in it, trees of fire; it was hot where they threw you down; hot and orange; how am I supposed to remember which flame, on which day, or what his name was, or how he did it, or what he said, or why, if I ever knew; I don't remember knowing. Or even if, at some point; really, even if. I lived in urban flame. There was the flat earth, for us gray, hard, cement; and it burned. I saw pictures of woods in books; we had great flames stretching up into the sky and swaying; moving; dancing; the heat melting the air; we had burning hearts and arid hearts; girls' bodies, burning; boys, hot, chasing us through the forest of flame, pushing us down; and we burned. Then there were surreal flames, the ones we superimposed on reality, the atomic flames on the way, coming soon, at a theater near you, the dread fire that could never be put out once it was ignited; I saw it, simple, in front of my eyes, there never was a chance, I lived in the flames and the flames were a ghostly wash of orange and red, as if an eternal fire mixed with blood were the paint, and a great storm the brush. I lived in the ordinary fire, whatever made them follow you and push you down, you'd feel the heat, searing, you didn't need to see the flame, it was more as if he had orange and burning hands a mile high; I burned; the skin peeled off; it deformed you. The fire boils you; you melt and blister; then I'd try to write it down, the flames leaping off the cement, the embodiment of the lover; but I didn't know what to call it; and it hurt; but past what they will let you say; any of them. I didn't know what to call it, I couldn't find the words; and there were always adults saying no, there is no fire, and no, there are no flames; and asking the life-or-death question, you're still a virgin, aren't you; which you would be forever, poor fool, in your pitiful pure heart. You couldn't tell them about the flames that were lit on your back by vandal lover boys, arsonists, while they held you down; and there were other flames; the adults said not to watch; but I watched; and the flames stayed with me, burning in my brain, a fire there, forever, I lived with the flames my whole life; the Buddhist monks in Vietnam who burned themselves alive; they set themselves on fire; to protest; they were calm; they sat themselves down, calm; they were simple, plain; they never showed any fear or hesitation; they were solemn; they said a prayer; they had kerosene; then they were lit; then they exploded; into flame; and they burned forever; in my heart; forever; past what television could show; in its gray; in its black and white and gray; the gray cement of gray Saigon; the gray robes of a gray man, a Buddhist; the gray fire, consuming him; I don't need to close my eyes to see them; I could reach out to touch them, without even closing my eyes; the television went off, or the adults turned it off, but you knew they were still burning, now, later, hours, days, the ashes would smolder, the fire'd never go out, because if it has happened it has happened; it has happened always and forever. The gray fire would die down and the gray monk would be charred and skeletal, dead, they'd remove him like so much garbage, but the fire'd stay, low along the ground, the gray fire would spread, low along the ground, in gray Saigon; in gray Camden. The flames would stay low and gray and they would burn; an eternal fire; its meaning entrusted to a child for keeping. I think they stayed calm inside the fire; burning; I think they stayed quiet; I mourned them; I grieved for them; I felt some shadow of the pain; maybe there was no calm; maybe they shrieked; maybe it was an agony obscene even to God; imagine. I'd go to school on just some regular day and it'd happen; at night, on the news, they'd show it; the gray picture; a Buddhist in flames; because he didn't like the government in Vietnam; because the United States was hurting Vietnam; we tormented them. You'd see a plain street in Saigon and suddenly a figure would ignite; a quiet, calm figure, simple, in simple robes, rags almost; a plain, simple man. It was a protest, a chosen immolation, a decision, planned for; he burned himself to say there were no words; to tell me there were no words; he wanted me to know that in Vietnam there was an agony against which this agony, self-immolation, was nothing, meaningless, minor; he wanted me to know; and I know; he wanted me to remember; and I remember. He wanted the flames to reach me; he wanted the heat to graze me; he wanted this self-immolation, a pain past words, to communicate: you devastate us here, a pain past words. The Buddhists didn't want to fight or to hurt someone else; so they killed themselves; in ways unbearable to watch; to say that this was some small part of the pain we caused, some small measure of the pain we made; an anguish to communicate anguish. Years later I was grown, or nearly so, and there was Norman Morrison, some man, a regular man, ordinary, and he walked to the front of the White House, as close as he could get, a normal looking citizen, and he poured gasoline all over himself and he lit it and the police couldn't stop him or get near him, he was a pillar of fire; and he died, slow, in fire, because the war was wrong and words weren't helping, and he said we have to show them so he showed them; he said this is the anguish I will undergo to show you the anguish there, there are no words, I can show you but I can't tell you because no words get through to you, you've got a barricade against feeling and I have to burn it down. I grew up, a stepdaughter of brazen protest, immense protest; each time I measured my own resistance against the burning man; I felt the anguish of Vietnam; sometimes the War couldn't get out of my mind and there was nothing between me and it; I felt it pure, the pain of them over there, how wronged they were; you see, we were tormenting them. In the end it's always simple; we were tormenting them. Others cared too; as much as I did; we were mad to stop it; the crime, as we called it; it was a crime. Sometimes ordinary life was a buffer; you thought about orange juice or something; and then there'd be no buffer; there was just the crime. The big protests were easy and lazy up against Norman Morrison and the Buddhist monks; I remember them, as a standard; suppose you really care; suppose the truth of it sits on your mind plain and bare; suppose you don't got no more lies between you and it; if a crime was big enough and mean enough to hurt your heart you had to burn your heart clean; I don't remember being afraid to die; it just wasn't my turn yet; it's got your name on it, your turn, when it's right; you can see it writ in fire, private flames; and it calls, you can hear it when you get up close; you see it and it's yours. There's this Lovelace creature, they're pissing on her or she's doing the pissing, you know how they have girls spread out in the pictures outside the movies, one's on her back and the urine's coming on her and the other's standing, legs spread, and she's fingering her crotch and the urine's coming from her, as if she's ejaculating it, and the urine's colored a bright yellow as if someone poured yellow dye in it; and they're smiling; they're both smiling; it's girls touching each other, as if girls would do so, laughing, and she's being peed on, one of them; and there's her throat, thrown back, bared, he's down to the bottom, as far as he can go; if he were bigger he'd be in deeper; and she's timid, shy, eager, laughing, grateful; laughing and grateful; and moaning; you know, the porn moan; nothing resembling human life; these stupid fake noises, clown stuff, a sex circus of sex clowns; he's a freak, a sinister freak; a monstrous asshole if not for how he subjugates her, the smiling ninny down on her knees and after saying thank you, as girls were born for, so they say. There's this Lovelace girl on the marquee; and even the junkies are laughing, they think it's so swell; and I think who is she, where's she from, who hurt her, who hurt her to put her here; because there's a camera; because in all my life there never was a camera and if there's a camera there's a plan; and if it's here it's for money, like she's some animal trained to do tricks; when I see black men picking cotton on plantations I get that somewhere there's pain for them, I don't have to see it, no one has to show it to me for me to know it's there; and when I see a woman under glass, I know the same, a sex animal trained for sex tricks; and the camera's ready; maybe Masta's not in the frame. Picking cotton's good; you get strong; black and strong; getting fucked in the throat's good; you get fucked and female; a double-female girl, with two vaginas, one on top. Maybe her name's Linda; hey, Linda. Cheri Tart ain't Cheri but maybe Linda's Linda; how come all these assholes buy it, as if they ain't looking at Lassie or Rin Tin Tin; it's just, pardon me, they're dogs and she's someone real; they're Hollywood stars too—she's Times Square trash; there's one of them and there's so many thousands of her you couldn't tell them apart even when they're in separate coffins. There's these girls here, all behind glass; as if they're insects you put under glass; you put morphine to them to knock them out and you mount them; these weird crawling things, under glass, on display; Times Square's a zoo, they got women like specimens under glass; block by city block; cages assembled on cement; under a darkening sky, the blood's on it; wind sweeping the garbage and it's swirling like dust in a storm; and on display, lit by neon, they have these creatures, so obscene they barely look human at all, you never saw a person that looked like them, including anyone beaten down, including street trash, including anyone raped however many times; because they're all painted up and polished as if you had an apple with maggots

297

and worms and someone dipped it in lacquer and said here it is, beautiful, for you, to eat; it's as if their mouths were all swelled up and as if they was purple between their legs and as if their breasts were hot-air balloons, not flesh and blood, with skin, with feeling to the touch, instead it's a joke, some swollen joke, a pasted-on gag, what's so dirty to men about breasts so they put tassles on them and have them swirl around in circles and call them the ugliest names; as if they ain't attached to human beings; as if they're party tricks or practical jokes or the equivalent of farts, big, vulgar farts; they make them always deformed; as if there's real people; citizens; men; with flat chests, they look down, they see their shoes, a standard for what a human being is; and there's these blow-up dolls you can do things to, they have funny humps on their chests, did you ever see them swirl, the woman stands there like a dead puppet, painted, and the balloon things spin. In my heart I think these awful painted things are women; like I am still in my heart; of human kind; but the men make them like they're two-legged jackasses, astonishing freaks with iron poles up the middle of them and someone smeared them with paint, some psychotic in the loony bin doing art class, and they got glass eyes with someone's fingerprints smeared on them; and they're all swollen up and hurt, as if they been pushed and fucked, hit, or stood somewhere in a ring, a circus ring or a boxing ring, and men just threw things at them, balls and bats and stones, anything hard that would cause pain and leave marks, or break bones; they're swollen up in some places, the bellies of starving children but moved up to the breasts and down to the buttocks, all hunger, water, air, distended; and then there's the thin parts, all starved, the bones show, the ribs sometimes, iridescent skeletons, or the face is caved in under the paint, the skin collapses because there is no food, only pills, syringes, Demerol, cocaine, Percodan, heroin, morphine, there's hollow cheeks sunk in hollow faces and the waist's hollow, shrinking down, tiny bones, chicken bones, dried up wish bones; and they're behind glass, displayed, exhibits, sex-women you do it to, they're all twisted and turned, deformed, pulled and pushed in all the wrong directions, with the front facing the back and the back facing the front so you can see all her sex parts at once, her breasts and her ass and her vagina, the lips of her vagina, purple somehow; purple. The neck's elongated so you know they can take it there too. They're like mules; they carry a pile of men on top of them. They're like these used-up race horses, you give them lots of shots to make them run and if you look at the hide there's bound to be whip marks. There's not one human gesture; not one. There's not one woman in the world likes to be hung or shit on or have her breasts tied up so the rope cuts in and the flesh bulges out, the rope's tearing into her, it sinks, burning, into the fleshy parts, under the rope it's all cut up and burned deep, and the tissue's dying, being broke apart, thinned out and ripped by pressure and pain. If I saw pictures like that of a black man I would cry out for his freedom; I can't see how it's confusing if you ain't K.K.K. in which case it still ain't confusing; I'd know it was a lie on him; I'd stand on that street corner forever screaming until my fucking throat bled to death from it; he's not chattel, nor a slave, nor some crawling thing you put under glass, nor subhuman, nor alien; I would spit on them that put him there; and them that masturbated to it I would pillory with stones until I was dragged away and locked up or they was dead. If they was lynching him I would feel the pain; a human; they are destroying someone. And if they put a knife in him, which I can see them doing, it ain't beyond them by no means, they wouldn't show him coming from it; and if they urinated on him he wouldn't be smiling. I seen black men debased in this city, I seen them covered in blood and filth, in urine and shit, and I never saw one say cheese for a camera or smiling like it was fun; I didn't see no one taking sex pictures

299

either; I myself do not go through garbage or live on cement to have an orgasm; be your pet; or live on a leash; I ain't painted red or purple; I seen myself; how I was after; on the bed; hurt; I seen it in my brain; and I wasn't no prize in human rights or no exemplar of human dignity I would say; as much as I tried in my life, I did not succeed. But wasn't nobody put me under glass and polished me all up as if I was a specimen of some fucked thing, some swollen, painted sex mule. This Linda girl, with the throat, who tormented her? In the end, it's always simple. I paid the dollars to go; to the film; to see it; if it was true; what they did to her throat; I figured the boy who did it to me must of got it from there; because, frankly, I know the world A to Z; and no one banged a woman's throat before these current dark days. I smelled bad and I was past being a whore and they didn't want me to go in but I had the money and I'm hard to move, because I'm more intransigent now; on cement; hungry almost all the time; hates men; an old woman nearly, hates men; and if you don't have a soft spot for them, you don't have no soft spot. I wanted to see Linda; if she was a creature or a person; I think they are all persons but you can't prove it, it's a matter of faith; I have this faith, but there's no proof. In the film she's this nice girl who can't have an orgasm so they line up hundreds of men to fuck her, all around the block, and they just keep fucking her every which way to Sunday to try to get her to have one and she's bored which, on the intellectual plane, would be true; but I fucked that many men, it's a week's worth, not one afternoon as they show, and no one gets an orgasm from such a line of slime acting as men, because it will tear you and bruise you inside as well as out and you will hurt very bad, but she just smiles and acts dis- appointed; and there's all this blah blah, talk with a supposed girlfriend, a hard-edged whore, by which I mean she been used so much already there's not too much left of her and it shows, how they've drained her away; and they talk about how Linda can't come; and the girlfriend puts a cigarette in her own vagina and I wanted to reach into the film and take it out; a burning cigarette in her vagina; but it was another joke; it was all jokes; the men around the block; the vagina huffing and puffing on the cigarette so smoke comes out; and the girl Linda's got big bruises all over her legs, real big bruises, high and wide, master bruises, have to be from feet and fists, it ain't in the story, no one hit her in the legs in the story but someone sure beat the hell out of her all over her fucking legs; I see the bruises; I feel the pain; I've taken such a beating; perhaps, Linda, we could be friends, you and me, although I'm unsavory now, perhaps you ain't no creature at all, just a girl, another girl, but they caught you and they put you under glass, in the zoo, you're a girl they turned the camera on but they had to beat you to pieces to do it; maybe you're just some girl; and then there's this doctor with a big cock who's pleased with himself generally speaking and he finds out she's got a clitoris in her throat, the big joke, and that's why she can't come from all these other sex acts so he fucks her in the throat to cure her, he fucks her hard in the throat but slow so you can see it, the whole distance in and out, the whole big thing, to the bottom of her throat; and she don't seem ripped apart, she's smiling, she's happy, shit, she's conscious, she's alive; think of it like an iron bar, a place in your throat where there's an iron bar, and if someone goes past it it don't give, you choke, you vomit, you can't breathe, and if he goes past it with a big penis he stretches muscles that can't be stretched and he pushes your throat out to where it can't be pushed out, as if the outsides tore open so there was holes so it could expand so the penis could go through, you'd rather have a surgeon drill holes in the sides of your throat than have him push it down, the pain will push you down to hell, near death, to coma, to the screamless scream, an agony, no voice, a ripped muscle, shreds swimming in blood in your throat, thin ribbons of muscle soaking up blood. But Linda smiles, and the camera doesn't let up, and the penis is big, it comes out so we can see how big it is in case we forgot and it goes down, her throat stretches like a snake eating an alligator or some boa constrictor with a small animal in it and the penis pushes hard to the bottom, it's in her neck by now bumping around her shoulders; again and again; and I'm crying myself near to death; the men are rubbing and moaning and ejaculating and someone's offering me money and I'm sitting there crying near to death for the girl; because I don't know where the blood is; but I know there's blood; somewhere Linda's shed blood and there's pieces of her floating around in it; Linda. They do all the things to her; glass in her vagina; from the front; from behind; all the things; and it's all big jokes and big moaning, the phony moans, ooh and aah and more and harder, stupid, false moans; and you think these men are crazy to think this is a woman moaning in sex; and then there's this guy with the world's biggest penis and he fucks her throat and she's in love with him because he's got this giant penis so he satisfies her, at last, completely, a romance, he fucks her throat, he is a cold creep, a sheet of ice descends over the screen, he fucks her throat; he's evil, even for these men who do these things to women in films; who will do anything; to anyone; present her to him; put her there; lights, camera, action; roll her over; stick it there or there or there; yeah, she's tied up like a trussed pig; he says darling and sticks it in. There's one decision, just one; and I have to make it; are we humans or not; the girls under glass and I or not. If we are not then there's these creatures kept properly under glass because who'd want them loose and the bruises on them or what you stick in them doesn't matter and they smile because they are sincere, this under-glass creature smiles when you hurt it, and you get to use them; and, logically, you get to use the five infants too, why not, and this girl from Camden too, why not;

because we're apples with maggots too, why not. Maybe this girl Linda really likes it; except there's this iron bar in your throat and nothing pushes past it without a destruction of some sort, this or that; or why don't they use machine guns or trees or they will, they just haven't yet, how'd they get that Linda girl to do it? Or if we're humans; if we are; the fire's got my name on it; at last, my name's spelled out in the fire and it is beckoning to me; because they are tormenting us, pure and simple, these men are tormenting us, they just do it, as if we are so much trash for where they want to stick it and it is simple in the end and they all get to live no matter what harm they do or if we hurt or how much, all these guys live, they do; face it; you can take some actual person and mess her body up so bad it's all deformed out of its real form and you can put things up her and in her and you can hurt her, shred her, burn her, tortures that are done like roping her breasts, and it's okay, even funny, even if they do it to babies or even if they beat you or even if they put things in you or no matter what they do, it's over and tomorrow comes and they go on and on and on and they don't get stopped, no one stops them; and people just walk by the girls under glass; or just ignore the infants who growed up, the suicidal infants who can't breathe but are trying to talk; or the women who got beat; no one stops them; it's true, they don't get stopped; and it's true, though not recognized, that you do got to stop them, like stop the War, or stop slavery; you have to stop them; whatever's necessary; because it's a crisis because they are tormenting us; I gave my uncle cancer but it's too late, too slow, and you don't know who they are, the particular ones; and even if there's laws by the time they have hurt you you are too dirty for the law; the law needs clean ones but they dirty you up so the law won't take you; there's no crimes they committed that are crimes in the general perception because we don't count as to crimes, as I have discovered time and time again as I try to think if what he did that hurt me so bad was a crime to anyone or was anything you could tell someone about so they would care; for you; about you; so you was human. But if he did it to you, you know him; I know; this Linda knows; the infants know; the day comes; we know; each one of them has one of us who knows; at least one; maybe dozens; but at least one. When the Buddhists were burning themselves you couldn't convince anyone anything was wrong in Vietnam; they couldn't see it; they saw the fire; and you couldn't forget the fire; and I'm convinced that the fire made the light to see by; so later, we saw. Now there's nothing wrong either; nothing nobody can see; each day all these thousands of people, men and women, walk past the women under glass, the specimens, and they don't see nothing wrong, they don't see no human of any sort or that it's wrong that our kind are under glass, painted, bloated cadavers for sex with spread legs, eyes open, glassy, staring like the dead; smiling; painted lips; purple; lynched or pissed on; or on our knees; I will die to get her off her knees; sperm covering us like puke; and we're embalmed, a psychotic's canvas; eventually fucked, in any orifice; some-day they'll do the sockets of the eyes. It's the church to our pain; a religion of hate with many places to pray; a liturgy of invasion; they worship here, the men, *Hot Girls* is Michael-angelo's *David*; *Lesbian Gang Bang* is Tintoretto; it's Venice and Rome and Jerusalem and Mecca, too; all the art; every-thing sacred; with pilgrims; the service, how I injured her and came; the ancient masses, how I made a perfect penetration; the ordinary prayers, I felt her up, I stuck it in, she screamed, I ran; this is the church here, they worship here, a secular sadism where we're made flat and dead and displayed under glass, fifty cents a feel for a live one in a real cage, behind the movies are the places where they keep the live ones they caught, you pay money, you touch it; you pay more money; it touches you; you pay more money; you can hurt it bad if you pay enough; you pay money, you can stick it in, you want to cut it up, it costs more money; you want it young, you want to stick it in, you want to cut it up, it costs more money; but see, my uncle, a true believer, worshipped at home; so you have to grasp the true nature of the system; here is the center; here is like the transmission center; here is where they broadcast from; here is where they put the waves in the air; here is where they make the product, the assembly line with mass production techniques and quality control, the big time, and they sell it to make it socially true and socially necessary and socially real, beyond dispute, it's for sale, in Amerika, it's true, a practical faith for the working man and the entrepreneur, rich man, poor man. It's the nerve center, the Pentagon, the war room, where they make the plans; map every move in the war; put the infantry here and move it here; put the boats here and move them here; put the bombs here and move them here; dildos, whips, knives, chains, punishments, sweat and strangulation, evisceration; they teach how to teach the soldiers; they teach how to teach the special units; they teach how to teach; they develop propaganda and training films, patriotic films, here's the target, take her out. Here's where they make the plans to make the weapons; and here's where they commission the weapons; and here's where they deploy the weapons; it's the church, holy, and the military, profane, backbone and bedrock, there's dogma and rules, prayers and marching chants, sacred rites and bayonets, there's everything you stick up them, from iron crosses to grenades; you pull the pin; stay inside them as long as you have the nerve; pull out; run; it makes a man out of a boy. There's a human being; under glass. If you see what's in front of you you see what's down the road: someday they'll just take the children, the pied piper of rape, they'll just use the children, it's so much easier, how it is now is so difficult, so complex, fun taming the big ones and seducing them and raping them but the children are tighter, you know; and hurt more, you know; and are so confused, you know; and love you anyway, you know. All the worshippers will be tolerant of each other; and they'll pass the little ones on, down the line, so everyone can pray; and the courts will let them; because the courts have always let them; it's just big daddy in a dress, the appearance of neutrality. I been living in Times Square, on the sidewalks, I seen all the marquees, I studied them, I have two questions all the time, why ain't she dead is one and why would anyone, even a man, think it's true—her all strung out, all painted, all glossy, proclaiming being peed on is what she wants; I do not get how the lie flies; or ain't they ever made love; or ever seen no one real; and maybe she's dead by now; they must think it's like you are born a porn thing; in the hospital they take the baby and they say take it to the warehouse, it's a porn thing. They must think it's a special species; with purple genitals and skin made from a pale steel that don't even feel no pain; or they think every girl is one, underneath, and they wait, until we turn purple, from cold, or a thin patina of blood, dried so it's an encasement, like an insect's carapace. And they get hard from it, the porn thing, flat and glossy, dead and slick, and after they find something resembling the specimen from under the glass and they stick it in; a girl in the rain; five infants; some girl. It's like how Plato tried to explain; the thing pure, ideal, as if you went through some magical fog and came to a whole world of perfect ideas and there's Linda taking it whole; and they wander through the pure world putting fifty cents down there to cop a feel and five dollars down there, and for a hundred you see a little girl buggered, and for fifty you do something perfect and ideal to a perfect whore or some perfect blow-up doll with a deep silk throat and a deep silk vagina and a rough, tight rectum, and you come back through the fog and there's the girl, not quite so purple, and you do it to her; yeah, she cries if you hang her or brand her or maim her or even probably if you fuck her in the ass, she don't smile, but you can hurt her enough to make her smile because she has to smile because if she don't she gets hurt more, or she'll try, and you can paint her more purple, or do anything really; put things in her; even glass or broken glass and make her bleed, you can get the color you want; you strive for the ideal. I fuck it up, I say the girl's real, but it don't stop them; and we got to stop them; so I take the necessary supplies, some porn magazines where they laminate the women, and I take the stones for breaking the glass, I will not have women under glass, and I take signs that say "Free the Women, Free Ourselves" and "Porn Hates Women" and I take a sign that says "Free Linda" and I have a sign that says "Porn Is Rape" and I take a letter I wrote myself that says to my mama how sorry I am to have failed at dignity and at freedom both, and I say I am Andrea but I am not manhood for which, mama, I am glad, because they have gone to filth, they are maggots on this earth; and I take gasoline, and I'm nearly old for a girl, I'm hungry and I have sores, and I smell bad so no one looks at all very much, and I go to outside *Deep Throat* where my friend Linda is in the screen and I put the gasoline on me, I soak myself in it in broad daylight and many go by and no one looks and I am calm, patient, gray on gray cement like the Buddhist monks, and I light the fire; free us, I start to scream, and then there's a giant whoosh, it explodes more like wind than fire, it's orange, around me, near me, I'm whole, then I'm flames. I burn; I die. From this light, later you will see. Mama, I made some light.

ELEVEN

April 30, 1974
(Age 27)

Sensei is cute but she's fascist. She makes us bow to the Korean flag; I bow but I don't look. We are supposed to be reverent in our hearts but in my heart is where I rebel. It is more than a bow. We bow. We get down on our knees and we bow our heads. It's the opening ceremony of every class. In karate you get down on your knees in a lightning flash of perfect movement so there's no scramble, no noise; it's a perfect silence and everyone moves as one; the movement itself expresses reverence and your mind is supposed to obey, it moves with the body, not against it, except for mine, which is anarchist from a long time ago and I never thought I'd bow down in front of any fucking flag but I do, in perfect silence and symmetry insofar as my awkward self can manage it; my mind's like a muscle that pulls every time; I feel it jerk and I feel the dislocation and the pain and I keep moving, until I am on my knees in front of the fucking thing. It's interesting to think of the difference between a flag and a dick, because this is not a new position; with a dick how you get there doesn't count whereas in the dojo all that matters is the elegance, the grace, of the movement, the strength of the muscles that carry you down; an act of reverence will eventually, says Sensei, teach you self-respect, which wasn't the issue with the dick, as I remember. There's an actual altar. It has on it the Korean flag, a picture of Sensei, and some dried flowers. When I was a child I had a huge picture of Rock Hudson up on the door in my tiny bedroom, on the back of the door so I would see it when I was alone, as if he was there, physically present with me, because the picture was so big and real and detailed, of a real face; I put it up with Scotch tape and kissed it good-night, a mixture of heat and loneliness; not quite as I would kiss my mother if I could but with the same intensity I wanted from her, as if she could hold me enough, or love me enough, or rock me forever; I never understood why you couldn't just bury yourself in someone's arms and kiss until you died; just live there, embraced, warm and wet and touched all over. Instead there was this photo I cut out of a magazine, and a lonely bed in a lonely house, with mother gone, sick, and father gone, to pay doctors. I built up all the love there was in the world out of those lonely nights and when I left home I wasn't afraid ever to touch or be touched and I never abandoned faith that it was everything and enough, a thousand percent whole, perfect and sensual and true. I thought we were the same, everyone. I thought Rock could hold me; hold me; as if he were my mother, against his breast. Of course, I also liked Tab Hunter's "Red Sails in the Sunset"; and Tab Hunter. I was indiscriminate even then but it was an optimism and I never understood that there was a difference with men, they didn't take the oceanic view; they didn't want whole, just pieces. I thought it would be a small bed like mine, simple, poor, and we'd be on our sides facing each other, the same, and we'd ride the long waves of feeling as if we all were one, the waves and us, we'd be drenched in heat and sweat, no boundaries, no time, and we'd hold on, hold on, through the great convulsions that made you cry out, and time would be obliterated by feeling, as it is. Facing each other and touching we could get old and die; then or later; because there's only now; it didn't matter who, only how it felt, and that it was whole and real past any other high or any other truth; I wanted feeling to obliterate me and love to annihilate me; don't ever make a wish. There weren't religious icons in a Jewish house; only movie stars. Sensei says it's paying respect to her karate tradition to kneel down in front of the Korean flag and her picture on the altar but I always wonder what the Koreans would think about it; if they'd like a woman elevating herself so high. She's not really a woman, though; and maybe they saw the difference and gave her permission, because she's got a male teacher, a karate master, a blackbelt killer as it were, and he wouldn't brook no vanity. If she were a girl per se she couldn't be so square and fixed, so physically dense, as if there's more of her per square inch than any other female on the planet, because anatomically she's female, I'm sure, although it *seems* impossible. She's like a thousand pounds of iron instead of a hundred pounds of some petite, cute girl. You expect lethal weapons to be big, six feet or more, towering, overpoweringly high, casting long, terrifying shadows, with muscles as big as bowling balls; so you notice she's small and you can't figure out how she got the way she is except that once she must have been a real girl, even in dresses, and so maybe you could stop being so curved and soft and flimsy. Each inch of her uses up the space she's in, introducing weight where once there was air; she dislocates space, displaces it, it moves and she takes over, she occupies the ground, as if she was infantry with a bayonet and the right to kill. She's nothing like a girl. For instance, her shoulders are square, they take up space, they are substantial and she don't make them round or underplay them or slump them, they don't look soft as if you could just walk up to her or in a conversation put your arm around her, everything's an edge or a hammer, not a curve. She reigns, imperial; butch, my dear, but transcending the domain of a bar stool, it ain't role playing, or a pretense, or a masquerade; if she were a girl she'd be a little doll; petite; and there'd be a bigger male one whose shadow would fall on her and bury her alive. She'd live small in perpetual darkness next to him. Instead, she's a certifiable Korean nationalist with an altar and a flag who considers a hundred sit-ups an insubstantial beginning, foreplay but, in the male mode, barely counting, and she don't care about the pain. I myself pretend it's coming from a man, because I know if he was on top of me I wouldn't stop; so I try to keep going by turning it into him on me; you fuck way past pain when a man's fucking you blind. I can do maybe fifteen; I put him on top of me and I get near thirty, maybe twenty-eight; I put him in the corner of the room laughing and I get to thirty-five; after that, Sensei just keeps you moving and you don't get to stop even if actually you think your heart is contracting along with your abdomen and it will convulse and cease, still you move, and she sees everything, including if you hesitate for half a second or stay still for half a second, or try to rest halfway between up and down because you think she can't see the difference but she sees the molecules in the air and if they ain't moving you ain't moving and her eyes nail you and she's firm and hard; finally, she will say your name to humiliate you; or assign you thirty more; and so you keep moving, the muscles are cramped, all twisted up inside, swollen and twisted and convulsing, and your heart's collapsed into your stomach or your stomach into your heart and there's only a bed of pain in the middle of you that moves, it moves, a half inch of space over a period of minutes while the others have done five whole sit-ups, six, seven, and you feel stupid and weak and cowardly but you move the teeny, tiny smidgen, you keep moving, you bounce yourself, you use your breath, anything you can get to make you move so it looks like you're moving, and the muscles are stuck stiff with pain, swelling in hardened cement, but you move; barely, but you move; and of course with my intellect I try to see if she's getting off on it because if she is that lets me off the hook, I can walk out self-righteous because she ain't no better than I am, she's just the other side of my coin, my decrepitude, and it's dominion she's after, tormenting the likes of me. But she don't get off on it so I keep moving even though I'm barely moving and you reach a point where if you shudder you feel the muscles move and a tremor is distance covered; if you shake, the muscles move; and helplessly you do shake. Sensei learned to count to a hundred in a school pioneered by Stalin; she don't allow for human flaws, which is mental, as he would have agreed; she fixes defects in the mind that are expressed as incapacities in the body; it's right thinking that makes the abdomen strong enough to shatter a normal man's fist should he deliver a punch at the top of his form; you can punch Sensei in the gut with everything you got and she stands still, straight, tall, she don't feel nothing in her gut but the hitter is hurt. Push-ups is different because women can't do them, because all we get to do in life is carry our breasts and shopping, and from childhood they make us stay weak in the shoulders but we don't even know it; and so push-ups take forever to learn; and even the best students take forever to learn them; to do one is an achievement, and you burn with fury that they incapacitated you so much. Sensei can do butterfly push-ups, a hundred or a hundred and fifty; it's push-ups but you do them on your fingertips instead of using your whole hand; your hands don't hit the ground, only the tops of your fingers. I never seen anything like it in my life. It's an unreal as flapping your wings and actually flying. Yet I seen Sensei do it; a hundred times; she says she can do fifty more. I can barely breathe thinking about what it would feel like to do it or to be so strong or so agile or so fucking brave, because I'd be afraid of falling; of breaking my fingers; of slipping; of pain. I love it; I live for her to do it; up and down, with the tips of her fingers taking all the weight of her body going down, then lifting her up. I can raise just the top half of my body, about five times, which is pretty usual and she says that's how to build the muscles and we have to have patience to undo the damage of being made weak; and I see it ain't just the penis they nail you with, they pin you down at both ends, and all the strength you could have in the upper part of your body is atrophied as if you was paralyzed your whole life; except you wasn't. I tell myself that whatever I can take from him, whomever, I can take for me; me; now; and when I get weak and fall back to my bad old ways because I never had a me and still don't except by forcing myself to think so I say I'm doing it for her; this me is pretty tenuous but I can take anything for him and a fair amount for her and I play with it in my mind, that it's for her, and I watch myself with interest, how physical pain changes when it is in the guise of sex or love or infatuation or even just seduction, I will get her attention by moving, moving, just a little more, just a little bit more; I pretend this is sex but I still never get past sixty and it is because I have wrong thinking and a girl's stupid life. By sixty I mean sixty of barely moving; I never got past seventeen actual whole sit-ups and I never got to one whole push-up; and I still don't know why her fingers don't break from the butterfly push-ups; and she teaches us to make a fist and we practice and my fingers are too stupid and weak even to do that right, I try to fold them under so every joint is folded under every other joint so it's solid and hard and not filled with air the way girls make fists but my fingers won't move right and I can't make the sections tight enough. The part I like is breathing. You take all the air in you, inert stuff, and you exhale like you is threatening God face-to-face; you push like the air itself could kill. All the air you took in during fucking, all that Goddamn spastic inhaling, all that panting like some desperate dog, you shoot out, like it's bullets; I got a lot of air to push out. Then there's the horse position, where you take a stance, your legs spread far apart so your thigh muscles are tearing from the weight of your whole body resting on them; your feet are pointed out and your legs are spread far apart and your knees are bent and pointing out and the rest of you is on your thighs, absolutely still, at perfect silence; and after about five minutes your calf muscles begin to bear the weight of your thighs which time makes heavier and somehow you feel the weight of your soul and your life in the muscles in the insides of your thighs, because if you're a girl you lived there and memory's stored there and the world banged up against you there, so you undertake to bear the burden of it with conscious knowledge, a physical self-consciousness, a remorseless, aching cognition; and the history in your body comes alive as the muscles in your thighs strain under the weight of your life; the life of the cell; a brilliant physical solitude with all of the self spread out along the fault line of the thighs, a bridge of muscle; and you are absolutely still, contemplative, in pain, yes, a located pain, a fierce ache of recognition and identity; you are still; until Sensei orders you to relax, which is only slightly less burdensome but feels like deliverance; and I think to myself that everything these thighs took they will get strong enough to give back; it is a promise I make myself in horse position to be able to bear it; it is a promise I make every time over and over; it is a promise my thighs will remember even if I forget. Sensei says women got an advantage with the thighs, more strength than we might expect, because of the high heels they make us wear; I got strong thighs because of the reason under the reason; I been in horse position on my back most of my life; I like it alone and standing up. Sensei says eat steak but I can only afford potatoes, or sometimes frozen squash, or sometimes cheese, or the free bar food, but the men are unbearable so I don't do that unless I am ravenous; sometimes I'm hungry too much. I take double classes twice a week because I want to be strong; I am dying to be strong; all my money goes to Sensei and I fail at sit-ups twice in a night and I fail to do one whole push-up twice in a night, two times a week; and I have to come up with a stupendous amount of money, because it is fifteen dollars a class, so that is fifteen times four, and Sensei berates me when I say I will have to take a single class twice a week for a month or two or even three because I cannot find the money to pay for double classes; I feel my serious word that this is so is enough but she takes it as if I am lying or I don't value her or I don't have devotion, as if it's an excuse; and I feel enraged; because it's as if she'd turn me out for her fucking money, if you want it you can get it she says like any pimp on the street; I am a writer, I am going to hurt men, I am a serious person; she knows it. Sensei says she's never seen anyone with a will like mine but it's a trick to flatter me so I'll be persuaded to get the money for double classes after I've said I can't and I'm feeling the indignity because I am pure will and I have not insulted her by uttering one frivolous word. I am engaged in the serious job of survival and the creation of a plan to stop men; hurt them, stop them, kill them; and I am not some fool who says insubstantial things and I don't have money to move around, as if I can take it from something I don't need, which I feel is an indignity to have to explain, and I feel rage because she is middle-class in this way that demeans me and the dojo's in a Victorian brownstone she owns with her lover, a woman with round shoulders and sagging breasts who does not do sit-ups or horse position standing up; there is a sudden horror in my heart, a queasy feeling of sickness and dread, because I ask her to be sober and treat me with honor and she degrades me because of money and I cannot forgive it. I am learning that inside something goes wrong when something wrong happens; I am learning to follow it, the feeling. I say I write and it is first and I have thirty dollars I can find, not sixty, and I do not say how much I give up to give her the thirty because to do so would be demeaning in my heart, the sick feeling would come on, and she belittles me and I leave and I never turn back. Do not mess with me. I am making a plan in writing to make the men shed tears of remorse and I cannot waste my time with someone insufficient; she has to deserve me too; I want respect; there's a piece missing in her—what's hunger, what's poor; it's the pieces I got; I can't explain how what's a blind spot in her blindsides me; I can't have her talk *money* to me which she measures one way and I measure in sucking dicks, the economy as I see it, how long on your knees, how many times, equals a meal, makes the rent. I ain't saying it to her, it's an inchoate rage, but I turn over inside; Sensei eats shit. I say nothing, because she's an innocent, she counts money dry, not drenched in sperm. I cut her off without another word. She is out of my life. I don't look back. I paid, sister, I am paid up in dues well into the next century, I have clear priorities, she was number two, pretty high on the fucking list; number one is that I am writing a plan for revenge, a justice plan, a justice poem, a justice map, a geography of justice; I am martial in my heart and military in my mind; I think in strategy and in poems, a daughter of Guevara and Whitman, ready to take to the hills with a cosmic vision of what's crawling around down on the ground; a daughter with an overview; the big view; a daughter with a new practice of righteous rage, against what ain't named and ain't spoken so it can't be prosecuted except by the one it was done to who knows it, knows him; I'm inventing a new practice of random self-defense; I take their habits and characteristics seriously, as enemy, and I plan to outsmart them and win; they want to stay anonymous, monster shadows, brutes, king pricks, they want to strike like lightning, any time, any place, they want to be sadistic ghosts in the dark with penises that slice us open, they want us dumb and mute and vacant, robbed of words, nothing has a name, not anything they do to us, there's nothing because we're nothing; then they must mean they want us to strike them down, indiscriminate, in the night; we require a sign language of rebellion; it's the only chance they left us. You may find me one who ain't guilty but you can't find me two. I have a vision, far into the future, a plan for an army for justice, a girls' army, subversive, on the ground, down and dirty, no uniforms, no rank, no orders from on high, a martial spirit, a cadre of honor, an army of girls spreading out over the terrain, I see them moving through the streets, thick formations of them in anarchy and freedom on cement. I keep practicing horse position and sit-ups and I kick good; I can kick to the knee and I can kick to the cock but I can't kick to the solar plexus and I can't kick his fucking head off but I can compensate with my intelligence and with my right thinking if I can isolate it, in other words, rescue it from the nightmares; liberate it; deep liberation. I practice on my wall to get my kick higher, never touching the wall, Zen karate, a new dimension in control and a new level of aggression, a new arena of attack as if I am walking up the wall without touching it; and I will do the same to them; Zen killing. My fist ain't good enough but my thighs needless to say are superb, possibly even sublime, it's been noted many times. Many a man's died his little death there and I made the mistake of not burying him when he was exactly ripe for it, not putting him, whole, under the ground, but I soaked up his soul, I took it like they always fear, I stole his essence to in me, it's protein, I got his molecules; and I never died. It is more than relevant; it is the point. I never died. I am not dead. If you use us up and use us up and use us up but don't kill us we ain't dead, boys; a word to the wise; peace now, or there's a mean lot of killing coming. I am torn up in many places and I am a moving mountain of pain, I have tears body and soul, I am marked and scarred and black-and-blue inside and out, I got torn muscles in my throat and blood that dried there that won't ever dislodge and rips in my vagina the size of fists and fissures in my anus like rivers and holes in my heart, a sad heart; but I ain't dead, I never died, which means, boys, I can march, I want to walk to God on you, stretch you out under me, a pathway to heaven. And I am real; Andrea one, two, three, there's more than one, I am reliably informed; the raped; Andrea, named for courage, a new incarnation of virility, in the old days called manhood and I'm what happens when it's fucked; we go by other names, Sally, Jane, whatever; but I had a prophet for a mama and she named not just a daughter but a breed, who the girl is when the worm turns; put Thomas Jefferson in my place, horse position on his back with a mob of erect rapists coming and going at will, at their pleasure; and ask what a more perfect union is; or would be; from his point of view; then. Put anyone human where I been and make a plan; for freedom. I will fill you with remorse because you fucked me to ground meat and because you buy it and you sell it and the hole in my heart is commerce to you; lover, husband, boychick, brother, friend, political radical, boy comrade; I can't fucking tell you all apart. You're pouncing things that push it in, lush with insult or austere with pain; I don't got no radio in my stomach like the crazy ones who get messages to kill and can't turn it off or dislodge it although you stuck enough in me, they say they hear voices and they kill, they say they are getting orders and they kill, and the psychiatrists come in the newspapers and call them long bad names and go to court and say they didn't know what they were doing; but they knew; because everyone knows. The psychiatrists miss it all but especially that there's information everywhere; the radio, the voices, are metaphors used by poets who dance rather than write it down, poet-killers; action poems; there's energy that buzzes, a coherent language of noise and static you can learn to read, you don't need to be subliterate on this plane, just receive, receive; there's waves you can see, you can take a fucking light beam and parse it for information or you can decode the information in the aura of light around a person or a thing; everything's coded; every-thing's whole; it's all right there, including the future, you can just pull it out, it's just more information, a buzz, a vibration, a radiance, even a smell in the air; and we are all one, sweetheart, which means that if I'm you I got your secrets including your dirty little rape secrets and your dirty little what you stick it in secrets, you can just pull the information out of the air as to who is evil and what is going on, how it works and what must be done; you can learn to see it and you can learn to hear it because you are flowing in an ocean of information and the information gets amplified by pedestrian events, for instance, you learn at karate school that they pin you down at both ends, they got different shoulders from you, which you didn't know, and they made yours useless like bound feet, which you didn't know; and they nail you, they plug you, the penis goes right through you on one end and screws you down, fixes you fast to some hard surface, and the shoulders are like a ton of metal dumped on you to keep you flat, it's information on the literal level, the pedestrian plane, a reminder of mechanical reality or a new lesson in it because girls don't learn mechanics or anything else that will help on the physical plane to rebel or get free so you got to read the cosmic information in the air, the molecular information, which could even come from other planets if you think about it, it could be moving towards you on light from far away, and you also got to be a student of reality as it is commonly understood. They fill your head with political theory because it's useless; it's dreams you can't have; of dignity that ain't yours; of freedom that ain't intended on any level for you; you take it to heart; they take you to bed; heartbreak hotel, the place where the dialectic abandons reality, leaving her barefoot and pregnant, raped and barefoot; these are the dreams that break your heart, the difference between what you wanted from Camus and what he would have given you; I always wanted to have a cup of coffee with him, on the boulevard; and how these men love whores; the thinkers, the truck drivers, the students, the cops; how they love you turned out, shivering in the cold, already undressed enough; no, they don't all rape; they all buy. I am an apprentice: sorcerer or assassin or vandal or vigilante; or avenger; I am in formation as the new one who will emerge; I am in a cocoon; but at night, being a girl, I just stroll; I am a girl who walks the streets at night, back to first principles, how I grew up, where I lived, my home, cement, gray, stretching out a thousand miles flat, a plain of loneliness and despair; my world; my bed; my place on earth; I will populate the dark forever, of course, night is my country, I belong here, I can't get free, I was condemned, exiled from daylight because survival required facing the dark; I am a citizen of the night, with a passport, a mouth used enough, it's vulgar to say but inside it changes, the skin gets raw and red and it blisters, it gets small, tight, white blisters, liquidy blisters, it gets tough and brown, it gets leathery, it sags in loose red places and there are black-and-blue marks, and your tongue never touches the roof of your mouth, instead there's a layer of slime, sticky slime, a white, viscous slime, a moving cement that never hardens and never disappears, a near mortar of awful white stuff, mucous and slime; you got a mouth crawling on top with slime; as if it's worms in you, spermy little worm things all laid out side by side all in a line lining the roof of your mouth; a protein shield, if you want to put the best construction on it, because you don't want his shit shooting to the top of your brain anyway, going through the roof of your mouth to your head, you don't want his molecules absorbed in your brain, planted there so his molecular reality grows in some hemisphere of your brain, you don't want him as weeds in your head, with his D.N.A. rolling all over behind your eyes; and of course you try to keep him as high in your mouth as you can, as close to the front, as little in; always give as little as you can; not just on principle, as in, give as little of anything as you can; but you give as little of yourself as you can in a literal sense, not as an abstract concept of self but as little of your mouth as you can; except for the one who rammed it down to the bottom, into your chest or your lungs or however far he got, he shattered muscles as if they was glass, splintered them as if they was bone, you could feel a smashed larynx swimming in blood, like a dead animal, all bleeding and cut open, I got a sexy voice now, something hoarse and missing, an absence, a bare vibration; but he wasn't a trick, he was a cute boy, true love and real romance, remember him I instruct myself because it's hard, rape's hard, remembering's hard, they have to break so much there's no deep deep enough to bury it in, they leave you with crushed bones, diced nerves, live nerves, sliced nerves as if someone took a knife to the nerve endings themselves, not so they are cut dead but so they are being sliced each minute of forever, and they don't go dead, there's not half a second of numbness or paralysis, the nerves are open and alive and being hit by the air, exposed, and the knife is cutting into them thread by thread, they're stringy and the knife's pulling them apart, and you got an acute pain and a loud scream, high decibels, ringing in your ears, a torture ringing in your ears, and it don't let you sleep and you don't get forgetfulness, your eyes cry blood and you got open sores, the lips of your labia get boils, big boils; you got a vagina with long, deep tears, an ass that rips open with blood every time you shit, because it's the penis again, oversized, pulling out after having torn its way in; and then you will remember rape; these are the elements of memory, *constant, true, and perpetual pain*; and otherwise you will forget—we are a legion of zombies—because it burns out a piece of your brain, it's the scorched earth policy for the sweetmeat in your head, the rape recipe, braise, sear, burn bare, there's a sudden conflagration on the surface of your brain, a piece of one hemisphere or the other is burned bare, blank, and you lose whatever's there; just gone; whatever; so rape's a two-pronged attack, on your body, in you, on your brain, in you; on freedom, on memory; you might as well bury yourself in the backyard, or throw yourself in a trash can, you're like some dumb cat or dog that got hit by a car, run over and died; only they let the shells of dead girls walk around because hell it makes no difference to them if what they stick it in is living or dead; what's left, darling, is fine, according to the formula, a girl frail and female, a skeleton with a fleshy pudendum, ready to serve, these girls are ghosts, did you see, did you notice, where are they, why ain't they here, present, on earth, why can't you find them even if you look for them in the light, how come they don't know anything or do anything, how come they ain't anything, how come they are shaking and flitting around and apologizing and begging and afraid and drugged and stupid even if they are smart; how come they are comatose even when they're awake? He pushes it in, she pushes it out, a dead spot in the brain marks the spot, there's a teeny little cemetery in her brain, lots of torched spots, suttee; we bleed both ends, literal, little strokes every time there's a rape, time gone, hours or days or weeks, words gone, self gone, memory wiped out, severely impaired; I cannot remember—how do you *exist*? The skills, the tricks; tie your shoes; wrap ropes around your heart, or was it your wrists; or was it ankles; neck; I'd make a list if I could remember; I'd memorize the list if someone else would write it down; or I try, I scribble big letters, confused, misspelled, on the page; or I look at the words, meaningless, and draw a blank; I make a list, misspelled words signifying I don't remember what; or I draw a picture, I use crayons, of what? I try to say what I try to remember; the skills, the tricks, language, yesterday. There are little rape strokes, erased places in the brain, eruptions of blood, explosions, like geysers, it's flooded, places on the brain, blood's acidic, did you ever sit in a pool of your own blood, it wears the skin off you, chafes, irritates, the skin peels off; so too in the brain, the skin peels off; I've been there, a poor, dear, quiet thing, naked like a baby, in a river of blood, mine, curled up; fetal, as if my mama took me back. There's wounds and you sit in the blood. Why can't I remember? I am a stroke victim, a shadow in the night, invisible in the night, a ghostly thing, in the night, amnesiac, wandering, in the night, not out to whore, just what's left, the remains, on the stroll; taking a walk, pastoral, romantic, an innocent walk, lost in memories, lost in fog, lost in dark; having forgotten; but I got muscles packed with memory; hard, thick, solid, from the positions reenacted, down on my knees, down on my back; I got memories packed in my bones, because my brain don't make distinctions no more; can't tell him from him from him; I have an intuitive dread; of him and him and him; there's a heightened anxiety; I'm a nervous girl, Victorian nerves, strain, a delicate constitution in the sense that my brain is frail, pale; but my muscles is packed, it's adrenaline, from fear; there's a counterproductive side to creating too much fear, it's a meta-amphetamine, it's meta-speed, it's meta-coke, it's more testosterone than thou, I got a body packed with rage, you ever seen rage all stored up like a treasure in the body of a woman? I don't need no full capacity brain, as you so eloquently have insisted; I got sunstrokes in my head, enough daylight to carry me through any darkness, I am lit up from inside, a bursting sun; brain light. I am a citizen of the night, on a stroll, no dark places keep secrets from me, I am drawn to them by a secret radiance, the light that emanates from the human heart, some poor bum, a poor man, poor fucking drunk somewhere in the shadows hiding his poor drunk heart in the dark, but I find him, I see the pure light of his pure heart, I find him, some asshole, a vagrant, clutching his bottle, and I like them big, I like them hairy, their skin's red and bulbous, all swelled from drinking, they're mean, they'd kill you for the fucking bottle they're clutching to them, sometimes they got it buried under them, and they're curled up on cardboard or newspapers on the street, all secure in the shadows, manly men, behind garbage cans, hidden in the dark; but the light in them reaches out to the light in me, my brothers, myself, I pick on men at least twice my size, I like them with fine shoulders, wide, real men, I like them six feet or more, I like them vicious, I pick them big and mean, the danger psyches me up but what I appreciate is their surprise, which is absolute, their astonishment, which invigorates me; how easy it is to make them eat shit; they will always underestimate me, always, from which I enunciate the political principle, Always pick on men at least twice your size. This is the value of practice as opposed to theory; they're so easy; so arrogant; so used to the world always being the way they thought it was. The small ones are harder. The small ones have to learn to fight early and take nothing for granted, the small, wiry ones you cannot surprise; when I am a master I will take on the small, wiry ones; or assign them to someone else, maybe someone who can step on them, a real tall girl who would get something out of it by just treating them like bugs; but now I take the big ones, and I fucking smash their faces in; I kick them; I hit them; I kick them blind; I like smashing their faces in with one kick, I like dancing on their chests, their rheumy old chests, with my toes, big, swinging kicks, and I like one big one between the legs, for the sake of form and symbolism, to pay my respects to content as such, action informed by the imperatives of literature. Sometimes they got knives or bottles, they're fast, they're good, but they are fucking drunk and all sprawled out, and I like smashing the bottles into their fucking faces and I like taking the knives, for my collection; I like knives. I find them drunk and lying down and I hurt them and I run; and I fucking don't care about fair; discuss fair at the U.N.; vote on it; from which I enunciate another political principle, It is obscene for a girl to think about fair. Every girl

324

needs a man, gets an itch, the nights are long, I'm restless, it's
not natural for a girl to be alone, without a man; instead of
locking the windows and locking the doors and waiting for
one to crawl in I go out to find him; not ladylike but self-
determining, another girl for choice; a girl needs someone big
and strong, a macho man, a streetwise, street tough, street
crazy man, a hero of freedom, a loose man, unattached, a
solitary poet of drink and darkness, a city prince; I have always
found that a girl needs a boy. These ones are old and mean;
none of them's innocent and who cares? I fucking don't care.
It's been justified up my ass. Besides it's just sport, recreational
training, some ways to get through the night, means and
methods, because I can't sleep, because if you go to sleep they
will hurt you, one of them or some of them or some other of
them; whoever these ones hurt, I'm taking her place, whoever
she was, they don't know us apart, cunt is cunt is cunt, I'm
taking her place now, when I choose, I'm standing in for her
now, when it's good for me; is it good for you? And there's
one will stand in for me. There's anonymous women moving
through the night; I have my husband here, right in front of
me, I have a gun to his head, I pull the trigger, it is an
execution, my right, any time, any place; his life is mine,
because he hurt me; dreadful; a dreadful hurt. I want him
executed so I can be free of fear; and if there was justice I could
do it any time, any place; I'd have the gun; I'd have the choice;
I'd have the right. I think I have a twin in the night, some girl
standing in for me; who will just smash his fucking head in. I
think one day they will gather, the women, outside where he
lives, I think there will be thousands of them, I think it will be a
crowd, a mob, a riot, a revolution, and I think they will chant
his name, and I think they will surround his house, and I think
they will block the city streets for blocks, and I think they will
stop traffic, and I think no one will be able to pass in or out and
they will stop the police from getting to him to protect him

because they will stretch for miles and someone, an unknown someone, will kill him, it will be one and it will be all and no one will ever know who except for her herself, they will smash him or shoot him or knife him, or fifty will knife him, or a hundred, but so it's final, not making a mistake, they will kill him good and real and quick, and no one will know who, because it will be all of them; for me; do this; for me; and when an indictment is read they will all stand up; for me; including the ones who heard me scream and including the ones who weren't born yet. My eyes work. I see. It is not a mystery. If it's in front of you you can see how it works itself out. It's not prophecy; it's simple seeing; what is there; now; naked from the lies. I see the future, a pretty place. The men make a sex circus, we are the performing animals. There are hoops of fire, we are chained in cages, they whip us to make us jump: high enough for them to look under. We jump, we hop, we spread our legs; they'll paint us purple underneath; or shave us so we look like babies; or put brands on us, or chains through us, underneath; they'll hurt us, more; more than now; more; killing won't be enough; rape will be the good old days, when it was simple, how they just forced us, in private, or how they just beat us, with fists, in private, or how they put fingers inside us, when we were too small, underneath; we'll be the dog-and-pony show; they'll leash us and they'll manacle us and they'll paint us pink and we'll have nostalgia for the good old days when the living was easy before they grabbed us off the streets in vans and gang-raped us and bashed us with baseball bats, smashing us not looking where, arms, head, chest, stomach, legs, and filmed it, and dumped us, some of us lived, some of us died, or before they set dogs on us to fuck us, and filmed it, or before they cut us open, to ejaculate on us, and filmed it, or before they started urinating on us, using us like common toilets, to film it; but I don't expect to be listened to or believed, certainly even the simplest things of an already distinguished life cannot be believed, I couldn't say anything simple in the whole course of my actual life and have there be belief; as if justice for me, from him to me, could count; but I been through that; my grievances on that score are between the lines, at least there, always read the white space; I'm tired from it and I'm sad; Walt could say blah blah blah this will come and this will come and this will be and he was venerated for dreaming, as if his dreams was true dreams of a true future; my nightmares are true dreams of a true future. I'm not alone; though I can't find them; in the dark raped girls wander; smashing drunks; sometimes someone sets one on fire; I see the flames; I smell the carcass; the raped have stopped being kind, generally speaking, though it's still a secret. I personally have done the following. I have blown up several rape emporiums. I don't have bombs or explosives but I cannot be stopped. I steal a car; I back it into the rape emporium when it's deserted; I make a fuse to the gas tank; I light the fuse; the whole thing blows; it's simple, if a bit extravagant. Any man will follow any feminine looking thing down any dark alley; I've always wanted to see a man beaten to a shit bloody pulp with a high-heeled shoe stuffed up his mouth, sort of the pig with the apple; it would be good to put him on a serving plate but you'd need good silver. You're the piece of ass; he's invulnerable, of course; it's his right, to come after you; so if he follows you and you have the urge to smash him to death he's asked for it, hasn't he? I mean, he actually did ask for it. The army of raped ghosts got together and we marched, we marched, we marched in Times Square and the Tenderloin and Soho; we marched; everywhere there's neon we've marched; we visit the slave auctions; we have the names of the pimps, addresses, photos, telephone numbers, social security numbers; I plaster their neighborhoods with pictures of them; I say they are pimps who slaughter women for fun and money; I say he's at your P.T.A., he's with your children; I pursue him; the army of raped ghosts stays on his tail; we drive him out. They hide; they run. One day the women will burn down Times Square; I've seen it in my mind; I know; it's in flames. The women will come out of their houses from all over and they will riot and they will burn it down, raze it to the ground, it will be bare cement; and we will execute the pimps. No woman will ever be hurt there again; ever; again; it is a simple fact. I threw blood all over their weaponry; their whips; their chains; their spiked dildos; their leashes; I have buckets of blood, nurses give it to me, raped nurses; and I cover everything, the slave clothes, the bikinis, the nighties, the garter belts, and the things they tie you down with and the things they stick up you and the things they hurt you with, nipple clips and piercing things; I drench them in blood; I make them blood-soaked, as is a woman's life; I think over time I will engage in a new art, painting their world blood red as they have painted mine; simple self-expression, with a political leaning but neither right nor left per se, the anti-rape series it will be called, with real life as the canvas; and I will try to make the implicit explicit; a poet said, make the implicit explicit; a political theorist said, make the implicit explicit; the blood of women is implicit in the weaponry; I will take the blood of women implicit in the weaponry and I will make it explicit; and from this I enunciate another political principle, which is, The blood of women is implicit, make it explicit. A woman I didn't know with the face of an angel approached me. She leaned over. She touched me softly on the shoulder. She whispered. She had serious and kind eyes. She had a soft and kind voice. Andrea, she said, it is very important for women to kill men. I contemplated this, shuddering; I meditated on it; I breathed in deeply; I drew pictures, stories of life with men, with pencils, with crayons; I dreamed; I understood yes; yes, it is. I enunciated a political principle, which went as follows: It is very important for women to kill men. His death, of course, is unbearable. His death is intolerable, unspeakable, unfair, insufferable; I agree; I learned it since the day I was born; terrible; his death is terrible; are you crazy; are you stupid; are you cruel? He can't be killed; for what he did to you? It's absurd; it's silly; unjustified; uncivilized; crazed; another madwoman, where's the attic? He didn't mean it; or he didn't do it, not really, or not fully, or not knowing, or not intending; he didn't understand; or he couldn't help it; or he won't again; certainly he will try not to; unless; well; he just can't help it; be patient; he needs help; sympathy; over time. Yes, her ass is grass but you can't expect miracles, it takes time, she wasn't perfect either you know; he needs time, education, help, support; yeah, she's dead meat; but you can't expect someone to change right away, overnight, besides she wasn't perfect, was she, he needs time, help, support, education; well, yeah, he was out of control; listen, she's lucky it wasn't worse, I'm not covering it up or saying what he did was right, but she's not perfect, believe me, and he had a terrible mother; yeah, I know, you had to scrape her off the ground; but you know, she wasn't perfect either, he's got a problem; he's human, he's got a problem. Oh, darling, no; he didn't have a problem before; now he's got a problem. I am on this earth to see that now he has a problem. It is very important for women to kill men; he's got a problem now. I was in the courtroom. The walls were brown. The judge wore a long black dress. God's name was written on the wall over his head. There were police everywhere. The rapist smiled; at the woman. He had kidnapped her. He had held her for nearly two days, or was it four, or were there five of them, each being tried separately? He had fucked her over and over, brutally. He had sliced her with a knife. He had sodomized her. He had burned her. She shaked; she shivered; she screamed; she cried. He walked; the jury found her guilty. I was in the court. The walls were gray. He beat the woman near to death; they were married; the judge didn't see the problem; she's the wife, after all; the guy walked. The judge wore a long black dress. God's name was written on the wall above his head. I was in the courtroom. The walls were green. The judge wore a long black dress. God's name was written on the wall above his head. The daddy had raped the kid, over and over, so many times, she was four, he wanted custody, he got it, it was a second marriage, the first kid was raped too but the judge wouldn't admit it into evidence, said it was prejudicial, you know, just because he did it to that one doesn't prove that he did it to this one; they keep saying that; with them all; the beaters and the rapers; just stack the women they did it to before, the past women, in piles, for garbage collection; don't want them to prejudice how we look at him this time, when he did it to this one who's a slut anyway which isn't prejudicial because it is axiomatic; how many times does he get to do it in his lifetime, to how many, whatever it is he likes doing, a beater, a raper, of women, of children; that's why they don't teach girls to count. I want each one followed. I want each one killed. It is very important for women to kill men. I know girls whose fathers fucked them; near to death; it's a deferred death sentence on her, she does it to herself, later. I know girls who been banged by thousands of men; I am one such girl myself. I know girls who been cut open and fucked in the hole. I know a girl who was kidnapped by a bunch of college boys, a fraternity, and kept for days; used over and over; beat her to blood and pus; sliced her throat and dumped her; I know her and I know another woman raped the same way, wasn't sliced, she escaped; I know so many girls who been kidnapped and gang-raped you couldn't fit them into a ballroom; I know so many girls who been tortured as children you couldn't fit them into a ballroom; I know so many girls who was fucked by their daddies you couldn't fit them into a ballroom. No one cares; how many times can you say *raped*; it don't matter and no one stops them. I throw rocks through the windows of rape emporiums; I destroy business properties of men who rape; or men who beat women; if I find out; sometimes I hear her screaming; there's screaming all over the cities; it travels up the air shafts of apartment buildings; I spray-paint their windows; I spray-paint their cars; I go to the courts; I follow them home; I follow them to work; I have an air rifle; I break their windows with it; I am seeking to blind them; the raped women come out at night, we convene, there's rallies, marches, sometimes a mob, we stomp on the rape magazines or we invade where they prostitute us, where we are herded and sold, we ruin their theaters where they have sex on us, we face them, we scream in their fucking faces, we are the women they have made scream when they choose, when they like it; do you like it now? We're all the same, cunt is cunt is cunt, we're facsimiles of the ones they done it to, or we are the ones they done it to, and I can't tell him from him from him; we set fires, to their stores, to them when they come outside from the Roman circuses, inside they are set on fire metaphorically, the pimp uses the woman to make them burn, she's torn to pieces and they get hot, outside we introduce the literal; burn, darling, using girls is hot; we smash bums and we are ready for Mr. Wall Street who will follow any piece of ass down any dark street; now he's got a problem; it is very important for women to kill men. We surge through the sex dungeons where our kind are kept, the butcher shops where our kind are sold; we break them loose; Amnesty International will not help us, the United Nations will not help us, the World Court will not help us; so at night, ghosts, we convene; to spread justice, which stands in for law, which has always been merciless, which is, by its nature, cruel. They don't stop themselves, do they? They get scared, even the bouncers at the rape emporiums, it's inspiring, they ain't used to mobs of girls who surge and kick and smash; let alone that we are almost ethereal, so ghostly, so frail and fucked out, near to death. You see one of the big ones afraid and it will inspire you for a thousand years. A girl alone or any mass of girls; kicking, pushing, shoving; you can tear their prisons down where they keep women caged in; you must, mustn't you? I have spent some years searching for words, writing, wanting to write, and I have spent some years now, writing a plan, a map with words, a drawing with songs, a geography of us here, them there, with lyrics for how to move, us through them, us over them, us past them; I published the military plan in haiku—Listen / Huey killed / Me too—and it was widely understood; among the raped; who do not exist; except in my mind; because they are not proven to exist; and it is not proven to happen; but still; we convene. I map out a plan, which I communicate through gesture, graphs and charts and poems and a dance I do alone after dark; a stark and violent dance; on his face; the raped will hear me. They don't stop themselves, do they? I enunciate a fundamental political principle; I write it down, in secret; I enunciate a plan; Stop them. I have looked for words. I have read books. I have tried to say some simple things that happened, with borrowed words, or old words, with sad words, words tacked together shamefully without art. I have sobbed for wanting words; because of wanting to say the simplest things; what he did and what it was, or what it was like, as if it would matter if it could be said, or said right; I have sobbed to him saying stop; I have begged person-to-person; stop. Walt was a poet of abundance; he had a surfeit of words; the ones I struggled for mean nothing, I looked for *raped*, was it real, was it Nazis, could it be; how much did it hurt; what did it signify; I wanted to say, it destroys freedom, it destroys love, I want freedom, I want love, freedom first, freedom now; rape rape rape; fucking 0; I found the word, it's the right word; fucking 0; no one cares; enough to stop them; stop them. I will never have easy words; at my fingertips as they

332

say; but I will stake my life on these words: Stop them. They don't stop themselves, do they? I'm Andrea, which means manhood, but I do not rape; it is possible to be manly in your heart, which I have always been, and not rape, I've always liked girls, I've made love with many, I've never forced anyone, don't tell me you can't, save it for them that don't know what it's like, being with a girl. I was born in 1946, after Auschwitz, after the bomb, I never wanted to kill, I had an abhorrence for killing but it was raped from me, raped from my brain; obliterated, like freedom. I'm a veteran of Birkenau and Massada and deep throat, uncounted rapes, thousands of men, I'm twenty-seven, I don't sleep. They leave the shell for reasons of their own. I have no fear of any kind, they fucked it out of me some time ago, it's neither here nor there, not good or bad, except girls without fear scare them. I was born in Camden, on Mickle Street, down from where Walt Whitman lived, the great gray poet, a visionary, a prophet of love; and I loved, according to his poems. I was poor, I never shied away from life, and I loved. I had a vision too, like his, but I will never write a poem like his, a song of myself, I count the multitudes and so on, the multitudes passed on top of me, sticking it in, I lost count. For the record, Walt was wrong; only a girl had a chance in hell of being right. A lot of men on the Bowery resemble Walt; huge, hairy types; I visit him often. It was the end of April, still cold, a brilliant, lucid cold. You could feel summer edging its way north. You could smell spring coming. You would sing; if your throat wasn't ripped. Your heart would rise, happy; if you wasn't raped; in perpetuity. I went out; at night; to smash a man's face in; I declared war. My *nom de guerre* is Andrea One; I am reliably told there are many more; girls named courage who are ready to kill.

Not Andrea: Epilogue

It is, of course, tiresome to dwell on sexual abuse. It is also simple-minded. The keys to a woman's life are buried in a context that does not yield its meanings easily to an observer not sensitive to the hidden shadings, the subtle dynamics, of a self that is partly obscured, partly lost, yet still self-determining, still agentic—willful, responsible, indeed, even wanton. We are seeking for the analytical tools—rules of discourse that are enhanced rather than diminished by ambiguity. We value nuance. Dogma is anathema to the spirit of inquiry that animates women's biography. The notion that *bad things happen* is both propagandistic and inadequate. We want to affirm the spiritual dignity and the sexual bonding we seek to find in women's lives. We want a discourse of triumph, if you will pardon me for being rhetorically elegant. I have heard the Grand Inquisitor Dworkin say that, as we are women, such discourse will have to be ambiguous. She is a prime example, of course, of the simple-minded demogogue who promotes the proposition that *bad things are bad*. This axiom is too reductive to be seriously entertained, except, of course, by the poor, the uneducated, the lunatic fringe that she both exploits and appeals to. It is, for instance, anti-mythological to perceive rape in moralistic terms as a bad experience without transformative dimensions to it. We would then have to ignore or impugn the myth of Persephone, in which her abduction and rape led, in the view of the wise ancient Greeks, to the establishment of the seasons, a mythological tribute, in fact, to the seasonal character of the menarche. It is disparaging and profoundly anti-intellectual to concentrate on the virtual slave status of women per se in ancient Greece as if that in and of itself rendered their mythological insights into rape suspect. In fact, intercourse, forced or not, is the precondition for a fertile, fruitful, multiplied as it were, abundance of living things, symbolized by the planting and harvesting seasons. I am, of course, not allying myself either with the right-wing endorsement of motherhood or family in making these essentially keen, neutral, and inescapable observations. We cannot say the Greek philosophers and artists, the storytellers and poets, were wrong, or dismiss them, simply because some among us want to say that rape is bad or feels bad or has some destructive effects. In fact, it has not been scientifically proven that the effects of rape are worse than the effects of gender-neutral assault and we are not willing to stew in our stigma. As one distinguished feminist of our own school wrote some years ago in a left-wing journal of socialism, and I am paraphrasing: we should not dwell on rape at all because to do so negatively valorizes sex; instead we should actively concentrate on enjoying sex so that, in a sense, the good can push out the bad; it is sex-negative to continue to stigmatize an act, a process, an experience, that sometimes has negative consequences; if we expand sexual pleasure we will, in fact, be repudiating rape—in consciousness and in practice. Further, in women's academic circles we reify this perspective by refusing, for instance, to have cross-cultural or cross-disciplinary discussions with those who continue to see themselves as victims. While we deplore racism and endorse the goals of women of color, we do not enter into discussions on the Holocaust with Jews or on slavery with Afro-Americans because our theory, applied to their experience, might well be misunderstood and cause offense. In fact, they will not affirm the agentic dimensions of their own historical experience,

335

which, we agree, is essentially an oppressive one. They denounce and declaim, and we support them in those efforts. But, as we find transcending affirmative values in women's experience under patriarchy, so too we can find concrete examples of the same dynamic in both Afro-American and Jewish experience. Ghetto Jews from Eastern Europe did, after all, learn to do physical labor in the concentration camps—these are skills that have value, especially for those essentially alien to working-class experience—intellectuals, scholars, and so on. Jewish elitism was transformed into a new physicality, however base and tortured; one can see a foreshadowing of the new Jewish state—the shovels and picks of the stone quarries transposed to the desert. Of course, one must have some analytical objectivity. Afro-Americans sang as a creative response to the suffering of slavery such that suffering may not be the defining characteristic of the Afro-American experience. The creation of a major and original musical genre, the blues, came directly out of the slave experience. It is absurd to suggest that slavery had no mitigating or redemptive or agentic dimension to it, that the oppression per se was merely oppressive. These tautologies demonstrate how the dogma of victimization has supplanted the academic endeavor to valorize theory, which, in a sense, does not descend to the rather low level of direct human experience, especially of suffering or pain, which are too subjective and also, frankly, too depressing to consider as simple subjects in themselves or, frankly, as objects of inquiry. We apply our principles on agency, ambiguity, and nuance exclusively to the experience of women as women. There is no outrage in the academy when we develop an intellectually nuanced approach to rape as there would be, of course, if we applied these principles to Jewish or Afro-American experience. It is inappropriate for white women to approach those issues anyway and thus we are insulated from

336

what I can only presume would be an intellectual backlash while we support the so-called victims in a political atmosphere that Ronald Reagan created and that is anathema to us—the cutbacks in civil rights and so on, funding for Afro-American groups and so on. Then, when we mount our fight for abortion, which rests firmly in the affirmative context of a woman's right to choose, we have the support of other groups and so on. Outside women's studies departments our theoretical principles are not used, not understood, and not paid attention to, for which we are, in fact, grateful. To be held accountable outside the sphere of women's studies for the consequences of our theoretical propositions would, of course, be a stark abridgment of the academic license we have worked so hard to create for ourselves. Simple-minded feminists, of course, object to a nuanced approach to rape but we can only presume that their response to the abduction of Persephone would have been to picket Hell. To understand a woman's life requires that we affirm the hidden or obscure dimensions of pleasure, often in pain, and choice, often under duress. One must develop an eye for secret signs—the clothes that are more than clothes or decoration in the contemporary dialogue, for instance, or the rebellion hidden behind apparent conformity. There is no victim. There is perhaps an insufficiency of signs, an obdurate appearance of conformity that simply masks the deeper level on which choice occurs. A real woman cannot be understood in terms either of suffering or constriction (lack of freedom). Her artifice, for instance, may appear to signal fear, as if the hidden dynamic is her recognition that she will be punished if she does not conform. But ask her. She uses the words of agency: I want to. Artifice, in fact, is the flag that signals pride in her nation, the nation of women, a chosen nationalism, a chosen role, a chosen femaleness, a chosen relationship to sexuality, or sexualities, per se; and the final configuration—the way she appears—is rooted neither in biological givens nor in a social reality of oppression; she freely picks her signs creating a sexual-political discourse in which she is an active agent of her own meaning. I do not feel—and I speak personally here—that we need dignify, or, more to the point, treat respectfully on any level those self-proclaimed rebels who in fact wallow in male domination, pointing it out at every turn, as if we should turn our attention to the very men they despise—and what? *Do something*. Good God, do what? I do not feel that the marginal types that use this overblown rhetoric are entitled to valoriza-tion. They are certainly not women in the same sense we are—free-willed women making free choices. If they present themselves as animals in cages, I am prepared to treat them as such. We are not, as they say, middle-class, protecting the status quo. It is not, as they maintain, middle-class to appreciate the middle way, the normal, the ordinary, while espousing a theoretically radical politics, left-wing and solidly socialist. It is not middle-class to engage in intellectual discourse that is not premised on the urgency of destroying western civilization, though certainly we critique it, nor is it middle-class to have a job. It is not repugnance that turns me away from these marginal types, these loud, chanting, marching creatures who do not—and here I jest—footnote their picket signs, these really rather inarticulate creatures who fall off the edge of the civilized world into a chaotic politics of man-hating and recrimination. Indeed, the sick-unto-death are hard to placate, and I would not condescend to try. Women's biography seeks to rescue from obscurity women who did not belong there in the first place, women of achievement made invisible by an unjust, androcentric double standard. These are noble women, not in the class sense, because we do valorize the working class, though of course often these women are upper-class, and not in the moralistic sense, although of course they often are pure in the sense of emblematic. But certainly one need not labor to describe the muck or the person indistinguishable from it. We affirm sexually active women, yes. We will not explicate either the condition or the lives of sexually annihilated women—they achieved nothing that requires our attention. The crime of rape is not an issue of sex. It is an issue of power. To recast it once again, in a revisionist frenzy, as an issue of freedom is painfully and needlessly diversionary. Of course, there is a tradition in existentialist philosophy of seeing rape as an expression of freedom, a phenomenon of freedom incarnate as it were, for the rapist of course, presumed male, presumed the normative human. But certainly by now the psychological resonances of rape for the raped can best be dealt with in a therapeutic forum so that the individual's appreciation of sex will not be distorted or diminished—a frequent consequence of rape that is a real tragedy. The mechanics of the two, rape and intercourse, have an apparent likeness, which is unfortunate and no doubt confusing for those insufficiently sex-positive. One is the other, exaggerated, although, of course, we do not know—*pace* St. Augustine—which came first. St. Augustine contends that there was sexual intercourse in the Garden but without lust, which he saw as debilitating once he stopped indulging in it. Of course, we all get older. The philosophical problem is one of will. Is will gendered? Clearly Nietzsche's comprehension of will never took into account that he could be raped. Sade postulated that a woman had a strong will—to be raped and otherwise hurt. It is the governing pornographic conceit, indistinguishable from a will to have sex. The problem of female freedom is the problem of female will. Can a woman have freedom of will if her will exists outside the whole rape system: if she will not be raped or potentially raped or, to cover Sade's odd women, if she will not rape. Assuming that the rapist qua rapist imposes his will, can any woman be free abjuring rape, her will repudiating it, or is any such will vestigial, utterly useless on the plane of human reality. Rape is, in that sense, more like housework than it is like intercourse. He wants the house clean. She does not want to clean it. Heterosexual imperatives demand that she bend her will to his. There is, of course, a sociology to housework while there is only a pathology to rape. I am dignifying the opposition here considerably by discussing the question of rape at all. Housework, as I showed above, has more to do with women's daily, ordinary bending of will to suit a man. I object to tying rape to women's equality, in either theory or practice, as if rape defined women's experience or determined women's status. Rape is a momentary abrogation of choice. At its worst, it is like being hit by a car. The politicizing of it creates a false consciousness, one of victimization, and a false complaint, as if rape is a socially sanctioned male behavior on a continuum of socially expressed masculinity. We need to educate men while enhancing desire. For most men, rape is a game played with the consent of a knowledgeable, sophisticated partner. As a game it is singularly effective in amplifying desire. Amplifying desire is a liberatory goal. We are stuck, in this epoch, with literalists: the female wallowers and the feminist Jacobins. It is, of course, no surprise to see a schizoid discourse synthesized into a synthetic rhetoric: "I" the raped becomes "I" the Jacobin. As the Jacobins wanted to destroy all aristocrats, the feminist Jacobins want to destroy all rapists, which, if one considers the varieties of heterosexual play, might well mean all men. They leave out of their analysis precisely the sexual stimulation produced by rape as an idea in the same way they will not acknowledge the arousing and transformative dimensions of prostitution. To their reductive minds prostitution is exploitation without more while those of us who thrive on adventure and complexity understand that prostitution is only an apparent oppression that permits some women to be sexually active without bourgeois restraints. Freedom is implicit in prostitution because sex is. Stalinists on

340

this issue, they see the women as degraded, because they believe that sex degrades. They will not consider that prostitution is freedom for women in exactly the same way existentialists postulated that rape was a phenomenon of freedom for men— striking out against the authoritarian state by breaking laws and, in opposition to all the imperatives of a repressive society, doing what one wants. They won't admit that a prostitute lives in every woman. They won't admit to the arousal. Instead, they strategically destroy desire by calling up scenarios of childhood sexual abuse, dispossession, poverty, and homelessness. Even the phallic woman of pornography has lost her erection by the end of the list. Rape as idea and prostitution as idea are of inestimable value in sexual communication. We don't need the Jacobins censoring our sexual souls. Meanwhile, in the academy our influence grows while the Jacobins are on the streets, presumably where they belong if they are sincere. I will keep writing, applying the values of agency, nuance, and ambiguity to the experiences of women, with a special emphasis on rape and prostitution. I have no plans to write about the Holocaust soon, although, I admit, I am increasingly irritated by the simple-minded formulations of Elie Wiesel and his ilk. Kvetch, kvetch. After I get tenure, I will perhaps write an article on the refusal of Holocaust survivors to affirm the value of the Holocaust itself in their own creative lives. Currently I want those who are dogmatic about rape and other *bad things* to keep their moralisms posing as politics off my back and out of my bed. I don't want them in my environment, my little pond. I won't have my students reading them, respectfully no less, or my colleagues inviting them here to speak, to read, to reproduce simplicities, though not many want to. I like tying up my lover and she likes it too. I will not be made to feel guilty as if I am doing something violative. I was that good girl, that obedient child. Feminism said let go. You can do what a man does. I like tying her wrists to the bed, I like gagging her, I like dripping hot wax on her breasts. It is not the same as when a man does it. She and I are equals, the same. There is no moral atrocity or political big deal. I like fantasizing. I like being a top and I like bringing her to orgasm although I rarely have one myself. I like the sex magazines, the very ones, of course, that the Jacobins want to censor, exept for the fact that these magazines keep printing pictures of the Jacobins as if they are, in fact, Hieronymous Bosch pin-ups. One does get angrier with them. One does want to hurt them, if only to obliterate them from consciousness, submerge them finally in the deeper recesses of a more muted discourse in which they are neither subjects nor objects. One would exile them to the margins, beyond seeing or sound, but strangely they are sexualized in the common culture as if *they* are the potent women. Everyone pays attention to them and I and others like me are ignored, except of course when the publishers of the sex magazines ask one or the other of us to write essays denouncing them. But then, of course, one must think about them. When I'm having sex I find that more and more I have one of them under me in my fantasy, I hear her voice, accusing, I muffle the sound of her voice with my fist, I push it into my lover's mouth, slowly, purposefully, easy now. My lover thinks my intensity is for her. I can't stand the voice saying I'm wrong. I really would wipe it out if I could. It makes for angry, passionate sex, a kind of playful fury. The Jacobin despises me. I have more in common with the so-called rapist, the man who makes love by orchestrating pain, the subtle so-called rapist, the knowing so-called rapist, the educated so-called rapist, the one who seduces, at least a little, and uses force because it's sexy; it is sexy; I like doing it and the men I know know I like doing it, to a woman; they are pro-gay. I'm an ally and I will get tenure. I'm their frontline defense. If I can do it, they can do it. The so-called rapists in my university are educated men. We like sex and to each his own. In my mind I have the Jacobin under me, and in my nuanced world she likes it. I am not simple-minded. Rape so-called is her problem, not mine. I have been hurt but it was a long time ago. I'm not the same girl.

Author's Note

In a study of 930 randomly selected adult women in San Francisco in 1978 funded by the National Institute for Mental Health, Diana Russell found that forty-four percent of the women had experienced rape or attempted rape as defined by California state law at least once. The legal definition of rape in California and most other states was: forced intercourse (i.e. penile-vaginal penetration), intercourse obtained by threat of force, or intercourse completed when the woman was drugged, unconscious, asleep, or otherwise totally helpless and hence unable to consent. No other form of sexual assault was included in the definition; therefore, no other form of sexual assault was included in the statistic. Of the forty-four percent, fully half had experienced more than one such attack, the number of attacks ranging from two to nine. Pair and group rapes, regardless of the number of assailants, were counted as one attack. Multiple attacks by the same person were counted as one attack. See Diana E. H. Russell, *Sexual Exploitation: Rape, Child Sexual Abuse, and Workplace Harassment*, Sage Publications, 1984; see also Russell, *Rape In Marriage*, Macmillan Publishing Co., Inc., 1982 and *The Secret Trauma: Incest in the Lives of Girls and Women*, Basic Books, Inc., Publishers, 1986.

Linda Marchiano, slave name Linda Lovelace, "star" of the pornographic film *Deep Throat*, was first hypnotized, then taught self-hypnosis by the man who pimped her, to suppress the gag response in her throat. She taught herself to relax *all* her throat muscles in order to minimize the pain of deep thrusting to the bottom of her throat. She was brought into prostitution and pornography through seduction and gang rape, a not uncommon combination. Her lover turned her over without warning to five men in a motel room to whom he had sold her without her knowledge. Neither her screams nor her begging stopped them. She was beaten on an almost daily basis, humiliated, threatened, including with guns, kept captive and sleep-deprived, and forced to do sex acts ranging from "deep throat" oral sex to intercourse and sodomy to being penetrated by objects both vaginally and anally to bestiality. Her escape from sexual slavery and her subsequent life as a mother, school teacher, and antipornography activist is a triumph of the human spirit—part of an unambiguous discourse of triumph. See Linda Lovelace with Mike McGrady, *Ordeal*, Citadel Press, 1980; see also Lovelace with McGrady, *Out of Bondage*, Lyle Stuart Inc., 1986.